Purrfectly Peculiar Pixie

PHLOX'S STORY

MJ MAY

Untitled

Purrfectly Peculiar Pixie
Phlox's Story
MJ May

Copyright 2024 MJ May

All rights reserved. This copy is intended for the original purchaser only. No part of this book may be reproduced, scanned, or distributed in any printed or electronic form without prior written permission from the author.

This book is a work of fiction. The names, characters, places, and incidents are either the product of the author's imagination or are used fictitiously, and any resemblance to actual persons, living or dead, business establishments, events or locals is entirely coincidental.

Cover design by cheriefox.
Edited by Hannah VanVels Ausbury

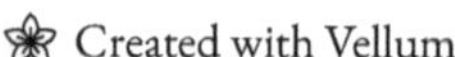 Created with Vellum

Chapter One

PHLOX

I checked the address a third time, verifying I'd put the information correctly into my navigation system. As I glanced down, my phone emotionlessly repeated, "You have arrived at your destination."

"Huh," I grunted while leaning over the steering wheel and peering out the front windshield. The house wasn't exactly what I expected, although to be truthful, I wasn't sure what that vision entailed. As far as homes went, this one was quaint. The outside was well taken care of. More than that, it was a home that gave off the impression of being well tended, or more to the point, well loved.

Late spring revealed a plethora of vibrant plants nestled close to rock-hewn skirting. Shutters framed every window and blooms spilled from window boxes. The setting sun gave the house an ethereal glow. No, not a house—a home.

I expected nothing less of a bonded home-and-hearth pixie. My confusion simply came from the size of the home. It was my understanding that Sedrick Voss was a wealthy alpha werewolf. My source's information was beyond reproach, which meant Alpha Voss wasn't one to flaunt his wealth. The were immediately went up a few notches in my opinion.

A different sound emanated from my phone. A quick glance at the clock told me I didn't have time to take the call, especially considering it was from my Auntie Tandra.

I was in the process of allowing the call to go to voicemail when yips and a sharp howl snapped my head up and drew my gaze.

"What the—" barely slipped past my lips before my eyes widened and my mouth dropped. Openly gawking, I stared as two wolves playfully romped toward the house. They were both large, the smaller one grayish brown, but the bigger, white one was ginormous. I'd never seen a shifted wolf that size before.

I sat there, stunned to silence while my eyes tracked their progress. The main door opened as they trotted up and swiftly closed after they scuttled through. I blinked, my eyes dry and my brain trying to make sense of what I'd just witnessed.

"Trust me, that never gets old."

I jumped and twisted. My wings senselessly beat against the car seat and my hair caught on my seatbelt. I stared through my window, unsure who I saw. I'd rolled the window down prior to turning the car off. Before I could register what happened, a hand shot through that lowered window.

"Hi, I'm Wendall."

His smile was so innocent it stole my breath. Blue eyes stared down at me, movement swirled within, rolling like the ocean tide. Wavy blond hair danced with the breeze, revealing slightly tipped ears. I couldn't see any wings.

Wendall. I mentally tossed the name around until recognition hit. *Fairy.* Sort of.

Reaching for that offered hand, I slid my fingers into his, the position awkward given I was still sitting in the car.

"Frost," I offered in return. "It's nice to meet you."

"And you." Wendall's grin grew. "You're the agent the Magical Usage Council sent, correct?"

I started to answer but another, cooler, voice interrupted. "Wendall, I believe our guest would like to exit his vehicle."

"Oh! Yes, I'm sorry." Wendall ran his fingers through his hair, nervously laughing and stepping back. "I got a little ahead of myself." Waving a hand toward the house's door, Wendall added, "Seeing Dillon and Ruthie in their fur always makes me a little flustered. In a good way," he tacked on. "It's so much fun watching them romp around. Thanks for reminding me, Ray."

"Of course."

Pushing the car door open, I stepped out into the fading sun. Arching, I stretched my back and fluttered my wings. It wasn't enough to raise me off the ground, but it got the kinks out. My loose pixie pants shifted around my legs, the soft fabric heavenly against my skin.

Deep crimson hair caught my attention causing my heart to skip a beat. Hellfire Rayburn. The fairy stood at Wendall's side, an arm wound around the smaller human-turned-part-fairy's waist. His back was to me, that long swath of bloody crimson hair falling to the swell of his rump. Even from this angle, I could easily make out his perfectly tailored suit.

As an agent for the Magical Usage Council, I'd been around more fairies than most pixies. Still, I retained a healthy respect for their power, especially this fairy. Hellfire Rayburn was a legend among fairies. Fairies didn't particularly like one another. Some got along better than others, but all respected power and every time I heard Hellfire Rayburn's name mentioned, it was with the utmost respect.

It was a lesson I took to heart.

"Oh, wow." Wendall's surprised voice slipped through my internal musings. "I've never seen a pixie with hair like that before. Or that type of wing color. It's really beautiful."

I didn't exactly preen. Unlike Auntie Tandra, I wasn't a social pixie. I'd taken after my mother's nature. However, all pixies, no matter their affinity, appreciated praise. Shaking my hair, I allowed it to settle, showing off its odd, horizontal coloring. My pixie hair started off white blond at the top and darkened to its tips. However, unlike typical pixies, my hair color was banded. Deep blue was the most consistent color, but varying shades of ochre and gray alternated with it. My wings had similar coloring, although they weren't banded so much as mottled. It was a color combination that shouldn't work but somehow did.

"Have you ever seen anything like this, Ray?" Wendall walked behind me, circling my body. I might have been nervous had I not been previously briefed on Wendall Galen—human turned zombie turned alive again. A human mixed with a healthy punch of fairy DNA. No one was certain what threat level Wendall posed. However, it was generally believed that whatever abilities he had, they were tempered by an agreeably tender soul.

I could not say the same about his lover.

"No." That one word was cool with little emotion. "However, I believe there is more to this pixie than is typical." Hellfire turned his head ever so slightly, allowing a glimpse of a black pupil ringed by a halo of crimson.

"More? How so?" Wendall cocked his head to the side, an air of innocence leaking from him in waves.

Again, I didn't get a chance to answer. A round ball of fur darted across the yard. I jumped back as it scurried up Wendall's leg, running across his arm and settling on his shoulder. A long tail wrapped around his bicep and Wendall leaned into the mound of fluff. Cooing filled the air. It was a sound I was completely unfamiliar with.

"Did you have fun? There are a lot of trees around here. Did you see the wolves?" Chattering erupted as the round fluffball tottered back and forth. "I told you not to engage with them, Trinket," Wendall admonished. "They're a lot bigger than you."

In answer, Trinket opened their mouth impossibly wide, showing off a row of razor-sharp teeth. My eyes widened but Wendall seemed nonplussed.

"Yes, I know you're fully capable of defending yourself, but I don't think Alpha Voss would be happy if you tore a chunk out of his niece or nephew. None of that. You know I'm right, and we're guests in Phil's house. He's a bonded home-and-hearth pixie. This is his home, and we'll respect it and the ones it protects."

Trinket's demeanor instantly quelled. Nestling deeper into Wendall's neck, their coos sounded apologetic.

Fingers disappearing into their deep fur, Wendall scratched what I thought might be their side. Gaze tracking to me, Wendall gave an apologetic shrug. "She's pretty young and still learning."

"Oh, I...what is she?" I asked the completely rude question.

"A scuttlebutt," Hellfire answered. "She is of Fairy." He said the last with warning.

"Ray gifted her to me." Wendall leaned into Hellfire, his eyes full of adoration. "She was the absolute best present in the world."

Hellfire's cheeks flushed, their color only slightly dimmer than his crimson hair.

"She has indeed proved her worth."

Wendall chuckled before going up on tiptoes and pressing his lips against Hellfire's cheek. "She has," he readily agreed.

"Come, I believe we've wasted enough time outside. The others are already here." Hellfire wrapped his arm around Wendall's waist again and made for the door. He didn't look back to see if I followed.

Before he could reach for the knob, the door swung open. Phil's protective barrier washed over me, tingling my skin and raising my hair. Inside, the house was awash in warm colors and enticing smells. Sound came from nearly every corner of the house, voices melding together in harmony.

"When will it be ready, Phil?" A young werewolf child bounced on her toes. Her brown hair was heedlessly bound on top of her head, little strands coming out here and there. "It smells soooo good." As if to prove her point, she leaned her head forward, nose in the air, and sniffed.

"Soon, Ruthie." I'd heard that Philodendron was large for a pixie. Sometimes, knowing something and seeing it in person are two totally different things. Phil was big. He was also beautiful. Pink ombre hair freely flowed down his back between two large pixie wings. Pink dust filled the air, mixing with a lingering glimmer of golden yellow.

"I want some too." A typical-sized pixie, golden yellow wings and matching hair fluttered nearby. Intel told me this was Peaches. "Goddess, you make the best cinnamon twists." Peaches clapped his hands. He looked more excited than the children.

"Peaches is right." A young werewolf male stood behind his sister, arms crossed and head raised in confidence. "Everything Phil does is the best," Dillon said with the authority of youth.

"Oh, I doubt that," Phil answered, ruffling Dillon's hair. On the surface, Dillon appeared miffed but the dusting of pink across his cheeks told a different story.

"Don't argue with an alpha were, Phil. That never turns out well." A large, burly were with a deep brown beard and thighs the size of tree trunks encircled Phil's waist, squeezing between his wings and nuzzling his neck. When Phil tilted his head, it exposed a pink diamond necklace, platinum surrounding those sparkling gems.

"I'm gonna agree with Sedrick on this one," Peaches said. "Especially where cinnamon twists are concerned." Turning, Peaches placed his fisted hands on his hips. "Lucroy, I really wish you could consume something other than blood. You're really missing out on Phil's baking."

The Southeastern vampire king's dark black eyes gazed at me as he answered, "With all due respect, beloved, I believe others are missing out on the sweet taste of your blood. I suppose that is a blessing considering I would tear out the heart of any other that drew your blood."

Peaches's golden eyes rolled skyward. "So possessive."

"Naturally," Lucroy calmly answered, his eyes still locked on me. I'd met more vampires than fairies and that cold stare barely made me twinge. If Lucroy Moony wanted to have a go, I'd happily give him a run for his money. I'd most likely be ripped to shreds, but my shifted form was more lethal than most expected. I might be small, but I was mighty and, when properly pissed off, quick and deadly. Lucroy Moony could best me, but he wouldn't come out of an altercation unscathed.

"Trinket!" Ruthie joyfully called and the little ball of fluff skittered down Wendall's body and shot toward the child. Going to her knees, Ruthie giggled as the scuttlebutt danced around her body before climbing her like a tree.

Wendall sighed and when I chanced a glance in his direction, he appeared pleasantly at ease. That ease dissipated slightly when Lucroy's cool voice broke through the calm atmosphere.

"Ray, would you care to introduce our guest?"

"Apologies," Ray returned, nearly as devoid of inflection. Despite the soft tone, or perhaps because of it, all heads turned toward me. "This is Frost. He was sent by the Magical Usage Council to assist in our endeavors."

"*Frost?*" Peaches flew forward and would have come closer

if Lucroy hadn't reached out and grabbed the edge of his shirt, pulling him back. Peaches didn't even turn his head to acknowledge the move. "I've never heard of that type of pixie name." Peaches didn't sound judgmental, simply confused.

"It is my work name, not my given one." I didn't expound upon what my given name was.

"Oh, I see." Only it didn't really seem like Peaches did.

"Welcome." Phil stepped forward, holding out his hand. I took those extended fingers and gratefully returned the gesture. I stood within Phil's home by his grace alone. Should Phil wish it, the house would kick me out.

"Thank you, Phil. Or would you prefer I call you, Philodendron?" I asked, wanting to be polite.

"Phil's fine," he answered with a smile. "Would you like introductions or do you already know all of us?" Phil asked, head slightly tipped to the side.

"I believe I already know everyone, but to be certain, I'd like to go around the room." When everyone remained quiet, I started with the fairies "Hellfire Rayburn and Wendall Galen."

"You may call me Ray if you desire."

"Thank you, Ray," I easily answered before moving on to my first pixie. "Peaches and his vampire beloved, Lucroy Moony, king of the Southeastern vampire nest." Peaches lit up while Lucroy merely inclined his head.

Turning toward my second pixie, I gave what I hoped was a polite smile. "Phil and his mate, Alpha Sedrick Voss." Shifting my gaze lower, I stared into prickly wolf eyes. "And this would be Dillon and Ruthie Voss. Dillon is an alpha in training, and it is my understanding that Ruthie is a dire wolf."

Ruthie's smile tugged her cheeks and scrunched her eyes. Dillon was far warier, just as I'd expect from an alpha. Grasping his sister's hand, Dillon placed himself slightly in front of her. Trinket scurried up his body, perching on his head and disturbingly wrapping her tail around his small neck. I tried not to let it bother me considering how calm and dismissive Dillon appeared.

Arms crossed, Dillon's gaze raked me up and down. Eyes narrowed, he ran a finger under his twitching nose. Eyebrows pulled down, a small v formed between. "You're awfully small, even for a pixie."

"Dillon," Sedrick scolded. "You know damn well size doesn't matter." Disappointment laced Alpha Voss's tone.

Dillon waved his uncle off. "I know Uncle Sed. I'm just pointing out he's kind of tiny. I've never heard of a pixie working for the Magical Usage Council." Dillon stretched his neck, sniffing my general direction. When he was finished, he looked even more confused. "He doesn't smell like a pixie. I mean, he does, but..."

Ruthie stepped in to help him out. "He smells kind of like a cat too. It's a weird mix. Do you have a pet cat?" she asked hopefully.

Grinning, I allowed a slight shift and my typically dark blue eyes flooded with yellow. I wasn't a trick pony and didn't plan on fully shifting, even to sate the curiosity of two adorable were children.

Dillon and Ruthie's eyes widened, and Trinket let loose a hissed spat that could rival any feline.

"Shit," Dillon cursed with awe.

"Dillon!" Sedrick scolded again. "What have I told you about using language like that?"

I heard Alpha Voss murmur something about troublesome dwarves and them having far too much influence on his young nephew.

"But look, Uncle Sed." Dillon wildly waved his hand my direction. "Did you see his eyes? That's not a *normal* pixie."

Ray took the opportunity to step in. "Young Dillon is correct. Frost is not your typical pixie. He is, however, a representative of the Magical Usage Council and is here at their behest. Frost is a seasoned agent and I believe we are fortunate to have his aid." Ray pointedly said the last part while staring Dillon in the eyes.

Dillon's ability to hold that gaze was impressive.

My eyes eased back to my pixie blue. Partial shifting was as easy as breathing. Sometimes, it was too easy. When I was stressed or excited, parts of my body shifted. When I was younger, Auntie Tandra often found me in rather embarrassing partially shifted situations. No doubt she has multiple albums filled with photos of those *adorable* instances.

Now that I was an adult and more in control of my emotions, I strived to remain in either full form. It was a point of pride.

Dillon hooked a thumb my direction. "You sayin' he's got what it takes, Ray?"

Wendall's lips twitched as he tried not to smile. Ray's grim mask never faded as he seriously answered, "I am."

Dillon seemed to think that over for a few seconds before he gave a confirmatory nod. "Okay. If you say so. I just want to make certain they sent the best. Those pixie traffickers need to be taken down." Dillon pounded his fist into his open palm. Agreeing, Trinket pranced on top of his head, shrilly cooing.

"Trinket wants her chance at them too. She'd rip out their throats without a second thought," Ruthie added, reaching up and giving Trinket a praiseworthy pat on what I assumed was her head. Given her round body and lack of distinct shape, it was a little difficult to tell. I thought about warning Ruthie off after I'd seen the row of impressive teeth but decided against it. The children were obviously familiar with the scuttlebutt and their uncle didn't have a problem with it.

Wendall's complexion went slightly pale, and Peaches choked on a sound I couldn't interpret. I had the distinct impression I was missing something but didn't press.

"Why don't you three head back outside and burn off a little more energy?" Alpha Voss directed.

Pouting for all he was worth, Dillon turned on his uncle, hands fisted at his sides, chin jutted out. "That's code for getting us out of the house so you can talk about grown-up stuff."

Sedrick shook his head while Phil fluttered beside him. "Nothing code about it. We need to discuss some things that aren't meant for your ears. You've both got too good of hearing to stay in the house, and it's a nice evening out. I know how much you like romping around in your fur, and Trinket would love playing with you."

When Dillon's chin jutted out even further, it was Phil that stepped in, or rather, knelt down.

With a gentle smile and even gentler hands, Phil cupped Dillon's face with one hand, and Ruthie's with the other. "Listen, this is stuff I don't want you worrying about, it's—"

"But it's about kidnapped pixies," Dillon protested.

"And holding them prisoner," Ruthie chimed in sounding devastated.

Phil swallowed and gave a firm nod. "It is and I'm grateful that both of you care so much. You don't know how much that means to me. I'd love to believe that when you're older, horrible things like this will no longer happen, but history doesn't point in that direction. So, one day, it will be up to the two of you to help keep everyone safe. But right now, it's up to us." Phil's gaze swept the room before landing back on Dillon and Ruthie. "And right now, the way you can help me the most is by enjoying the time you have as children." With a wide and generous smile, Phil's eyes danced with unshed tears. "That's what gives me joy, what chases away all the bad and makes me hopeful. I love seeing the two of you carefree and happy. I wish I could bottle it up and keep the bad part of the world from you both.

You've already been through so much. Don't take on this mantle. Not yet. One day, it will fall to your shoulders. Don't rush it, okay?"

Leaning in, Phil kissed each of their foreheads. Ruthie fell into his arms, hugging him tight. Dillon's stubborn jaw relaxed, and he offered an agreeing nod.

"Okay, Phil. But if there's anything you need, if we can help in any way—"

"I'll be sure to let you know. Right now, the best way you can help me is to shift and have a good time. When I'm feeling down, all I have to do is imagine the two of you in your fur, playing and romping around the house and yard. Thinking of that makes me smile. There's no greater gift."

Dillon's cheeks dusted pink. Trinket slid off his head, landing on his shoulder like a furry growth.

Without another word, Ruthie grabbed her brother's hand and headed for the door. Just as before, the front door swung open, softly closing behind them.

The room remained hushed until Peaches broke the silence with a heartfelt "well done, Phil."

Rising, Phil's wings fluttered, spreading pink dust. Thankfully, he was far enough away that no one sneezed. It was interesting that Sedrick walked through that wall of pink without so much as a sniffle.

Phil shrugged before answering. "Everything I said was true."

The oven timer went off and Phil immediately heeded the call. Taking out a tray from the oven, Phil laid it on the counter to cool. Looked like the kids just missed the finished cinnamon twists.

As if he read my mind, Phil waved a hand over the hot twists and said, "It's just as well they got out of here before the twists were done. Last time it took Dillon two shifts to heal his burned mouth."

Sedrick chuckled while tucking a section of pink hair behind Phil's pointed ear.

"Perhaps we should begin," Lucroy announced, breaking through the heavy atmosphere. "I believe Vander is expecting our call."

"That he is," Sedrick easily answered before heading to a nearby laptop. "Vander's going to join us through an online conference call." I got the distinct feeling that explanation was for my benefit alone. It seemed like everyone else in the room was already aware. "I'm assuming you know who Vander Kines is," Sedrick said, this time pointedly looking at me.

"I do. Warlock Vander Kines, bonded in both the pixie and warlock way with Parsnip." Parsnip was legendary. A social pixie with a hit television show on the Home and Kitchen network. Parsnip had his own *coming out* when he announced on air that he'd been lying about his aqua colors. The irony was that Parsnip's gray tones shot through with streaks of his original aqua color were eye catching and beautiful in their own way. Auntie Tandra would be all kinds of jealous when she learned I had a case involving Parsnip. Parsnip was legendary in the social pixie world.

"That's them," Sedrick answered, his grin pulling the thick strands of his beard. "They're currently in Tibet filming the latest edition of *Interspecies Habitat.*"

"Ooh." Peaches flew closer. "Phil told me they were in the Himalayas, but he didn't tell me who the couple is."

"Yeti and...what was it, Phil?" Sedrick glanced at his mate while typing something into the computer.

"A phoenix," Phil answered.

The room went silent again until Wendall said, "That might be kind of tough. I'm not exactly sure what kind of temperature phoenix shifters like. I suppose yetis like the cold, so..."

"It sounds like an interesting episode." Peaches sounded

wistful. "Not as interesting as the one Lucroy and I shot, but still good."

No one contradicted Peaches's confident statement. When I chanced a glance at Phil, he sported a fond smile.

"Anyway," Sedrick continued, "Vander and Parsnip are in Tibet and it's not that easy to get from there to here. Correct me if I'm wrong, Ray, but I think you could have fetched both of them."

"I said that too," Wendall offered. "Tibet sounds so exotic. I really wanted to go, but Vander didn't want that."

"We will go another time," Ray easily placated. "However, now is not the time. As you said, that was not Vander's desire."

"You're right about that." The voice was new and sounded oddly disembodied.

"Hey, Vander. How's Tibet?" Sedrick leaned toward the computer, turning it so everyone else could see the screen. Vander Kines was a handsome warlock. He was young enough that most of his hair was still dark black, however his temples were shot through with gray. Hands clasped below his chin, Vander also had the typical blackened fingertips warlocks were known for. His tenor was deep and husky, another warlock trait.

"Cold as fuck. I'm still waiting for this show to go somewhere with a warm beach. I wanna slather my body with sunscreen and fry. Is that too much to ask for?" Vander's words were harsh, but they hummed with fond amusement.

Sedrick chuckled and even Lucroy's features softened. Genuine affection easily filled the room. It was an odd mix, to be certain. It was also a mix that worked and that's what we needed.

"How is Parsnip?" Phil asked. Peaches scooted closer. He and Phil shared a concerned glance.

Vander's sigh was heavy. "Depends on who you ask. If

Parsnip were here, he'd tell you he's fine. But he's not here, so I'll tell you the truth. And the truth is he could be a hell of a lot better. That's why I wanted to do this meeting without him. His brother, Parsley, currently has two pixies recovering at his place. There was supposed to a third but...he didn't make it. They got there too late, and he'd faded too far." Vander swallowed and for the first time, I noticed the dark circles under his eyes. "It hit Parsnip hard and far too close to home. It's not his fault. None of it is, but he feels responsible. Don't ask me why because I've got no clue. All I know is that it's true."

"I'm so sorry," Peaches said, head hanging and wings drooped. Lucroy was instantly at his side, pulling him close.

"Not your fault, Peaches," Vander easily answered. "But I appreciate your concern."

"I wish I could be there," Peaches answered.

"I think we all do," Phil added.

"And he'd like that, but you know how Parsnip is. For a social pixie, he's not really that—"

"Social," Peaches interrupted.

"Exactly. I think he needs some time alone. I'm trying to do that for him, but I'm also trying to make sure he knows he's supported and that I will never allow anything like that to happen to him again." Steel laced Vander's voice and I pitied the fool who tried to take Parsnip from him.

Stepping forward, I saw the opportunity to introduce myself. "That is exactly what we are all trying to prevent, Warlock Kines."

Vander's attention snapped to me. Eyes narrowed and assessing, he asked, "Are you the representative from the Magical Usage Council?"

"I am. Agent Frost."

"He's a pixie," Peaches needlessly added before he softly amended, "I think. I mean, I know he's a pixie, but he's also something else. Dillon and Ruthie say he smells like a cat, and he did something with his eyes earlier, but..." Peaches's voice faded as he ran out of descriptive words.

What I was or wasn't was not the important bit of information. "The council thought I would be the best choice. I assure you, I'm here to put a stop to this disgusting operation. Pixie trafficking is illegal and carries an immediate death sentence to anyone who's not addicted to their dust." Pixie dust was addictive to ogres and, as such, they were sent into rehabilitation programs. It was the ones who profited off that addiction that fairy law was truly after.

"Glad to hear it," Vander said, voice deep and resonant despite the distance. "Like I said, this is all hitting a little too close to home for Parsnip. I told him I'd take care of the meeting and fill him in later. I think the fact he's letting me get away with that says all we need to know."

No one offered an ounce of argument.

"Now that we are all present, perhaps we can share information and formulate a plan." Ray stepped in and moved the meeting forward.

"Indeed. I'm inclined to agree with Hellfire," Lucroy answered.

Sedrick grunted. "Well, that should be easy on our end. Unless Ray's got something to add, so far, we've got jack shit. Oh, we've got lots of feelers out and there have been a couple of times we've gotten a promising lead or two, but they haven't panned out. Or rather, the lead disappears."

"Or, more likely, is eliminated by a larger fish," Vander said darkly.

"Someone higher up the power chain," Lucroy agreed.

"That's some damn fine micromanagement there. Whoever's in charge, they've got their finger on the pulse of their operation and haven't missed a beat yet." Sedrick's rumbled growl filled the room. The lights momentarily dimmed before flaring brighter. The low fire roared and burned hotter.

Rubbing his hands up and down Sedrick's arms, Phil's wings fluttered as he snuggled in closer.

"Sorry, Phil," Sedrick apologized. "I didn't mean to make the house upset."

"Don't worry about that," Phil reassured. "Our home is only concerned, as am I. Besides, I think it was more a reaction to my emotions. I can't help but feel threatened by what's going on and I can't hide those emotions from our home. It's who I am."

"And I adore who you are, Phil. It's fine. We'll figure this shit out."

"Sedrick is correct, Philodendron." I wasn't sure if Lucroy was referring to Phil's home-and-hearth nature or the fact Sedrick had promised to solve the current pixie trafficking horror. Either way, I agreed.

"In this instance, I hate to agree with Sedrick, but he is not wrong regarding our stymied investigation. Queen Silvidia is most dismayed by the lack of progress and continued loss of life. Even with multiple resources and several individuals on task, Fairy hasn't had any better fortune. I do not believe I have ever seen Hamish so...annoyed."

Sedrick's growl was an even lower tenor this time.

"Sedrick," Phil scolded lightly. "Hamish is trying to help, and he did save Peaches and Lucroy's lives when Aurelia was under Arthur's control."

"I know," Sedrick grumbled. "That doesn't mean I have to forgive him for what he tried doing to you."

"As a fairy lawyer, Hamish was doing his job," Ray defended.

Wendall's wide eyes stared up at Ray, their peaceful seas turning turbulent.

"Yeah, but he did it in a sneaky, underhanded way,"

Sedrick huffed. "And don't try and tell me any different. Even you didn't agree with what he tried doing to Phil. Phil could have died." His last words were laced with so much pain I felt my chest constrict.

"But I didn't die, and everything is fine. Besides, I think I'm just as responsible, if not more so, than Hamish. I should have realized I'd bonded with the house—with you and the children. It was my own stupidity, I—"

"No more of that." Peaches flew to Phil, golden dust filling the air. Ray barely covered his nose in time. Wendall didn't and sneezed a couple of times. "I won't stand here and listen to you call yourself stupid. You were naïve and didn't know better. That's a far cry from stupid." Peaches crossed his arms and flew a little higher, wings mercilessly beating and spreading even more dust.

"Beloved," Lucroy calmly cajoled. "While I love your passion, I'm afraid the non-pixie, breathing among us are having a little trouble with all the dust."

"Oh! I'm sorry." Peaches's wings stopped so suddenly he nearly dropped to the ground. Lucroy's hands grabbed his waist and eased his descent.

"It's okay. If you hadn't scolded him, I would have," Sedrick said, laying a hand on the side of Phil's cheek. Inhaling deeply, Sedrick released a heavy sigh. "The point is it's difficult for me to hear Hamish McIntyre's name and not sprout claws."

Ray sounded perfectly agreeable when he answered, "While that is understandable, Hamish excels at whatever task he has agreed to take on. We are fortunate to have him on our side. The fact he has been unable to trace this trafficking ring is more than disheartening. This particular group is far more organized and well controlled than past iterations."

"Most likely that is because it isn't ogre run," I added, pulling all eyes toward me.

"We already knew that," Vander said, his voice a little hollow coming through the computer speakers.

"Yes." I nodded. "The Magical Usage Council in conjunction with the Ogre Addiction Organization has confirmed this. We've managed to arrest two ogres that we believe are involved, however, they are so low down within the operation that they have no pertinent information regarding those higher up. The bottom line is we need to get closer. The Magical Usage Council has tried infiltrating the group, but whoever's in charge is far too cagey, or perhaps, paranoid to gain any inroads. In short, that plan has failed. Miserably."

Grunts, groans, and dispirited sighs filled the air.

"Then what's the plan?" Sedrick asked, his gaze flitting around the room, amber orbs lit from within, his wolf close to the surface.

Instead of answering directly, I turned my attention toward Ray. The slight tilt of his head was permission enough. This was a plan approved by both Fairy and the Magical Usage Council. It was the reason I was here.

"The plan," I said, licking my suddenly dry lips, "is bait."

"*Bait?*" Phil and Peaches echoed in unison.

"Who would..." Phil's words faded, his wide, pale green eyes staring at me, a soft "no" drifting from his lips.

I didn't wait for the others to catch on. I simply nodded and grinned. "No better bait than a tiny, defenseless pixie."

My prospective kidnappers would learn I wasn't as *defenseless* as I appeared.

Chapter Two

Leon

It was a typical Wednesday night. We were in the time of year where the sun went down later and later, which meant my nestmates didn't amble into the bar as early as a couple months prior. It was the way of our kind. Except for Lucroy, every other vampire I knew lived and died by sunrise and sunset. It was so ingrained within our vampiric nature that we couldn't be roused when the sun was at its most deadly zenith.

I'd spent the day inside Dusk, using Lucroy's underground den. As a typical rule, vampires didn't like sharing their resting spaces. Few, if any, were allowed inside. Lucroy and I'd known each other for centuries. I was his second and current heir of the Southeast nest. To my knowledge, Peaches and I were the only ones he'd ever allowed into his private sanctuary. So, while I didn't feel unwelcome there, it wasn't home either. What it was was convenient.

Understandably, Lucroy spent more time at his beloved's orchard. The completion of the underground addition to the home only solidified this fact. With every passing day, the running of Dusk fell increasingly under my control. It was a position in which I found comfort and was pleased my king and friend trusted me so completely.

Johnny was behind the bar proper. The faun had been with Lucroy nearly as long as me. Of course, that was an exaggeration. Fauns didn't live nearly as long as vampires. Not that everyone considered us *alive*. We were far more alive than zombies, but I didn't begrudge those who questioned my living status. Fairy law saw vampires as equal creatures, deserving of all the same rights as those who required air to continue their existence. For me, that was enough.

"Evenin', boss-man." Johnny had taken to calling me boss-man since Lucroy's frequent absences. Knowing Johnny, his choice of nicknames could have been far worse. I neither encouraged nor discouraged the term.

"Good evening, Johnny. Any issues tonight?"

"Not that I've seen," Johnny answered with a headshake. Hands spread on the bar top, Johnny leaned closer. Standing on the riser behind the bar, the shorter faun was nearly eye level. "Got a couple of werewolves in the corner that I haven't seen before. Probably some of Arie's pack but so far, they haven't given cause to boot their furry asses out."

With an understanding nod, I picked up the warm glass of blood Lizbeth inconspicuously slid my way. I raised the glass her direction in thanks before draining half the glass in one go. Like most vampires, I had my own preference. Human made up the bulk of nearly every vampire's diet. But a little extra *something* added a kick now and again. Before claiming Peaches as his beloved, Lucroy's favored drink was human with a hint of ogre. If I'd still been human, I would have shivered at the thought. While I cared for and respected my king, I did not share his blood palate.

"It's becoming a trend," I needlessly said, now sipping my drink.

"A damn irritating trend," Johnny agreed. "I don't like it."

Johnny said some variation of that sentiment nearly every evening.

"Nor I. Lucroy isn't fond either. However, as long as they do nothing untoward, we have no cause to remove them. Dusk is open to all." Even humans came by, although I often wondered about their mental health. Lizbeth notwithstanding, humans didn't typically mix well with other species. Or, at the very least, they often found themselves at the unpleasant end of an old-fashioned fairy tale—the distinctly non-Disney variety.

"Arie Belview's up to something." Johnny's voice was barely above a whisper.

I nearly snorted my blood. "Of course he is. Alpha Belview is always up to something. It would go against his nature to do otherwise." Not all alphas acted like Arie Belview. In fact, I doubted most of them did. One need look no further than Sedrick Voss for Arie's polar opposite.

"True enough," Johnny readily agreed.

"Johnny," Lizbeth interrupted. "We just got an order for licorice liquor. It's up on the top shelf. You want me to get it?"

Johnny grumbled. "I miss Wendall. That boy's too busy to work in here as often as I'd like. Off at some damn meeting tonight with Ray." Johnny stomped a hoof before waving his towel Lizbeth's direction and saying, "That'd be great."

Lizbeth grabbed the ladder and scurried up, snatching the bottle and wiggling back down. The ladder rungs were hell on Johnny's hooves. He could use the ladder, but it wasn't graceful and took a lot longer.

"Must be a group of brownies here somewhere. They're small enough I probably missed them. We don't get a lot in the bar and they're the only ones who like that licorice stuff. I've got it up top, along with the virgin tears. Used to have the burnt rum up there too, but I moved it down when Vander began coming around more often. Now that he's off wanderin' the globe with Parsnip, it might be time to stick it back up there. We don't get a lot of warlocks knocking down our doors either."

Johnny was correct. I wasn't certain if that was because warlocks weren't all that plentiful or if they simply didn't like socializing with others. Most likely it was a combination of both.

While I'd grown fond of Wendall and felt his absence, Johnny was the one who missed him the most. I didn't think it was simply the fact Wendall was agile and shimmied up and down ladders with ease. Johnny truly liked the young zombie turned living humanoid fairy.

"This time tomorrow you'll have a new trainee. As I understand it, a pixie. They'll be able to fly up to the top and get what you need, just like Phil."

Phil's brief stint as a bouncer hadn't gone well, but he'd made a decent bartender and had pulled in a unique crowd. Dusk had acquired a reputation for pixie viewing. Pixie bars drew most of them. It was a place they could fly, drink, and dance without complaint of patron nasal complications. If you wanted to see pixies at play, one needed to mask up and head for a pixie bar.

Dusk was different. We had our own set of pixies and Dusk was large enough that when they were here, a section could be cordoned off for their enjoyment. Pixie dust dissipated quickly enough that if Dusk's other patrons were far enough away, the dust was gone before it had a chance to infiltrate their delicate noses. No matter the species, one couldn't help but smile when in the presence of a dancing pixie. Pixies might be hell on the nose, but they were pure joy to the eyes.

"I heard that. Do you know anything about them?" Johnny asked.

"Not much. Lucroy could not share information he did

not have. I know they are being sent from the Magical Usage Council."

Johnny grunted. "I can't say that I've ever heard of a pixie agent before." Rubbing his chin, Johnny appeared as doubtful as I felt. "Pixies aren't really known for their..." He waved a hand in the air, unable to put his thoughts into words.

"Aggressive nature?"

"Yeah, something like that. They're not really a deceptive lot. I know Parsnip lied and covered up the fact he'd faded, but it wasn't like he took any joy out of it. In fact, I think that deception hurt him the most."

"Agreed." When Lizbeth walked by, I scooted my empty glass her way.

"You want more?" she asked and hurried away to get it when I nodded.

"I assume the council has its reasons." Most councils did. The vampire council certainly claimed to. I'd met their members once and didn't care for a repeat experience.

Johnny shrugged. "I suppose. You know me, as long as they're friendly, work hard, and don't start shit, then I'm all good."

My lips twitched, itching to grin. "It is one of your finer qualities."

Johnny threw a nearby towel my direction. I didn't bother dodging and allowed the slightly damp cloth to hit me in the chest.

Chuckling, Johnny said, "I've got the apartment cleaned out and ready. Wendall already got rid of most everything." Nose scrunching, Johnny said, "You know I love that boy, but I'm glad I didn't have to clean out the fridge. Brains are bad enough, but rotten brain is probably worse, not to mention what Trinket eats." Like all fauns, Johnny was a vegetarian. "You know I'm not prejudiced. You gotta eat what your body needs, but that don't mean I gotta like cleaning it up." With a dramatic shiver, Johnny's tension dissipated. "Anyway, it was a moot point. Wendall cleaned everything up. I didn't have to do much. Wendall's a good lad."

Wendall was far more than a *lad*. In point of fact, none of us really knew what Wendall was now. Mostly human with a dash of fairy. Thanks to Aurelia, that *dash* of fairy was now more like a *splash*. I wasn't overly concerned. Wendall's good nature would quell anything else that came along.

"Do you know when they're expected?" Johnny asked.

"The pixie?"

"Mm-hmm."

"Not precisely. I am uncertain how long the meeting at Sedrick's will last or if Lucroy will bring the pixie here directly after." As inconspicuously as possible I glanced the direction of the wolves sitting on the other side of the room. Even their excellent hearing couldn't overcome Dusk's music and distance.

A fresh, warm glass of blood appeared before me. By the time I picked it up, Lizbeth was off, her lavender hair reflecting the overhead lighting and making her glow. Despite my original misgivings and despite her unfortunate humanity, Lizbeth was an excellent hire.

Now that my appetite was sated, I savored my second glass. I might have a third before the night was over. I would be fine without it, but I saw no reason for hunger. A hungry vampire did not make congenial conversation.

Another employee stood behind Johnny reluctant to interrupt, and patiently waiting for our conversation to end

"Duty calls," I told Johnny before slipping out of my chair and into the crowd. I might not be Lucroy Moony, but as his second, most of our nestmates took comfort in my presence. Vampires could be solitary creatures, but we often retained our living, human personalities. As such, some vampires were sociable and required interaction with others. Dusk was here to fulfill that need. Lucroy had a few simple rules. No nestmates went hungry. No nestmate lacked for a safe place to sleep during the day. No nestmate need pay tithes. No nestmate had to perform any task they did not wish. Vampires within the Southeastern United States had luxuries other nests did not and are ranks were growing because of it. Lucroy's style of leadership was very appealing, and our increased diversity strengthened our nest.

I spent the rest of the evening being available to nestmates in need. Most of that need came from small, nearly insignificant requests or inquires. The evening turned into night which rolled into early morning. The bar cleared as patrons found their way home. The group of brownies stayed until nearly three in the morning. I was staring at them when they suddenly blinked out and were gone. That was the way of brownies and I'd seen it enough over the centuries that I barely found it disturbing now.

Johnny, Lizbeth, and a handful of other staff went around the bar, cleaning tables and putting the bar to rights. Sliding out of my corner booth, I decided to make a final round, making certain all was well, and I was no longer needed. Most nights, I felt as if my presence was little more than window dressing. Lucroy was right, as long as Johnny was present, Dusk basically ran itself.

"You headed downstairs, boss-man?" Johnny asked.

"Soon." I'm not sure why I lingered. Johnny didn't need me. Being alone didn't bother me. Maybe it was staying in Lucroy's home. Maybe I should have left earlier so I could sleep in my own den. Only that space wasn't as comforting as I'd once found it.

I was unsettled, had been since Lucroy found his beloved. I didn't begrudge Lucroy his happiness. In fact, I was relieved he'd found Peaches. Before Peaches, I'd begun observing disturbing habits. It was early, but I was wary. I'd lost my maker to depression and ultimately, the sun. She'd walked out into the early sunrise, finding a level of peace she'd lost in her second life. I did not want to lose Lucroy the same way.

A vampire at loose ends danced a fine line, one that did not always end with centuries but a pile of ash.

"Leon." Lucroy's cool voice danced across my skin. He wasn't my maker, but he was my king. He was also a good friend.

I turned, surprised when I didn't see Peaches by his side.

Aware of my gaze, Lucroy said, "My beloved was away from his orchard too long this evening. I took him home before stopping by Dusk."

"Is he well?" Concern tickled my brain. As a bonded nature pixie, being away from his orchard could kill Peaches. A few hours were fine, any longer and the consequences would be devastating. We all knew that firsthand.

"He is fine. A small headache and decreased energy, but nothing being back on his land won't cure."

The tightness around my chest eased. While I cared for Peaches, my larger concern would be his death's impact on Lucroy. Depending on the circumstances, Lucroy would either lose himself to madness, becoming a danger to everything in his path, or he would simply cease to exist. Neither outcome was desirable.

Before I could inquire further, Lucroy turned his head, tilting it just so as he listened to the hall leading to the parking garage. Seconds later, I heard what had caught his attention—the flutter of pixie wings.

I blinked before my eyelids managed to glue themselves open. My heart thudded, a dull drum that reverberated through my body and yet I remained statue still. I'd seen my fair share of pixies. All of them were beautiful. None of them had ever caught my attention like this.

"Leon, this is Agent Frost. He is the representative the

Magical Usage Council sent. Frost, this is my second, Leon McMillon."

"Nice to meet you, Leon. Looks like we'll be working together for a while."

Tingles swept through my body like shards of ice. Frost was extraordinary and yet the only thing that managed to exit my mouth was an insulting "fuck, you're tiny, even for a pixie."

Chapter Three

PHLOX

I bristled and pixie dust scattered. It was a good thing I was surrounded by vampires that didn't need to breath. Then again, I thought right about now that Leon asshole deserved a good sneezing fit.

Chin jutting out, my inner cat pulsed, pushing at my skin and begging for release. Of course, that form was smaller than my pixie body, but that form also had claws and teeth. Mister High and Mighty Vampire wouldn't see that coming.

Clamping my jaw tight and clenching my fists, I put on my biggest, fakest smile. Auntie Tandra would be so proud if she could see me now.

"Haven't you heard? Good things come in small packages," I barely refrained from hissing, going for snark instead of outright hostility. Did this asshole think he was telling me something I didn't know? I'd been petite all my life. Auntie Tandra said it was probably because of my father's genes. According to her, my mother had been typical pixie size. Pictures I'd seen certainly backed up Auntie Tandra's claim.

Leon appeared taken aback. A low, alarmingly warm

chuckle slipped past his lips. "Apologies, that was a shitty opening." A lazy grin tilted his lips, not even close to showing fang. Still, it was more emotion than I typically witnessed in vampires. Maybe this one was young yet. Although, I found that difficult to believe considering Lucroy introduced him as his second. Surely you had to be a little older to earn that title.

"It was," I breezily agreed, refusing to sweep the comment under the rug. "The council does not view my size as a detriment, and neither should you."

Leon held up his hands, palms out. "No, you are right. I—"

"What have we got here?" A faun appeared from behind the bar. A connecting door to a back room swung in his wake. His kilt swayed around his thighs, revealing fur-covered legs that ended in hooves.

"Johnny, this is Frost. He is—"

"My newest employee," Johnny said, interrupting Lucroy mid-sentence. "Excellent." Johnny clapped his hands, nearly making me jump. "Since Wendall's not here as often, we could use the extra help and those wings will make getting supplies off the top shelf easy-breezy." Clomping forward, Johnny held out a hand. "Nice to meet you, Frost. I'll tell you the same thing I told Phil. You work hard, follow the rules, and don't cause any trouble and we'll get along just fine."

Auntie Tandra would tell him I hadn't always been good at following the rules. Truth be told, I found a lot of rules were itching to get broken. However, I knew the stakes and took my position seriously. I had a job to do and part of that bigger job was playing the part of bar employee. I needed to be convincing and planned on playing my part well.

"I've got nothing against hard work," I truthfully answered.

"Fantastic." Moving his attention to Lucroy, Johnny said,

"I'm heading out, boss. It's been a long night and my hooves could use a soak. I already sent everyone else home."

"As always, your work is impeccable, Johnny," Lucroy easily answered. I had to admit, Lucroy Moony was one of the most agreeable vampires I'd ever met, or at least he was the most praiseful, especially for a king. Most vamps were expectant divas. Glancing Leon's way, I sincerely hoped he wasn't one of those. If that were the case, I couldn't guarantee Johnny that I wouldn't cause trouble. I refused to continue swallowing insults from self-important vamps.

"Leon, you want me to show Frost to his apartment before I leave?" Johnny asked.

"That won't be necessary. As you said, you are tired and I am more than capable. I will see you tomorrow evening. Have a good rest."

Throwing Leon an odd two-finger salute, Johnny turned and headed back toward the door he'd entered through earlier.

"See you later, Frost. Be down no later than six p.m. Lizbeth and I will get you up to speed and useful in no time flat." Johnny chuckled as he walked away.

"Leon, do you require anything further?" Lucroy politely asked.

"No. I've got it. You head home to Peaches. The sun will be up soon. I know it is not dangerous to you any longer, but I also know you are not used to it and the sun makes your skin itch."

"Too true. Thank you, Leon. If you need me, call. I will stop by tomorrow evening to check on things." Turning to me, Lucroy kept his hands tucked away, his face a mask of perfect vampire emotionlessness. "Frost, should you require anything, please let Leon, Johnny, or me know. I wish for your stay here to be a comfortable one."

"Thank you," I sincerely answered. Although I still hadn't

seen the apartment, I felt confident I'd been forced to stay in worse places while working for the council.

With nothing further, Lucroy turned and silently walked down the hall leading to the garage and his vehicle. My rental was parked in the same lot, taking up a tiny fraction of space. I had a couple bags containing my belongings I needed to get and asked, "You want me to get my things before or after you show me the apartment?"

Leon's facial features mimicked Lucroy's. Vamps were uncannily good at that unsettling uncaring façade.

"Now would be fine. Do you require assistance?"

"No. I've got it."

"I will wait here then."

Zipping down the hall, I made quick work of getting to my car and pulling out my bags. Thankfully, pixie clothes were lightweight and nothing else I had was much heavier. Reaching in a final time, I snagged my cell phone. I had another missed call from Auntie Tandra. I really needed to do more than send her a quick text message letting her know I'd arrived and was fine. I owed the pixie who'd raised me so much more than that.

Back inside, a bag in each hand, I said, "Ready."

Leon's lip twitched. His blacker-than-night eyes flicked over my hovering form. Part of me wished I knew what he was thinking. An even bigger part of me wasn't sure I wanted to know. He'd already said I was *tiny*. Some might not see it as an insult. It wasn't a compliment either. Why I wanted one of those from this ginger-haired vamp I had no idea.

"This way," Leon said, sweeping an arm toward a set of stairs tucked behind the bar. "The apartment is on the second floor. It is recently vacated, and Johnny assures me is clean and ready for a new occupant."

Leon led the way, and I flew behind him. I could have walked and if we were in the company of those who needed to breathe, then I would have. Most pixies preferred flying. We liked being off the ground, even if it was only by a couple of feet.

The stairs were a little steep, not that I minded given I flew and didn't climb them. My position gave me an excellent view of Leon's backside. He wore black, fitted jeans and a dark gray three-quarter length sleeve shirt. It was casual and immaculate all at the same time. Those jeans hugged a firm tush.

My cheeks heated and I shut down my lusty thoughts. Vamps and pixies didn't really co-mingle. At least, that used to be true. As word circulated about Lucroy and Peaches bonding, that was slowly changing. I wasn't sure if that was for the better or worse. The Magical Usage Council reached out to the Vampire Council. Thankfully, it appeared we were all on the same page regarding pixie safety. Nirgal was very clear on this. The ancient vampire did not want any pixies harmed in vampires' quest for the sun. No one knew if Lucroy and Peaches were an isolated case or not. Did all pixie blood allow vampires to walk in the daylight? Was it just nature pixies? Did the pixie have to be the vampire's beloved?

There were too many unknowns for anyone's comfort. Time would tease the answers free, but until then, it was anyone's guess. The lure of the sun was a powerful mistress and pixies were becoming increasingly concerned that it wouldn't be only ogres we had to worry about.

The opening of a door pulled me from my inner thoughts, and I followed Leon into a small, but well-appointed one-bedroom apartment. A quick glance around confirmed my earlier thoughts. I'd definitely stayed in worse.

"There is a small galley kitchen with a two-burner stove, microwave, and refrigerator. Our last resident had little need for more than the fridge and microwave."

"Who lived here last?" I casually asked while setting down my meager belongings.

"Wendall."

I perked up. "Wendall Galen?"

Leon nodded. "He was a zombie then and his dietary needs were...sparse."

I chuckled. "I'll bet."

"To my knowledge, Wendall was happy here and found the apartment agreeable. The bedroom is just through there and it has an attached bathroom. The apartment has its own thermostat. You may make the area as warm as you desire."

Pixies did like being warm. More to the point, we liked not having to wear heavy clothing to protect us from the cold. Pixie skin was sensitive. I wasn't sure if mine was as sensitive as typical pixies. I knew I didn't get cold as easily and even preferred it over heat which wasn't pixie-like at all. I got my cold affinity honestly from my mother and father.

"As Lucroy said, should you need anything, you have but to ask."

"Thanks, Leon. This isn't bad. I'm sure it will be more than adequate for the time I'll use it." How long that would be was anyone's guess. Truth be told, no one even knew if using me as bait would work. As much as being captured scared the hell out of me, I also wanted it to happen. It needed to happen. This pixie trafficking ring needed to be shut down in the worst way and the ones in charge needed to be put down in the most egregious way possible. Most likely, I wouldn't participate in that side of things. I wasn't averse to bloodshed, but that didn't mean I craved it either. I was, however, vindictive—something else pixies weren't supposed to be.

Auntie Tandra said I got my vindictiveness from my father's genes. She was probably right. I hadn't known my mom either, but I'd heard enough stories to know that my mother, Perovskia, wasn't the type to hold a grudge. According to Auntie Tandra, my mother was never upset with my father's abandonment. In fact, she didn't view it that way at all. It had been a fling, one that no one could have expected a child from. Some species mixed okay and offspring were expected. Pixies and shifters weren't two species known for their genetic compatibility.

Some might call me a freak of nature. Auntie Tandra never made me feel that way. She'd claimed the opposite—that I was a fortuitous gift. She said my mother felt the same. I only had Auntie Tandra's word on that, but I'd seen photos of my mother holding me in the few precious months we'd had together, and she looked happy enough. More than happy. I was probably prejudiced, but as Perovskia's child, I had a right. My mother had been gorgeous and in pictures with the two of us together she radiated unmitigated joy.

Auntie Tandra was right. I'd been wanted. I'd been born with an abundance of love. Maybe my mom had a sixth sense that she wouldn't be around and felt the need to shower me with as much of it as time allowed.

It was a silly notion. My mother hadn't known she'd be captured by an addicted ogre. She hadn't known she'd be placed in the hot sun, withering and fading faster than a typical captured pixie. My mother had been a rare nature pixie —one that thrived in the cold and wilted in the heat. My mother's affinity for cold was how she'd met my father. The frigid Mongolian cold isn't a place most pixies vacation. I doubt my father had ever seen a pixie up close and personal. According to Auntie Tandra, my father had been mesmerized.

I'd been ruminating, stuck in my head, and hadn't realized Leon was just standing there, his blown pupils a black abyss of emotionlessness.

At some point I'd stopped flying and my bare feet comfortably rested on a soft rug. Shifting toward the couch, I cautiously asked, "Is there something else you need?"

Instead of verbally answering right away, Leon's head tilted ever so slightly to the side. It was a barely-there movement, something I wouldn't have noticed if I hadn't been so observant.

Was he trying to intimidate me? My wings instinctively fluttered, scattering a fresh batch of dust. If that was his game, then he'd have to try a hell of a lot harder than that. This wasn't my first vamp rodeo.

Building up a huff of steam, I was getting ready to lay a verbal smackdown on this vamp when he finally uttered, "You are a uniquely marked pixie."

Was that another insult? My brain struggled. There was no tone to attach to the words. It was like getting a text without an emoji.

Deciding to go with the words themselves, I nodded and answered, "So I am."

Leon blinked, his long, red lashes briefly covering his obsidian eyes. I waited for him to say more and was on the verge of kicking his vampire ass out of my new apartment when he walked toward the door, a casual "I like unique," whispered past his lips.

Leon's parting comment flushed my cheeks. I opened my mouth a couple of times, ready to say goddess only knows what at the now closed door, Leon well on his way down the stairs. In the end, the only sound that made it past my lips was the rattle of my teeth as my jaw tightly clamped shut.

Ignoring my hastened heartbeat, I turned from the closed door and crassly said, "Weirdo." I wasn't really sure what I meant by that singular word, only that I hoped it stilled my stupidly racing heart. "Vampires are trouble," I reminded myself. "Blood drinking, emotionally constipated, scary as fuck trouble."

Snagging my bags, I headed for the bedroom. My phone rang again, the tone letting me know it was Auntie Tandra. This would be call number three. One more unanswered call and she'd be on the warpath. Auntie Tandra had contacted the

Magical Usage Council on more than one occasion when she couldn't get ahold of me. I needed to spare them the tirade.

Tossing my bags on the bed, I hit the accept button and followed my paraphernalia's decent. The bed was firm, just the way I liked it.

"Hey, Auntie. Sorry I didn't—"

"Are you okay, Phlox? I've been so worried. You promised you'd call when you got to your location, and you also said it wouldn't be later than five p.m. It's after midnight." Underlying the obvious scolding was a wealth of fear. That fear halted the inkling of ire that worked its way free.

"Sorry, Auntie. I planned on calling but the timing didn't work out. I couldn't miss my rendezvous."

Auntie Tandra's sigh whispered across the line. "I understand, but I also worry."

I swallowed hard. The last thing in the world I wanted was to make her worry. "I'm sorry," I apologized again.

"No, no. I understand." Auntie Tandra's musical laughter eased my soul. "I'm glad you answered this time. I'm sure the council is getting fed up with me and I would have embarrassed myself again."

"Nonsense," I half lied. "They like you." That comment wasn't even a partial lie. Despite how demanding Auntie Tandra could be, members of the Magical Usage Council were just as smitten with her as Auntie Tandra's adoring social media fans. Truth be told, I believe some of them were starstruck when *the* Peltandra, stunningly golden social pixie maven, personally called them.

"Hmm, I suppose. Still, I'm sure they have more important issues to deal with than an overprotective auntie. I'm afraid Perovskia would have been much calmer than me. Your mother had a way about her. Sometimes I think that's why we got along so well. I was all splash and drama and your mother was a dash of cool water that tamed my fiery personality.

Perovskia evened me out. I try and channel your mother's natural Zen qualities but…" She sighed again. "I suppose it's a constant work in progress."

I wished Auntie Tandra could see my grin. "Mom would have been proud of you." I'd told her that a hundred times, maybe a thousand. Maybe I hadn't known my mom, but I was as certain of that statement as I was the sky was blue.

"That's my line," Auntie Tandra predictably bantered back. "She would be so proud of the work you're doing. Not that I really know what that is."

"Auntie, I wish—"

"No. I understand and I'm not fishing."

That was good. I could rarely tell Auntie Tandra what my missions were, not even when they were over. I was especially glad the council had forbidden me from discussing this one with her. After losing my mother to capture and fading, Auntie Tandra would be beside herself knowing I was actively seeking capture. It was a worry she didn't need, especially when I fully planned on making it out of my eventual capture alive, whole, and with the weight of the Magical Usage Council, the Vampire Council, and Fairy law ready to fall like an axe on the perpetrators.

"Can you at least tell me if you've got a comfortable place to stay?" That was always one of Auntie Tandra's concerns. I was happy this time I could genuinely relieve one of her fears.

"It's a good place. I'm sitting on a perfectly firm mattress as we speak." I bounced up and down a little, relishing in the lack of mattress movement.

"That's a relief. If there's a nice mattress, then that implies a roof over your head."

I chuckled, the sound a little raspy. "That's true." I was glad Dusk was closed and the music turned off. I wasn't sure how loud it was in the apartment but didn't want to take the chance of Auntie Tandra hearing the sound. She'd be too curious to let it go and despite what she'd said earlier, Auntie Tandra would indeed go information fishing.

"I suppose I should let you go. I'm not sure what time it is where you currently are." Auntie Tandra was on the West Coast, four time zones earlier than Rutherford Haven, Virginia. "Please contact me when you can." I nearly folded under the begging tone lacing her request. I'd had my share of missions where I couldn't contact her. Until my expected capture, this mission wouldn't be like that.

"I should be able to contact you regularly for a while. If things go well, there will be a time when I can't." Hopefully, that time would be minimal. While I might *want* to be captured, that didn't mean I planned on being a long-term prisoner. Quite the opposite. Then again, the best laid plans and all that.

"Okay. I'll try not to worry, but I suppose we both know that will be impossible." There wasn't an ounce of reproach in her voice, merely concern beating around a core of unconditional love. Once again, I was reminded how lucky I'd been that Auntie Tandra had willingly taken me in when my mother died. Auntie Tandra never made me feel like anything other than a blessing.

"I'm sorry I worry you so," I sincerely apologized. While I loved my work, I regretted the emotional toll it took on her.

"Nonsense. I'm fine. I've got thousands of adoring fans to soothe my wounded soul." Although that was true, I knew Auntie Tandra would trade them all in to have my mother back and me safe.

"I saw your latest post. That new hair sparkle product looks beautiful, and the lighting was perfect." Auntie Tandra was a social pixie through and through. She lived for compliments. Like nearly all social pixies, she could be vain and self-centered. What nearly every other species missed was that social pixies were also devoted parents who doted on their children. While we weren't related by blood, Auntie Tandra viewed me as her offspring. She would burn the world down for me.

"Thank you, dear," she gushed. "The sparkle is divine. It's a bit pricey, but worth every penny. I've still got it in. I'm seeing how well it holds up in different conditions. I'll add that information to my blog later."

I didn't mind stroking Auntie Tandra's ego. I rarely gave her false compliments. Such things weren't necessary.

"I'll be curious to hear how this new product performs." If it wound up being as good as she thought, I might purchase some for Parsnip. If I could get a signed autograph out of it that would be even better. A signed photo of Parsnip would certainly give Auntie Tandra something to crow about.

"I'll be sure to post a few messages on there to you as well, sweetie. Take care and be careful. Don't forget who you are. You are Perovskia's blood and my chosen child. Your father's blood runs through those veins—a proud and powerful shifter. Call on your blood, Phlox. Your heritage will not let you down."

Dampness filled my eyes. It took an embarrassingly long time to eliminate the quiver from my voice enough for me to answer, "I won't forget."

"I know you won't. Goodbye for now, sweetie. As always, I'm sending you all my love." Auntie Tandra ended the call before I could say the words back to her. Deep down she knew. The ones you loved should always know. After all, none of us knew when the goddess deemed our time up. Sometimes she granted decades. Sometimes she stingily doled time out in preciously packaged tragedies. Ultimately, the choice was hers. But I'd fight her on it. I'd fight tooth and claw to eke out as much time as I could greedily grab.

Chapter Four

LEON

My usual blood blend tasted stale. Reheating it didn't help. Swirling it didn't help. I had a sinking feeling nothing would. I hadn't tasted Frost's blood and yet, instinctively, I knew nothing could compare. Was this what Lucroy had felt? Was this what had driven him so hard to buck centuries of cautionary vampire lore?

Perhaps.

The sun would rise soon. I could feel it deep in my core. It was survival instinct, hardwired into every vampire. Lucroy said he could still feel it, knew when it was time to go to ground. The sun no longer threatened Lucroy's life, but he also didn't feel on friendly terms with her either. Lucroy said he believed the sun merely tolerated his existence in deference to his beloved.

I had no idea if Lucroy was correct or not. Gaia was not my mistress. Vampires had no god or goddess we prayed to. Perhaps in our first lives, but not our second ones. Gods and goddesses ruled the living. They cared not for the dead.

Red rimmed my otherwise clear glass, coating the edges as I

swirled the warm blood, aerating it, hoping against hope that it would improve the flavor. Another sip proved my hopes futile.

Forcing the fluid into my mouth and down my throat, I drank my meal like a shot, grimacing when finished. Staring at nothing in particular, I thought back to the unusual pixie two floors above me. Frost was up there. Unlike me, he could leave the premises any hour he wished. Frost leaving without me rankled. It was ridiculous and completely unlike me. I'd known the pixie for less than an hour.

"Foolish," I said into the empty room.

Allowing my stoic mask to fall, my lips pulled into a deep grimace. Fingertips dancing along the armchair, my mind refused to settle. This pixie should be nothing to me. Unlike other vampires, I hadn't fallen on the pixie bandwagon. I didn't frequent pixie bars, hoping one would grant me a sip or two. While I enjoyed Phil, Peaches, and Parsnip's company, I did not seek them out either.

"Why this pixie?"

Expectedly, the room had no answer and my voice merely echoed in the quiet.

It was a puzzle. Typically, I enjoyed puzzles. While I'd managed to keep my life from becoming too stagnant, I could admit numbness had crept in, encroaching along the edges of my existence. I should welcome this new, tantalizing conundrum. And, in a way, I did. What I did not appreciate was the *concern* that accompanied it.

Frost was here by order of the Magical Usage Council. He was an agent. Frost wasn't even his true, given name. I hadn't had the opportunity to speak with Lucroy long enough to learn the general plan. He'd simply told me to expect an agent and that they would be working in the bar with Johnny. At the time, the details seemed trivial.

Not so now.

Sunrise inched closer, making my mind and limbs increasingly sluggish. If I didn't make it to bed soon, I'd uncomfortably awaken in this chair come sunset.

Pushing out of my seat, I rinsed my glass and set it in a nearby drying rack. I'd essentially taken over Lucroy's home. It was still decorated to his tastes. Only the blood in the minifridge spoke to my occupation. The space was safe and functional but didn't feel like home. Honestly, nowhere inspired that feeling.

Slipping off my shirt and jeans, I crawled into bed in little more than my boxer briefs. Pulling the sheet up, I barely had time to cover myself before the sun's arrival slowed my reflexes, muddying my thoughts and movements.

"What can you tell me about Frost's mission?" Lucroy's ass barely hit the booth seat before the words slipped past my lips.

With a slightly raised eyebrow, Lucroy settled into a comfortable position before answering. "I do not believe there are any restrictions I am aware of."

Good. That was very good. Waking had not diminished my desire for more details. Watching Johnny show Frost around the bar had only fueled the need.

"Is there anything specific you wish to know?" Lucroy apathetically questioned.

Twirling the fresh glass of blood Lizbeth dropped off earlier, I attempted to mimic my old friend's demeanor. "I was only curious how Frost's presence might impact Dusk, our nest, and our customers." Inwardly I congratulated myself on my logical reasoning.

"I see." I could tell nothing from Lucroy's tone. "That is

reasonable. I should have considered this when I accompanied Frost here last night. It was an oversight on my part."

I waved Lucroy off. I hadn't meant to imply anything nefarious. "It is understandable. You needed to get back to Peaches."

"Indeed. When it comes to my beloved, I am afraid I become singularly focused. It is fortunate I have you to remind me of my duties toward our nest."

Lucroy was a different type of vampire king. As far as I was concerned, other kings and queens could take a few lessons. I couldn't think of another nest where their ruler referred to the nest as *ours*. Traditionally, vampires lorded over their territories and didn't share power. While most had seconds and underlings that held more power than others, Lucroy Moony was the only vampire that I knew of that truly thought of those underlings as equals.

"I did not mean to imply otherwise."

"Of course not, Leon. As for your earlier inquiry, the Magical Usage Council is as dismayed as the rest of us regarding the lack of progress into the latest pixie smuggling ring. They have had no more success in their attempts to reach the masterminds than us. As such, they have decided to approach the issue in a decidedly different way."

My already slow heart skipped a beat. I suspected I would not like this new approach. "How so?" I reluctantly asked.

"We have all been attempting to infiltrate the group from the angle of conspirator. The Magical Usage Council decided to send someone in a bit more covertly. From my understanding, their intention is to use Frost as bait."

This time, my heart came to a dead stop. "*Bait?*" The tips of my fingers itched, my talons ready and waiting for release.

Lucroy interwove his fingers, casually placing his clasped palms on the table. "Indeed. It is an intriguing plan. Sedrick,

Vander, and I spoke of this option but none of us could fathom willingly placing a pixie at such risk."

"Does Peaches know?"

"About the Magical Usage Council's plan or that we considered the idea previously?"

I had meant the latter but answered, "Both."

"He was at the meeting last evening and is aware of the risk Frost is taking. As for our earlier thoughts on the matter... No, he is unaware. Sedrick, Vander, and I believed it unwise."

It didn't take a genius to figure out why. "Peaches or Phil would have volunteered." Given Parsnip's history, I doubted he would willingly place himself in that situation again. While undeniably brave, Parsnip's underlying fear would likely impede his cognitive abilities.

"All too true." Lucroy's eyes briefly bled crimson before he regained control.

My gaze drifted toward Frost when Johnny let out a happy "whoop" followed by a round of applause. Johnny eagerly put Frost's wings to good use and had him restocking the top shelf. A mix of shaded blues and ochres surrounded Frost in a haze of pixie dust. It truly was a unique combination.

"And what protections have been offered to Frost?" Centuries of practice kept the growl from my voice.

"According to Frost, two implanted tracking microchips along with a charm of Vander's making and hair clips provided by his brownie ward, Byx. It is my understanding these charms are tracking devices as well."

Such devices could be removed, and I said as much. "Microchips and charms are easily discovered."

Lucroy's grin stopped short of showing fang. "I believe Warlock Kines found a way around that problem. The charm is imbedded within Frost's skin—below the surface. According to Vander, the charm will be impossible to remove and nearly as impossible to locate."

A tiny fraction of my unease subsided. I still wasn't a fan of this strategy, but I understood it.

"Forgive me, Leon, but you seem ill at ease with this plan," Lucroy said.

Body stilling, I considered my words. "Perhaps my control is slipping."

"Only I would notice, my friend."

Lucroy's words pulled my gaze from Frost. Lucroy was right. We could read each other better than most. I doubted any other, besides Peaches, would be able to parse out his current concern.

Relaxing, I offered a weak "I am unsure I understand and am even less certain I can explain it." Being truthful and indicating vulnerability was not a typical vampiric trait. Vulnerable vampires didn't live long within our harsh society. My relationship with Lucroy—the trust we'd built over the centuries—allowed me to show that quality now.

"Understood. Should you require a listening ear, mine are always available."

"Thank you," I answered sincerely.

Lucroy waved me off. "Think nothing of it. You have been a solid and reliable confidant over the years."

While that might be true, I still valued Lucroy's offer.

Another round of clapping, laughter, and clomping hooves filled the air. My gaze automatically shifted, zeroing in on the latest pixie to grace Dusk's floor.

What was it about Frost that captured my attention and made me crave his blood?

Chapter Five

"Damn, I'd forgotten how much I missed Phil," Johnny lamented as I flew back down to the floor. "Before I spent much time with pixies, I didn't give a thought about wings and how handy being able to fly is. Makes me wish for a pair."

Lizbeth snorted. Fisted hands on her hips, Lizbeth's lavender hair caught in the light. She was small, even by human standards and although I'd known her less than an hour, it was enough time to instill a healthy dose of respect. Human or not, Lizbeth was a force to be reconned with.

"Stop complaining, Johnny." Lizbeth rolled her eyes. "Wings are great, but I'd kill for your legs." As if to prove her point, Lizbeth stuck out her shorts-clad leg, twisting the lean appendage back and forth.

Running a hand down a fur-covered leg, Johnny's answering grin was wicked. "I always said you had good taste, Lizbeth."

With another eye roll, Lizbeth threw a dirty towel at Johnny before loudly huffing and flouncing away.

Chuckling, Johnny picked up the towel and offered a

warning. "Bit of advice, don't go poking that particular human. First time I met her, I made the mistake of thinking she was a weak, pink bag of human flesh. The boss thought the same. Lizbeth proved us wrong by climbing Bax like a mountain, wrapping her arm around his neck, and putting the big-ass troll in a head lock. Bax passed out and went down like a sack of potatoes. The boss hired her on the spot."

I grinned, liking Lizbeth even more. My gaze followed her as she wove around the still empty tables, tidying up and checking every last detail before Dusk opened its doors. Leon and Lucroy were nestled together in a corner booth. Johnny told me it was their usual spot, or at least it was Lucroy Moony's typical area. From what I understood, it was the same space Lucroy, Peaches, Sedrick, Phil, Vander, and Parsnip occupied when they were around. When they weren't, it was Leon's spot. In other words, the biggest fish in the building ruled from that little corner.

Leaning an elbow on the bar top, I stared at Leon. His attention was taken by Lucroy. My inner pixie didn't like that Leon's attention was elsewhere. Compounding that problem was the fact I was irritated that it bothered me in the first place. Two negatives didn't equal a positive.

"Got a question?" Johnny intuitively asked.

"Not really," I lied.

"The way you're starin', seems like you might," Johnny argued.

I hated being so obvious. Adding a third negative in there and I was well and truly in a downward spiral.

Gritting my teeth, I finally settled on a question that might be rude but was relevant where vamps were concerned. "How old is Leon?"

Johnny's eyebrows shot skyward. Despite his obvious surprise, he answered, "To the best of my knowledge, around three hundred, give or take a couple of decades. If I were a betting faun, I'd say older rather than younger."

Three hundred. It wasn't ancient by vampire standards, but it was impressive. It meant Leon had made it through the dangerously moody teenage vamp years. He was considered well-seasoned. Leon also had to be powerful. Not as powerful as Lucroy Moony, but nothing to sneeze at either.

"That all you want to know?" Johnny asked.

Was it? It should be and yet I found myself asking, "What kind of a boss-man is he?" I'd heard Johnny refer to Lucroy as *boss* and Leon as *boss-man.*

Johnny shrugged while polishing a glass. "In the simplest terms, the good kind. Leon's got Mr. Moony's back. He's got mine and everyone's back in this bar too. I've worked for Mr. Moony for a lot of years, and I've seen a lot of vamps come and go. Lucroy's a different kind of king. I wouldn't work for any of those other asshole vamp kings and queens. Trust me when I say the boss didn't want that shit in a second either. Goddess forbid something happen to Lucroy. But if it did, the nest's in good hands with Leon. It adds stability and a second layer of protection. That's a big part of why the Southeast vampire nest is one of the fastest growing in the US."

Johnny offered up a lot more information than I expected, and I offered a nod of thanks. His reassurance should have settled that twisted feeling in my gut. It didn't. If anything, my insides twirled and turned a little more.

"Anything more personal and you'll have to ask the boss-man himself," Johnny added.

"Understood and appreciated," I answered easily.

"So, that's the vampire side of things. What's your story?"

I blinked, expression doing an excellent vampire impersonation.

Johnny's chuckle sounded more like a coughed wheeze. "I don't mean the real story. I mean, what is the bullshit line we're supposed to tell our customers when they ask?" Pointing his glass in my direction, Johnny assured, "Because they will ask. Trust me on that one. This bar's got a pixie reputation and now we've got a fourth one—all shiny, new, and unattached."

"Ah...yes, an excellent question." The council and I'd gone over my cover story. I needed to look like easy pickings and the best way to go about that was to make others believe I wouldn't be missed.

"We're gonna take the KISS approach," I answered.

"Keep it stupid simple." Johnny nodded.

"Exactly. My backstory is sweet and simple. Or maybe sad and simple. No family. A smattering of loose friends. I'm originally from the West Coast and moved to Rutherford Haven hoping for a new start in life. Feel free to make up some hazy, tragic history that no one truly knows the details of. You can just say it's not something I like to talk about." The key to a successful lie is building it around a core of truth and keeping the facts minimal and easily subject to understandable change. No one would think twice when hearing different theories regarding my tragic past. Nearly every species had an innate need to gossip, to fill in knowledge gaps with questionable theories.

Johnny's eyes momentarily scrunched before he answered, "I can do that. Sounds easy enough. I'll let Lizbeth know. She's not aware of why you're really here. She's not a gossip and when she tells others to shut up and mind their own damn business, it will add a touch of reality to things."

In Lizbeth's case, it would be reality. Unaware of the underlying deception, Lizbeth would an unwitting accomplice.

"I don't like lying to her, but in the end, she'll understand," Johnny stated. It sounded like he was trying to convince himself more than me.

"Settling in well?" Lucroy asked as he glided toward the bar. Vamps had a way of doing that. They were so damn graceful that sometimes they appeared to float rather than walk. Despite his innate silence, I'd seen he and Leon's approach.

I nodded, temporarily ignoring Leon. "I am. Johnny and Lizbeth are catching me up to speed." I'd never worked in a bar before, but I had a fair amount of experience being a patron. "Learning different species' liqueur preferences will be the hardest part."

Johnny scoffed. "That and knowing what beverage will get one species high and another dead."

I blinked.

"Don't worry about it. Lizbeth and I've got your back. You'll learn quick enough and if you've got any questions, just ask. Mostly it's the humans you've gotta watch out for." Johnny shook his head. "I swear, if I live a thousand years, I'll never understand humans."

Lizbeth walked past and uttered a quiet "ditto."

Ignoring her, Johnny said, "If I had a dime for every time a human came in and asked for some dangerous shit on a dare, I'd be a rich faun. Their lives are short enough, you'd think they'd take a little more care." With that final lament, Johnny walked away, heading to the washing station and storage area. The washing station was one of my first lessons. From what I understood, it was Wendall's spot when he was here. When he wasn't, that would be one of my designated areas.

"Although colorfully said, Johnny, as usual, is correct," Lucroy said. "Please take care of our less *hearty* and *wise* customers. The paperwork is endless when there is a death within the bar. If possible, should someone do something foolish and get themselves killed, please see if you can direct them off Dusk property before they expire."

Thinking Lucroy was making a joke, I released a light chuckle. It died on my lips when I realized he was dead serious.

"Leon, I will leave Dusk in your capable hands. Peaches wanted to come in tonight, but he was gone from his orchard longer than he should have yesterday. He needs to stay there today. If I linger longer, I do not put it past my beloved to call Phil and ask for a ride into town."

It sounded like Lucroy knew his beloved well.

"Frost, Peaches wanted me to tell you he'd like to visit, get to know you better. I do not believe I can keep him at home two nights in a row. Most likely we shall both see you tomorrow. As I said before, do not hesitate to let Johnny, Leon, or myself know if you require further assistance."

"Thank you, Mr. Moony."

"While appreciated, your thanks are not needed. My beloved is most distraught regarding this pixie smuggling ring. If your sacrifice gives him a modicum of peace of mind, then it is I who owe you thanks."

I thought I caught a flash of crimson in Leon's eyes but couldn't be certain. Maybe he was as disturbed by the word *sacrifice* as me. I didn't plan on dying on this mission. Fading had stolen my mother. I refused to follow in her footsteps.

"Have a good evening, Leon," Lucroy said before heading toward the parking garage, leaving Leon and me alone again.

Silence stretched between us, widening to an uncomfortable gap. Music started from somewhere. The sound was low, little more than a background murmur. I stood there, twiddling my proverbial thumbs, wondering if I was supposed to say something or not. Leon was statue still.

Irritated at myself for expecting more from this odd vampire, I swallowed a huff. The hair clips Byx gave me fed off my poor mood, reflecting my exasperation by standing on their hind legs and barking their distress.

My irritation only grew when Leon responded to my hair clips while he'd all but ignored me.

"Is that some kind of canine?" Leon asked while leaning forward, obsidian eyes fixated on my head.

"Meerkat." Touching one of the clips, I inhaled deeply, forcing calm into my core. The hair clips responded by backing down. "According to Byx, they're one of her new creations. They're supposed to bark out a warning when a predator is nearby." Reflecting on the choice, I grimaced. "Probably not the best option considering my current working environment."

A single crimson eyebrow soared. "And they believe I am such a threat?"

I shrugged. "No idea." I wasn't about to tell Leon they'd probably fed off my unsettled mood rather than his lurking presence. "Vander pulled me aside and informed me some of Byx's creations don't always go to plan. Like I said, this is a new one. I offered to be the guinea pig." The hair clips were adorable. I'd go to my grave before admitting that was the reason I'd agreed.

"Interesting." Leon leaned back into his own personal space, evidently nothing more to say.

Tired of whatever the hell this was, I said, "If that's all, I've got work to do." I didn't get far. Leon's hand shot out, latching onto my wrist. His grip was just shy of painful. With a pointed glare at his hand, I slowly shifted my eyes until our gazes locked. When he didn't release me, I asked, "Is there a reason for *this*?" I pointedly glanced back at his vice-like grip.

"You are not a sacrifice," Leon stated, tone so cold I thought the bar top might turn to ice.

"No, I'm not. On that we can easily agree."

Leon's grip eased and his fingers slowly slid from my skin. I hid my shiver, absorbing it into my body. Interestingly, the meerkats didn't so much as twitter.

Leon didn't seek forgiveness for his rash act. "I am pleased we are on the same page."

Pulling my arm to my side, I narrowly avoided rubbing the tender flesh he'd touched. Tilting my head to the side, I studied this odd vampire and stated, "You're worried."

Leon's apathetic mask remained firmly in place. "Worried would be a strong word. I am...concerned. I do not relish the thought of any weaker species placing themselves in such a position."

"*Weaker*?" My lip twitched, my emotions battling between humor and pissed off. "Because I'm a pixie," I flatly stated.

"I did not mean to imply pixies are incapable. Recent events have offered me the opportunity to interact with your species enough to learn you can be very stubborn and protective. However, pixies are not known for their offensive abilities. You are a peaceful species by nature."

While that was true of most pixies, I wasn't *most*. Tapping my fingertips along the countertop, I allowed a very unpixie-like grin. "Oh, Leon. I think you'll soon learn I'm not your average pixie." With a flirty wink, my wings fluttered to life. Spinning, I flew in the direction of the washroom, leaving a very flummoxed vampire in my pixie dust wake.

Chapter Six

LEON

I should head home when the bar closed. I had more than ample time before the sun rose. And yet, I sat, ever the voyeur. True to his word, Lucroy and Peaches came into the bar tonight. Sedrick and Phil stopped by for a short time also. What they did not do was have more than a cursory, polite interaction with Frost. Lucroy explained that upon further consideration, he did not believe it wise. The idea was to make Frost appear an easy target and part of that plan was weaving a tale involving few interpersonal relationships. The fewer individuals there were to miss Frost, the less likely the fuss when he disappeared.

Lucroy instructed Johnny not to act too fondly toward our newest pixie addition. If anything, Lucroy said we should act dismissive, if not outright hostile toward Frost. Nothing too obvious, just enough that if anyone were watching, they'd get the impression we cared precious little regarding Frost's comings and goings.

If only that were true.

I glanced at the clock, not that I needed an outward sign of time to reference the sun's cycles. Over three hundred years hadn't quelled that particular habit. Regardless, I still had time. I could stand up, walk out the door, drive home, and be comfortably in bed long before the first rays crested the horizon.

I didn't move.

I wasn't the only one sticking around. The bar was busy, although this time of the early morning, several species began filtering out. Most of my nestmates would stay another twenty, maybe thirty minutes before they left too. The younger vampires were often the first to leave. The sun was their boogeyman, and they were often a twitchy bunch when it came to safety. I remembered those days well and was glad I'd mentally moved past that overwhelming fear.

My gaze ticked to my left. I'd kept a weather eye on the group of three werewolves passively lounging at a table on the outer fringe of the dance floor. Although not as gluttonous as dwarves, werewolves were known to enjoy their cups. Sedrick guzzled beer as if the fount would never run dry. They had high tolerances for alcohol and generally liked enjoying themselves. These wolves barely drank one beer apiece the entire evening.

Admittedly, Dusk's werewolf population was more anemic than most bars. Arie Belview was the alpha of the local pack and for some unfathomable reason, he didn't like mingling with vampires. Especially, Lucroy's nest.

Keeping my internal grin just that, I silently chuckled at Arie Belview's discomfort. It was a small victory, but a victory nonetheless.

So, the question was why were Arie's wolves coming into the bar now? It wasn't always the same group. There was never just one. They came in pairs, trios, or occasionally four-packs. They were exceedingly polite for werewolves, let alone Arie

Belview's wolves. Much to Pete and Bax's dismay, the wolves never gave our troll bouncers cause to intervene.

"That group doesn't do my sense of calm a bit of damn good," Johnny lamented as he sat next to me. "I don't like it, boss-man. They're up to something." Johnny kept his voice low, and the blaring music helped cover his words, keeping them from sensitive werewolf ears.

"Hmm, an accurate assessment, Johnny," I easily agreed. Maybe that was why I didn't want to go home, why I stayed at the bar and would most likely spend another day nestled within the safety of Lucroy's underground dwelling.

Johnny huffed. "I hate this waiting game shit. You know, I thought we were done with all that when that jackass, Arthur Stover died. Now that Aurelia's asleep again, I'd hoped we might get a longer reprieve." Johnny ended with a discouraged sigh.

Stagnancy was a vampire's Achilles' heel. It was a gentle pull, a lie that lulled one into dull complacency and before a vampire knew it, they were little more than a shell of their former self. Life lost all meaning and there was absolutely no reason to continue. Peace and quiet were the death nail of most vamps. Perhaps that is why, traditionally, we were such a brutal race. Maybe we'd been forced into that role, if only to perpetuate our second lives.

But there were different levels of peace and quiet, and I found, like Johnny, that a longer run of peace would not have been detrimental.

With the djinn on his mind, Johnny twisted a nearby napkin and said, "You know, we could ask Peaches to wake her up. He could just wish for Aurelia to find who's in charge of this pixie trafficking ring. The whole thing would be done and over with like that." Johnny snapped his fingers.

While Johnny's idea held a lot of appeal, it was a dangerous road. More dangerous than our current path.

"Djinn are not a species to so callously use."

"It's not callous. It's about saving lives," Johnny rightfully argued.

"You are correct. I chose my wording poorly. What I meant is that while your thoughts have merit and sound reasonable, one cannot count on a djinn to conform to those thoughts, even a djinn as mentally stable as Aurelia appears to be. It would be a dangerous ploy and one I would not invoke unless the situation were truly dire."

As much as I hated the idea of Frost playing bait, I feared the idea of waking Aurelia more. The djinn had seemed to be on our side last time, but there was no guarantee she'd feel the same now. While the one controlling her object of attachment held Aurelia's leash, that tether was, at best, precarious, and at worst, little more than a wispy cloud.

The best the world could hope for was that djinn faded from memory. That they became little more than a fairy tale— something precious few believed truly existed. The more we used Aurelia's abilities, the less likely that was to happen.

Elbows planted on the table, Johnny set his chin in his cupped hands. "You're right. I hate that you're right, but that doesn't make it less true."

Little yips met my ears and Johnny turned just in time to welcome Trinket onto the table. The scuttlebutt scurried up his arm and settled into the crook on Johnny's neck. Uproariously laughing, Johnny patted Trinket on the head.

"Hey, that tickles."

Trinket heard the words and saw them as an invitation to wiggle more. Johnny laughed even harder.

"Sorry about that, Johnny." With a half-full bin of dirty glasses on his hip, Wendall blew a section of bangs off his forehead. "It's been a couple of days since we've been in, and Trinket's missed everyone so much. She just can't help herself." Wendall's words were full of affection.

"It's okay. I missed our little lady too." Knuckles roughly rubbing against her skin, Trinket leaned into the deep massage and let loose a round of gurgles that sounded somewhere between pain and pleasure.

"Hey, Leon," Wendall greeted as he reached over and grabbed my empty glass of blood. It had taken me an embarrassing long time to force the liquid down my throat tonight. "Busy night?" he asked while clearing the table.

"Typical," I easily responded. When I caught Wendall's gaze, I was momentarily mesmerized by the blue waves rolling within. Aurelia's intervention not only saved Wendall's life but boosted his fairy DNA. None of us were sure what that fully meant.

Scanning the bar, I didn't see Wendall's other half and asked, "Is Ray here?"

Wendall shook his head. "He had to see Aunt Silvidia."

Wendall's casual mention of his aunt, otherwise known as the Fairy queen, was a constant source of amusement.

"Is everything all right in Fairy?" I asked.

"As far as I know. I think he mostly went to fill her in on the latest plan." Wendall leaned over and whispered the last part. "She's pretty concerned." He frowned, holding out his arm. Trinket easily jumped from Johnny to Wendall, racing up his arm, nesting on his shoulder, her long, prehensile tail safely wrapped around his bicep. "To be honest, I'm not sure if she's more concerned about the pixies or the fact that someone's so blatantly ignoring fairy law. That's not exactly fair. Aunt Silvidia's really worried about the pixies, it's just...you know, she's not really used to being so..." Wendall waved a hand in the air, struggling to come up with the right word.

I understood. Attempting to quantify Queen Silvidia's thoughts was not a prospect I envied.

"Anyway, she's not happy," Wendall finally finished.

Johnny grumbled. "An unhappy fairy queen is a risky

affair."

Wendall nodded. "Yeah." Shifting his bin of glassware, Wendall perked up. "Ray should be here soon. He said he'll come directly to Dusk when he's done." Wendall's cheeks flushed, and his voice filled with delight. Outward signs indicated that relationship was going well.

"I'm glad I was able to come in tonight. I got to see Frost again. He's doing a great job." Wendall beamed. "I know I'm not supposed to let others see that I like him, but I don't think it's a problem to show him when we're alone."

If I didn't know Wendall Galen was already well and truly spoken for, I might have lost control of my transformation. Logically, I understood Wendall's phrasing was innocent. Logic was a difficult mistress to obey when instinct took over.

"He's doing great," Johnny agreed happily. "He's quick on the uptake." Johnny tapped a finger to his temple. "I've only gotta show him something once and he's off and running. Truth be told, I'd like to have about three of him come the weekend."

"If it'll help, I can work this weekend."

"Indeed, that would be fine," Ray agreed, casually walking to our table and instantly wrapping an arm around Wendall's waist. Without a word, Ray took Wendall's bin, easing it out of Wendall's arms and carrying the burden. Wendall didn't protest. It was a common occurrence.

"Good meeting?" Wendall inquired, eyes wide and nearly begging Ray not to disagree.

Conflict raged within Ray's crimson ringed eyes. "It was... expected," Ray finally settled on. "Queen Silvidia sees the merit in our current strategy and will not interfere. My queen assured that her services and assistance are available when needed. Queen Silvidia did request she be given the honor of dispatching those involved personally."

I considered Ray's answer and said, "I would expect

nothing less."

"Nor I," Ray easily agreed.

Johnny grimaced. "Well, I have to say, I don't necessarily want to be around when this all goes down. Hearing about it secondhand will be good enough for me." Fauns weren't known for their bloodthirsty ways.

"Looks like our were friends have had enough for the evening," Johnny said, gaze fixed on Dusk's exit.

"Friends?" Wendall questioned and then nodded when he figured out Johnny was being sarcastic.

"They are coming in more frequently," Ray added.

"Nearly every night now," I agreed.

Ray's eyes narrowed. Typically, beyond the law, fairies didn't care much about the comings and goings of other species. Hellfire Rayburn was different.

"Yo, Johnny, you gonna sit on your ass all evening or are you gonna help me?" Lizbeth shouted from a nearby table. "The bar's backing up. Frost's doing a good job, but he's not as quick as you and me."

Slapping his hands on the table, Johnny stood. "Duty calls. You spending the day here again, boss-man?"

I nodded without thought. I'd definitely spend the day here. Something inside wouldn't allow me to go elsewhere. Logically, that didn't make sense. I was utterly useless during the day. My body was inert, and my mind would not wake.

My gaze found Frost. The pixie was behind the bar, scurrying back and forth. Pixie dust surrounded him like a heavenly haze. He grinned, winked, and fluttered about like he hadn't a care in the world. Frost was focused on his work.

As if he could sense me watching, Frost's head lifted, our gazes meeting across the still busy bar.

No. I wouldn't leave the bar. I'd stay, locked in my safe little dungeon, as close to the living as I could be without risking the sun's wrath.

Chapter Seven

Two and a half weeks later and no progress. Summer in Virginia settled in, and my body protested. I wanted to stay inside by the air-conditioning vent. I would have sat on top of the damn thing if possible. Peaches and Phil loved this weather. Parsnip probably did too. I'd been told he and Vander would be back soon. I'd gladly switch places with them. The snowy Himalayas sounded like heaven right about now.

Flopped out on my bed, I lay across the sheets in nothing more than a pair of loose, deep blue panties. They were silky smooth and barely left anything to the imagination. I didn't care about all that. I wasn't trying to be sexy. I was aiming for cool. I'd cranked the air-conditioning up as high as it would go. I wasn't sure if Lucroy would charge me or not.

"Fuck it, he can bill my hot ass," I said, only the constant whirl of the air-conditioning witness.

I was currently at loose ends. I'd called and reassured Auntie Tandra that I was alive. I'd also contacted the Magical Usage Council. Six more known pixies had been abducted and were listed as missing. Unfortunately, I wasn't one of them.

Time was running out. Unlike previous pixie trafficking operations, few of these pixies were found before they faded. Pixies only lasted so long in captivity. Each victim had five, maybe six months and no pixie had ever survived in captivity more than seven months. As far as I knew, Parsnip held the dubious record of longest captured pixie to survive. Another day, maybe two, and he wouldn't have survived.

I slammed my fist into the mattress. What else could I do? I'd gone out at night, after my shift or on days I had off. I'd wandered the streets alone, the perfect, easy target. Letting loose a growl, my inner shifter begged for release.

"Not so alone." Those words came out garbled. "Leon," I hissed. The vamp followed me. It was ridiculous how he thought I didn't know he was there. And if I knew he was there, then so did others. Leon was sneaky. All vamps were. He didn't know I had better hearing than your typical pixie. Considering no one knew who was behind the pixie thefts, there was a good chance that whatever the species was, they had just as good of hearing as me. And if not hearing, other senses that allowed them to pick out Leon's meddling.

Vampires hunted humans for a reason. They were the easiest prey.

I'd sort of been flattered at first. Or maybe smitten. I'm not sure what the right word was. Now, I was just pissed. Leon all but ignored me while I worked in the bar. The sexy vamp barely said two words to me in a night, but the fucker followed me all over town when I wasn't on duty. What kind of sense did that make?

None.

Tossing my head, my hair spread out behind me, I stared at the ceiling. When had my life gotten so confusing? I was used to working cases alone. This one shouldn't have been different and yet it was. While everyone was careful not to outwardly appear too concerned, that was as far from true as could be. It was strange, working in an environment where I felt genuinely cared for. I was conflicted. My pixie side relished the attention. My shifter side not so much.

"Ugh. Enough!" Sitting, I pushed off my bed and grabbed a pair of my loosest, coolest pants and top. Shoving Byx's clips in my hair, I headed for my door and the street. I'd avoided going out alone during the day, mostly to avoid the heat. Also, nearly every report of captured pixies took place during the dark. Daylight wasn't the prime time to meet my goal. It was, however, vampire free.

Stomping down the stairs, I gave the door leading to Leon's underground nest the one finger salute. "This is all your fault," I ridiculously accused. "You're making me go out in this goddess forsaken heat."

Quickly raiding Dusk's main fridge, I grabbed a couple bottles of cold water. If I had to do this, then I'd need hydration. Heading across the bar, I threw Dusk's door open and released an internal growl. The heat was even worse than I expected. This was going to be a long, steamy day.

"Thanks, Leon," I grumbled before slamming the door and locking it behind me. Despite my anger there was no way anyone was getting into Dusk during the day. Vamps always had a lot of security around the entrance of their private, daylight dwellings. That didn't mean I had to make it easier for some asshole with a vampire axe to grind.

No one was getting near Leon. Not on my watch.

Goddess, it's hot. I caught my appearance in a nearby shop window and grimaced. I appeared wilted. Pixies flew around me now and again, chatting it up and happy as warm clams. A couple inquired about my health but flew off with a few well-placed reassurances.

I'd ducked into more than half a dozen shops, seeking air-conditioning and a moment to cool off and collect myself. Inevitably, I'd have to head out into the heat again. The setting sun hadn't cooled the area off. If anything, it was just steamier than it was earlier. I was convinced humidity was a curse upon the world.

Dusk rose in the distance. Bright oranges, deep russets, and mellow yellows lit up the sky around it. The building wasn't all that impressive. It wasn't meant to be. Johnny explained that Dusk was built like a fortress, able to withstand all that nature, humanity, and anything every other species could throw at it. Dusk's beauty lay within its walls.

Unlocking the door, I didn't have to type in my security code. Lizbeth was already behind the bar, doing inventory and getting things ready. Her eyes widened and her skin paled when she saw me. Lizbeth's bubblegum-pink hair belied her worry.

"Jesus, what happened to you?" Lizbeth scurried around the counter, quickly pulling out a stool and directing me into it. "Sit down before you fall down. I'll get some water." She darted off and I thanked the goddess that she was there and on a water mission.

"Here," she said before sternly ordering, "drink."

I didn't hesitate and downed the contents in less than two minutes. Lizbeth was ready with a second bottle. I drank this one much slower and even managed to savor its cool feel.

"Thanks," I huskily managed.

"No worries." Her eyebrows scrunched, creating a tight V of skin in between. "Scratch that. I *am* worried. Why do you look like something the cat coughed up on the rug?"

I chuckled, relaxing into the cooler room. Dusk wasn't as cold as my apartment, but it was a damn sight better than outside.

"Thought I'd go for a walk." Johnny told me Lizbeth

could be trusted, but for her own safety, they tried to keep her out of the loop regarding the more dangerous escapades troubling Rutherford Haven's residents.

"Yeah?" Lizbeth tilted her head, eyebrows still scrunched in concern and confusion. "Not a bad plan. Pixies thrive in this kind of weather, but you don't look like you did a lot of *thriving* out there today."

I waved a dismissive hand, my wings too tired to stir up a speck of dust. "I'm not your typical pixie."

"So you keep saying." Leon's cold tenor made me shiver more than the air-conditioning. Leon's joints popped, the telltale sound of a vampire on the cusp of transformation. My exhausted body immediately went on alert.

"Lizbeth, you wanna give us a minute here," I said, never once taking my gaze off the livid vampire fuming a few feet away.

Lizbeth hesitated. Bless her human heart, she really was concerned. "I-I don't know, Frost. I'm not sure this is the best time to do that."

"It's the perfect time," I reassured.

"Maybe I should call Mr. Moony."

I considered Lizbeth's suggestion and shook my head. "Not yet. I'll let you know if it's necessary. Now, go on. I've got this." I had no idea if that was true, but whatever had crawled up Leon's dead ass and died, I didn't want Lizbeth caught in the crossfire. She was too human-fragile to risk.

"Okay. I've got Mr. Moony's number on speed dial and my finger on the button," Lizbeth reassured as she walked away, the sound of the swinging door leading to the washroom quickly following.

Sitting on my stool, I reached inside myself. I didn't have to dig deep. My inner shifter was ready, waiting, and impatient for release. Interestingly, Byx's hair clips remained silent. I'd need to have a discussion with her. I didn't think this design worked out the way she planned.

Silence fell like a heavy cloud. Leon stood there, nails shifting to talons before easing back into nails. The process repeated twice before he finally said, "You left the building."

"Sure did, Captain Obvious. I leave the building all the time."

Leon tilted his head, and I heard the distinctive popping of his joints elongating. "During the day," he growled.

"Yup. It's hot as hell out there." I reached for my water, stupidly or valiantly ignoring my pounding heart.

"The sun is up," Leon answered.

I rolled my eyes. "Again with the Captain Obvious. Yes, the sun is up. Well, not now, but it was earlier. I don't see the problem." The problem was that I'd nearly expired in the heat. But I didn't think that's the angle from which Leon came at the problem.

"You could have been injured. Or captured."

"That's kind of the point." It was the wrong word choice.

Leon lost control of his transformation and soon a scary-as-shit vampire towered above me. Call me an idiot, but I still didn't scream for Lizbeth to call Lucroy. Did it really matter, though? Lucroy would never get here in time. Either I handled the situation or I was a bleeding husk on the floor.

Hunched, Leon's eyeteeth elongated to the point they hung past his lower lip. He snapped them at me but didn't move closer. I could see his internal war, struggling behind his obsidian eyes.

I could shift. I'd have a better chance that way. I'd probably still end up as mincemeat, but I'd get in a few good swipes. Right now, I needed reason, not claws.

"Leon." I kept my voice calm and steady. "I'm not injured. Maybe a little dehydrated and hot, but not hurt. No one took me. I'm perfectly safe."

Leon's roar shook the building. He snapped his fangs, eyes now blown crimson. His talons clicked as he flicked them together.

Call me crazy—and others had definitely accused me of that and worse—but I got off my stool. I must be losing my mind because I didn't exactly feel threatened. Leon was mad— beyond livid—but that anger wasn't directed at me. It was *for* me. Leon was worried. I still wasn't sure why. There was so much about this vampire I didn't understand. That didn't mean it wasn't true. It was why he followed me at night, why he stayed at Dusk every day and didn't go home, why he was so angry now. When I'd taken off earlier, I hadn't anticipated this level of fear. And it *was* fear. It leaked from every one of Leon's pores. My shifter side recognized the scent, knew it for what it truly was.

With deliberate slowness, I took one small step, followed by another. I kept my limbs loose and as nonthreatening as possible. I didn't think Leon wanted to hurt me, but right now, he was running on instinct and sometimes the innocent got caught in the fray. I wasn't sure I qualified as *innocent*, but the analogy worked well enough.

Leon fidgeted, as if he couldn't get comfortable in his own transformed skin. Crimson slowly leaked from his eyes, leaving them a familiar, calm sea of black. Hand outstretched, I settled my palm against Leon's cheek, rubbing my thumb along his alabaster skin.

"I need you to calm down, Leon. Can you do that? For me?"

Seconds ticked by and Leon's body remained still. Finally, his joints popped, and his body shrank. Leon still towered above me, but he didn't loom. When his hands returned to normal, his fingers wrapped around my wrist, holding my palm in place.

Leon's large eyes blinked, slowly covering onyx in crimson

fringed alabaster. There was no inhale, no tension releasing deep breath. Leon stood there, only the methodically slow beat of his heart indicating he hadn't expired a second time.

"You back?" I asked, making sure my voice remained even and without a hint of fear.

A handful of seconds passed before Leon managed a cold "I am."

"Good. Lizbeth was worried." I didn't mention how concerned I'd been. Never show fear. It was a mantra I tried living by. Some days I managed better than others.

"Only Lizbeth?" Leon tried calling me out on my bullshit.

"She's the only one I'm admitting to." I tried pulling my hand back, but Leon wouldn't release me.

"Leon, I—"

"You will not leave the premises again during the daylight," Leon demanded, voice still icy.

"Says who? You?" I made a sound somewhere between a hiss and scoff. Only my handler on the Magical Usage Council told me what to do.

"Yes." Simple. Direct. And painfully to the point.

"Yeah, well, I don't remember when you were designated my keeper. Oh, there's a reason for that. You're not my keeper." I yanked my hand back, and thankfully, Leon let me go. I had no illusions that if he'd wanted to hold onto me, he would have.

Lips pulled back, the tips of Leon's fangs peeked through. It was a very emotional vampire response. "You placed yourself in danger today. Did you even tell anyone where you were going?"

"No. There was no need. I'm a grown pixie, I can—"

"It is dangerous out there." Leon threw his arm out, pointing beyond the building.

"No shit, Sherlock. That's kind of why I'm here." I took a step back. When Leon didn't follow, I took another until I backed into the stool where I'd been sitting. Leon's arm slowly dropped. Don't ask me how I knew, but the look in his black eyes was mutinous.

Fuck, I was too damn tired to deal with this. Not to mention I had to work tonight. Plopping down on my barstool, I grabbed what was left of my water and downed it. Elbow resting on the bar top, I placed my forehead in my palm.

Unlike Leon, I needed to breathe and after three good inhales and exhales I felt put back together enough to converse like a grown up.

"Listen, Leon," I started, hoping against hope he didn't interrupt me. "While I appreciate the concern, I'm honestly not sure what to do with it." Or where it came from. "Pixies are dying." I lifted my gaze. "Dying," I repeated. "The longer that goes unpunished, the more pixies we'll lose and it's a horrible death." I swallowed hard thinking about what my mother went through. "I don't have a death wish, but if I can do something to help stop it, then that's what I'm going to do. And, unfortunately, that means getting captured." Leon's chest rumbled but he didn't interrupt. "It's my job. No one twisted my arm, I volunteered. I've got the best tracking available. Two chips, a warlock charm etched into my skin, and brownie-created hair clips." I pointed at the silent meerkats lounging within my hair. "Like it or not, I'm the best chance we've got."

Hands tightening into fists, Leon muttered, "I do not like it."

"No?" I raised an eyebrow. "I never would have guessed." A grin teased the edge of my lips before I sobered. "You wanna explain why that is?"

Leon twitched. The movement was slight but the equivalent of vampire pacing. When he settled, Leon answered, "I am uncertain." He licked his lips and his gaze tracked toward my neck. "Your blood...it sings to me." Leon sounded just as confused saying those words as I was hearing them.

"Huh?" I didn't have anything more eloquent.

Leon's dark eyes gazed everywhere but at me when he said, "I do not know how to explain it. Lucroy was equally confused when he met Peaches."

"What does—" My body stilled, doing a respectable imitation of a vamp. My brain tumbled through his words. They were deceptively simple at face value. Inhaling again, I said, "Peaches is Lucroy Moony's beloved."

"I am aware."

"Are you saying—"

"I do not know." Leon allowed a hint of irritation into his voice. I didn't think he was irritated with me so much as the situation. I could kind of relate.

My empty water bottle's plastic crumpled within my death grip. "Is it just my blood you want?" I asked.

Leon's gaze finally came back to me. "The packaging is appealing as well."

"*Packaging?*" I lifted an eyebrow.

"I have already said you are unique." Leon said those words as if they explained everything.

"You did. Forgive me for not understanding your meaning," I sarcastically answered.

"Vampires crave uniqueness. I was offering a compliment."

"Oh." I didn't know what to do with that. Evidently my cheeks did because they flushed with a different type of heat. My pixie form was pretty. All pixies were. Compared to Auntie Tandra and photos I'd seen of my mom, I was downright drab. I was also petite. Other pixies didn't really hold that against me. I figured it was more of an internal issue than external one.

Leon took a cautious step forward. When I didn't pull

back, he took another, and then another until I could reach out and touch him if I wished. I thought about it but kept my hands planted within my own personal space bubble.

"Perhaps I should use more common terminology. You are very attractive, Frost. Every part of you is enticing—the scent of your blood, your intense coloring, your bravery, your wit and determination, your smirk, the way the light shimmers through your blue eyes, the hint of yellow that bleeds through when your emotions are high—there is not an inch of you I do not find appealing."

Oh. Oh! What did I do with that? My lips parted, shallow pants filling the air. Absently, I wondered if that yellow Leon just described lit my eyes because my emotions were high. Very high.

Clearing my throat, I attempted speech a couple of times before anything decipherable came out.

"I-I...I'm not sure what to say. I don't think... I mean, I'm pretty sure no one's ever described me in those terms." I'd never suffered insults for my size the way I'd heard Phil had. I'd never been afraid my colors were too dull like Parsnip. I'm not sure I would have given a shit if they had. That wasn't completely true. I *was* a pixie, but that was only half my heart. My other half couldn't care less what others thought.

Still, it was nice—no, better than nice—hearing someone else describe you in such appreciative terms. It was even nicer coming from someone who made my dick stand up and pay attention.

Leon's lips twitched. He palmed my cheek, his talons long gone, his blunt nails gentle against my skin. Leon wasn't exactly cold to the touch, but he was cool. I leaned into his skin, relishing the feel on my overheated flesh.

"Reciprocation is most likely too much to expect at this point." The cold indifference typically lacing Leon's words was absent, replaced by a tinge of playful warmth.

"Hmm...maybe not," I practically purred, leaning into his touch even more. "You're not so bad yourself." I left off "for a vampire." Leon knew what he was. He didn't need my reminder.

"*Not so bad*? I suppose I've worked with less."

I chuckled, the sound rumbling through my bass purr. The sound brought Lizbeth from the washroom. She cautiously peeked through the door. She must have been satisfied by what she saw because she was gone nearly as quickly.

Leon and I stayed that way for a few more precious seconds. His thumb touched my lower lip, running his pad over the surface. I gasped but couldn't manage much more. Deep in my core, I knew this moment somehow changed everything. My life path was immediately picked up and realigned. The weaving road was now straight as an arrow, wide, and sure. It wasn't a sensation I could easily describe and yet it was as true as anything I'd ever known.

Leon's dark gaze slowly slid from my eyes toward my tilted neck. I hadn't even realized I'd done that. Did he see it as an offer? It was amazing how expressive his onyx eyes were when I paid closer attention.

And if that's what he wanted, was I ready to offer up a vein? Peaches did it. Previously, questioning him seemed rude. Current circumstances made me reevaluate that decision.

My pulse pounded. I could only imagine what that looked like to a hungry vampire. In that instant, I knew I wasn't ready. The first niggle of fear rolled through me. It wasn't overwhelming, simply that spark of self-preservation nearly every individual had. Something must have shifted in my eyes or maybe my demeanor. Whatever it was, Leon stiffened and dropped his hand. I immediately missed the coolness and pressure.

"I will not force you," Leon said, tone frigid once more.

"I know," I answered confidently. I shouldn't have sounded so sure. "I don't know why I know that, but I do."

Leon relaxed a fraction. "Good. I do not wish to frighten you."

I grinned. I just couldn't help it. "Trust me, I've seen a lot scarier than you."

I'd thought Leon would understand the amusement. Instead, his eyes flared crimson before settling into black again.

"That does not put me at ease, Frost."

"Sorry." Given Leon's reaction to my leaving the building during the daylight, I should have figured that out. What I also figured out was that I didn't like Leon using my agent name. Coming from his lips, it didn't sound right. Staring at my fingers, I said, "Phlox."

"Pardon?" Leon leaned closer but refrained from touching me.

I cleared my throat. "Phlox. That's my real name. When we're alone, I'd like you to use it." There wasn't a lot of difference between the two names, and yet, Phlox felt so much more personal.

"Phlox." Somehow, Leon made my given name sound sexy. "I will enjoy using your true name when we interact." Just as he'd made my name sound different, when Leon said the word, *interact*, it sounded positively filthy.

"Nice, Leon."

Leon's answering grin barely avoided showing fang tips.

The sound of Johnny's hooves eased into the little bubble Leon and I'd wrapped ourselves in. The sound of the washroom door swinging open, followed by Johnny's loud "you two are up early" popped our bubble completely.

"No offense, Frost, but for a pixie, you look like shit. Not sure what you've been up to today, but I'm sending you upstairs to clean up before you head back down here. Go on, shoo." Johnny waved me off.

"Aye-aye, Johnny." I gave a little salute before sliding off my chair. My wings were recovered enough that I could fly, adding a little dust to the air. Johnny quickly covered his nose. Leon's dark gaze followed my exit. I could feel that lusty stare bore into my back. Johnny might think I looked like shit, but Leon was a different matter. Leon was a different matter altogether.

Chapter Eight

"Is there something you wish to tell me?" Lucroy asked as he lounged against the booth seat opposite me. Peaches was at the bar, socializing with Johnny and Lizbeth. He offered a cursory greeting to Phlox but managed to keep the interaction to a minimum. Peaches was exhibiting a generous amount of self-control.

"I don't follow." Lucroy and I were friends, but that didn't automatically mean we shared everything. I rarely offered information without knowing what the one doing the questioning truly knew.

Lucroy's gentle smirk signaled he was game to play. "I see. Perhaps I should be more specific." Still at his leisure, Lucroy tapped his slender fingers along the back of his seat. "I spoke with Lizbeth...or perhaps the more accurate description would be Lizbeth spoke with me. It seems our human bartender was rather concerned earlier this evening."

"Was she?" I took a sip of blood and barely concealed a cringe. My human blend tasted increasingly foul. I hadn't taken a sip of Phlox's blood and yet it was all I craved. No wonder Lucroy had been so set on tasting Peaches. At the time, I'd viewed it as ridiculously risky. I had a new appreciation regarding Lucroy's need now.

"Mm-hmm. It seems you did something completely out of character and lost control of your transformation. It also seems Frost was at the center of that mishap."

It sounded odd hearing Lucroy call Phlox *Frost*. Now that I knew his true name, Frost seemed wrong. And yet, it also seemed right. At least, right for everyone else.

When I remained silent, Lucroy said, "I do not ask out of a need for gossip. I am truly concerned. If there is a problem between the two of you, then I—"

"There is no problem." I rarely interrupted my king, and yet I could not hold my tongue. "At least, there is not a problem like you believe. I assure you, Frost is completely safe within my care." Per his desire, I used Phlox's agent name when speaking with Lucroy. It tasted wrong on my tongue, but I would do as he asked.

Lucroy arched a single eyebrow. "Forgive me, but that is not the way Lizbeth saw things."

We both trusted the human, so I did not take offense. "I do not fault Lizbeth's recall. From her perspective, I am sure the situation was...uncomfortable."

Lucroy's second eyebrow met the first. "*Uncomfortable?*"

Had I been a younger vampire, I would have squirmed. Ignoring the purposefully understated word, I said, "Frost and I worked through our issues." That wasn't completely true. Phlox and I had a lot that still needed to be verbalized. Or perhaps, words were overrated, and action was what was truly needed. I would not drink from him until Phlox was ready. However, there were other ways we could enjoy each other without sharing blood. Swapping other body fluids hadn't been discussed yet.

"That is good to hear, but I must ask what prompted this *uncomfortable* event?"

As king of the Southeastern nest, it was Lucroy's duty to question me. Understanding the need did not diminish the irritation.

"He left the building." When Lucroy only stared at me, I added, "During the daylight."

Lucroy's slow blink was purposeful. "And that was a concern why?"

My fingers dug into my palms. A quick glance toward the other end of the bar reassured me Phlox was fine and unharmed. He was currently cleaning a four top. Wendall was in the back washing glassware.

"I could not follow," I ground out. My teeth desperately wanted to lengthen, and I fought the transformation urge with everything I had.

Lucroy stared, his dark eyes revealing nothing. His casual posture belied his sharp mind. We remained silent, Dusk's surrounding music a pounding base drum constantly beating in the background. I knew the moment Lucroy understood. I doubt another would have noticed the subtle uptick of his brows.

"I see," Lucroy stated, and I knew, without a doubt, that he truly did understand. "Will this be a problem?"

"As I said, Frost and I discussed the situation. I believe he is wary but not unamenable to my affections."

The corner of Lucroy's lip barely twitched. "While that is excellent news, it is not what I meant. Frost is important to you. If the situation is as I believe, then I cannot imagine willingly allowing Peaches to place himself in danger. I would... It would not be pleasant."

I wanted to huff. It was an antiquated reaction, a leftover instinct from my human life. "I will admit that I am struggling with Frost's mission. I am uncertain if I can allow his capture.

While I understand the importance of shutting down this ring, I do not relish the idea that Frost is being used as bait."

"So far, very unsuccessful bait," Lucroy said.

"I believe that was the reason for his daytime trip. Frost is attempting to appear as fragile and alone as possible."

"Most reports are of pixies being taken at night or in the early morning hours before dawn. I find his daytime choice odd." Lucroy cocked his head to the side.

Somehow, I managed not to squirm under his scrutiny. "There could be a reason he chose that time."

"Oh? Has he learned something I am unaware of?"

"Not in the way you imagine," I hedged before giving in. "Frost has gone out in the dark, alone, on several occasions. It is difficult, allowing him to appear so vulnerable with no one there to watch his back. I might have followed him previously." I'd followed on every occasion but did not feel the need to reveal myself so completely.

"I see," Lucroy answered after a few tense seconds. "Indeed, it appears we do have a problem then."

Golden pixie dust filled the air before Peaches flew over the back of the booth seat, plopping down beside his beloved.

"What did I miss? You two look tensor than usual." Peaches's eyes widened as he brought his cup of honeysuckle mead to his lips. "Goddess, that is heavenly," Peaches's eyelashes fluttered, and he relaxed into Lucroy's outstretched arm, snuggling in. Jealously slammed through me hard and fast. I wanted that.

I'd been jealous before, but it was a mere echo of the green monster currently stirring my soul. I did not begrudge Lucroy his happiness. I simply wanted something similar. Now that I'd found Phlox, I realized just how badly I not only wanted but needed it.

I craved the intimacy, the casual knowledge that I'd never be alone again, that there was a being within this world that treasured my existence as much as I treasured theirs. It was a clawing need, desperate for release.

Lucroy was correct. We had a problem, and that problem was me.

I tried not following, but it was impossible. Phlox went out again tonight. He didn't tell me his plans. He didn't need to. Every sense in my body was attuned to his every move and intention. I could call it what it was—obsession. It was as dirty word, one that I hated, and yet it seemed the most appropriate. Had circumstances been different, I do not believe Phlox would have minded my obsession. But right now, he was irritated.

"I know you're there, asshole." Phlox stood below a streetlight, leaning against the dirty surface, hands stuffed into the pockets of his loose pants. There weren't a lot of souls out and about at five a.m. Most vampires had gone to ground. For those who enjoyed the night, the coming daylight also had them crawling back to their chosen homes.

Phlox huffed. "And if I know you're there, then you can bet I'm not the only one. Goddess, Leon, this is never going to work with you breathing down my neck all the time."

I wanted to say, "Good, because I don't want it to work," but Phlox would view that as selfish. That vice was difficult for a vampire to wrap their head around. As a general rule, selfishness was not considered a poor quality in my kind.

Throwing up his hands, Phlox stomped his foot before taking to the air again. "This is pointless. I'm calling it a night. Do you hear me, Leon? I'm going back to Dusk." True to his word, Phlox's flight plan headed back to Dusk. Stepping out of my darkened corner, I followed. I caught a few mumbled comments regarding overprotective vampires, stupid vampires, meddling vampires, and a litany of other disparaging words placed before my species designation.

I ignored them all while remaining stubbornly silent. Phlox added that dubious trait to his list as well.

Suddenly twirling, Phlox pointed a finger at my chest. Yellow rimmed his blue eyes, a sure sign he was furious. "You have to stop this. No one is going to go after me if you're shadowing my every damn move."

I gave a slow blink and remained silent.

"Goddess, you're infuriating." Phlox smacked his hand against my chest before wincing. Shaking out his hand, Phlox mumbled, "Fucking made of stone."

"Are you injured?" I finally broke my silence.

"Just my damn pride," Phlox grumbled. Sometimes my pixie didn't sound very pixie-like.

Shoulders slumped, Phlox tilted his head toward Dusk and said, "Come on. Let's get you home before the sun rises and fries your vampire ass."

I followed, this time a little closer than before. I didn't crowd Phlox, but it was a near thing. My pixie smelled divine. Not just his blood, but him.

"You are concerned?" I asked, fishing.

"Of course I'm concerned. Knowing you, you'll push things right up to the limit and the sun isn't anything to mess with, not if you're a vamp."

While Phlox was correct, I answered, "The early rays would only cause severe irritation. I would survive their touch."

Phlox blew out an exasperated breath. "And you think the thought of you in pain is better?" He held his hand out flat and tilted it back and forth. "That's only marginally better than thinking of you as a pile of ash."

"It is good to know you care," I deadpanned.

"Ass." Phlox backhanded me, the touch far gentler and

more reserved than his previous whack. Head down, Phlox glanced my direction, his eyes uncertain as he chewed on his bottom lip. "Seriously, Leon. We have a problem. I was sent here with a mission and your attentions are interfering with that. Honestly, at this point, I don't even know if this would work without you following me. It's damn frustrating." Phlox stopped flying and his bare toes landed on the sidewalk. Pixies didn't seem to mind a little dirt and who knew what else on their bare skin.

Running his fingers through his hair, Phlox looked horribly dejected. "I hate failing." Those words were barely above a whisper. "Especially this case. I... My mom, she..." Phlox angrily shook his head. "It doesn't matter. That was a long time ago. This is now and this shit's still going on. It's even worse this time."

"Because other species are involved?" I guessed.

Phlox nodded. "Greed's a bitch. I'll never understand how anyone can be okay with profiting off another's suffering or death."

Vampires had a different moral code. Some might say we had no moral code. That wasn't completely true. Our second lives were much different than our first ones. The rules were different, the game was different, and success and failure were measured differently. One had to change or one quickly succumbed. Defeat often meant permanent death.

Head tilted, Phlox's gaze found mine. His eyes were warm and understanding and a gentle smile tilted his lips. "I'm not sure you feel the same."

"I do and do not. I do not relish suffering when it is unearned or has no greater purpose. Suffering and death are wasteful. Vampires do retain the urge to protect. It is only that what we value and deem worthy of that fierce protection often changes during our second lives." I didn't know how else to describe it. "Loyalty is a trait nearly every vampire admires."

Nearly didn't mean *all*. Lucroy and I knew that better than most, and by the time a vampire reached my age, they were also keenly aware.

"You're loyal to Lucroy," Phlox said.

"I am. I am also loyal to our nest and his beloved."

"Peaches."

"Unless Lucroy has acquired another beloved I am unaware of," I teased.

Phlox reached out to smack me again, but this time I caught his wrist and pulled him close. Phlox came willingly, not an ounce of protest on his plump lips. He didn't pull away when I dipped my head closer. He didn't tell me to stop when I was mere inches away from his lips, and he didn't so much as utter a whispered decent when I lowered my head.

Warmth exploded across my skin. I could feel the pulse of Phlox's blood bounding through his flushed lips, the sound louder as it raced up his neck, flushing his cheeks. Needy sounds swam up from deep within his chest, escaping here and there as I licked and plundered his mouth. Rumbling began, reverberating through Phlox's throat and pouring into the early morning air.

Phlox leaned into me, pushing his body against mine. I could easily feel the thick, solid length of his cock press against my leg. I'd managed enough blood earlier that my own erection answered the call.

Reluctantly pulling away, Phlox tilted his head back and gasped. "Air...fuck...need to breath." I didn't have such constraints and immediately began licking his luscious neck.

"Shit, that feels good," Phlox panted. That odd rumbling continued. It was pleasant and spurred my actions. I dove in, nipping at the flesh and bringing that delicious blood closer to the surface. I wouldn't bite, no matter how badly instinct told me to. I'd wait for Phlox's permission. That didn't stop me enjoying the taste of his flesh on my tongue. Nothing could stop that immense pleasure. Nothing except the sun.

Yanking away, I slapped my hand over my face. That stopped the stinging pain in my cheek, but my hand began sizzling.

"Shit! Goddess, Leon. Come on."

Phlox grabbed my arm and pulled. He flew like a maniac, tugging me after as the sun continued rising. A few cups of blood and a day or two of rest and I'd be right as rain. But right now, the sun's rays stung like a son of a bitch.

"Almost there," Phlox shouted, barely tilting his head enough to look back at me. I could see Dusk rise up in the background. My body felt increasingly sluggish. It was still early enough that I wouldn't fall asleep, but my body wasn't as reactive as it should be.

I heard the jingle of keys as Phlox dug out the one for the front door. He dropped them once, cursed, and picked them up. Shoving the key into the slot, I heard the click of the door before Phlox grabbed ahold of my wrist and said, "Got it. Almost safe, just a—"

Phlox didn't finish. Blindingly white light surrounded us. My stomach rolled and then I knew no more.

Chapter Nine

PHLOX

I keeled over and vomited all over the floor. My stomach cramped and I did it again, emptying everything and then some. I think I might have whimpered but couldn't be sure. The scent of my own sick made my stomach role again.

"Nasty," I heard someone lament. "That must be a really shitty way to travel."

"Shut it. You have no idea the level of magic a transportation spell requires." The person speaking did sound kind of drained. Not that I really gave a shit right now. "It worked. We got the pixie."

"Yeah, and we got somethin' else too."

Something else? My brain screamed. Leon! I'd been holding Leon's wrist when...when whatever the hell happened happened. Had he been taken with me?

Unfolding my body, I managed to get up on my knees. Leon lay beside me, body stiff and unmoving. Thankfully, I hadn't lost my guts all over him.

I lunged, falling on him and shaking his body like mad. This wasn't supposed to happen. I was the only one that was supposed to be taken, not Leon. I had no idea where we were, if the sun was out, if Leon was in danger, if he was even still alive.

"Leon," I rasped, my throat sore from my previous vomiting. "Leon," I repeated, a little more impatient when he didn't so much as twitch.

"*Leon?* What have you done?" All exhaustion fled that voice, a shrill quality taking over. "Do you even know who that is? Gaia, you're a moron. That's Lucroy Moony's second. He wouldn't have batted an eyelash about the pixie, but Leon's another matter."

My head snapped up. "What did you do to him?" I demanded. Thankfully, we were in an enclosed room. The only light was artificial. The room was crowded by a troll. A smaller woman with ash-blond frizzy hair and more bangles, necklaces, and rings than I'd seen outside a market stall stood to his side. Hands on hips, her pleated skirt floated midcalf.

I'd only seen two species wear that much jewelry, most of it charmed. Witches and warlocks. This one looked female so witch was the first thought that came to mind.

My wings fluttered as they channeled my anxiety. Dust scattered. The witch sneezed first, quickly followed by the troll.

"Keep those things under wraps." The witch waved a hand in front of her face before covering her nose with the scarf draped around her neck. I wanted to keep them moving, but the pointed look she threw Leon's way made me snap my wings closed.

"Better," she cooed. "Good to know you can take instruction. It might make this whole thing easier."

I bristled but tried keeping my cool. Losing my shit wouldn't do Leon or me any favors. I repeated, "What did you do to him?"

"Me?" The witch gave a false look of innocence. "Oh no,

honey. That's all the sun's doing. Thank Gaia, it's high in the sky. Leon's out for the count." She laughed like she'd made a funny joke.

I didn't find her humorous. At all.

"What do you want?" I thought I knew. That bit about "getting the pixie" was sufficient tip-off.

The witch grinned. She'd either had braces as a child or more likely, charmed her teeth to brilliant white perfection. Hands on hips, she leaned forward. Her multitude of necklaces and bracelets jingled.

"Oh, honey. What we want is you. Or more precisely, the money we'll get for you." The witch rubbed her thumb and forefinger together.

I fought my transformation. It was too early to show all my cards. Leon's capture hadn't been figured into the plan. Get caught, get taken, learn all I could, escape if I could when the time was right. If I wasn't back within a week, a rescue party would be sent. Glancing down at Leon's still body, I wasn't at all certain we had the luxury of one week.

Vampires were tough to kill, but only when the sun was down. They were intolerably vulnerable when the sun was on this side of the horizon. That's why they protected their sleeping dens so fiercely.

Running my fingers over Leon's face, I pushed some of his ginger hair to the side, revealing blistered skin. I winced while remembering his earlier painful hiss. He'd stayed outside too long. He'd stayed out trying to protect me. And now here he was, temporarily dead to the world and easy pickings.

Leon was still mobile when I touched Dusk's doorknob. Knowing that was the case meant wherever we'd been transported had to be east of Virginia—somewhere the sun was high in the sky. We'd traveled time zones. That wasn't a good sign.

Staring down at Leon's vulnerable body, I swallowed my

continued nausea. I didn't think this gut churning was from being yanked through a witch-created portal.

"You've got me." I tried playing innocent. "I don't know what you want, but from what you said earlier, you don't want Leon. You're right. King Moony will hunt you down to get Leon back." I raised my chin, attempting to look fierce. It was a hard look for a pixie to pull off.

Neither the witch nor her troll companion appeared impressed.

"It's a complication," she said, scrunching her face and twisting her lips. "But it's a complication we might be able to work to our advantage." Her perplexed features eased into another sickening grin. "Yes, I think this might work out very well. I've got a feeling our buyer might be interested in this little vampire morsel. Pick him up, Oxley."

"Just 'cause I'm big don't always mean I gotta do the grunt work," Oxley complained while moving to do exactly as the witch said.

"Yes, yes. I know. But if you hadn't noticed, my magic's a little tapped out after that transportation. I could drag him, but it'll take longer."

"Outta the way, pixie." Oxley tried shooing me away from Leon. I didn't budge.

"Not until you promise me you're not going to hurt him." If I didn't get that guarantee, Oxley was going to have to carry both of us because I planned on plastering my body to Leon. If they planned on putting him in the sun, I'd do my damnedest to shield his body with my own.

Oxley grimaced, pulling his lips back and revealing yellowed, peg-like teeth. "I said get outta the way, runt."

"Not a chance, asswipe."

Oxley looked as if he was about to rip my wings off, but the witch intervened. "Oh for love of Gaia. The vampire is safe. For now. He might be worth something. Whether that's dead or alive remains to be seen. Until I find out for certain, we'll keep him out of the sun."

My brain quickly processed her words and found a modicum of comfort in them. These assholes were all about the money. If there was one thing I could trust, it was their greed.

Slowly, I pushed off Leon, standing on shaky legs. That transportation spell really did a number on me.

"Careful, he got burned earlier," I chastised when Oxley picked Leon up and threw him over his shoulder like a bag of produce.

"Sylvie said he'd live. She didn't say nothin' about bein' gentle. He's a vamp. A little blood will fix him up." Oxley didn't even sound winded with Leon slung over his shoulder.

"Trolls can be terribly literal," Sylvie chuckled before becoming deathly serious. "Now, are you going to come along peacefully or do I have to drug you?" Sylvie pulled out a little bag filled with magenta dust. She held it in the palm of her hand, lips poised to blow the stuff in my direction. Between being drugged unconscious and keeping my wits about me, I knew which one I'd chose.

"I'm coming," I said, rolling my shoulders inward and appearing as nonthreatening as possible. There'd be time for teeth and claws later.

I followed Oxley. I didn't want to take my eyes off Leon, but I needed to look around. Knowing where we were and how we got to our next location might be important. Head down, I did my best to look absolutely dejected. In a way, it wasn't that difficult. My brain tumbled through scenarios, each one just as bleak as the previous. I was used to doing things on the fly. Plans were great and all that, but a fabulous plan was meaningless when things went to shit. It was time to work the problem. I just wished each calculation didn't end in the same disastrous outcomes.

Traveling down corridor after corridor, the air became increasingly damp and cool. We were headed deeper underground. At least we had that going for us. Unless there was a tunnel leading up to the sky, Leon should be safe enough. At least for now. The future was another matter.

One problem at a time, I reminded myself. Get through this and move on to the next step. That was the only way to get through and get out.

I pretended to shiver. I was a pixie, and they'd expect it as the temperature dropped. The cool air felt like heaven on my heated skin. Sylvie and Oxley didn't need to know that.

Leon swayed as Oxley turned a corner. I wasn't sure if blood could rush to a vampire's head or not. If so, it was a good thing Leon was dead asleep. I could only hope Sylvie was correct and that when the sun went down, Leon would wake. I squashed the fear that his state had more to do with the transportation spell.

We finally emptied into a room. Calling it large would be kind, but it was big enough to contain three pixie-sized cages. Phil would have had trouble fitting inside. Given my smaller size, it wouldn't be so bad.

"Go on." Sylvie pointed toward the closest empty cage.

My instinctual hesitation wasn't an act. No one wanted to willingly walk into a cage they may never come out of again.

"Walk in or get tossed in. It makes no difference to me. As long as your wings work and you can produce dust, that's all I care about," Sylvie warned.

Clenching my fists, I stepped inside. The sound of metal clanging closed behind me was deafening. My heart raced and my inner shifter paced. That part of me liked being caged even less than my pixie half.

"What do you want me to do with him? Those cages are made for pixies, not vamps. This one will be able to bust out as soon as the sun sets," Oxley said.

"Over there, against that wall," Sylvie ordered. "I've got enough juice to charm the shackles."

I watched as Oxley tossed Leon off his shoulder, none too gently sitting him on the cold, stone floor. Sylvie grabbed one manacle and Oxley the other. The metal snapped closed before Sylvie reached for a third, clasping it around Leon's neck. With her back to me, I couldn't see what she did, and I didn't understand the words she used to cast her spell. I did feel the initiation of magic as it settled into the iron.

"Th-there," Sylvie panted, bent over and hands on her knees. "That should hold him until we figure out what to do."

"You okay?" Oxley didn't sound overly concerned, more curious than anything. "You need me to carry you too?"

He reached out and Sylvie batted Oxley's clumsy hand away. "I'm fine," she insisted. "Just tired. Doing that spell was a little too soon after the transportation one, especially since there were two of them and not just one." Straightening, Sylvie said, "Check his pockets. Grab his phone."

Oxley fumbled through Leon's coat pocket, pulling out his phone and crushing it in his palm. Sylvie hadn't told him to do that but since she didn't lose her shit over it, I assumed she was fine with Oxley's self-motivation.

"What about tracking chips?" Oxley asked, making my spine stiffen. "A lot of pixies have them nowadays. You know that last one did, and we had to cut it out of her." He nodded in my direction. "You want me to get the scanner?"

"No need." Sylvie waved him off. "The last pixie we got didn't go through a transportation spell like this one." She hooked a thumb my direction. "That kind of magic scrambles the chips. If he's got one, it's worthless now."

Byx's hair clips rustled, my supposed meerkat protectors finally stirring from their slumber.

"Hush," I whispered, attempting to get them to settle and

stay quiet. While I was relieved Byx's magic survived Sylvie's spell, I didn't want them revealing just how special they were.

Thankfully, they stilled.

"You don't look so good," Oxley said while leaning down and scrutinizing Sylvie's complexation. "You're kind of gray around the edges."

"I need rest," Sylvie snapped. "And food." She shivered. "Somewhere warm would be helpful also. Come on. Let's get topside and get in touch with our contact. I want to see if this vamp is as juicy a piece of meat as I think he is." Sylvie kicked Leon's leg. It wasn't a hard insult, but it was enough to make me growl. Thankfully, it was too low for either of them to hear.

Finally turning from Leon, Oxley followed Sylvie as she made her way back toward me and the exit. Oxley's eyes remained fixed on Sylvie, watching her as if she might keel over any second.

"Rest up, little pixie." Sylvie grinned. That malicious movement was tempered by her waxen complexion. Oxley was right, Sylvie didn't look good. She'd magically overextended herself. Good for her. I couldn't think of a better witch to feel like shit.

I shifted to the back of the cage, shaking with false fear. Only, it wasn't as false as I wished it were. While I wasn't afraid for myself, I was very afraid for Leon. What happened if her contact didn't think Leon was worth keeping around? If he was more trouble than he was financially worth?

When I thought of that, my fear was all too real.

"Not as pretty as some, but that's not what's important to our client. You can make dust, that's what counts. You'll be worth a pretty penny to a desperate, drug-addicted ogre."

I threw my hands over my face, feigning shock. I could have said something, begged for release. I didn't. I just couldn't lower myself to useless groveling. Nothing I said would make a bit of difference to this greedy pair. Even if I were independently wealthy and offered them what they coveted most, they wouldn't release me.

I knew who they were. They'd made no effort to hide their identities. Only those who didn't expect their prey to live did that.

But they were as wrong as wrong could be. This little pixie wasn't about to roll over, flap my wings, and produce dust for some addicted ogre until I faded. Oxley and Sylvie were in for a painful wake-up call. And as far as I was concerned, the more painful, the better.

Chapter Ten

LEON

Awareness came by slow, painful degrees. My head felt fuzzy, as if my senses were coated in thick wax. Feeling came first, sharp and cruel. The left side of my face prickled with little needles of fire. Those same agonizing bolts of pain radiated from my hands and the left side of my neck.

Memory is a tricky mistress. Mine flickered, little pieces coming into focus only to be replaced by the next jump in the reel. The picture finally presented itself in all its bitter glory...only that picture didn't include my current circumstances.

"Leon? Are you awake? Please tell me you're awake."

The waxy coating covering my ears instantly fell away.

Phlox.

My eyes flew open, and only then did I realize they'd been closed. Opening them didn't improve my situation. In fact, opening my eyes made me instantly furious.

"Phlox." My voice should have been garbled. I could feel my teeth pushing against my gums, but they remained stubbornly the same and nearly useless. Similarly, the press of transformation uselessly pushed against my limbs and joints. Even my nails refused to obey my instinctual need.

I growled, low and far too human. "Phlox, what is going on?"

"Nothing good," Phlox grunted. "Although, you being awake is a start in the right direction."

I wasn't so sure about that. I was on the floor. Metal manacles trapped my wrists and neck. There was a single bulb illuminating an otherwise dark and dank room. Instinctually, I realized the sun had recently set. Phlox and I were deep underground, and worst of all, Phlox was trapped within a metal cage.

Yanking, my bondage remained stubbornly in place. I could feel the uncomfortable prickle of magic against my skin. It chafed my already singed flesh.

"Stop it," Phlox scolded, worry softening his order. "You'll only hurt yourself. The cuffs are charmed."

"Witch or warlock?" I asked. Their magics were different but not something I could discern.

"Witch," Phlox hissed. "And a nasty troll," he added. "Best I can tell, the witch, Sylvie, spelled Dusk's doorknob. When I touched it, I was transported here. Since I had a hold of you at the same time, it seems you were pulled along for the ride. Sorry about that."

"Not your fault."

"No, but it does make this situation more complicated." Phlox huffed. "I finally get captured and now I've got to get us out of here way earlier than planned."

My head snapped his direction. "Get us out of here? How do you plan on doing that while trapped inside that metal cage?"

Phlox stood, stretching his slender arms above his head and arching his back. His wings fluttered and he lifted off the cage bottom as far as the confines allowed.

"I'm not a typical pixie," Phlox said with a mischievous grin.

A lesser vampire would have rolled their eyes. "So you say. I still fail to see how you plan on getting out of your confinement."

Phlox rolled his shoulders while his gaze skimmed over the bars. "Why do other species always underestimate pixies?" He shook his head, his ombre hair floating around his shoulders. Despite the circumstances, I was entranced. Phlox was stunning. Ignoring my burning skin, I soaked him in like a human dying of thirst lusting after an oasis. Given how long it had been since I'd fed, the analogy hit far too close to home.

"First things first. Time to get out of here. I was waiting for you to wake up."

"I don't see how—" The words died on my lips. Phlox's body changed, decreasing in size, shrinking in on itself. His marvelous wings disappeared along with his flowing hair. The air around his body shimmered and when that shimmer died, a small feline was left.

My mouth dropped open, my eyes shot wide. "Phlox," I whispered and got a guttural mew in answer.

Sitting on that cold stone floor, I watched Phlox walk up to the metal bars. Their spacing was meant to keep a pixie inside, not an eight-pound cat. Wiggling through, Phlox easily came out the other side. Shaking his plush fur out, Phlox padded my way.

The closer he got, the more stunning he looked. Phlox's fur was gray with hints of ochre and reddish hues. His head was round and full with small, curved ears. Phlox's tail whipped around, a dense appendage ringed with narrow black bands interspersed with gray, the tip black.

Crawling onto my lap, Phlox's eyes were pure yellow, his pupils circular instead of slit like a typical feline.

The more I gazed at him, the more I realized Phlox's shifter form wasn't a typical house cat. While I wasn't certain what he was, that much was clear. What was also clear were the claws kneading my chest.

"You're stunning," I said in a hallowed whisper. Those words earned me a hearty purr and a rough tongue swipe along my jaw. Phlox was considerate and stuck to the side of my face that wasn't sun scorched.

Another shimmer of light and I had a lap full of pixie.

"Bet you didn't expect that," Phlox said smugly.

"No. Not that," I easily agreed. "I've never heard of a pixie-shifter before."

Phlox shrugged as if it weren't important. "Not sure if there are any others. You told me I was unique. I guess you just didn't know how right you were." Glancing off to the side, Phlox's wings fluttered. He looked nervous and sounded unsure when he asked, "Is it okay? I know it's a little...different."

I hated my shackled arms more than ever. "Free me of these restraints and I'll show you just how *okay* I think you are."

Phlox's grin lit his face. "You got it." Holding up his right hand, Phlox raised his index finger and flicked out a single claw. "Partial shifting has its benefits. One of the first things I learned when I became an agent was how to pick a lock. Magical or not, I've got this."

One by one, my shackles fell, slipping away and falling to the ground with an unceremonious clang. The itchy feel of foreign magic fell with them.

"Better?" Phlox asked hopefully.

In answer, I wrapped my arms around the amazing pixie I planned on making my own. "Better," I agreed before tasting his lips. Phlox melded perfectly with my body. Knees on either side of my hips, Phlox plastered our chests together. I ignored the stinging pain radiating from where our lips touched. My scorched skin wasn't nearly as happy as the rest of me.

Finally pulling away, Phlox rested his forehead against mine. "It wasn't supposed to happen this way. It was just supposed to be me."

Rubbing my hands up and down his arms, I whispered, "I'm not sorry. I couldn't fathom the idea of you being taken. If you were gone and I had no idea where you were..." I couldn't finish that thought, let alone sentence. Most likely Lucroy would need to take drastic measures if that were to happen.

Phlox sighed and pulled away. His gaze was stern with a little V formation between them. "That's all well and good, but we've got a problem."

"Just one?" I questioned, raising a single eyebrow.

"One that's bigger than the others. Like I said, you weren't part of the plan, and believe it or not, there was a plan." Phlox blew out a breath that sounded like a raspberry. "And it's not just my plan blown to pieces. Oxley and Sylvie didn't expect you either."

"Oxley?"

"The troll. Anyway, the point is, they don't know what to do with you either, but they've got ideas." Phlox filled me in on what he'd heard. "They haven't been back since dumping us in here, so I don't know what they've decided about you." Phlox sniffed and raised his chin. "Really, the service here is deplorable. They didn't even offer me a glass of water. Not that I would have drank it if they had. Sylvie's already threatened to drug me a couple of times."

This time, my teeth extended, and my eyes tingled letting me know they'd flooded in crimson.

"Hey, I didn't say she *had* drugged me." Phlox gave me a

winning grin. "I played along well. It's easy to fall into expectations. Oxley and Sylvie expect a passive pixie and that's exactly what I gave them."

"I would say I am sorry I missed the performance, but I doubt I could have contained my rage." Ripping those two to shreds sounded well and good, but that wouldn't prove informative.

Sitting back on my lower thighs, Phlox tilted his head to the side, his long hair flowing over his shoulder and pooling around my legs. Without thought, I ran my fingers through his silken strands. The banded colors played along my fingers. Realization hit me that his hair was a play on his shifted form.

Which reminded me... "What kind of a cat are you?"

This time, Phlox's grin accompanied lightly flushed cheeks. "Pallas's cat."

I blinked. "Forgive me, I do not know the species."

Phlox waved me off. "Not many do. They're not native to this part of the world. My pixie mom ran into my dad somewhere in Mongolia. Auntie Tandra said it wasn't a love match, but they did have a spark and *viola*." Phlox waved a hand down his body. "Here I am."

"Yes. Lucky for me." I pondered what he'd told me and verbally rolled the name over my tongue. "Pallas's cat. Your other form is beautiful."

Phlox's flushed cheeks deepened in color. "Thanks, but, uh...Pallas's cats aren't known for their tameness. They might be pretty, but they don't do domestication. If you're ever in that part of the world and come across a true, wild Pallas's cat, steer clear. They might look cute and cuddly, but they're anything but."

"Thank you for the warning. I believe I have my hands full with the Pallas's cat sitting in my lap. I have no need to quest for more."

"Oh...well..." Phlox spluttered, and I enjoyed his discomfort. Had the circumstances been different, I would have continued teasing him. As it was, we most likely could not afford the time.

"You've been awake longer than me and know the situation better. Given your escape routine, I assume you have a plan."

"Eh...sort of." Phlox filled me in on the original plan, the one my capture had upended. "I don't think we can wait the week. If Sylvie's to be believed, her magic fried my tracking chips. I've still got Vander's mark and as far as I know, it's still in working order. I can't contact him through it, but he should be able to find me. Same with Byx's hair clips." He touched the quiescent meerkats slumbering away. "So, they can find me, but shouldn't show up for a week. Like I said, I don't think we can wait that long. It's better if you're worth something to them, but even then, I don't think it's wise sticking around. You can take the troll. A witch might be a different matter. She's weaker right now. I'm not sure how long it will take Sylvie to regain her magical mojo, but I don't think we want to be here when she does."

Unfortunately, Phlox was correct. As far as strength and speed were concerned, no species could best a vampire. But magic was a different matter. And right now, I wasn't as nearly as certain as Phlox that I could take down a troll. My body was weakened and my flesh scorched. I needed to feed.

I don't know if Phlox could read my thoughts or had figured my state out on his own. Regardless, with barely a questioning glance he tilted his head, exposing the heavenly slope of his neck.

My body stilled. My eyes locked onto that flesh and the blood flowing below. I could hear the delicious sound of it speeding through arteries and veins, that pulse increasing as Phlox's heart rate thrummed.

"Phlox." I licked my arid lips. "You do not need to do this. I am not so desperate for sustenance." I craved his blood, and it took all I had to offer him this out. But what I said was correct. It was not life or death. Not yet.

"I know I don't *need* to, but I want to. You're thirsty and my blood will help heal your wounds. I need you as strong as possible if we're going to make it out of this in one piece."

Phlox's words stung. Was he offering simply out of duty? While practical, that option didn't sit well with me.

Clamping my mouth shut, I acted like a teenage vamp, turning stubborn and mulish. "I can manage just fine," I protested.

Phlox rolled his eyes. "Just feed, Leon. I know you want it, and I don't mind."

He didn't mind? I squirmed, valiantly keeping my mouth closed.

"Goddess save me from prideful vampires." With a flick of the newly formed claw on his finger, Phlox sliced open a thin line of skin. Crimson slowly seeped to the surface trickling down his neck. The scent hit me like a nuclear bomb. Phlox always smelled divine, but this...his blood exposed and so very close.

My lips parted and my eyeteeth dropped. Still, I made no move.

"Come on, Leon. Drink. Let me do this for you. I *want* to do this for you."

Those magic words stirred me to action. I'd like to say I didn't lunge for him, but that would be a bald-faced lie. My teeth struck home, piercing Phlox's delicate skin. I shamelessly moaned around the warm blood flooding my mouth, slipping down my throat and quenching a hunger I'd fought for weeks.

No other blood could ever be this delicious. I was done, hooked on a single donor source. Should Phlox deny me, deny our bond, I would wither away to little more than a starved husk. Most likely I would walk into the sun before that day happened. It wasn't just Phlox's blood I needed to survive; it was the whole package I held within my arms. Pixie or Pallas's cat, Phlox was mine.

Phlox was my beloved.

Chapter Eleven

PHLOX

Fuck, that hurt. Leon's fangs sank into my skin with a flash of searing pain. It was short lived. I'm not saying it felt good after, just not nearly as painful. Was this what Peaches went through at every feeding? The way he cuddled up to Lucroy and leaned into him when Lucroy passed his fingertips over the bite marks on his neck made me think not.

I stayed there, perfectly still as Leon took pull after pull of my blood. I wasn't lightheaded. Yet. If he didn't stop soon, I wasn't sure how long that scenario would hold true. While I needed Leon strong, we couldn't afford for me to be too weakened either.

I was just getting ready to say something when Leon pulled away. His tongue tenderly swiped over the area he'd damaged and his embrace gentled. Knowing it was over allowed me to finally relax.

"Forgive me," Leon roughly whispered. "I did not take proper care. I was gluttonous."

Considering I didn't feel all that faint, I disagreed. "I don't think you took too much."

Leaning away, Leon cupped my head in his palms, his black eyes swimming in a ring of crimson. Rubbing his thumbs along my jaw, Leon continued staring, fixing me with his gaze. "That is not what I meant. I was too rough with the bite. It has been decades since I drank directly from the source."

I mulled that over. "Bottled blood?"

"Mm-hmm. It is never as good, even when warmed, but it is safer. For all our strengths, vampires have far too many weaknesses and one of them is the need to feed. Clever humans discovered ways of weakening and even killing us by polluting their own bodies."

I flinched. "You're kidding."

"Unfortunately, no. Vampire blood sources are carefully monitored. Under fairy law, it is an automatic death sentence if you're caught tampering with vampire blood."

I knew that but had never considered the devious reasoning behind the law.

"Do not think too harshly on humans, at least not for this. They are prey and for many centuries, fell victim to draining. Back in the day, it was common practice for a vampire to glut themselves on a single individual. Draining a whole body in a single feeding isn't wise. Some individuals were kept against their will and slowly killed instead. It was not unlike what ogres do to pixies. The method might be different, but the results are the same."

The shiver racking my body wasn't from the cold. "That's...disturbing," I settled on.

Leon grinned and I noticed his skin didn't look as bad. In fact, it was nearly healed. "Thankfully, vampires haven't condoned such practices in nearly two centuries. I am pleased to say that even before fairy law, vampires policed themselves. I will not claim such incidents no longer happen, but they are few and when the culprit is found, punishment is swift."

I figured that punishment resulted in a trip to a dust bin, followed by the garbage.

"Come on." I jumped when Leon patted my rump. "We better get a move on if we're going to put your plan in motion."

Wings snapping open, I flew up, eye level with a now standing Leon. It was amazing how quickly he moved. I'd barely seen a blur. Looked like my blood really had revived Leon.

"By the way, what is the plan?"

Leon's question snapped my attention back to the here and now. "What time of day do you completely lose consciousness?" Vampires slept throughout the daylight hours, but they could be roused during sunrise and toward sunset. The sun's zenith was a different matter.

Leon's slow blink let me know he'd been thrown by the question. "This time of year, 10:17 a.m. I am capable of regaining consciousness at 2:47 p.m. I cannot say I would be useful while the sun is up, only that I can be made aware."

Well, that was more exact than I'd expected.

"Each century has shortened my unconscious time by twenty-three minutes."

"Wow, I...that's interesting." And again, painfully succinct. I suppose if the sun's movements ruled my life like it did Leon's, I'd pay close attention too.

"Why do you ask?"

"Because you were sluggish but still up and walking when I touched Dusk's doorknob but when we arrived here, you were out. That means—"

"We were transported to a different time zone."

I nodded. "Exactly. Most likely east. Since we were in Virginia, that probably places us out of the US."

Leon glanced around the room before saying, "The sun has fully set here."

I didn't question how he knew. It was a vamp thing.

"If I hadn't been injured and weakened, I would have stirred prior to the setting sun."

"Understood. That means we're at least four hours different than Rutherford Haven. The sun's probably still up there which means no one knows you're missing yet. Like I said, I don't have a way to contact the Magical Usage Council, Vander, or Byx, but I bet when they figure out we're both gone, they won't wait the full week to track me down. Fingers crossed on that one, otherwise we'll need to scrounge up a phone. That might not be too difficult." I shrugged. "I just don't have enough intel to say one way or another." I hated being uninformed. Knowledge wasn't just power. It often got my pixie ass out of trouble. Brainpower almost always trumped physical strength.

I headed for the door. As far as I'd been able to see, unless you were fairy, brownie, or a juiced-up witch, there was only one way in or out of our underground prison. Maybe a mole shifter could tunnel their way out. Next time I saw Agent Griffon, I'd ask.

"I don't think it's locked, but just in case, I'll probably need you to bust it down since the lock will be on the outside." I doubted our captors had bothered. The lack of security cameras and the fact neither Oxley nor Sylvie had bothered checking on us spoke to their confidence. It was understandable. Caged pixies didn't typically escape on their own.

"Understood." Leon moved in front of me and lifted the door latch. Just as I'd thought, it opened with ease. Leon carefully pulled the door open. Pale light filtered in, matching the atmosphere of our small room.

Leon leaned out, his gaze running along the doorjamb and surrounding walls. "There are sigils in the wall and along the doorframe, but they are not activated. Curious. Or perhaps, overconfident."

"Or maybe Sylvie used too much magical juice bringing us here and then charming your restraints. She was pretty wiped when she left. I was kind of hoping she'd fall on her face, but that didn't happen, at least not that I could see." I was hoping Sylvie's magical burn out would work to our advantage. If we were lucky, she'd slept the day away while trying to recover.

"Should we run into the witch, we will need to inquire as to the reason," Leon said, sounding one part indifferent and three parts anticipatory. I wasn't sure about our chances against a fully charged up witch, especially one powerful enough to use a transportation spell. Again, I could only hope Sylvie's magical tank was still running on empty.

Leon led the way. The tunnel was poorly lit. Shifting my eyes, I allowed my inner Pallas's cat visual reign. Nooks and crannies I hadn't seen before suddenly became clear, including the sigils Leon mentioned. Like him, I couldn't feel so much as a whisper of magic against my skin.

We came to a fork in the corridor and Leon asked, "Do you know which way?"

"I know how to get back to where we first arrived. I'm not entirely certain that's the way out or if that's the way to where we might find more information. I can tell you that room was closed up tight. Not sure if it was completely underground, but there weren't any windows. Gotta say, I was exceedingly grateful for that fact." I reached out and touched Leon's arm. The contact was probably more for my benefit than his. I didn't want to think back on those terrifying moments when I thought Leon would crumble into a pile of ash before my very eyes.

"That was exceedingly fortunate," Leon agreed, understating the situation like only a vampire could.

"We can start with the way we came." I pointed to the

right, and Leon and I cautiously started down that path. Although the tilt was minimal, the ground's upward angle was unmistakable.

The corridor we traveled was eerily silent. I'd shifted my ears along with my eyes. My Pallas's cat form could also hear a lot better than my pixie half.

Within a matter of minutes, the corridor emptied out into the room we'd arrived inside. I was dismayed to find it still stank of my earlier sick.

"Sorry," I offered when I saw Leon's nose twitch. "You were unconscious when we arrived, so I don't think you felt the full effects. Let me just say, traveling by way of witch translocation isn't recommended." I rubbed my empty belly. With my nausea well and truly passed, hunger gnawed at me.

"Looks like Oxley and Sylvie aren't really into cleanup." Most likely Sylvie had a magical solution to the mess on the floor. Once she was recovered, she'd probably use her innate abilities to do the dirty work. If we were in Phil's home, he would have already cleaned it up by now. He viewed it as inconsiderate to the house. As a home-and-hearth pixie, Phil's bonded home was sacred.

By silent agreement, Leon and I separated and began wandering the room's perimeter. It didn't look much different than I remembered. There also wasn't much there. Another door lay opposite the one through which we'd entered. I already knew what was behind us, which left only one direction to head.

"I can still feel the residual magic," Leon said, his emotionless tone belittling the heaviness of that observation. It took a lot of magical mojo for a witch to do a transportation spell and the fact he could still feel its remnants was telling.

Nodding toward door number two, I said, "You ready to head out?"

Leon held out a sweeping arm. "After you."

I inwardly preened. Flying so I could reach his face, I kissed Leon's smooth cheek. "Thank you for not treating me like a fragile pixie in need of protection. Maybe old vamps really can be taught." I'd fought all my life for recognition and to be considered capable. As the only pixie agent with the Magical Usage Council, the road hadn't exactly been difficult, but it hadn't been easy either.

Leon's palm cupped my cheek and I leaned into his cool skin. "Do not mistake my belief in your abilities as a willingness not to protect you. I will always do so. To ask me otherwise would mean you seek the impossible."

I rubbed against his hand, relishing the strength I found. A purr rumbled through my chest and Leon's eyes widened, expanding their inky black depths as his fingers brushed against the fur lining my shifted ears.

"Interesting," Leon said while the pad of his fingers tickled my ear. A couple of weeks ago, I would have found his comment irritating. Now I saw it for what it was. Leon cherished the interesting and unique and I happened to be a healthy combination of both.

My heart pounded and my purr deepened. Where this vampire was concerned, I was definitely in over my head. I could only imagine what Auntie Tandra would think of my heart's latest desire.

Pushing sexy thoughts of Leon away, I focused on the job at hand. "I suppose we better get a move on."

Leon's hand dropped to his side, releasing my cheek. I immediately felt the absence.

Spinning midair, I flew to the door. Thankfully, it too was unlocked. While I wasn't certain where Oxley and Sylvie were or if there were others waiting on the other side, I figured busting a door off its hinges would bring more attention than we wanted.

Stealth was our friend. Thankfully, we didn't need Leon's

brawn and the door slid open, revealing a much different scene.

Shifting my eyes back to their pixie form, I waited for my eyesight to adjust to the improved lighting. Unlike the previous corridors and rooms Leon and I'd been through, the hall beyond was finished like a proper home. The air was dryer, the musty dankness retreating behind the door we closed behind us.

The hall was windowless, and I wasn't certain if we were above ground yet or not. I thought I scented fresh air ahead and Leon agreed.

"I smell salt."

Lifting my nose higher, I sniffed again and agreed. "We must be near an ocean."

"Perhaps an island," Leon mused.

An island could be more of a problem than I currently desired. While pixies could fly, we were sprinters, not marathon flyers. There was no way I could make it across an ocean. I wasn't sure how well Leon could swim. Then again, it might not matter. Since vampires didn't need to breath, maybe he'd just sink and walk along the ocean bottom. I wasn't sure what the pressure would do to him. Maybe it depended on just how deep the ocean was.

I was about to ask when sounds caught my attention. It was barely a murmur, but I couldn't decipher the words. Zeroing in, I turned to Leon and placed a finger over my lips, indicating the need for silence. Leon didn't disappoint. If there was one thing vamps were experts in, it was silence.

We made our way down the hall, the sound growing. The words became increasingly distinct, as did the owner of that voice. Raspy, deep, and rattling didn't fit with Sylvie. Oxley was near.

Holding up a closed fist, Leon stilled as I leaned against a cracked doorway. Oxley's gruff voice drifted through the slightly open door. It sounded like he was on the phone given that, from Leon and my perspective, it was a one-way conversation.

"...fucked up. Sylvie thinks it might not be so bad though," Oxley said with a bit of indifference. "I don't see what the big deal is. He's a vamp. If he gets outta hand, I'll just toss him into the sun."

I stiffened and my feline teeth pushed against my gums. Leon must have felt my tension and laid a hand on my shoulder.

"Yeah, I know, but they don't even know where we are. I think Sylvie's making a lot more of it than she should." I could visualize Oxley's eye roll. "Yeah, I'm just the dumb muscle. She doesn't care what I think. If the money weren't so good, I'd ditch the witch." Oxley chuckled at his rhyme. "Hmm...no, I don't think so. Yeah, she said she's gonna contact someone." There was a pause before Oxley huffed. "Of course she didn't tell me who. You think Sylvie would trust me with that?" Another pause. "Yeah, you're right. Probably not a matter of trust. More like she doesn't think I'd have anything to contribute. Dumb troll." If Oxley wasn't our kidnapper and planned to profit off my eventual death, maybe I'd give more of a shit that his feelings were hurt.

"Nah, I don't think she's heard back yet and if she has, she wouldn't come runnin' to tell me. I tried askin' earlier but Sylvie shooed me outta her room. She won't admit it, but she sort of shot her magical load gettin' that pixie." Oxley chuckled again, this time louder. Yeah, the troll was fucking hilarious.

"She's all shut up in her room. I think she's been asleep most of the day. Maybe she'll hear back soon. Chances are she'll only tell me if we need to haul that vamp outta the cellar and dump his undead ass on the east side of the island."

I swallowed hard at the confirmation that we were truly on

an island. Leon's fingers tightened on my flesh, but his grip wasn't painful.

The one on the other end of the call must have said something Oxley found hilarious if his booming laughter was any indication. The conversation soon devolved into sexual innuendo and debates regarding the best kind of rotten meat. My stomach churned, my earlier hunger receding.

Waving my hand, Leon and I silently crept by the open door, Oxley none the wiser. At least we'd confirmed one thing —it didn't look like anyone knew that we'd escaped our cells.

The house turned out to be a maze of corridors and tiny rooms. It was bigger than I would have imagined, but not a mansion. A set of stairs led upward, and Leon silently walked up them while I flew. A new voice caught my attention, and I instantly recognized it as Sylvie's. It was muffled, her door closed. Leaning my ear against the solid wood surface didn't help. I couldn't make out what she said. Her words were sparse and if she were talking to someone, then it was sporadic. I also thought I heard the clack of computer keys, but again, I couldn't be certain.

I looked around the small foyer, working the problem and attempting to find a way in. While I wasn't certain of the time, I figured ours was dwindling. We were fighting against the sunrise and hopefully rescue. I couldn't let this opportunity go to waste.

My gaze caught on an airduct. It was small and my current form wouldn't be able to fit. Good thing I had a second form. Motioning toward a nearby, empty room, Leon and I ducked inside and quietly closed the door.

I pointed toward the nearby airduct and quietly whispered my plan. "I think I can fit." I shimmied my body, trying to convey my idea of wiggling through the duct.

Leon did little more than raise an eyebrow and give a nod. "Be careful. If you are in danger, I will not be responsible for my response. I doubt the witch will live long enough to be useful."

Hearing someone's willing to kill for you shouldn't be such an aphrodisiac. Flying up, I pecked Leon on the lips. He turned that little touch into an inferno when he deepened the kiss. I came away breathless and Leon and I were both hard.

Palming his interest, I said, "We'll need to explore this later." And there would be a later. We were both getting out of this mess, and we'd do it with enough information to nail this asshole to the wall.

Leon palmed my ass before releasing me. "Give me a hand up?" I asked and Leon nodded. I could sprout pixie wings in my Pallas's cat form. I'd done it before, and Auntie Tandra had pictures as proof. Of course, I'd threatened my auntie within an inch of her life if she ever showed them to anyone. She'd gushed about how adorable I was—a cat with wings, capable of flight. I had no doubt I was as cute as she thought. I didn't want to be cute. A plush cat with a pair of pixie wings didn't exactly inspire trepidation.

I shrank down, becoming smaller and smaller until I was the size of a typical housecat. My dense fur made me look larger than I truly was.

Leon scooped me up, motions gentle as he lifted me into the air. I heard his joints pop as his arms elongated. He kept his talons in check, and soon I was at the level of the duct. The cover was easy enough to pry off, and Leon snagged it before the metal could tumble to the floor.

With a little shimmy and a smidge of contortion, I wiggled into the narrow duct. It was a tight squeeze, but I managed. Slinking along, I followed my ears and made my way closer to Sylvie's voice. The first opening I came to didn't allow me to see much. Thankfully, there was a second. Scurrying through another duct, I came out with a much better view. I was practically on top of Sylvie. More importantly, I had a direct view of her computer. And what a view it was. I grinned. It was too bad no one was around to see it. No one would see me as anything but the badass agent I was if they could see my sharp teeth and wicked grin.

Jackpot! I silently whispered.

Chapter Twelve

LEON

I thought I'd learned patience over the centuries. Currently, those lessons evaded me. Full transformation allowed me to peer into the air duct, but Phlox was beyond my sight. I'd been able to barely hear him while he'd scurried about. I could only assume he'd found what he was looking for and was currently stationary. I hated him out of sight and auditory range.

Tilting my head and cracking my neck, I relaxed back into a more human personage. I fought the urge to pace. Would I be able to hear as well if I were moving? I didn't know and that kept my feet planted. I could barely make out the clicking of computer keys on the other side of the thick wall. The sound was dull, and I doubt I would have mentally clocked it if I weren't so hyper aware.

I stood there, drifting into a dark, welcoming headspace. I needed to find that core of patience and pull from it. Phlox would be fine. He had to be fine. Now that I'd found him, I could not conceive of a life without him.

Beloved. That singular word whispered through my brain

and danced on my tongue. Could Phlox really be the one? I don't know why I questioned it. I'd been suspicious before. Now that I'd tasted his blood, there was no doubt.

The only true question was if Phlox would consent to being my beloved. It was not as forgone of a conclusion as I would like. I would not force him. The very idea made me recoil with disgust. Phlox was precious. He was my everything and harming him would only serve to harm me.

Vampires lived their second lives in search of a purpose. Why were we allowed more time? What was the point in living decade after decade, century after grueling century? I'd been struggling with that question of late. It was an early warning sign. The answer was now so very clear.

Phlox.

Phlox was my reason for existing. Everything I did from now on would be with him in mind. Was this what it was like for Lucroy? I could only imagine it was. I'd thought I understood before, but that understanding was a pale imitation of my current knowledge. It was frightening how completely thoughts of Phlox consumed me and yet that fear was tempered by overwhelming joy. I wanted to scream to the heavens that I'd found my beloved, that, if Phlox was willing, I would never suffer loneliness again. This damn confinement restricted my voice, but it could not quiet my delight, nor the overwhelming peace such thoughts brought.

I would need to speak with Lucroy. Given how much his work meant to him, I could never ask Phlox to give up his position with the Magical Usage Council. However, my protective instincts would not allow him to do perform that job alone. Given how much Phlox had to travel, that might require me to give up my position as Lucroy's second. The thought gave me pause, but I was not overly concerned. If anyone would understand, it would be Lucroy Moony.

Time floated by. My internal clock tracked the sun's path.

We had a little over an hour before the sun's rays tipped the horizon. That gave me four and half hours before I would be completely useless and little more than undead meat for the slaughter. Whatever came, Phlox and I needed a plan before that happened.

Faint scratching sounds met my ears. The soft sound of fur sliding against metal became clearer and clearer. Transforming again, I stretched until my eyes tipped over the edge of the duct. I was met with Phlox's large, yellow eyes. Reaching forward, I plucked my beloved from the duct, cradling his dust-covered fur against my chest as I eased back down into my humanoid form. My actions garnered a rough tongue against my cheek before Phlox fully transformed, leaving me no longer holding fur and claws, but a petite pixie. No, scratch that, I was holding a busting-at-the-seams pixie.

"You have discovered something?" I inquired, keeping my voice low.

"Oh, hell yeah." Phlox wiggled and his body slid to the floor. He immediately began the equivalent of pixie pacing—flying back and forth, spreading dust all over the room. Fisted hand to his chin, Phlox's joy turned pensive. I allowed him to mull, but we didn't have a lot of time to waste.

Thankfully, Phlox came to some type of decision and flew toward me so fast he nearly slammed into my chest. "We need to get out of here. The council needs to know what's going on." Phlox tapped his head while his eyes scanned the room. Disappointment replaced his earlier excitement. "I'd really hoped someone would be here when I got back. Someone from the council," Phlox clarified when I gave him a questioning look. "It should be dark in Rutherford Haven by now. They should know you're gone too. Surely someone can put two and two together."

I thought Phlox was most likely correct but didn't say so.

He chewed on his bottom lip before his gaze fell to the window. "How much time do we have?"

"Thirty-six minutes before the sun crests the horizon. Sluggishness will set in immediately. It will be possible to wake me for another three hours, but after that..." I shrugged.

Phlox gave an understanding nod. "That leaves us two options." He shook his head. "No, really just one." He blew out a deep breath. "The good news is that you're worth something." He frowned. "The bad news is that you're evidently worth as much dead as alive. I got a good look at Sylvie's online conversation, but the username is bound to be a fake. The point is, whoever Sylvie spoke with...they want your demise recorded." Phlox swallowed hard and he appeared torn between rage and terror. "I'm not sure when they plan on doing the deed, but I can't imagine they'll wait out another twenty-four hours. Most likely they'll wait until you're immobile and take you outside to await the sunrise. Either that or they'll cut off your head. The method wasn't specified, only the need for proof that it is truly you and that you're nothing but a pile of ash when it's done." By the time he was finished, Phlox's throat was clogged with emotion.

"That certainly doesn't sound pleasant."

Phlox slapped my chest, yanking his hand back with the sting. "Damn, I keep forgetting you're made of granite or something equally hard. Anyway, don't sound so flippant. I could hardly... I could barely sit still when I learned that. I..." Phlox turned from me, dull fingernails turning into lethal claws.

Moving between his wings, I allowed them to settle along my sides as I slipped my arms around him, pulling Phlox in tight. "I do not plan on expiring this day. Obviously, slipping back into the underground cavern and awaiting execution is not a viable plan."

"No, it isn't." Phlox's silken hair shifted against my skin.

"Then what do you propose?" I knew what I wanted to do but wasn't certain it would have the desired outcome.

"We need to take Sylvie and Oxley out. If possible, we need to keep one of them alive. Sylvie will be more dangerous, but she's probably got more information than Oxley. By his own admission, Sylvie hasn't shared much with him. But—"

"Witches are unpredictable."

"Exactly." Phlox blew out a breath, and the gentle beat of his wings hemmed me in. "She's not as dangerous as she could be. Sylvie still looks wiped, but she's probably got a litany of charmed paraphernalia at her disposal. The odds aren't in our favor nearly as much as I'd like."

I kissed the top of his head, relishing in his scent. "Well then, I suppose we will need to be extra careful."

"Yeah. Very careful. Once we've got them contained, you can go back underground where it's safer. I can grab Sylvie's computer. She's also got a cell phone on her desk. As long as I've got a good signal, I can contact help and by tomorrow night, we should be out of here."

"Did you learn where *here* is?" I asked, more curious than anything.

"I did. I'm not sure which one exactly, but it seems we're in the Canary Islands."

"Hmm...a beautiful locale. Perhaps we can enjoy an evening stroll along the beach tomorrow."

Given his wings, Phlox couldn't turn in my arms. He did lean over his shoulder and tilt his lips up for a kiss. I was more than happy to oblige.

"Troll first?" Phlox asked.

"Troll first," I easily agreed.

Eliminating Oxley as a threat was easier than even I'd thought. Although large and powerful, Oxley was no match for me now that I'd supped from my beloved. A fatal blow might not have been necessary if we'd had a better way to contain him. As it was, we could not take the chance of him recovering during the day while I was so vulnerable.

Phlox barely batted an eyelash at the carnage.

With the troll taken care of, we made our way back to Sylvie's door. Our efforts were met with silence on the other side. I thought it too much to hope she was asleep. Sunrise was mere minutes away. I had seven, maybe eight minutes before the cresting rays impacted my capabilities. Speed was of the essence.

Phlox pointed to the room we'd used earlier and whispered. "I'll crawl through the ducts again. You come at her in a frontal attack. I'll be the surprise."

His plan sounded as good as anything I could conceive. Hastily following our previous actions, I lifted Phlox into the open duct. This time I maintained my vampire form and left the room. I attempted to wait the allotted time I knew it would take Phlox to get into position. The wave of intense magic that suddenly filtered into Sylvie's closed door erased my patience.

I'd figured the door would be locked. While the magical barricade wasn't completely unexpected, its strength was.

A hellacious growl rumbled through my chest. I wasn't sure if she'd been tipped off somehow or if her door was always magically blocked. It was possible she'd heard us dispatching Oxley. Either way, I couldn't get inside. Not this way at least.

I stared at the thick plastered wall. If this witch thought she could keep me out, keeping me away from my beloved, then she had another thing coming.

I scanned around the area, feeling my magical way along the wall. Sylvie's magic didn't extend past the doorway. If Phlox and I were lucky, the reason Sylvie hadn't reinforced the surrounding walls with magic was because she was still too drained from the transportation portal she'd used to bring us here.

The sound of a metal grate hitting the floor followed by Sylvie's high-pitched scream heightened my need to get into that room. Arm pulled back, talons extended, I slammed my razor-sharp appendages into the wall. The old plaster cracked and crumbled. Five more punches shattered the wall, and I ran inside.

My entrance immediately drew Sylvie's attention. Lips curled back in a snarl, words I didn't understand flew from her lips and fiery light sparked from her fingertips. Taking advantage of the distraction I'd created, Phlox, still in his Pallas's cat form, launched himself off the bed, claws extended and aimed for Sylvie's turned back. With her attention on me, she'd ignored a very small, yet potent threat.

Sylvie's pained screech pierced my ears. Her hands flew to her back as she squirmed, attempting to dislodge Phlox's claws. Phlox was having none of it. Reeling back, his head shot forward and, fast as a snake, his teeth sank deep into Sylvie's flesh.

Her second scream of pain was far worse than the first. Efforts increasing, Sylvie stopped trying to dislodge Phlox's claws and teeth and instead ripped his body off. Holding him by the scruff, Sylvie threw my beloved across the room.

An unholy roar tore through my chest. I didn't think. I just moved. Instinct is a damnable thing. Thoughts of keeping the witch alive fled my mind. Thrusting my arm forward, my talons punched a hole through Sylvie's chest. When my hand came out the other side, it held Sylvie's dying heart.

The witch gurgled, incomprehensible words twisting

through her lips. Sylvie expired where she stood, my impaled arm the only thing holding her upright. Pulling my arm back eliminated that last vestige and her body crumpled to the floor, her bloody heart still in my hand.

My bloodlust satisfied, the roar filling my brain faded and the sounds in the room slowly filtered back in. The rapid beat of wings hit my senses before Phlox's pixie dust entered my vision. But when I glanced up, it wasn't what I expected.

Sylvie's heart slipped from my hands, landing with a splat as it joined her body. My crimson washed eyes receded as did my vampiric form. I would challenge any vampire to retain their battle form when faced with a plush kitty with fluttering pixie wings. The wings were proportional to Phlox's Pallas's cat form and dust filled the air around him. The scene would have been sickeningly sweet had it not been for the disappointed rage filling his yellow eyes.

Head purposefully pointed down, Phlox's gaze shot to Sylvie's very deceased form before that glare focused back on me. I stared at the carnage littering the floor and dripping from my hand.

"I thought she harmed you," I said defensively.

Phlox rolled his large, yellow eyes before light shimmered around him and he transformed back into his pixie form.

"But she didn't harm me." He pointed over his shoulder to his wings. "I can fly, remember."

It was difficult to forget. "You were in your cat form." The implication was clear enough. Phlox's dusty cheeks and averted gaze told he me understood.

"Yeah, well...as you can see, I can fly in that form too." Phlox got in my face and jabbed a finger into my chest. "But if you tell anyone what you just saw, I'll make your second life a living hell. You got that?" He jabbed a little harder for emphasis.

"My lips are sealed," I promised.

Phlox folded his arms over his chest and heavily sighed. "Well, this is a big fucking mess."

"Indeed. It appears I got here a little too late." I tensed at the new voice. Wrapping my hand around Phlox, I pushed his body behind me, only relaxing when my eyes caught up with my ears.

"Nice to see you, Ray."

Phlox shoved me and moved to my side. "Yeah, but it would have been nice to see you about twenty minutes ago," Phlox scolded.

"Forgive me. It seems Byx's hair clips did not work as precisely as she hoped."

Phlox touched the sleeping meerkats and sighed. "Yeah, I wondered about that."

"She was able to track you to a general location, but it was not precise enough. Vander and Parsnip were on a plane heading back to the United States. It is difficult translocating to a plane while it is in flight. I had to wait until it landed to contact Vander so he could track you better. I'm afraid that took longer than desired."

"It's fine." Phlox blew out a relieved breath. "You're here now and that's what matters. The sun will be up soon and—"

"It has risen," I interrupted.

Phlox's wings beat and dust filled the room. Whirling on me, he said, "You should have said something! We need to get you underground." Phlox's hands fluttered over my chest, patting me here and there as if he couldn't figure out exactly what needed done.

"It is fine. I still have a few hours before I am completely incapacitated. As long as I stay out of the direct sun, I will be fine."

Phlox's lips pulled tight before he shook his head. "It is not fine." Twirling back around, Phlox asked, "Can you get

Leon somewhere safe or do we need to head back down into the underground tunnels?"

"I do not have enough intel regarding this location. Staying would not be ideal." Ray's gaze fell on Sylvie. "I will have someone watch the premises. Is there anyone else present?"

"No one alive that I am aware of. There is a troll downstairs. I have not been able to detect any other heartbeats. There are several tunnels below ground. It is conceivable others are there and beyond my senses," I answered.

"The area will need exploration," Ray answered as his gaze fell on Sylvie's computer.

"We need to take that with us," Phlox directed, pointing at the computer. "With both of them dead, it's our only source of information." Phlox sent an irritated scowl my direction.

"I will take care of the computer and return shortly." Ray barely got the words out before he created an atmospheric tear.

Turning again, Phlox reached around my neck, pulling himself up instead of using his wings. "You look tired," he said, sounding worried.

"I am, but it is not too bad." I raked my fingers through his silken hair. Phlox leaned into my touch, rubbing his cheek into my palm.

"I was worried," he said. "Don't scare me again, okay?"

I hated to make promises I couldn't keep, so instead of agreeing, I answered, "I'll do my best."

It was all the truth I knew.

Chapter Thirteen

PHLOX

Goddess, it was amazing how good a shower felt. There was nothing like getting clean after being dirty. While I craved the cold, a warm shower felt like heaven. It was an odd paradox. The shower both woke me up and made me sleepy all at once. Sleep was going to win out soon. I'd made myself stay awake while Leon and I'd been captured. He'd been so vulnerable. I couldn't afford to sleep. I'd had no idea if Oxley or Sylvie would come back for him while he was still unconscious. And then when the sun went down, there'd been no time to waste.

There was also the little matter of my blood donation. Rubbing my neck, I was amazed how well the wound had healed. There was only the slightest tingle left behind. I winced while remembering the pain. I needed to speak with Peaches and ask if it always hurt that much. I could probably ask Leon too, but that seemed rude.

My phone rang, and Auntie Tandra's name popped up. I wish I had time to talk, but I needed to debrief the team and they were all waiting for me in the bar downstairs. The sun hadn't risen in Rutherford Haven yet, so Leon was still awake. I wondered if he had the vampire equivalent of jetlag. I needed to get a move on so I could fill them in before the sun came up.

I allowed the call to go to voicemail but sent Auntie Tandra a text, letting her know I was okay and would call later. I added on that I was really tired and would probably crash soon so it would be later before I called. I got a quick thumbs-up emoji in response.

Goddess, whoever invented texting was a genius.

Throwing on fresh clothes, I headed downstairs. Voices hit my ears as soon as I opened my apartment door. Ray managed to rouse the crew. I'd taken a shower while we waited on Phil and Sedrick to make it to Dusk. They'd offered to pick up Peaches too. Vander and Parsnip were in California, waiting on their connecting flight so they wouldn't be here yet.

Leon was waiting on me when I reached the bottom of the stairs. My smile was automatic. If I kept grinning like this, my cheeks were going to be sore soon.

"Hey," I managed, feeling like a teenage pixie with my first crush.

"Hello," Leon answered. I was a couple of steps from the bottom, our gazes even. Without hesitation, Leon leaned forward, grabbed my waist, and pulled me toward him. His lips were soft, and he kissed with abandon. There was no question in his touch, just heady surety.

Pulling back, I inhaled, taking in Leon's crisp, clean scent. Vampires didn't sweat and didn't have any body odor. Some found their scent unpleasant. It wasn't the same decay as zombies, but it favored them more than the living. I found Leon's scent comforting.

"I could get used to greetings like that." I grinned, licking Leon's taste off my lips.

"Only from me," Leon huskily answered.

"Only from you," I agreed.

Leon's fingers squeezed my waist before he lowered me to the ground. "Phil, Sedrick, and Peaches just arrived," Leon said, cupping the back of my neck as we turned and made our way into the bar.

It was an odd time of day. It was late enough that the patrons were gone. It was the time when the bar staff stayed to clean, getting everything prepared for the following night. The sunrise was an hour away, maybe less. Most vampires had already scurried to their hidey-holes. Thankfully, Leon's safe zone was mere feet away.

As I walked by the bar, a furball zipped past, quickly followed by Wendall's cry. "Trinket, get back here. You're soaking wet."

Wendall scooted past me, towel in hand. Trinket ignored him, merrily tittering as she scrambled around the floor, crawling up and over tables, and leaving a trail of dirty dish-water in her wake.

Ray's bellowed, "Trinket," finally put an end to her play.

"Thank you, Ray." Wendall sounded exasperated or maybe just out of breath. "I'm not sure what bug's gotten into her bonnet, but she's all fired up tonight." Wendall threw the towel over her and vigorously rubbed. Trinket didn't seem to mind. She cooed and wiggled around until he was satisfied then scrambled up Wendall's arm, perching on his shoulder with her long tail wrapped around his upper arm. She looked a bit like a drowned rat or, in this case, a drowned and scraggly scuttlebutt.

"I think she's just trying to blow off steam. She was really worried earlier when you left, Ray." Wendall went up on tiptoes and pressed his lips against Ray's cheek. Trinket leaned in too, nuzzling against Ray's neck.

"I was perfectly fine," Ray answered but didn't sound miffed.

"I know, but none of us knew what you were walking into." Wendall shot a concerned look my way. "We were all so worried. We didn't know who or what we'd find."

"Wendall's right." Peaches flew past me and embraced Leon. My vampire stood there, a little frozen and unsure what to do. "I don't know what Lucroy and I would have done if something happened to you. Don't you ever do something so silly again." Peaches smacked Leon on the shoulder before zipping away. A bright, whirling light shot out from Peaches hair, spinning around the room and chittering in a voice too high-pitched for me to understand. In fact, it kind of hurt my ears.

I stared at the whirly-gig until it dawned on me what it was. "Is that a sprite?"

The little thing buzzed before diving toward me. It ground to a halt when Peaches scolded it. "You need to ask permission first."

The bright light danced in the air, its chittering louder. Fisted hands on hips, Peaches shot me an apologetic glance and said, "They'd like a taste of your dust. I know some pixies don't like them eating their dust, so I told them to ask first."

"They eat mine all the time," Phil offered. "It's not like I need it for anything."

I gave a slow nod before making sure, "Is it the only one?" I wasn't certain how I felt about a horde of sprites enveloping me.

Peaches nodded. "The rest are at my orchard. This one occasionally comes out with me."

"Then it's okay." From what I knew, sprites didn't get addicted to pixie dust the way ogres did. They liked it and could live off the stuff, but they ate other things and it was more delicacy than addictive drug.

Fluttering my wings, I produced a little dust. The sprite dove in and out, zipping around me before getting its fill and heading back to Peaches. It settled on the crown of his head and fell asleep.

I stared at the place I knew the sprite was though I could no longer see it. Lucroy quickly found his way to Peaches's side. Mr. Moony was in the bar when Ray dragged Leon and me there. Their reunion had been exactly what I'd expected—low-key with barely a hint of relief. Neither one of them were fooling me. I'd seen and experienced enough with the two of them to understand just how important they were to each other. Lasting, deep friendships were difficult to find. Loyal ones even harder. I was glad Leon had someone like Lucroy Moony in his second life.

Sedrick cracked a yawn, his mouth opening wide. Scratching his thick fingers through his beard, Sedrick shook his head like a dog. "I need some fucking coffee if we're gonna talk about stuff this early in the morning."

"You already had two cups," Phil innocently said.

Sedrick just shook his head. "Not enough."

"Oh." Phil sounded stricken as he glanced around the bar. Johnny must have already gone home because he wasn't anywhere to be seen. "If we were home, I could—"

"Don't worry about it." Sedrick sank his fingers into Phil's long, pink ombre hair. "I'll be fine. I'm just bitching."

"The hour is an odd one," Lucroy agreed. "I believe that holds true for all of us."

I wasn't sure about Ray and Wendall. From what I understood, fairies didn't require as much sleep as other species. Even if that were the case, I had no idea how Wendall fit in. He was fairy, but also human. Aurelia boosted Wendall's fairy side, but no one knew just how much she'd skewed his genetics. Wendall had been changed recently enough that I doubt he knew much either.

"Apologies," Ray said, even though he didn't sound very apologetic. "I thought it best to debrief while Frost and Leon's memories are fresh. While Frost's capture did not go to plan, he was able to get closer than any other."

Inhaling, I made to step away from Leon. My vampire was having none of it and followed me. His hand slipped from my nape to my lower back. It was a comforting weight.

It was amazing how hours of capture and intrigue could be condensed down into a ten-minute tale. Everyone stayed quiet and attentive until the very end.

Contemplative silence reigned until Wendall finally asked, "You said you got a look at Sylvie's computer, is that right?"

"I did." My grin was back, this time for a whole new reason. "She was online, chatting with someone important, someone who sounded like they were high up in this scheme." My grin slipped and a low growl slipped out. "Whoever it was knew who Leon was and had a pretty big hate on for him. They..." I shook my head, hating the words lighting up my memory. They'd been stark against the unfeeling computer monitor. "What they suggested—no, what they *wanted*—wasn't kind. It wasn't even humane." I swallowed hard. I'd wanted to slip through that vent and slice Sylvie's neck open from one side to the other.

Lucroy's body went completely still before he asked, "Do you know who she was chatting with?"

"No, but we got her computer." I glanced at Ray for further explanation.

"Frost is correct. Sylvie's computer was confiscated. Queen Silvidia sent others in to investigate the property more thoroughly. I will pass along that information when it is forthcoming. I've given the computer to Hamish."

Sedrick grumbled, the sound just shy of a growl. Phil patted his chest and soothed Sedrick's inner wolf.

"Hamish is the best when it comes to newer human technology. I would not have given it to him otherwise," Ray said.

"I know, Ray. But I'll never like that fairy." Sedrick sounded resolute.

"I am not asking you to like him. I am certain Hamish couldn't care less. What I am asking is that you trust my actions." Ray's tone was cool but cutting.

"I do." Sedrick nodded. "It's just hard not to react to the name."

"Understood." Ray seemed appeased.

"It is unfortunate about the witch," Lucroy said. "However, Leon's actions are understandable. I trust there will be no punishment forthcoming."

I hadn't even considered that. My mouth snapped open, ready to defend Leon's actions when Ray calmed my rising fears.

"Pixie trafficking is an automatic death sentence. My queen has no qualms regarding Sylvie and Oxley's demise. She only regrets the timing. Interrogation prior to death would have been ideal, but as Lucroy stated, Leon's actions are understandable and considered justifiable in the eyes of fairy law."

I released a sigh of relief. That relief couldn't squash all my frustration. We'd been so close. Sylvie had to know more but we'd lost the opportunity to squeeze her for information. I wasn't certain if Oxley knew anything else or not. With both of them dead, we'd never know.

Unless... "Are Oxley and Sylvie past the point of a necromancer?" I asked, gaze tracking around the room. While we had a menagerie of species here, a necromancer wasn't among our numbers.

"Muriel might be able to do something." Wendall didn't sound certain.

"She is a priestess," Ray said. "You were an exceptional zombie, Wendall. Muriel would not be able to revive the troll or witch with their memory or mental capacities intact."

"Yeah, I figured." Wendall deflated and Trinket nuzzled deeper into his neck. I wasn't sure if Wendall realized he was petting Trinket or not. "I don't know any necromancers though."

"Vander most likely does. Or at least knows where to find one," Ray answered. "But I would not recommend involving a necromancer unless absolutely necessary." Ray didn't explain why. Honestly, he didn't need to. Necromancers were... It was difficult to put necromancers in a conversational box. They were few—fewer in number than warlocks. There was probably a good reason for that.

"Okay. So, we wait on that." I thought back and asked, "Do we even still have Oxley's and Sylvie's bodies?"

"I did not bring them back with us, but the fairies Queen Silvidia sent will keep them safe and preserved for the time being. When it is certain their bodies are of no use to us, they will be returned to their families."

I shuddered thinking Oxley and Sylvie had families. Oxley was speaking on the phone to someone when Leon and I eavesdropped. I didn't know who that was, but it sounded like they knew each other well. Would Oxley be missed? I shouldn't care. The troll had made his own bed and now he was eternally lying in it.

Silence permeated the space again before Phil muttered, "She used a transportation spell. Isn't that hard to do? I mean, when Parsnip was taken, Letty was juiced up on borrowed magic." Phil chewed on his bottom lip. "I don't like the implications."

I didn't either. If the silence going around the room was any indication, none of us did.

"This is bigger than we thought, isn't it?" Peaches asked

while clinging to Lucroy.

"I am afraid it might be." This time, Ray did sound apologetic or at least as apologetic as I thought fairies were.

Peaches let loose a heady sigh before slumping into Lucroy's hold. "I don't even know what to think any longer. I mean...who would want to hurt others like that? And for something as cheap as money."

Money wasn't everything, unless you were someone who desperately needed it. I figured several of the lower henchmen fit that bill but doubted those at the top did. It was all about greed to those selfish fuckers.

We stood and sat around, discussing a few more details and ins and outs of the last thirty-six hours. Interestingly, so far, no one else had been found at the compound Leon and I'd been taken to. There were no other captives or captors. It really had just been Oxley and Sylvie. That didn't really surprise me much. Afterall, how many did you really need to take down and control your typical pixie? The sad answer was not many.

Leon sagged. By now I'd witnessed the change enough to know what it meant. The sun was up. It was past time for all good little vampires to go to ground.

Lucroy knew too and said, "I believe we have learned as much as possible. The sun is up." All eyes tracked to Leon.

"Sleep does sound appealing." Despite those words, Leon didn't release me. If anything, his arm tightened.

Wendall left Ray's side and said, "I've got one tub of dirty glasses to wash and then I'm done." He started for the washroom, Ray hot on his heels.

Sedrick's lip twitched. "Never thought I'd see the day when a fairy volunteered to wash dishes."

Lucroy's grin barely avoided showing fang. "It is certainly an interesting development."

"Brilliantly understated as usual, Lucroy." Sedrick shook

Lucroy's hand before he and Phil headed for the hall leading to the parking garage. Peaches flew off after them and gave Phil a crushing hug before zipping back to Lucroy's side.

"Leon, you would inform me if you were unwell or adversely affected in any way." It wasn't a question and bordered on a command.

"I would," Leon easily answered. "It is nothing that a good day of rest won't solve." I wasn't so certain about that. I figured rest and blood and was curious why Leon left that latter part out.

Lucroy gave a single nod and said, "If you are ready, Peaches, I believe I would enjoy going home."

With a friendly wave, Peaches flew off, keeping close to Lucroy's side, leaving Leon and me alone. I could hear the faint sounds of glassware clinking in the sink, along with Wendall's soft hums as he sang a tune I didn't recognize. I didn't hear Ray but knew he was there, at Wendall and Trinket's side.

Leon's gaze drifted toward the door leading to his underground sanctuary. He stood there, staring yet not moving an inch.

"Leon?" I finally questioned, unsure what his hesitancy was about.

"I find the thought of descending into that room unpalatable. I do not wish to leave you."

Oh. "I think that can be remedied." Honestly, the thought of walking up my apartment stairs and sleeping alone in the bed wasn't nearly as appealing as it had been earlier. "I just need to grab some food, water, and my phone."

Leon's black eyes sluggishly blinked. "You would not mind?"

I shrugged. "I don't see why not."

This time, Leon's gaze drifted down and to the side. "Many find sleeping next to a vampire during the height of the day unpleasant. Or, perhaps, disturbing. I would not wish to make you uncomfortable."

I considered Leon's words. The height of the day would mean when the sun was highest in the sky, when Leon was essentially *dead* to the world.

"You will not be able to wake me. It will be like sleeping next to a statue."

"I've slept next to worse."

Leon's low rumble told me exactly what he thought of that.

"I'll be back soon. Do you want to wait or head down first?"

"I'll wait. There are security measures of which you are unaware. You will not be able to enter once the door is closed. Only Lucroy, Peaches, and I have access."

I raised an eyebrow. "Not even Johnny?"

"No."

"I'll be back soon," I reassured before flying off to my room. I quickly grabbed my phone and a premade sandwich from the fridge. A bottle of water finished off my hasty meal and I made quick work of getting back downstairs to Lucroy. He was in the same position I'd left him, heavily leaning against the bar.

"All ready," I assured, holding up my sandwich, water, and phone as proof.

"Excellent." Leon walked toward the reinforced double doors. His gait was steady but more languid than I was used to witnessing. While he could be awake at this time, it didn't look pleasant or comfortable.

The doors swung open, and Leon headed down the stairs first. The chilled air hit me, and I relaxed into the feel.

"I can turn the heat up if you'd like," Leon assured. "Lucroy made certain the heating system is in good working order since joining with his beloved."

"It's fine," I reassured. "I like the cold."

Leon turned, a half grin lifting his lip. "Not a typical pixie, are you?"

I laughed. "Not even a little."

Chapter Fourteen

LEON

I woke with a thirst that was difficult to control. It was tempered by the warm body snuggled up at my side.

Phlox. Phlox was beside me. He'd followed me downstairs and stayed the day. In the quiet space I could hear the rush of his blood as it flowed through his arteries and veins. Phlox's heart rate was steady and languid. Unless one were in the throes of a nightmare, sleep often did that.

My fangs itched, desperate to drink from the delicious fountain lying beside me. Were I a younger vampire, I might have succumbed to that desire. I don't know if it was my age or my greater desire to protect Phlox, even against my baser needs, that stayed my instincts.

Nuzzled into the crook of my arm, Phlox's cheek pressed against my upper chest, the crown of his head tucked into my neck. His wings were spread out behind him and fluttered every once in a great while. One arm was stretched across my chest. My cold, unconscious form hadn't bothered him a bit. That knowledge eased my mind.

Phlox's long hair lay across my arm, its silken feel wonderous. My fingers curled into those strands, allowing them to dance and skitter as they slipped through. Perhaps it was the flex of my fingers or maybe it was simply time for Phlox to wake because not long after, he stirred.

Stretching like a cat, Phlox snuggled in closer. Licking his lips, he sighed and whispered, "Good evening. Sleep well?"

"Like the undead."

Phlox lightly smacked me on my abs before stretching again and rolling back. He couldn't complete the motion without sitting up and readjusting his wings.

"How about you? Did you sleep well?"

"Mm-hmm. Like a baby." Phlox yawned. His wings fluttered. It seemed more instinct, or perhaps that was his own way of stretching his wing muscles. Turning, Phlox slipped his legs over the edge before pushing off the mattress. He stretched which made me wonder if it had more to do with his Pallas's cat side than pixie.

Cracking his back, Phlox loosened a grateful sigh that went straight to my dick. He was a vision. If I could wake to this every evening for an eternity, it still would not be enough time. How had I lived without this? Had it even been living? At the time, I'd thought so. I'd enjoyed much of my second life. Now, looking back and not seeing Phlox there, I realized that *living* was an overestimation of what I'd been doing. Existing now seemed more apt.

Phlox shuffled across the room. His wings twittered now and again but not enough to lift him off the ground.

"Do you keep blood in here or do we need to head upstairs for that?" Phlox didn't wait for an answer before he pulled the refrigerator door open and let out a happy sound. "Ah-ha! Found it." Phlox pulled out a chilled bottle that once would have been appealing. Now, thoughts of drinking its contents curdled my borrowed blood and made my stomach cramp.

"Do you like it heated up?" Phlox questioned innocently

while looking around the small kitchen. "I see you've got a microwave and there are some cups in the drying rack." He grabbed one and set it upright on the counter.

I lay there fighting my nausea. "It is of no importance. I am not currently hungry," I blatantly lied.

Phlox turned, the bottle neck grasped within one hand. "Not hungry?" He glanced at the bottle then back at me, his eyes narrowed, and nose scrunched in confusion. "Vampires are always hungry when they wake up and you can't tell me what you took from me yesterday was enough to last through today. Especially when you needed extra energy to heal the wounds from the sun."

"Regardless, I am not currently hungry." I sat up, forcing my legs over the mattress edge but not standing. "Although, I would imagine you are. I will let you out and so you can—"

"Stop." Phlox held up a hand before setting the bottle down on the counter with a loud thud. Fisting that hand and settling it on his hip, Phlox's wings sprang to life, lifting him off the floor. His bare toes dangled. His toenails were a deep, dark blue with a halo of ochre at their tips.

I swallowed, my throat dry. Phlox's heart rate sped up, and his blood gushed through his body, loud and tempting.

Tapping the side of his nose, Phlox flew a little closer. "You know, I've got a pretty good bullshit detector and right now it's blaring loud and proud. So, you wanna start over and tell me what's really going on? Because I'm not going anywhere until you spill."

Tilting my head, I tried to look anywhere but where he hovered. I did not wish to frighten Phlox and yet that is exactly what I was afraid I was about to do. He'd been so understanding. Phlox had lay by my body all day and even cuddled close. Would he still feel the same way when I told him that I could only drink his blood now? Would Phlox understand what that meant? Was it too soon? Would he run from me?

Those thoughts swirled through my brain, leaving me dizzy and even more nauseated. I could barely comprehend the idea that Phlox would walk up those steps and out of my life. He had no reason to stay. He'd completed his mission. Phlox had been captured. He'd gained information that would hopefully prove valuable enough to track down the ringleaders we were after. Would the Magical Usage Council call him back in? Would the assign him another mission, somewhere far from me?

Those thoughts swirled and tumbled with abandon, free-falling through my brain and bottoming out somewhere low in my gut. I'd never felt so cold before.

"Hey. Tell me what's going on in there." Phlox gently tapped my temple before following the motion with an equally gentle kiss. "In case you don't remember recent events, we make a pretty good team." Phlox leaned back and gave me a wry grin. "I'd like to think I can be helpful now too."

He had no idea just how helpful I wanted him to be.

Resting my hands on his hips, I cherished the feel of Phlox's pert bottom resting on my bent legs. His flesh was warm, yet not too hot. It was just the right amount of comfortable.

Still unable to look him in the eyes, I stared at something over Phlox's shoulder as I asked, "Will the council send you somewhere else now?"

Phlox blinked, his eyes currently a dazzling shade of the darkest blue. "I...I'm not sure." He swallowed and all traces of humor fled. "I haven't fully debriefed yet. It probably depends on what can be learned from Sylvie's computer." Placing his hands on my cheeks, Phlox cradled my face. "Is that what's bothering you? You're afraid I'm about to leave."

It was one of many fears currently holding court within my psyche. I'd been a vampire too long to put all my cards on the table or at least to show what those cards truly meant. Downplaying my fear, I said, "It is a concern."

Phlox scoffed, calling me on my bullshit. "*Only* a concern, huh?" His smile was back. "I think I've been too tired to really think things through, but listen, this thing between you and me, I want to explore it more. I've probably got some vacation time so even if I'm officially done with this mission, if you want, I can stick around a bit longer."

Although minimal and probably not noticeable, my arms trembled with relief. *A bit longer* wouldn't be enough, but it would be a start. It would give me time to figure out how to tell Phlox just how important he was to me. Somehow, I'd make do with whatever time we had.

Raising the chilled blood bottle, Phlox tilted it back and forth. "Now that we've got that settled, how about breakfast?"

Phlox's ringtone saved me. Slipping from my lap, Phlox took the dreaded blood bottle with him. Carelessly setting it on the counter, Phlox picked up his cell and answered, "Frost."

Easing back into bed, I rested my head against the wall. Phlox's voice rose and fell but I found it difficult to focus on his exact words. My mind buzzed and my body ached for sustenance. But that discomfort was minimized simply by the cadence of Phlox's voice. If Peaches's voice had a similar effect on Lucroy, no wonder he didn't mind hearing his pixie talk.

Done with his conversation, Phlox flew back to my bedside. He didn't exactly appear upset, but he wasn't happy either.

"Is there news?"

Phlox held up his hand and toggled it back and forth. "Kind of. Hamish is still working on Sylvie's computer. He's not sure how helpful it will be. It's more than we had, but perhaps not enough."

I internally grimaced. If I'd had better control, we'd have a witch to interrogate.

"Stop beating yourself up," Phlox ordered. "If the situation had been reversed and I'd thought she'd really hurt you, I can't be certain what my actions would have been." Phlox shifted, as if the admittance was uncomfortable.

"Still, I find my actions regrettable."

"Yeah, I've got a lot of those situations cluttering up my past. We make the best decisions we can at the time. That's all we can do, Leon. Only oracles see into the future, and I wouldn't wish that burden on my worst enemy."

I wasn't certain I wouldn't wish an oracle fate on my worst enemy, but I understood the sentiment. Oracles didn't remain sane for long. It was more curse than gift. Caught between ever shifting timelines, oracles were never certain if they were living in the present or future. Their world was built upon grains of ever shifting sands instead of solid rock.

Running his fingers down the side of his phone, Phlox's voice was low when he said, "Ray's thinking about bringing a necromancer in."

Phlox's words temporarily abated my raging thirst. Given Ray's previous comments regarding necromancers, the move seemed extreme. "He believes that is necessary?"

"Necessary enough that he's going to speak with Vander. I guess we really shouldn't have killed Oxley and Sylvie. Or, at least, we shouldn't have jumped to killing Oxley as quickly as we did."

"*We* did not kill him. I did."

Phlox waved a dismissive hand. "Semantics. I agreed with the action. At the time, it seemed safest. It's doubtful he knew much, but I have a feeling he would have cracked easily. You never know, Oxley might not have even known he held important information. You and I both know it's easy to slip around those we don't think are competent enough to figure out what were up to. Some of my most successful rouses have been playing naïve and brainless. You fade into the shadows, little more than background noise. You're not important enough to care about and pretty soon others are talking like you aren't even there. Most likely Oxley was the same."

"A valid point. Regardless, we cannot venture back in time. What's done is done."

Clearing his throat, Phlox said, "Warlock Vander Kines and his one and only, Parsnip, arrived at the Richmond airport six hours ago. Peaches said Ray wanted to give Vander and Parsnip a little time to recover from the long flight. We'll be contacted as soon as Ray finds out if Vander can recommend a necromancer."

Phlox sat down beside me, shoulders slumped, elbows on his knees, and head hanging. Placing a hand on his thigh, I gently squeezed. "You are concerned."

"I am. I don't know much about necromancers beyond the Magical Usage Council echoes Ray's sentiments."

"Warlock Kines is conscientious. He will do his best to recommend a reputable necromancer, should one exist." My necromancer knowledge was woefully inept. "Vander can be trusted. He was very useful during recent events concerning a djinn."

"Yeah, I've heard a little about that. Not as much as I'd like, but enough to know I'm glad I only heard about it after the djinn was contained."

I wasn't certain Aurelia was as *contained* as Phlox hoped. She was currently peacefully napping, but one wish from Peaches would wake her and bring Aurelia back on the playing field. It was anyone's guess what her disposition would be. Her hatred of Professor Arthur Stover made us *friends*. Djinn had a long history of killing their masters. I could only hope the same fate would not one day befall Peaches.

Slapping his thighs, Phlox flew off the bed, pushing my

hand aside as he moved. "Well, we're not going to solve the world's problems by staying down in this underground hole. Time to go up and see what kind of trouble we can get into today."

I grabbed Phlox's outstretched hand, my larger one dwarfing his. "Give me a moment to dress," I said before lifting his hand and kissing the back. Phlox flushed bright red and spluttered something incoherent. That was just fine with me because somewhere along the line, Phlox had completely forgotten about the warming blood bottle taking up space on the counter. I'd take the reprieve while I could. I could go without for another few days. It would hurt and I'd have to watch my temper. Hungry vamps had notoriously short fuses. Regardless, it was worth it. I'd suffer through anything for my beloved. I just needed a little more time, a few more hours to figure out how to tell him without risking him running for the nearest airport.

Chapter Fifteen

PHLOX

Twenty-four hours had never felt so long. Given my recent capture and subsequent escape with Leon, that wasn't quite true. Pixies weren't known for understating situations and in that respect, I hadn't fallen far from the pixie tree.

We'd heard very little from Vander and Parsnip's camp. The only information we'd gotten was that Vander was "working on it." I don't think any of us understood exactly what that meant or the timeframe we were looking at.

"I wish Parsnip would give me a little more information," Peaches lamented while staring at his phone. His fingers flew across the screen as he typed something back to Parsnip.

"If he knew more, he'd tell us," Phil said, tone eternally dripping with understanding. "It's not like necromancers advertise their services. At least, true necromancers don't." Phil looked decidedly uncomfortable. "I talked to Sedrick about it last night. His knowledge is second, or maybe, third-hand. Sedrick said his grandmother told him a story about a necromancer their pack used once." Phil shuddered. "If half the things she told him are true, then we need to be very careful. I'd rather Vander take his time."

Peaches's fingers tapped along the wooden tabletop. His face was scrunched, and his nose looked like he'd scented something foul. "I hate how right you are."

Leaning into the bench, I spread my wings out, much like my pixie tablemates. Arms crossed, I glared at Peaches's phone, willing it to ping with more information. I'd been mulling something for the past few hours and finally decided to ask, "Do you think Sylvie's strength while alive will affect her..." I waved a hand in the air, unsure what to call what we were planning. It wasn't reanimation. That's what priests and priestesses did with zombies.

"When we bring her consciousness back from the dead?" Phil thankfully filled in.

"Yes, that," I agreed. "She was powerful enough to enact a transportation spell. That's no small feat. And she did it using her own magic."

Phil shivered. "Parsnip's told me about the one Letty Fox used on him. He said it was horrible and made him vomit."

"Parsnip's not wrong."

"Ugh, I'm glad I just got a face full of sleeping dust." Peaches took a long drink of his mead. "That was bad enough and as close to magic as I want to get."

I raised an eyebrow at that. Pixies utilized magic all the time. The way we did it was different than other species, but we wouldn't be who we were without it. Pixies weren't fairies or brownies. Those species *were* magic. There was a difference. A Grand Canyon-sized difference.

Phil rubbed his forehead and Peaches leaned in and asked, "Are you okay? Have you been away from the house too long?" Worry laced Peaches's voice and he looked ready to spring into action if Phil so much as hinted that was what was wrong.

"No, it's not that. At least not yet. I just hate this whole situation. I hate thinking about pixies being taken and…" Phil couldn't finish his thought. "I'm so fortunate to have never experienced something like that. I can't imagine what it must have been like for Parsnip."

By now everyone who knew anything about Parsnip understood his past and why he only had a smidgeon of his natural aqua color remaining.

Peaches reached across the table and clasped Phil's hand. They interlocked fingers and essentially held hands. Sedrick and Lucroy were across the floor, near the bar. They were talking with Johnny and Leon. The three of us had stayed behind. My gaze wasn't the only one that kept straying toward them. With his hand clasped within Phil's, Peaches's head was turned toward the bar, exposing the length of his neck and the fading bite marks there.

I stared at that patch of skin, unaware of how rude I was being. When Peaches reached up and covered the area with his hand, I finally blinked and drew my eyes away. Peaches's chin jutted out and he had a stubborn pout fixed upon his face.

"Problem?" Peaches asked as if begging me to say yes.

I aggressively shook my head. "No. I'm sorry, I know I was staring, but it's probably not what you think." I reached up and unconsciously rubbed the healed patch of skin on my neck. Clearing my throat, I said, "You see, I, uh… While we were captured, Leon needed to feed. Prior to our transport, he'd been caught in the early morning sun. His skin was burned, and he need to be at full strength if we wanted to get out of there. Plus, I didn't like seeing him in pain."

Peaches's hand dropped, exposing his neck. He now appeared more confused than confrontational.

"That sounds reasonable." Peaches's golden gaze flicked from me to Phil. Our larger than average pixie companion simply shrugged.

"Yeah, I know, it's just...it hurt."

Peaches's eyebrows and nose scrunched. "*Hurt*? The bite?"

I nodded. "Yeah. I mean, I don't know why I was exactly surprised. Leon's teeth sliced through my flesh. I just thought...I figured vampires had a way to make it *not* hurt." I waved a hand in Peaches's general direction. "You seem to like it well enough. Or, at least, you don't seem to mind."

Phil made the mistake of taking a sip of his honeysuckle mead, promptly choking when he processed my words. When I looked over, his cheeks were nearly as pink as the tips of his magenta hair.

Glancing back at Peaches, he had an odd, amused twinkle lighting his eyes. "Well, I suppose you've got that right. Lucroy's bite is far from painful. In fact, it's orgasm inducing."

Phil groaned while placing his forehead in his hand. "Peaches, we don't need to—"

"Oh, I kind of think we do." Peaches leaned over the table, gaze fixed on me. "I think Frost is very interested in how vampire bites feel."

"I..." I swallowed and uncomfortably shifted. "Leon and I have gotten kind of close." My cheeks heated and I figured they might be as pink as Phil's. That warm feeling fled when I thought back to this evening and waking up in Leon's lair again. Tonight was no different than last night. Leon didn't drink when he got up. He told me he'd get something at the bar, but I'd yet to see him so much as lift a glass to his lips and I'd been watching—insistently so. His cheeks were hollower, and Leon's body felt more chilled this evening.

"I don't think he's feeding," I blurted.

Humor fled Peaches and seriousness rapidly took its place. Phil perked up too, sitting straighter and leaning in. He glanced at Peaches before settling his gaze back on me.

"Leon hasn't been feeding? From you or…?"

"I haven't seen him drink anything," I clarified. "And believe me, I've offered him the bottled blood in his fridge the past two evenings. He keeps giving me bullshit excuses why he's not drinking it. I know my vampire biology and he needs to drink. I know Leon's old, but he's not old enough that he doesn't need to feed daily."

"That's true," Peaches agreed. "Typically, Leon feeds multiple times a night. I don't think he needs that much, but vampires enjoy sipping their blood. I've never known Leon to abstain." Peaches threw a concerned glance Leon's way. I watched as Lucroy caught his beloved's gaze, a single eyebrow raised in question.

Peaches gave a slight headshake before returning his attention to me. "I don't think Lucroy knows. Or if he does, then he hasn't said anything to me. That means he either doesn't think it's a problem or he's keeping quiet out of respect for Leon. I couldn't tell you which right now." Peaches huffed. "He's my beloved, but sometimes I still can't tell what Lucroy's thinking. Vampires are sneaky that way."

"Werewolves can be that way too," Phil chimed in. "Sedrick doesn't like to upset me. I keep trying to convince him that I get more upset when I think he's keeping things from me. I'm not sure about Mr. Moony, but I think where Sedrick's concerned, it's part and parcel regarding his alpha nature. Protect, protect, protect. It's part of his DNA."

Peaches shot Phil an understanding smile before focusing back on the problem at hand. "Leon needs to feed. He'll get weaker and increasingly unpredictable. First, he'll get snippy. Or as snippy as a three-hundred-year-old vampire gets. They've got a pretty good lock down on their emotions." Peaches's eyebrows pulled down and he tapped his fingertip along his chin. "Have you offered him your blood again?" Peaches asked.

I jerked back, flattening my wings on the bench. "No. I... the last time I offered, it hurt. I can't say that I'm ready to head down that road again yet."

"Understandable. Did Leon say anything after he fed from you? Did he apologize about it hurting?"

I searched my memory. There'd been a lot going on at the time and much had happened since. I forced myself to think hard and remember. I brought up the memory and nodded. "He did. He said something about not having enough control to make it painless. Or something along those lines."

Peaches nodded in understanding. "Whatever pain I've felt when Lucroy feeds from me is fleeting and quickly replaced by pleasure. But Lucroy's never been in desperate need. He's never required blood to heal injuries or in a time of distress. I'm not sure if it would be different then or not. I could always ask him, but I think he'd find the thought of harming me too horrid to contemplate. I'm his beloved. He cherishes me and would never—" Peaches suddenly stopped speaking. His eyes were wide as saucers. That earlier twinkle was back with a vengeance.

"Peaches?" Phil cautiously questioned.

Peaches licked his lips. They parted once or twice before he finally got enough breath together to whisper, "You said you and Leon have gotten closer?"

"We have. I've slept in his bed the last couple of days. We haven't really... I mean, we haven't done anything beyond kiss and some heavy petting, but I..." I tried mentally arranging my thoughts and corralling my emotions into something I could relate. But my thoughts were as wild as the mustangs running along the prairie.

"But you want more?" Peaches guessed correctly. "And so does Leon."

"He's concerned the council will call me back and send me off on another mission. So far, they're keeping me put and I told him if they do call an end to this mission, I've got some vacation time I'm happy to use up. I don't know how to explain it, but I don't want to leave him just yet."

I was still struggling with why. Not that Leon wasn't attractive. Just the opposite was true. But I'd seen my fair share of drop-dead gorgeous individuals over the years and never felt this connected to any of them.

Sucking on his bottom lip, Peaches fiddled with his phone. He kept shooting glances Phil's way. They seemed to have some kind of silent communication going on. While I really liked the two of them, being out of the loop was starting to piss me off.

"What's going on?" I asked, sitting up and leaning forward enough to free my wings. "If something's wrong with Leon, then I need to know." *Need* might have sounded like a strong word, but it felt right.

"Nothing's *wrong*," Peaches hedged. "At least, I don't think so. In fact, from the vampire perspective, it's probably something very right."

"I don't think just the vampire perspective," Phil amended.

"No." Peaches's smile was soft. "You're right, Phil."

I could feel my inner cat growl, its claws scratching for release. Funny how frustration brought out my more feral side.

Sucking in a deep breath, I counted to five. I should have gone to ten but didn't have the patience. "I need clarification. What are the two of you—"

Peaches's phone dinged with an incoming text and his attention was immediately pulled away. "It's Parsnip," he said before quieting and reading the text. It must have been short and to the point because he quickly said, "They're on their way here." Peaches sounded confused and added, "There's a thinking face emoji along with one of those green-faced nauseous ones. I'm not sure what that means. Do you think Vander's sick?" Warlocks were closer to human genetics and became ill sometimes. Pixies were fairly impervious to ailments unless they were away from their bonded too long.

I didn't know if Vander was ill or not. Regardless, I wanted to continue our previous conversation but couldn't. Evidently the others had gotten a similar message from Vander.

"Did Parsnip contact you, beloved?" Lucroy eased down next to Peaches and glanced at his phone when Peaches tilted it his way.

Sedrick must have gotten a glimpse because he huffed and said, "We got something equally colorful from Vander. Those two were definitely made for each other."

I got up and allowed Sedrick to scoot in next to Phil. He gave me a gruff thanks before sidling in close. Sedrick's thick fingers were gentle as a feather as they swept over Phil's pink diamond choker, skimming across his mating mark before Sedrick replaced his fingers with his lips.

Phil leaned into the touch. The happy contentment radiating from him made me shift uncomfortably. It seemed like too private of a moment, as if I should avert my eyes and wipe the memory from my brain.

Leon didn't give me a lot of time to contemplate my reaction. Sitting down beside me, his thigh ran the length of mine, slightly warming my skin. His arm snaked around my shoulders as he stretched his arm along the length of the back of the booth.

With a tray balanced on his shoulder, Johnny headed our way, setting down fresh cups of honeysuckle mead and a beer for Sedrick. At the end of the table he set down a glass of amethyst-colored fluid.

When he caught me staring, Johnny huffed and said, "Burnt rum. Vander loves the stuff. Don't ask me why. Personally, I think warlocks have some messed-up tastebuds." Johnny shrugged while setting another cup of honeysuckle mead beside it. "I figure Vander will need that"—he pointed toward the burnt rum—"when he gets here. I've got another full bottle in the back. You tell him if he wants more to ask." Johnny gave a sympathetic headshake. "I think he's had a shit last twenty-four hours."

Johnny clomped away, leaving our little group alone.

"Do we have an ETA?" Sedrick asked before taking a large swallow of beer.

"No. Although I do not believe it will be long. From what I understand, they are already on the road and..." Lucroy stopped mid-sentence, body still and black eyes dark.

"Lucroy?" Leon asked, leaning slightly over the table. I felt Leon's body stiffen. "What is it?"

"Wolves." A layer of disgust laced that singular word. Knowing Lucroy's comment wasn't directed toward Sedrick, I figured we had other company.

Sedrick's low growl rumbled through his chest. "How many?"

"Three," Lucroy answered. He had the best vantage of any of us. While I hated having my back to the door, the U-shaped booth hadn't offered a lot of other options.

"New?" Leon calmly asked.

"I am uncertain. You or Johnny would most likely know better than me."

"Or Wendall," I offered. I might recognize them too. "Lizbeth might know too."

"I would prefer to keep the human out of current affairs," Lucroy answered. I didn't think it was because he thought little of Lizbeth. I knew it was the opposite. Lucroy Moony had a soft spot for the human and viewed her as part of his nest. Though capable for a human, Lizbeth was still that. She was the most vulnerable of Lucroy's nestmates.

"Understandable," I agreed.

"Have they been coming in often?" Phil asked. None of us turned. We didn't want to draw attention to the fact we noticed or, perhaps, cared.

"More often than they used to," Leon answered.

"Part of Arie's pack?" Phil asked, a slight hitch to his voice.

"Most likely," Lucroy answered. "Arie Belview is the unfortunate alpha of the largest werewolf pack in the area." Lucroy offered Sedrick the barest hint of a smile. "It seems like the other alpha in the area enjoys the company of a different type of packmate."

Far from offended, Sedrick lifted his mug and saluted Lucroy. "I've got the best pack hands down. Vampires, warlocks, pixies, dwarves, humans, and sprites. Come one, come all. As long as you're not a shithead bent on world domination, you're welcome in my pack."

A low chuckle sounded close by and someone I'd only seen through video chat walked up to the end of the table, dragging two chairs behind him. "Couldn't agree more, Sedrick."

Gray pixie dust tinted with hints of aqua filled the area as Parsnip followed close behind. "What are we agreeing with Sedrick about?" Parsnip asked as he sat in the chair Vander pulled up for him, capping off the end of our booth.

"That he's got an eclectic pack full of awesome members." Vander took a great deal of liberty with that paraphrase, but no one called him out on it.

"Oh. Well, yes, then I heartily agree." Parsnip snagged his cup of honeysuckle mead and downed its contents in one go. Vander reacted similarly with his burnt rum. I stared, a little starstruck. Auntie Tandra would lose her shit if she could see me right now.

Thinking of Auntie Tandra, I sheepishly asked. "Goddess,

I know what this sounds like, but can I get a picture of you and Vander together? My auntie is a huge fan."

Parsnip instantly perked up, a smile spread across his face, lighting it up and erasing some of the recent wear.

"Sure. I don't look my best, but I think it should be fine." Squeezing in next to Vander, Parsnip grinned and posed like the superstar he was. Vander did a fair job of faking it and managed to erase a little of his half-dead appearance.

I took a couple of pics and quickly sent them off to Auntie Tandra. She didn't always have her phone on her, so I wasn't sure if I'd get a response right away.

"Thank you," I said honestly. "This will make her week."

"No worries." Parsnip waved me off. "I'm a social pixie. If anything, your request gave me a little energy boost." Parsnip rubbed his hand over Vander's bicep. "I wish I could do the same for you."

Vander sighed, leaning heavily back into his chair. He rubbed the back of his neck, the strain of the last few days obvious.

Leaning in, Peaches asked what we were all wondering. "Were you able to find a necromancer?"

Vander winced. "Finding one isn't exactly the problem, at least not if you know who to ask. Finding one who might be willing to help is another matter."

Silence filled the table until Vander's tense shoulders relaxed. "Fuck it. It's not like it's a hush-hush secret. It's just not something warlocks talk about a lot. Necromancers are kind of like our dirty little secret." Vander shook his head, seemingly upset with himself. "No, that's not true. They're our fear."

"Fear?" Phil asked, twisting his head toward Sedrick before glancing back at Vander, worried. "Warlocks are scared of necromancers?"

"Not exactly. Shit, this is tough to talk about."

Parsnip leaned into Vander's shoulder, placing his hand on Vander's chest. "Take your time."

"Indeed," Lucroy agreed before his attention shifted over our shoulders and his eyes narrowed a fraction.

"I'll keep an eye on things," Leon offered, already standing. His fingers gripped the edge of the table, and I knew it wasn't simply my imagination that his skin was paler than usual. It was chalky white, not the luminous moonglow I was used to.

"Thank you, Leon."

Leon gave a faint nod before walking away. He didn't even turn and look my way before he left. Leon didn't pat my hand or run his fingers through my hair. He was stiffer than usual. Something was definitely wrong.

I wanted to get up and follow him, demand that he spill whatever secret he was keeping, but I couldn't. I was still the agent on this case, and I needed to hear what Vander learned.

Frustration filled me. Sedrick's askance glance hinted I'd probably lost a little control and allowed a growl to slip through.

"Back again?" Vander asked as Lizbeth slipped another glass of burnt rum in front of him. "Ah, perfect timing." Lizbeth shot him a grin before slipping back into the crowd. Vander took a sip before repeating, "Arie's wolves—they're back again?"

"It appears that way," Lucroy coolly answered. "From what Johnny and Leon have told me, it is a much more common occurrence."

"Always the same ones?" Parsnip asked.

"No. There are often repeats, but it is not always the same group, nor the same number. From what I understand, occasionally Arie himself shows up, but those instances are rare."

"You could always kick them out," Vander said casually.

"I could, but that would indicate I harbor concern," Lucroy answered.

Vander raised an eyebrow, eyeing Lucroy. "But you do harbor concerns. A shit ton of concerns."

"Of course, but Alpha Belview need not know that." Lucroy sounded very matter of fact.

"Vampires," Vander grumbled but it lacked heat.

Sedrick agreed. "If it were my bar, I would have kicked their asses out a long time ago."

"Thankfully, Dusk is not werewolf owned." Lucroy's tone remained pleasantly cool. "As long as they do not cause trouble, Dusk is open to all."

"As you said, it's your bar. You can do whatever the hell you want with it." Sedrick drank down the rest of his beer.

"How magnanimous of you, Alpha Voss." Lucroy sounded more amused than annoyed. Truly, they had an interesting relationship. In fact, it was an odd conglomeration of species. And yet, somehow, it worked. The affection was clear. The Magical Usage Council would find this interesting.

Moving past Lucroy's choice of patronage, the vampire got us all back on track by asking, "Are you capable of explaining further?"

Vander took another drink before nodding his head. "Yeah, I'm capable. It's not really that bad, just not something warlocks like talking about. Mostly because we hate thinking about it."

Setting his glass back on the table, Vander started with a history lesson. "Long ago, before the rift between warlocks and witches, we often mated each other. Female children were witches and male children were warlocks." Vander shrugged. "I'm not certain what gender had to do with it, but it influenced the way we bend magic. From what I understand, the witches and warlocks of those times were more powerful than your current garden variety."

"Is that what allowed witches of that time to create djinn?" Sedrick asked.

"Most likely. It's what also caused the rift between the species. Witches and warlocks hated each other. They couldn't move past their mistrust to even talk, let alone procreate. That began easing in the past century or so, but we're still a long way from producing offspring." Vander took another drink before continuing. "Anyway, obviously, there are still little witches and warlocks running amuck. So, who do you procreate with?"

"Humans," I answered. It was a known fact that most warlocks and witches produced children with humans.

"Exactly," Vander agreed. "Our genetics are closest. The magical bloodlines were diluted, but the species survived. Sometimes, a witch child will be born with lesser magical abilities. Rarely none at all. But warlock children are a different matter."

I leaned forward, completely enthralled by what I heard. While much was known about individual species, there was a hell of a lot that wasn't. All of us had secrets we'd rather not share.

"It's a small percentage, but some children born of warlock blood don't have the same capabilities as their fathers. Those children are necromancers."

Sedrick drew in a deep breath while Lucroy remained statue still. Peaches's mouth opened in a surprised O while Phil's light green eyes were filled with a well of sympathy. As for me, I was simply curious.

"And warlocks are ashamed of this?" I asked. I didn't want to be uncouth, but I couldn't deny my curiosity.

"No. Not in the way you think. It isn't shame in what they are, but heartache. Warlock life spans are centuries long. Necromancers'...aren't."

"Oh, Vander," Phil whispered.

"Nearly all of them are human short. I'm ashamed to say that many warlocks abandon those children when they're born and realized what they are. It is not due to shame, but emotional self-preservation. Children are precious and warlocks aren't a fertile species. The joy of a successful pregnancy is tempered with the fear that that child might be born a necromancer, that they will die while the warlock has many years left. It is a pain many turn from."

"And the children are abandoned?" Peaches asked.

"By the warlock, not their human mother. Warlocks will financially provide, but most refuse to emotionally engage. I do not defend the action. I merely say I understand it. Unfortunately, what this often creates are resentful children who do not fully understand their capabilities. They feel shunned by not only their fathers but the world. Necromancers find it difficult to integrate into society and so many go to ground, fading into difficult-to-find nooks and crannies. An unfortunate few are so mentally traumatized that their sanity fades and they become dangerous not only to themselves, but to society at large. Those unfortunates are what give necromancers a very poor reputation."

I swallowed, throat parched. My mouth opened, only to close on words I couldn't find, let alone articulate. It was a tragedy all around.

Inhaling, Vander pulled Parsnip close, laying a kiss on the top of his head and breathing his scent in. When he'd gotten his emotions under control, Vander said, "I know of a few necromancers, but most of those are in the wind. I do, however, know of a warlock who refused to follow tradition and did not abandon his necromancer son." Vander's lips contorted and I couldn't figure out if he found the situation humorous or endlessly irritating.

"Nikodemus Holland is a pompous asshat," Parsnip

supplied. "I only heard Vander's side of the conversation and it was enough for me to figure out."

"He's got reason to be pompous. Nick's the most powerful warlock west of the Mississippi. He's got the juice to back up the pomp." Vander sort of, kind of defended the other warlock.

Parsnip rolled his eyes. "Whatever. That's west of the Mississippi. You're the best one east of the Mississippi. As far as I'm concerned, you're on equal footing."

Vander's eyebrows shot high upon his forehead while his lips twitched, finally forming an oddly fond smile. "That's sweet, if not one hundred percent accurate."

Parsnip waved him off. "Says you. I happen to know it's a fact and no one, not even you, is going to convince me I'm wrong, so don't waste your breath trying."

Chuckling, Vander leaned in and planted a kiss on Parsnip's temple. "Have I told you recently how much I love your sass?"

Cheeks flushed, Parsnip answered, "Not in the past couple of hours."

"Well then, looks like I need to pick up the pace, Sassy Pants."

"Ohh, I like that one." Peaches bounced in his seat, wings twittering and spreading dust around the table. Vander and Sedrick covered their noses but neither said a word of reprimand.

When Peaches calmed, Vander uncovered his nose and leaned back. Arm thrown around Parsnip's shoulders, he causally took another sip of burnt rum before returning to the topic of interest. "As I was saying, Nikodemus didn't abandon his son. He's been an integral part of Erasmus's life."

"Are Nikodemus and Erasmus's mother still together?" I asked, wondering if that was part of the reason he'd remained in touch.

"Not that I'm aware of," Vander answered with a shrug. "She's not his one and only, that much I know."

"So, besides being a *pompous asshat*," Sedrick said, and Parsnip raised his cup of honeysuckle mead in the air, saluting Sedrick's wording, "was this Nikodemus helpful?"

Vander sighed while running his black tipped fingers through his graying temples. "I think so. At the very least, he's going to ask Erasmus if he'll help. There'll be a fee."

"Naturally," Lucroy said.

"It will exorbitant," Vander assured us with a hint of embarrassment. "Nick made that fact very clear."

Lucroy sounded nonplussed. "Whatever the amount, I am certain I can cover the cost."

"*We* can cover the cost," Sedrick corrected. "We're in this together, Lucroy. I've got the means and the will."

"I did not mean to offend," Lucroy offered.

"I didn't think you did," Sedrick reassured. "And, to be truthful, I appreciate your willingness. Not so long ago, I wouldn't have been able to offer."

Lucroy and Sedrick shared a glance, and both grew quiet with unstated understanding.

"When will we know if Erasmus is willing to help?" Phil leaned forward and asked.

"Nick said he'd get back to me by tomorrow. He might be an ass, but Nick wouldn't lead me on about something like this. Plus, from what I understand, he's got a good relationship with his son. They speak on the regular, so I don't have any reason to doubt Nick's word."

The table grew quiet. Peaches's soft voice cut through that silence as he asked Vander what was most likely on all our collective minds. "Have you been around a necromancer before?"

Vander's jaw worked and his lips twisted before he gave a

slow, solemn nod. "I have. Twice. The first time was with Georgiana."

"Byx's mother," Parsnip added while looking at me. "Georgiana helped Vander hone his warlock skills and when she passed, she left her daughter in his care."

I touched my meerkat hair clips. They might not work exactly like Byx hoped, but they'd at least led to my general direction. Plus, I'd kind of grown fond of the little fellas. Parsnip saw the motion and grinned. "I've got a few pairs myself. Byx is very creative."

"That she is," Vander agreed. "But as to your question. I'm glad Georgiana was with me the first time. Seeing a necromancer in action is...disturbing." Vander swallowed hard before turning his attention to Lucroy. "No offense, Lucroy, but seeing a dead body come back to *life* is creepy as fuck." Vander shivered dramatically.

"I do not take offense. While I have not witnessed a necromancer raise the dead, I do not believe it is similar to my second awakening. No one was in control of my consciousness and once I awoke to my second life, it was mine to live as I pleased. That is not so when a necromancer is in charge."

"No, that's true," Vander said. "Necromancers are akin to puppet masters, pulling the strings of a dead corpse's consciousness. And once they're done"—Vander snapped his fingers—"they cut the cord and the body falls to the ground, little more than an empty shell, its soul and consciousness sent back to wherever the necromancer pulled it from. It's all very...undignified."

"From the way my grandmother told it, the one brought back is confused too," Sedrick said, his tone low and raked across thick gravel. "Let's just say the process left an impression on her."

"Hmm, I don't doubt it," Vander agreed. "I do not relish

the thought of repeating the experience. However, I agree this is the best course of action."

I suddenly felt the need to apologize again. "I'm sorry. Leon and I should have kept Oxley alive. And Sylvie..." I shook my head. "I don't blame Leon for killing her. She was a threat and he thought she'd hurt me." While I was frustrated Sylvie was dead, I wasn't angry with Leon. I'd gotten over that emotion quickly.

Vander leaned in, elbows planted on the table and gaze fixed on me. "Listen, I haven't gotten the complete lowdown on what happened, but trust me, whatever actions you and Leon took were justifiable. I've been on the end of the captured stick. It sucks ass and sometimes you just gotta do what you've gotta do. Hindsight's great and all, but not real useful while you're in the moment trying to make snap decisions and fighting for your life. Nikodemus will come through, as will his son, Erasmus. We'll pony up whatever insane payment they want and see if Sylvie and Oxley can be more useful in their deaths than in their lives."

"Here, here," Parsnip cheered. Holding up his cup of honeysuckle mead, Parsnip leaned across the table. Peaches, Phil, and I all raised our own cups, clinking them together and hoping against hope that Erasmus could get something more out of Sylvie or Oxley.

We all swallowed, hoping the goddess heard our toasted prayer.

Chapter Sixteen

The thirst was an untamable beast. Had my throat ever felt this dry? My lips so parched? My gut so hollow? Surely there had to be a point in my past, when I was a freshly turned vampire and hunting was so difficult I'd thought I'd go insane from hunger.

If there was such a time, I couldn't remember it. Perhaps it had been so horrid I'd blocked the memory. It was doubtful, but currently, it was a hope I desperately clung to. Because if I'd survived such thirst in the past, I could surely hold out now.

"They look far too at ease." Johnny tossed his hand towel over his shoulder, draping it across his shirt. "Smug too."

I glanced at the wolves currently preoccupying all our minds and time. They were a distraction I could hardly currently afford. I'd assured Lucroy I would keep a weather eye on them, but preoccupied as I was with my current circumstances, I was hardly the pillar of observation I typically was.

With a distinct uneasy feeling, I realized Johnny was correct. The wolves did look smug. Had they appeared that way before? I wasn't certain. On closer observation, I realized only one of the wolves held that expression. The other two simply looked wary as their eyes forever shifted around the room, as if constantly on alert and expecting someone, or something, to pounce on them any second.

"I put Lizbeth on their table. She's damn observant and those cocky bastards will underestimate her the most," Johnny said. "She can't get a good read on them. Just like all the other groups that have come in and sat in the bar. Werewolves are supposed to be a social, rowdy bunch. Arie's wolves couldn't be more different. When they come in here, they're sullen and quiet as the grave. They certainly aren't coming into Dusk to let off some steam and relax."

Again, Johnny wasn't wrong.

Huffing, Johnny shook his head and asked, "You want me to get you something to eat?" Johnny turned as if he was ready to head for the fridge and pour me a glass of blood.

I swallowed but had little saliva to work with. Giving a reluctant head shake, I said, "Thank you, but no."

Johnny's head cocked to the side and his eyes narrowed in puzzlement. "You sure? I haven't seen you drink anything tonight and—"

"I said no thank you," I snapped, voice low and cold.

Johnny straightened. His puzzlement morphed into stunned silence.

Silently cursing my hasty remark, I said, "Apologies, Johnny. I did not mean to snap at you."

He waved me off. "It's okay. I suppose we're all wound a little tight." Johnny said the right words, but his wounded eyes told a different story.

"While true, that does not give me the right to take that frustration out on you. Again, I beg your forgiveness."

Johnny's tight shoulders relaxed, and his face softened.

"Nah, it's okay. You just let me know if you change your mind."

Johnny left to take care of Dusk's customers. I stood there, staring after him. I'd done well so far but that brief altercation was the first blow across the bow. With my thirst riding me, my temper was on a hair trigger, and it would only get worse. If I never took another sip of blood again, I'd survive, if one could call it that. Boxing was the worst punishment a vampire could suffer. Sealed inside an impenetrable crate and left for days, weeks, months or sometimes years to decades. Given enough time without feeding, there was little more than a husk left, the mind inside tormented by thirst to the point of insanity. The vampire could be revived with blood, but what came back was a mental time bomb.

Boxing a vampire was worse than death. It was cruel and only the vilest among us deserved that degree of punishment. If I could not convince Phlox that he was my beloved and that I needed to feed exclusively from him, I could only hope another took pity on me and either beheaded me or gave my body over to the sun.

Leaning my elbows on the bar, I fought the exhaustion pulling at my mind and body.

"Leon." Lizbeth's anxious voice pulled me from my dark thoughts.

"Yes?" I couldn't manage much beyond that simple word.

Lizbeth stood there, a folded piece of paper in her hand. She stared at the outstretched piece of paper as if it might explode if not handled gently. "I found this tucked under a glass. It was at the table with the weres. Someone left it."

I eased the paper from her pinched fingers before glancing at the now empty table. I hadn't even noticed their absence. I was doing a piss-poor job keeping an eye on our unwanted guests.

Pushing my failure from my mind, I concentrated on the

scrawled writing and felt my eyebrows pull tight as my brow pinched. The note was for Sedrick or, more specifically, Alpha Voss.

"I thought about taking it over myself, but the boss looks like he's in deep conversation with everyone. I didn't know if it was okay to disturb them or not."

"I'm sure it would have been fine, but I understand and appreciate your hesitancy. I will make sure Alpha Voss gets the message."

"Thanks, Leon." Lizbeth sagged with relief before ducking behind the bar.

The paper was little more than a folded sheet, so light I barely registered the weight. I had no idea what the contents were but given it was addressed to Sedrick, whatever was on the note was not intended for my eyes.

Lizbeth was correct. Lucroy was ensconced in a meeting of sorts. Hellfire and Wendall were missing but whatever was said, I knew they'd be filled in soon. Or perhaps they were already aware of Vander's news.

With the wolves gone, I headed toward the table, easing into my previous seat beside Phlox. Being this close was agony and bliss all rolled into one complicated package.

"Leon," Lucroy addressed, voice soothing and cool as always. "I noticed our *guests* vacated the property."

"They have, but one left this behind." I slid the note Sedrick's way. I had to lean closer to Phlox to do so. The blood rushing through his arteries and veins sped as I neared. I scented arousal, not fear. What I also scented was confusion. Now was not the time to explore those feelings further.

"What's this?" Sedrick asked as he snatched the paper from my fingers. His eyes widened as he stared at his name. "You said one of Arie's wolves left this behind?"

"Lizbeth found it on the table, tucked under a glass." It was obviously left on purpose.

Sedrick's deep brown eyes briefly glinted gold as they scanned the table, finally resting on Phil. His mate could only shrug.

"I suppose we won't know until you open it," Phil wisely said.

"Yeah, but knowing Arie, there could be a nasty surprise waiting inside," Sedrick just as wisely replied.

"Give it here." Vander made a gimme motion with his fingers. Sedrick didn't hesitate passing the note over. Running his fingers over the note, Vander closed his eyes. I'd seen him do that before. It meant he was concentrating, searching for magical threads.

"Anything?" Parsnip asked.

Vander shook his head. "Nothing I can sense. As far as I can tell, it's clean." Vander's lips twisted. "I wish I could give you a hundred percent guarantee, but all I can say is that I don't sense anything nefarious."

Vander leaned across the table and handed the note back. Sedrick grabbed it and flipped the folded paper between his thick fingers. "Just because there's no magic doesn't mean the words inside aren't toxic as hell."

"A valid observation," Lucroy agreed.

With a heavy sigh, Sedrick said, "Best get on with it then." Opening the folds, Sedrick's eyes scanned the brief message. As he read, his eyebrows shot up before scrunching down.

"What's it say?" Peaches asked, wings twittering.

Phil leaned over Sedrick's arm, eyes scanning the scant words. His mouth opened once, before he cleared his throat and read, "Help us, Alpha Voss. Alpha Belview has gone mad."

The table went silent before Phlox finally asked, "That's it?"

Sedrick gave a solemn nod. "That's all it says." He flipped

the paper over, scanning it to make certain nothing else was there.

Again, silence settled in. None of us knew what to make of it. Lucroy said, "If it is a trap, it is far too vague to be useful. Unless..."

"Unless he's trying to rile me up, get me to start poking around his pack. To what end, I'm not certain. This is Arie Belview we're talking about." Sedrick tapped his temple. "Logical thought isn't a trait I associate with him."

"Agreed. However, I do not believe I have ever thought of Alpha Belview as *mad*. The usage of the word in this instance implies insanity, or at the very least, a break with reason. In the past I have always found Alpha Belview filled with reason. While I may vehemently disagree with the thought process behind that reason, I'd hardly call him *mad*." Lucroy glanced around the table finding agreeing nods.

"What in the goddess's name is going on with him?" Phil asked.

Refolding the paper, Sedrick answered, "I have no idea. I just wish I didn't need to speculate. Moon goddess, I just want Arie Belview to disappear. I want him out of our lives for good." Sedrick rubbed his forehead. Phil leaned his head on Sedrick's shoulder while wrapping his arms around his mate's chest.

"I suppose I need to talk to Ray about this," Sedrick said, his voice a little defeated. "I doubt fairy law can do much. This seems more like a werewolf matter to me, but I'd like to keep him in the loop."

"Speaking of information loops..." Vander held up his phone. "I just got a text from Nick. Looks like Erasmus is willing to help out. As expected, the fee is...generous." Vander swallowed hard. "Shit, if Byx saw this, she'd zap my damn phone."

Parsnip leaned over Vander's shoulder and whistled.

"Bold, but it's difficult to haggle when they've got us by the balls."

Phil choked on a sip of honeysuckle mead. His face flamed and I wasn't certain if that was due to embarrassment or asphyxiation. I did not miss breathing.

"When can the necromancer be here?" Lucroy asked, ignoring the financial sting.

"Nick says Erasmus is in Mississippi, so it won't take as long as I thought. Once we give the okay, he'll hop on a plane. I'd say tomorrow at the earliest. I'm assuming we're all in agreement here?"

"Give him the go-ahead," Sedrick said. "The sooner we get this sorted, the better." He gave a heated stare that should have lit the note on fire. "Between this pixie trafficking ring and Arie's continued bullshit, my wolf's getting restless." The last was said as little more than a growl.

"I am afraid I agree with Sedrick," Lucroy replied smoothly. "When it comes to either topic, I find it increasingly difficult to control my more feral side. Without my beloved, I doubt I would be able to maintain such an amiable façade."

Peaches nuzzled Lucroy's neck. While I doubted the full truth of that statement, it was clear to see the calming effect Peaches had on the Southeast vampire king. I longed for that same peace and contentment. While Phlox sat hip to hip beside me, that level of bliss had never seemed so far away.

Chapter Seventeen

PHLOX

Dusk was nearly empty and I was on the last bin of glasses. Johnny left about five minutes ago and Lizbeth only a few minutes before that. All the other workers left even earlier. Sedrick and Phil went home about the same time as Lucroy and Peaches. Both pixies had been away from their bonded areas a little too long and were beginning to show signs of wear by the time they left.

Parsnip didn't have that problem. Bonded to Vander, as long as his warlock was near, Parsnip could go anywhere he wanted for as long as necessary. Given his profession and need for travel, that was a very good thing.

Leon was on the phone. After the meeting broke up, he'd immediately gone into work mode. The vampire had barely spared me a glance the rest of the night.

A glass slipped from my fingers, crashing into the sink. My inner cat huffed at my clumsiness, but in truth, it was my shifter agitation that probably caused it. My cat wasn't happy with Leon or, I suppose, the way Leon was ignoring us. I was so confused I wasn't sure which way was up. Leon was so damn hot and cold. I couldn't get a read on him. At first, I was upset. Now I was just angry.

"What the fuck's his problem?" I groused at the dirty dishwater. "I mean, in the beginning, he couldn't keep his hands off me. He's transforming and being all huffy and protective and shit and now..." Now what? What happened? And why in the hell wasn't Leon feeding? His skin held an unhealthy luminescence, his cheeks were hollower, and I'd heard him snap at a couple of employees. That wasn't the vampire I knew and... I couldn't exactly finish that statement, despite the fact I knew the word that fit.

I rinsed the final glass and laid it on the counter to air-dry. I'd put them all up tomorrow evening before Dusk opened.

Drying my hands on a towel, I tossed it into a nearby bin. Hands fisted and firmly planted on my hips, I stared at the clean washroom. My wings fluttered and lifted me off the floor, leaving my tapping foot connecting with little more than air.

"This is ridiculous," I huffed. "I've had it. Enough is enough. I'm not spending another day sleepless and wondering what's going through his head. We've got too much shit going on to deal with that too."

Decision made, I flew toward the door, slamming my palms into it. The door swung open, banging into the wall. My eyes quickly scanned the empty bar. Last I'd seen, Leon was sitting at the back booth, phone in hand and taking care of Dusk's business.

That's not where my vampire still was. Leon was at the door leading to Lucroy's underground sanctuary.

Rage flared. I caught my reflection in a nearby mirror, my eyes no longer deep blue but burning yellow.

"You're going down without me?" I accused. I wanted to fly at Leon but stayed where I was, hovering in a cloud of angry pixie dust. "Were you even going to tell me? Or are you just slinking off to hide for the day." I didn't have independent access to Leon's hidey-hole. Once he was locked inside, I'd be locked out.

Leon shifted, one hand still on the now open door. If he wanted to dart inside, I'd never be fast enough to get there before the door shut and locked.

Arms crossed, I huffed. "I never took you for a coward, Leon."

Rage, unmitigated and fierce filled Leon's eyes, turning them into shimmering rubies. "*Coward?*"

Oh, he didn't like that. Good. "I call it like I see it. And right now, you're scurrying into a vault to get away from me."

Leon's mouth opened in a snarl. His fangs elongated and he snapped them. Joints popping, Leon's transformation wasn't far off. I'd definitely pulled the tiger's tail.

With deliberate purpose, Leon's eyelids slid closed, covering that scarlet glow. His body went eerily still. Seconds morphed into minutes and somehow, I managed to hold my tongue, waiting for Leon to get his emotions in check. It shouldn't take him this long. Leon had far better control than what he currently exhibited. His current state confirmed all my earlier thoughts. Something was wrong and that something needed fixing ASAP.

Flexing his fingers, Leon's voice was deceptively cool when he finally said, "Forgive me. I should not have reacted so—"

"Dramatically?" I finished.

Leon gave a slow nod. "That is certainly one word for it."

I could have kept pushing that angle, but instead I aimed for a direct hit. I was tired of beating around this thorny bush. "What's going on, Leon?"

"I don't know what you—"

"Don't you dare finish that bullshit statement." I flew forward and punched a pointed finger into his granite-like chest. "You haven't been feeding. Even by vampire standards, you're pale. You're short-tempered, irritable, and wholly unpleasant. And you've been purposefully ignoring me all night. Now, what the fuck is going on? I swear to the goddess, if you don't tell me, I'll find a way to make you. Don't ask me how. All I know is that I'll figure something out." It's what I excelled at.

Leon's stoic countenance fractured, and his lips twitched on the verge of the first smile I'd seen all night. "That might be...entertaining." His hand raised, as if he wanted to touch me, only to fall to his side, a flash of pain lighting his otherwise onyx eyes.

I moved in closer. Maybe Leon questioned if he should touch me, but I had no such qualms. Placing my hands on his chest, I stared up into his troubled eyes and begged. "Tell me what's wrong. Please. I'm worried about you." I was more than worried.

Leon's body shivered, its granite surface slowly relaxing beneath the weight of my palms. Swallowing appeared painful for him and yet he repetitively did it, as if it was more reflex than thoughtful action.

Leon's fingers gripped my shoulders. For a moment I wasn't sure if he would push me away or pull me in. Making his decision for him, I leaned in and whispered, "Don't push me away. If you do, I'll just be here tomorrow evening. When the sun goes down and you walk up those steps and open the door, I'll be the first thing you see."

With a needy groan, Leon pulled me to his chest, holding me tight. His lips were next to my ear, his whispered words tickling my skin. "If I tell you, I could lose you forever. Perhaps I am a coward. I cannot bear the death of the illusion."

Leon allowed me to pull back enough that I could see his face when I answered, "I'm not an illusion. I'm right here and I'm not going anywhere. Now, drag me to your lair. We've still got a few minutes before the sunrise. That should be enough time for you to explain."

While he didn't exactly drag me, Leon did hold me as he descended the stairs. The thick, metal double doors silently closed behind us. The locking mechanism wasn't so silent and sounded immensely final. It was a good thing I wasn't bothered by confined spaces.

Treating me as if I were the most precious creature in all the world, Leon deposited me on a soft, backless chair. He'd told me yesterday the chair was purchased with Peaches in mind. I had Lucroy's beloved to thank for my agreeable accommodations.

I'd hoped Leon would head to the mini-fridge and grab a bottle of blood. He didn't. Instead, my vampire paced the confined room. His slender fingers slid through his ginger hair, ruffling and displacing the otherwise immaculate strands.

I allowed his pacing, attempting to patiently wait. But time was not on our side. The sun would rise soon and while Leon would remain coherent for a few hours, he would be sluggish and perhaps not thinking as clearly as I'd like.

As Leon made another pass, I reached out and snagged his wrist. He could have easily pulled free but didn't. Instead, he stood there, allowing my hold.

"My auntie Tandra always says to just spit it out. The problem is generally halved simply by giving it airtime." I was paraphrasing but thought Auntie Tandra would approve. "Besides, the sooner we start, the sooner we can come up with a solution." And I was positive a solution could be found. I couldn't imagine a different scenario.

Dropping his head, Leon moved to the seat across from me. Releasing his wrist, I scooted until my rear barely touched my chair. A part of me wanted to shift, crawl in Leon's lap, and nestle in close. For now, I fought that instinct and gave Leon his space. When he continued sitting there, silence filling the air, I grasped his limp hands and entwined them with mine.

"Hey, I said I wasn't going anywhere and I'm not. Nothing you can tell me will be that bad. I promise."

Leon's mirthless chuckle sent shivers down my spine.

"You say that now, but I do not know if that is a promise you will be able to keep."

"You let me worry about keeping promises. Now, let's start with something simple. Why aren't you feeding? Are you ill?"

Leon attempted half-heartedly to pull his hands free. I clamped down harder and he gave up quickly.

"That is not as easy of a question as you believe."

"No, probably not, but considering it's the one with the most lethal possibilities, I think it's the most important one." I'd wanted to start with asking why he was ignoring me, but Leon's health was more important than my wounded heart.

Leon's gaze slowly lifted, first to my eyes and then to my neck. He licked his lips and his fangs dropped. I almost released his hands and pulled back. It took all my self-control to remain where I was.

"Fear. I can feel it radiating from you in waves." Leon's tone was soft with despair.

I swallowed hard. I could deny it, but what was the point? Leon could feel it and I couldn't exactly hide it. Honesty, that's what I expected from Leon and that's what he needed from me.

"The last time you bit me, it hurt."

Leon's soulful wail ripped a hole in my heart. "I would not wish to harm you for the world. To think I hurt you, I—"

"Hey." I scooted until I was nearly off my chair. "None of that. You were in pain and needed to feed. I asked Peaches about it earlier tonight. He said the bite typically isn't painful and probably only was because you didn't have as much control that time."

"It is still no excuse. Causing you pain is the last thing I would ever wish for. I would rather walk into the sun than—"

"Don't you even joke about that," I scolded, my emotions heavy. "You don't want to cause me pain. Well, that works both ways. Tell me you understand that."

Leon gave a reluctant nod. I wanted to ask for more but didn't feel it was the time to push. Ignoring the lingering, instinctual fear, I tried assembling the pieces of the puzzle that were slowly falling into place. My conversation with Peaches earlier, the fact I hadn't seen Leon drink since he'd fed from me, and then when I did ask him about feeding, his eyes automatically tracked to my neck.

Realization is a damning thing sometimes. While I might not completely understand the picture I was creating, I thought I knew enough to say, "You want to feed from me."

"Want. Need." Leon's words scratched through his throat.

Need? I licked my suddenly dry lips. "Are you...are you telling me you can *only* feed from me?" Could that really be it? And if so, what in the hell did that mean?

This time, when Leon tugged his hands, I allowed him to pull free. He leaned back into his chair, allowing the frame to take his weight. His silence was answer enough.

Following suit, I scooted back, sitting properly so I could contemplate what I'd just learned. "Are you certain?"

"Without a doubt," he quickly answered.

"Well, shit." It wasn't my finest verbal moment, but it was all I could contemplate. "What...? I mean, why? Do you know why you can only drink from me now?" Compared to most pixies, I probably had a better, general working knowledge of vampire physiology. That still didn't mean I knew everything. Besides, currently, my brain seemed to be on hiatus in a location with no cell service.

Leon's gaze traveled around the room, landing on everything but me. Just when I thought he'd keep his silence, Leon dropped his bombshell. "You are my beloved. Even contemplating drinking another source is revolting."

I reared back as if I'd been physically slapped. *"Beloved?"* I knew Leon was interested in me, that we had something I wanted to explore, but that wasn't a word vampires casually threw around. It was also a word vampires didn't often use. As far as I knew, few vamps ever found their beloveds. Lucroy Moony and Peaches were the first recorded vampire/pixie bond. Was Leon seriously sitting there telling me we were about to be the second? Maybe there had been others I wasn't aware of. Word was slowly leaking through the vampire and pixie communities. The possibility opened up all kinds of squirmy cans of worms.

Weighty, nearly suffocating silence tried to steal my breath. I tried thinking through the problem only to wonder if this was truly a problem. I mean, I liked Leon. I thought I might even love him, but for me at least, there simply hadn't been enough time. I wasn't a terribly sociable pixie. Most who knew me considered me a loner. I'd never truly contemplated settling down. Pallas's cats mated and settled to a degree, but they didn't seek out other company.

A wickedly wry half grin settled on Leon's face. "Do you regret your earlier promise?"

I didn't have to think twice and answered an easy "no. I don't regret it."

"But you'd like to run," Leon accused.

"Honestly, I'm not sure what I want to do, but running isn't at the top of the list. It's just... It's a lot to take in." My mind tumbled over what Leon's words meant. Sometimes words were weightier than the heaviest elephant. I closed my eyes, breathing deeply. I was used to solving situations. This one was no different and I needed to approach it like I did everything else life threw my direction—one issue at a time.

Thinking into a far-off future was too overwhelming. The immediate concern was Leon's health. He needed to feed. He needed to feed from me. Pain wasn't a foreign concept. I wasn't one to seek it out, but I didn't shy away from the possibility either. Currently, it wasn't my pain I worried over. It was Leon's. If he bit me and it hurt again, would he be able to get past that? Would the guilt overwhelm him to the point he couldn't feed?

Looking at his sallow cheeks and dejected spirit, I decided I couldn't risk it. But as with nearly everything, where there was a will, there was a way.

Standing, my toes dug into the plush rug below. Again, I assumed I had Peaches to thank for my considerately soft surroundings. Leon didn't try and push me off when I straddled his lap. He didn't wrap his arms around me either. It was like crawling into the lap of a marble statue.

Fingertips pressed to Leon's chin, I lifted my vampire's face. As always, Leon could have resisted the move. I counted it as a win that he didn't.

Running my hands across his cheeks, I pushed a strand of hair behind his ear, sifting those strands through my fingers. "Leon, look at me." It took a few seconds, but Leon's onyx eyes rounded to focus on mine. There was so much desperate want hidden within those deep depths.

"I do not wish to harm you. I—"

"Shh." I pressed a fingertip to Leon's lips. "I know you don't. And you're not going to. Here's what we're going to do." Pulling my finger away, I shifted the nail into a sharp claw. Leon's eyes widened when he realized what I was about to do. I didn't give him time to object. In one quick motion, I sliced through my opposite wrist. Blood welled to the surface. I'd probably cut a little too deep, but I wanted to make certain the wound was large enough to fulfill Leon's needs.

"Drink," I ordered, holding my wrist to Leon's lips.

A groan, guttural and monstrous tore through Leon's chest. There was a half-second hesitation before he grabbed my arm and pulled my wrist to his lips. I felt the press of his fangs, but they didn't pierce my skin. His tongue worried the wound's edges. It wasn't horrid, but the sensation was far from pleasant.

Leon sucked, mouthing the wound, pulling my blood deep into his mouth and greedily swallowing. The flow probably wasn't as good this way, but it was safer for me and him. At least, for now. I had no idea what the future would hold. That was a problem for later. Right now, I had one objective and that was feeding Leon.

I gripped the back of Leon's head, encouragingly pressing his mouth against my skin. "That's it. Take what you need," I softly whispered into his ear while skimming my blunt nails along his scalp. "It's okay, Leon. Everything is going to be okay." I had no idea if that was true. Right now, it didn't matter. Right now, the only thing that mattered was this moment, feeding Leon, making sure he was healthy and strong.

Did I love Leon McMillan? My brain wasn't certain. My heart was positive.

Chapter Eighteen

So good. Groans of appreciation and need filled the air, all of those sounds coming from deep within my soul. Not even the first sip of blood I'd ingested after being turned had tasted this divine.

I drank and drank. Licking and teasing the wound to keep it open. The vague feeling of Phlox's fingers brushing along my scalp soothed me, his whispered words little more than a background melody. I could feel the beat of his heart, pounding fast and hard at first, then slowing into a more languid rhythm. His skin was cool to the touch, but that wasn't strange. Phlox ran colder than the typical pixie.

The black hole of craving faded and reason slowly took its place. Phlox's fingers no longer brushed my skin and his head now lay against my chest. Sealing the wound, I finally pulled away, licking every last drop of my beloved's precious liquid from my lips.

I sighed, the ache in my throat and chest finally eased. I wouldn't go so far as to say I was sated, but the gnawing hunger had abated.

Wrapping my arms around Phlox, I pulled his languid body close. His wings didn't so much as twitch. They lay there, as unmoving as him. Panic didn't slam into me. I could still feel and hear the steady beat of Phlox's heart along with the gentle rise and fall of his chest. I'd taken a little too much, but nothing beyond repair.

"Phlox." I stroked his long hair, relishing the way it draped over both of us like a silken blanket.

"Hmm," Phlox responded lightly.

"Apologies for taking too much." I waited for the guilt to slam into me. That feeling never came.

"'S'okay," Phlox mumbled. "Sleepy." His jaw cracked and he widely yawned.

Standing, I felt the weight of the sunrise, my body sluggish and weak. Regardless, I made it to the bed and placed Phlox beneath the covers. Ever careful of his wings, I arranged them so they laid against the bed at a comfortable angle.

"I'm going to get you some water. I want you to drink the whole glass before falling asleep."

"'Kay," Phlox muttered, scooting further into the covers.

Making my way to the mini-fridge, I found something better than plain water. There were still a few sports drinks, full of electrolytes and sugar. Quickly grabbing one, I twisted off the cap then helped Phlox sit up enough to safely drink the liquid. He protested a little when I shifted him but nothing terrible.

Phlox managed half the bottle before he pushed it away. Resettling us, before I could pull him closer, Phlox lay half his body over mine and with a contented sigh, he drifted to sleep. I stayed awake as long as the sun allowed, marveling at the magnificent creature willingly cradled within my arms.

I woke before the sunrise, although I knew it wouldn't be far off. I'd slept a little longer than typical. Phlox was in the same position he'd been when I'd finally succumbed to the sun's power.

A quick perusal eased any concerns. Phlox's heart still beat a steady rhythm and his breathing was even and without labor. His warm breath drifted across my skin sending tingly sparks of contented desire all the way to my toes.

With my arm wrapped around his waist, my fingers toyed between his delicate skin and the silky loose pants that drifted a little farther down his rump. Phlox, I quickly concluded, had a very nice rear.

"Are you going to keep fondling my ass?" Phlox sleepily asked.

I started to pull my hand away, but Phlox reached back and held my palm where it was. "I didn't tell you to stop. I just wanted to know if you were going to keep doing it."

"I see," I answered, continuing my earlier ministrations. My answer wasn't completely truthful. "I was uncertain if my attentions would be welcome."

"Hmm..." Phlox stretched, laying his palm on my chest and snuggling in closer. "So you were just going to feel me up while you thought I was asleep? Kinky vampire," Phlox scolded but his snicker told me he wasn't concerned. Or upset.

Cracking a yawn, Phlox asked, "What time is it?"

I wasn't certain of the exact time, only that the sun would set soon. "The sun should set within the next fifteen, maybe twenty minutes." I'd know the instant it did.

"Okay." Phlox settled down and I thought he might fall asleep again, but his increased heart rate told me that wasn't the case.

"How do you feel?" I asked, nearly afraid of the answer.

"Fine. A little thirsty and really hungry, but not bad otherwise. I'll let you know more when I try and get up. We'll see then if I'm woozy or not."

I appreciated Phlox's honest answer. He didn't sugarcoat things to preserve my feelings. I wasn't certain if he understood how much I appreciated that.

"Thank you for honestly answering me."

Phlox shrugged within my arms. "I don't see a reason to lie. It's not like I could hide it if I pass out when I stand up. Seems like that would be more alarming than if you knew it was a possibility."

"A very accurate statement." Practical. I liked that.

Staring at the ceiling, I wondered if Phlox could see anything in the pitch black of the room. Perhaps I should turn on a light. Unfortunately, that would require me moving from my very agreeable position.

Still, I would do anything for my beloved and asked, "Would you like me to turn on a light?"

"Nah, I shifted my eyes. I can see okay."

Twisting, I altered my position enough to see Phlox's eyes. A warm, yellow glow beautifully illuminated them. I offered an appreciative smile and said, "That seems to be a useful ability."

"It comes in handy now and again." Phlox grinned before laying his head back on my chest. There was no rise and fall, no breath to move my chest up and down.

"You are hungry. We should get up. It will be safe enough to leave by the time we are ready." Phlox had food in his apartment on the second floor. Beyond the sports drink, I had little to offer my beloved. I should have planned better. Then again, the overriding thirst had made practical thinking nearly impossible.

"I'm okay for a little longer," Phlox protested. "I'm good where we are." As if to prove the point, he snuggled in deeper.

Blissful silence filled the air, but it was not a maintainable silence. Words needed to be spoken. They were words which should have been uttered before the sunrise.

"You're thinking too hard, Leon." Phlox tapped a finger against my temple. "I can practically hear the wheels in your brain cranking."

"It is thanks to you that I am able to think again at all. The thirst was...all encompassing. It was becoming difficult to contemplate anything else."

I got a whack on the chest for that comment. Phlox shook out his hand, lamenting his forgetful nature regarding the hardness of my body.

"You should have told me sooner. I can't believe you placed your life in danger like that. Moron." There was little heat or true anger. Fear was the overriding emotion haunting those crass words.

"I was unsure what your response would be."

Phlox shot up, wings beating at warp speed. "You thought I'd let you die?"

"No," I soothed. "I did not wish you to feel obligated. I could not fathom the idea of causing you harm—be that physical or emotional. I did not wish to place such a burden on you."

Phlox's wings slowed, a constant shimmer of dust falling around us and dissipating as it landed on the sheets. "And you thought I'd be okay with you dying? How is that logical? Did you not think that would hurt me worse?"

"I... As I said, practical thinking is difficult with the thirst riding you. Besides, I would not have died from lack of blood."

"No?" One of Phlox's eyebrows shot skyward. "What? You would have dwindled, fallen into a husked-out shell, barely alive and constantly in pain. You think that makes me feel better?"

When stated that way... "No."

"Exactly. If this is the kind of nonsense you come up with when you're hungry, then I'm definitely going to need to keep you fed."

I stiffened, body going still. My reaction didn't go unnoticed. Sitting and leaning against the wall, wings spread out, Phlox pulled the sheets closer, twisting the top blanket.

"It's a lot to take in," Phlox softly muttered. "I think I said that earlier this morning. It doesn't seem as big and daunting as it did, but there's a lot to work out. I'm not going to sit here and tell you I have all the answers, Leon. I don't. I probably don't even have half the answers. What I do know is that I can't bear the idea of you suffering, especially when I can stop it. You told me I'm your beloved." Phlox stared at me, eyes wide, pupils rimmed in brilliant yellow.

"You are," I answered easily.

Phlox's lips twisted. "And you're positive?"

"I am." I'd said this earlier in the morning but evidently it bore repeating. Maybe Phlox thought I'd changed my mind.

"But how do you know?" Phlox sounded more curious than upset.

"I cannot answer that. All I can say is that I am certain. I doubt Lucroy could explain it either. It was something he simply came to realize. I would wager my realization came quicker than Lucroy's, but that could be because I understood the possibility more than Lucroy. When he met Peaches, it was widely thought pixie blood toxic to vampires." I was grateful Lucroy found Peaches first and was strong enough to debunk the myth.

Phlox stared off into the distant room. "Pixies don't really have beloved's. Well, that's not entirely true. Pixies bond, mostly with land or homes, but as you know, some bond with others. Phil's an unusual home-and-hearth pixie in that he not only bonded with the house and land, but the occupants as well. Social pixies will sometimes bond with others, but it's not common. Parsnip and Vander are more the exception than the rule."

"And you are a nature pixie." I wasn't completely certain.

Phlox gave a slow nod. "I am. Although I'm not really that typical either."

"Because of your shifter side?"

Phlox waved me off. "That too. But even without my Pallas's cat, I wouldn't be typical. My mom, Peroviskia, was a nature pixie. She had an affinity for the cold." Phlox gave a wry grin. "It's odd. Pixies love the heat, but not my mom and not me. I get it honestly from both sides."

"Your mother has passed?" Pixies lived long lives and didn't suffer illness like some other species. Given Phlox's age, it seemed odd his mother was already gone.

Phlox's eyes glowed and I realized they glistened with tears. The scent of salt water tickled my senses. "She was captured by an addicted ogre not long after I was born. The ogre placed her out in the heat thinking it would be a good environment for a pixie. For nearly any other, it would have been. Not my mother. She faded quickly. Too quickly to be rescued."

Anger, swift and vicious surged through me. My beloved should not have been made to suffer such a loss. Hot on the heels of that rage was realization. "That is why you volunteered for this assignment."

"It is. Not that I had a lot of competition." Phlox gave a wane smile. "But, seriously, this is important. I can't typically tell Auntie Tandra about my missions, even when they're over. Right now, that's a blessing. I couldn't put her through that kind of pain. She already lost my mother to that fate. She'd be worried out of her mind if she thought I was willingly trying to get captured."

I'd heard the name but wasn't certain of the exact relationship. "Your auntie Tandra is related to your mother?"

"Not by blood. They were best friends. Auntie Tandra—

Peltandra to her adoring social media fans—took me in and raised me. Auntie Tandra's a social pixie. She kept my mother's memory alive. The house was filled with pictures of my mom, and Auntie Tandra put me to bed with tales of the mischief they'd gotten up to."

Phlox wadded the blanket up even tighter. Finally sitting, I pulled him into my arms. Phlox came willingly. Phlox's soft hair fell around us, cocooning our space.

"My human mother passed when I was eleven. My father lived on, but he was a shadow of the man he'd once been. When I was turned, I found comfort in the knowledge that my maker was immortal. Marian was not like typical vampires of her time and cared for me as one might a child."

"*Was?*" Phlox gently questioned.

"Immortality is not what many believe it to be. Marian grew tired and lost the will to continue. I saw the signs and yet there was little I could do. She and Lucroy were friends. He tried as well, but in the end, Marian succumbed to her indifference and made the choice to walk into the sun."

"Oh, Leon. I'm so sorry." Phlox wrapped his arms around my waist and squeezed.

"As am I. It was over a hundred years ago and I still mourn her loss. It is a fate many vampires face. Eternity is not a concept our human minds can understand. The first few decades are filled with wonderous opportunities. Everything is new and adventure abounds. The shine begins fading. Monotony settles in and soon one finds themselves at loose ends. Those ends fray with each passing day, month, and year until one day, there is nothing left to hold on to." I considered telling Phlox that I'd begun feeling the first twinges of that looming fate, that meeting him had upended that path and set me on a new one, but I did not wish to add that level of pressure.

"Promise me you'll never do that."

"Walk into the sun?"

I felt Phlox nod against my chest. "I couldn't bear it, Leon. Just the idea of something happening to you, I...."

"Hush." I cradled Phlox's head. "I have no plans to end my second life just yet."

Phlox squeezed me again before he pulled away. I allowed the movement. The sincerity filling his eyes nearly broke what was left of my heart.

"I told you earlier that this is a lot to take in and it is. Give me time to process the situation. There's a lot to consider. No matter what, I won't allow you to die, Leon. My blood is yours."

Phlox hadn't offered up his heart, not yet. For now, his blood would need to be enough.

Chapter Nineteen

PHLOX

Erasmus wasn't what I expected. Then again, having never met a necromancer, I wasn't really certain what to expect. Black on black clothes? Dark eyeliner and eyeshadow? Sallow cheeks and a morose demeanor? Yeah, none of those things seemed to fit the man casually sitting in Peaches's living room. The area was small, Erasmus even smaller, but the diminutive necromancer sucked up all the space.

Erasmus's shaggy, dark brown hair gave the appearance he'd just rolled out of bed. His clothing did nothing to persuade me from that opinion. Erasmus's faded t-shirt looked like it was a couple washes away from falling completely apart. His baggy cargo pants were equally worn with frayed edges kissing his tennis shoe-clad feet. Dark leather straps covered his wrists and his fingertips ended in dark blue painted nails.

"Pops said you need my services." Erasmus smiled easily, showing off perfect white teeth. Erasmus leaned forward, placing his elbows on his knees. "I saw the amount he said he's charging, but the thing is, this is my business, not Pops's."

"Are you asking for more?" Parsnip asked, tone biting.

"Nah. Less, actually. I'm not greedy. You've got a problem and I'm a possible solution." Erasmus leaned back and shrugged.

"Maybe he's not as much of an asshat as his father," Parsnip said, cocking his head to the side, taking in Erasmus's comfortable posture.

Far from offended, Erasmus's grin widened. "I'll pass your opinion on to Pops. It'll make his day."

"I've no doubt," Vander lamented. "Gaia, I need a beer if I'm gonna get through tonight."

"Sorry, Van. I've got apple cider and water. No beer," Peaches apologized.

Vander waved him off. "No worries. I'll self-medicate when I get home."

Parsnip rolled his eyes but didn't say anything else.

While Lucroy didn't appear terribly impressed with our latest visitor's attire, he seemed a bit mollified by Erasmus's words. "Your father led us to believe you are the correct necromancer for the job."

Again, Erasmus shrugged. "I suppose that remains to be seen, but I'll see what I can do." He spread his arms wide and added, "That's the best I can offer."

"Well, it's a damn site better than what anyone else in the room can say." Vander rubbed his hands over his facial scruff before sighing. "I wish Sedrick could be here. Phil too," Vander offered Parsnip. "I hope the problem in the mine isn't bad."

"And that Ruthie's truly on the mend," Peaches said, and Parsnip eagerly nodded.

Sedrick and Phil were supposed to be here but there'd been an unexpected issue with the Voss mine and Sedrick's presence was needed. Phil could have driven out to Peaches's on his own but evidently Ruthie got into a little trouble and had to shift a few times to heal a broken leg. She was still a bit hobbled and with Sedrick gone, Phil didn't want to leave Ruthie and Dillon alone also.

"We can fill them in later," Peaches said.

Lucroy remained silent, gaze fixed on Erasmus. The sun wouldn't set for another three hours. While it might not be a physical threat, I'd noticed Lucroy was a bit grumpier when he had to be up during the daylight. The time of the meeting definitely ruled Leon's presence out.

Erasmus's gaze swept the room. "Not that this isn't fun and all, but vampire company excluded, I don't see anything dead around."

Peaches sucked in an angry breath. His wings sped, filling the room with golden dust.

"Whoa." Erasmus dramatically covered his nose. "Can you ease up on the pixie dust. I didn't mean any offense."

"Gaia save us." Vander pressed his thumb and forefinger against the bridge of his nose.

"Ray and Wendall should be here soon," Parsnip attempted to soothe. "They just had to snag Sylvie's body. They travel a lot faster than—"

The air vibrated, a bright vertical slit ripping the air. Ray's head popped through. He took a moment to peer around the room before simply stating, "We will take this outside." The atmospheric tear sealed shortly after he disappeared.

"Shit, that's impressive." Erasmus's eyes widened, bright green and wide.

"Yeah, yeah. Fairies are all that. Come on, Parsnip. Let's do what the pretty fairy says and head outside where there's more room." Vander pushed out of his chair and Parsnip followed. I motioned Erasmus to go before me, and Peaches and Lucroy brought up the rear. When we exited the house, Lucroy kept to the shadowed porch.

We'd no more stepped outside than a flurry of bright lights

swarmed toward us. Seeing one was impressive, but a cloud of twinkling stars was something to behold.

"They'll want some of your dust. Are you okay with that?" Peaches asked me politely.

"It's fine. I'm not sure I'm ready to be swarmed, so maybe just a few at a time."

Peaches's smile was near angelic. "They can abide by the rules. They'll be thrilled." Peaches met the horde a few feet out and laid down the current law. Thankfully, they seemed eager to abide my wishes.

"Fuck, it's been an age since I've seen sprites," Erasmus said, lifting his hand so one could perch. His grin appeared natural and completely at ease. "Pops has a colony in the forest surrounding his house. I used to play with them when I was a kid. I still go out and visit when I can. I've got no idea what they're saying, but I like the high-pitched language."

Personally, I thought there was something wrong with Erasmus's hearing. But I suppose to each his own.

The air shimmered again, and Ray walked through the portal he created. Wendall wasn't far behind and in between them was Sylvie's limp corpse.

I drew in a deep breath. The witch looked like she'd just had her heart ripped out moments before, not days ago. Fresh blood still leaked from the wound.

"Stasis spell," Wendall helpfully supplied when I gasped. "I know, I was surprised too when I saw her. The fairies Aunt Silvidia sent to the compound placed a stasis spell over the entire place. No one's getting in or out, and nothing decays or decomposes. It's like time stood still inside." Wendall shivered. "It was weirdly uncomfortable being inside."

"I should have had you remain in the garden outside," Ray said. His tone was cool but there was a niggle of concern that softened it.

"No. It was fine. Weird, but okay."

Trinket danced on Wendall's shoulder, cooing and chirping her agreement.

"What the hell?" Erasmus leaned in and unwisely poked a finger in Trinket's direction. The little scuttlebutt puffed up and opened her mouth but didn't lunge. "Holy shit!" Instead of being afraid, Erasmus's grin took up his whole face. "Those are some impressive chompers."

Ray closely monitored the situation. "Scuttlebutts are very discerning. It is fortunate she does not believe you a threat, necromancer."

Pulling his arm back, Erasmus stuffed his hands into the deep pockets of his cargos. "Nah, not a threat to anything living, that's for sure. Now the dead, that's a different matter."

Ray placed Sylvie's body on the ground, face down. While he wasn't rough with her corpse, he wasn't overly respectful either.

Crouching, Erasmus placed his elbows on his bent knees. "I'm assuming this is the witch you want brought back. I thought there was a troll too."

"If necessary, will retrieve him when we are finished with the witch," Ray answered.

"Whatever. Makes no difference to me." Erasmus shrugged but remained crouched where he was.

We waited, standing in silence as we ringed the dead witch and necromancer.

"Do you require anything else?" Ray calmly asked.

"Nope. Just me," Erasmus answered. "No chicken sacrifice, blood, verbal mojo, or anything else. Quiet sometimes helps, but I don't think that'll be a problem with you lot."

Erasmus wasn't wrong. No one seemed willing to speak, not even Peaches. He'd flown back to Lucroy's side and was snuggled in close. I don't think any of us were looking forward to today. Curious, yes. Eager, not so much.

"Okay. Times not really wasting, but I think we can all

agree the sooner this is done, the sooner everyone can relax."

"Anytime you are ready, necromancer," Ray said. Erasmus bristled but didn't contradict what he was.

Eyes slipping closed, Erasmus took two large breaths, exhaling deeply. I was no necromancer, but he appeared to be centering himself. When he said, "Gotcha," I wondered if what I'd thought was correct or not.

"Time to wake up and spill what's left of your guts, Sylvie Tabitha Danube."

I'd been unaware of her last name, let alone middle. When Sylvie's body jerked, it took every ounce of self-restraint not to do the same. It was incredibly unsettling.

"I think I'm going to be sick," Parsnip said and when I glanced up, he did look a little green. Vander wrapped his arm around Parsnip's waist and took a couple of steps back. Given Parsnip's reaction, I was glad he was to her back. I had a frontal view and couldn't say it was pretty.

Standing on shaky legs, Sylvie slowly rose. Head lifted, her glazed eyes traveled the area, attempting to make sense of the nonsensical. The hole Leon punched through the center of her chest continued leaking. If I lowered myself to just the correct angle, I'd probably be able to see clear through to the other side.

"Who are you?" Sylvie asked, and this time I did shiver. I knew she was dead, that Leon and I were safe, but I couldn't forget the casual way she spoke of ending Leon's life or her plans to sell me to the highest ogre bidder.

Sylvie's eyes locked on me. "I know you." Confusion gave way to recognition, and she drew in a hissed breath. Hands flying, she began chanting words that sounded familiar and yet remained foreign.

"Ah, ah, ah." Erasmus waved a naughty finger in front of Sylvie's face. "None of that if you please."

Sylvie's hands dropped and her mouth hung open, words

lost. She stared. I think we all stared, waiting to see what Erasmus would do. His crossed arms and causal stance were underwhelming and more than a little disappointing.

"Thank you," Erasmus said, sounding endlessly polite. "Sylvie Tabitha Danube," Sylvie flinched when Erasmus spoke her full name. "These individuals are going to ask you questions and you will answer them." Erasmus's tone changed when he said the word *will*. There was a weight to that singular word that wasn't present in the rest of them. Sylvie must have felt it too if her full body shudder was anything to go by.

"Who are you?" Sylvie asked, teeth gritted. The twin bloody trails leaking from the corners of her lips made her appear even more macabre.

"Someone who's in control of your very essence," Erasmus answered.

Sylvie's sucked in breath wheezed through her damaged body. "Necromancer." The word came out more curse than statement.

Erasmus gave a slight bow. "I take it you have some idea the situation you're in?"

Mouth slamming closed, Sylvie's jaw worked from side to side. I wasn't sure if she'd been aware she was dead when Erasmus brought her consciousness back or not. If she hadn't and just figured it out, Sylvie didn't seem nearly as disturbed as I thought she should be.

"I will answer nothing. Send me back across the vale." Sylvie's lips twisted with hatred. "You are a vile, unnatural creature. Your warlock sire should have put you in the ground when you were born."

I flinched at her words wishing Leon was next to me, holding me like Vander held Parsnip, like Ray placed a comforting hand on Wendall's shoulder, like Lucroy ran his hand up and down Peaches's back, easing his wing muscles. I'd never felt the need for another so sharply as I did in that moment.

Far from visually offended, Erasmus rubbed the back of his neck and let loose a weighty sigh. "You seem confused, Sylvie Tabitha Danube. You are not the one in control. *I am.*" Again, those words carried weight. It was difficult to tell in the sunlight, but I thought I saw Erasmus's eyes gleam when he said those words. "Now, they will ask you questions, and you *will* answer them truthfully."

"Or what?" Sylvie sneered. "I'm already dead. You can do nothing to me, necromancer."

Erasmus was quiet for a few seconds. He stood there, hands stuffed deep into his pockets, eyes locked on Sylvie's corpse. When he finally spoke, his words were laced with underlying confidence. "Looks like you wanna do this the hard way. That's okay. It'll take more time and it'll be hell on you, but I don't really care. The opinion of a witch who'd participate in a pixie trafficking ring means nothing to me." I'd yet to hear Erasmus's voice so cold. "Now, as for what *I* can do to you..." This time, the glow lighting Erasmus's eyes was unmistakable.

An unholy scream erupted from Sylvie's mouth. Head thrown back, she wailed into the sky before bending over, hands clasped over the hole in her chest. The scream went on and on, repeating without relenting.

Vander's jaw was taut while Parsnip's lips were parted in horror. Peaches buried his face in Lucroy's chest while the vampire stood statue still, his hands clasped over his beloved's ears. The sprites flew away, fast and furious. And Erasmus, he just stood there, hands still stuffed in his pants' pockets, shoulders loose and posture at ease. His eyes retained that ethereal green glow.

Following Lucroy's example, I slapped my hands over my ears, not that it helped much. Sylvie's scream tore through my brain. My jaw clamped tight, teeth grinding while I prayed to the goddess for the sound to stop.

"Enough," Erasmus finally said, his eyes fading back to human green. Sylvie's screams trailed off into intermittent whimpers. At some point, her corpse had fallen to the ground leaving her on hands and knees.

Erasmus crouched down in front of her, much like he'd done before bringing her consciousness back.

"You said I couldn't do anything more to you. I believe I just proved that I can and will. I can make you relive the pain of your death again and again and again. Since I'm not immortal, I can't do it for eternity, but I can maintain it as long as I'm alive. I don't even have to be nearby. I can be on the other side of the world, and it wouldn't matter." Placing the tip of his finger under Sylvie's chin, Erasmus lifted her head so he could stare into her eyes. "And that's just a taste of what I can do. I assure you, Sylvie Tabitha Danube, I can do far worse. I can rip apart your soul until there is nothing left. You will cease to exist. Or I can send your soul to a place where it will be tormented for eternity. The choice is yours."

Erasmus removed his hand, allowing Sylvie's head to drop. Standing, he shoved his hands back into his pockets.

"Now, I believe there are some questions my associates would like to ask. It would be infinitely easier on them if you would *stand*, Sylvie Tabitha Danube."

Sylvie stood. Her legs were shaky, but she managed. I honestly didn't think she had another choice.

"Will you answer their questions honestly?" Before she could answer, Erasmus held up a halting finger and added, "Fair warning, I will know if you are lying."

Hatred, pure, hot, and all-consuming glared through Sylvie's eyes. Through gritted teeth, Sylvie agreed. "I will answer."

"Excellent." Erasmus's gaze scanned our group. "Not sure

who's up first, but she's all yours."

I immediately looked to Ray. His slightly inclined gesture let me know the floor was mine.

Stepping forward, Sylvie's hatred found a new target in me. *Yeah, right back at you,* I thought while pushing my own disgust into my gaze. Whatever miniscule sympathy I'd felt earlier dissipated when I stared into her cruel eyes.

I started out with the obvious. "You performed a transportation spell with the direct aim of capturing me, a pixie, to sell for profit. Is that correct?"

"Obviously," Sylvie spat.

"And you got someone extra, someone not expected."

"Lucroy Moony's second."

"Yes, Leon. At first you were upset but soon figured out you could potentially profit from his capture. You contacted someone to see if Leon was worth more dead or alive." Those words felt like ash on my tongue. "Who did you contact?"

Sylvie's lips twisted into a sneer. Fresh blood no longer leaked to the surface. Now the dried substance cracked and flaked with her skin's movement.

"I don't know." Her grin was monstrous with its joy.

My wings snapped open, and I flew to her eyelevel. "You do know."

Sylvie's laugh was more cackled glee than joy. "Oh, but I don't. All I have are code names and server contacts. I don't know for certain who's on the other end. I don't know who pays my bills or who is in charge." Sylvie's hate-filled eyes traveled to Erasmus, focusing on the necromancer. "He knows I'm telling the truth. You've done all this for nothing," she spat.

I turned, hoping Sylvie was lying. One glance at Erasmus's face along with an abbreviated head shake let me know she wasn't.

Furious, I spun and began pixie pacing. Hands gripped

into tight fists, my brain fought for calm. There had to be more we could get from her. I knew Hamish was still working on her computer. He might still be able to track the IP address but there was no guarantee. Frustration threatened to consume me. I needed to calm the fuck down and think. I needed to—

"If you'll allow me." Ray's frosty voice cleared a path through my mental cloud.

"Go for it." I waved a hand in Sylvie's general direction.

"Thank you, Agent Frost." Ray didn't bother moving from Wendall's side. He remained at Sylvie's back when he asked, "How many pixies have you captured and sold?"

I braced myself for the answer, but a collective pixie gasp filled the air when Sylvie casually answered, "Seven."

Seven. Seven pixies. Even if she considered me one of them, that left six unaccounted ones out there. I grasped the fabric over my chest, the ache in my heart nearly unbearable.

"And you sold them all to the same buyer?" Ray asked.

"No."

"Were all the buyers associated with the same organization?" Ray asked, undeterred.

"Yes." Sylvie was sticking with one-word answers but so far she was being truthful.

"I see," Ray calmly said. "A lot of money has changed hands. Money can be a precious commodity to some, but the current scale seems exorbitant, especially considering the risk. Should they be found out, death will be swift and immediate."

Sylvie said nothing. She stood there, staring out into the distant orchard and lips little more than a thin line.

"I am curious what one would need with all that money. What would make the risk worth it?" Ray mused out loud but still hadn't asked Sylvie a direct question. He corrected that calculated mistake when he asked, "Do you know the purpose of those misbegotten funds?"

Sylvie hesitated before she answered, "I'm sure I wouldn't know."

"Lie," Erasmus flatly stated. "You get one warning, Sylvie Tabitha Danube."

Sylvie's hatred only grew and for a minute I thought her head might explode with all her barely suppressed rage. "I do not know exactly, only that they are seeking something rare, something powerful, something that can even destroy your precious Fairy."

Wendall gasped, Trinket wailed, and Ray remained stoically silent.

"Something that can destroy Fairy?" Vander shifted closer, fingers still entwined with Parsnip's. "What in the hell could that be? The only thing I can even think of is... Gaia, no. That can't be it." Vander's head turned toward Ray. "She can't be talking about what I think she is."

"I believe it is entirely possible," Lucroy said, walking closer to the porch edge. The sun was lower in the sky, its rays not as potent. Leaving the porch, Lucroy walked into those dying rays without hesitation. Peaches flew by his side, yellow-gold pixie dust trailing in his wake.

"Shit, fuck, and damn," Vander cursed while palming his forehead.

My attention snapped between each of them, wondering what I was missing. "What?" I asked. Beyond brownies, I couldn't think of anything that might be a threat to a fairy, let alone the land of Fairy. "What am I missing?"

"I'd like to know that too," Erasmus said. He didn't sound nearly as casual as before. "Anything that threatens Fairy gets my attention."

Ignoring Erasmus and me, Ray asked Sylvie, "Is that their goal? The destruction of Fairy?"

She shrugged. "I have no idea what their objective is, only

that whatever it is they are looking for is the most powerful weapon ever created."

"Djinn." Parsnip's voice was so low I barely parsed the word.

Erasmus's shoulder snapped taught. "Djinn? They don't exist." Eyes wide, Erasmus gaze fell on each and every one of us. While I'd not been involved in the incident with Aurelia, I knew of it and knew that djinn did indeed exist.

"I mean, they used to, but that was a long time ago and..." Erasmus's words drifted while he came to terms with the fact djinn were real and still present within the world. "Well, fucking fuck." Erasmus threw his hands in the air and twirled, walking away while his mind processed the fear assaulting his heart.

Sylvie's grin was nothing short of evil. "If that is what they seek, you are all dead. Including you, necromancer." She raised her voice, allowing it to travel the distance Erasmus walked.

"Yeah? Well, looks like you bit the big one first," I spat. It wasn't a very good comeback, but it was all I had.

Ray was more professional than me and asked Sylvie a few more questions she didn't know the answers to. Erasmus confirmed she wasn't lying. Sylvie didn't know where the other pixies she'd kidnapped were. She didn't know the true name of any of her contacts. She didn't know how many others were involved in the ring. In the end, she didn't know a hell of a lot and what she did know only served to scare the shit out of me.

"I believe we are finished," Ray finally said. "You may do with her as you will, necromancer."

"His name's Erasmus," Wendall scolded. I was glad he spoke up. I didn't know Erasmus well enough to say if I liked him or not. What I could say was that he'd done what we'd asked and not charged as much as his father *requested*. What I also knew was that his abilities were scary as fuck. Could he really do all the things he threatened Sylvie with? I wasn't certain. The very idea was horrid. While Erasmus himself wasn't so bad, what he was capable of was. I could understand why others were so leery of necromancers.

Erasmus gave Wendall a fist bump as thanks before becoming serious. Erasmus exhaled deeply before he said, "Sylvie Tabitha Danube, I release you. May your afterlife be a reflection and judgement of your living days."

Sylvie's eyes shot wide before her corpse crumpled to the ground, little more than an empty husk once more.

We all stood there, staring at the Sylvie's unmoving remains.

"Ray, do you—" Wendall started.

"Peaches, I believe it is time to revive Aurelia," Ray interrupted.

Peaches's wings fluttered. "Do you really think that's necessary? I promised her she could rest and that I wouldn't contact her unless absolutely necessary."

"Wait." I held up my hands, palms out. "Hold up. Aurelia, the djinn? You want to wake her up?" I gazed around the group and gawked, "She's here? You have Aurelia on the land?"

"You have a djinn?" Erasmus gawked, his voice a couple octaves above its typical cadence. "Are you serious right now?"

"Erasmus." Ray used the necromancer's name this time. "You have our thanks. We may wish to revive the troll at a later time, but not immediately. You may go if you wish." I was halfway surprised Ray didn't order Erasmus to leave. I think Erasmus was just as surprised.

"Are you kidding me? I'm not going anywhere. Until about five minutes ago, I didn't know djinn truly existed and now you're telling me you've got one and are about to bring them out. Yeah, not about to miss that."

Vander grunted. "Listen, kid, djinn aren't something you

want to get involved with. Aurelia's..."

"Not that bad," Parsnip finished. "We think," he added with less certainty.

"Regardless, Peaches will have control of her object of attachment," Ray attempted to reassure.

"That is little comfort when all of Aurelia's previous masters are deceased," Lucroy coldly replied.

"It's okay," Peaches attempted to soothe. "It's not like I'm going to ask her to do anything beyond maybe give us some information. I probably won't even need to make a wish."

Wendall left Ray's side, Trinket on his shoulder as he made his way toward Peaches. "You know, I'd like to see her. I never got the chance to thank her for saving my life."

"A djinn saved your life?" Awe was clear in Erasmus's voice. "You've got to be shitting me."

"Not in the least," Wendall happily answered.

"Gaia, this is insane." Erasmus plopped down on the ground, legs crossed. "Pops is never going to believe this."

"No, he will not. He will also never hear of it," Ray said, tone stern.

Erasmus's head snapped up, his gaze harsh. "Are you telling me I have to keep quiet?"

"If you value your life, then yes," Ray answered easily.

Erasmus's jaw snapped closed, and his eyes narrowed.

"Ray, you really need to work on your delivery," Wendall tsked before crouching in front of Erasmus. "He really doesn't mean to be so direct and scary." Wendall's fingers wiggled when he said the word, *scary*. "He's actually a big softie," Wendall whispered even though all of us could hear him, including Ray.

Erasmus eyed Wendall as if he were crazy. "Hellfire Rayburn is not a *softie*."

"Indeed, I am not," Ray agreed.

Wendall waved him off. "Okay, maybe that's an exaggeration. I was just trying to point out that we need you to keep quiet about this for everyone's safety. We've already got one crazy out there possibly searching for a djinn. We don't need it getting out that they truly exist and have others going off the deep end trying to find them. And for Peaches's and Lucroy's safety, it's best no one know they've got a djinn stashed somewhere nearby."

Erasmus raised an eyebrow. "You're telling me I shouldn't worry about a vamp having ready access to an all-powerful djinn?"

Lucroy looked as annoyed as a vamp can. "I assure you, necromancer, I have no use for such. I have found my beloved. Peaches is all I require. My second life is well and truly fulfilled. There is nothing a djinn can offer that I do not already have."

"And I've got Lucroy and my bonded orchard." Peaches flew up and kissed Lucroy's temple. "I've got all I need too," Peaches defended even though Erasmus hadn't seemed bothered by the knowledge that a pixie had access to a djinn.

Blowing out a breath, Erasmus hung his head. "Gaia, this is surreal."

"Tell me about it," Vander agreed. "But it is what it is."

"You didn't tell the Magical Usage Counsel that Aurelia's object of attachment remains on Peaches's bonded land." I wasn't sure if I should be irritated by that or not. In the end, I thought I understood and said just as much. "Unless something changes, you've got my word I won't mention it." It was as much of a promise as I could make.

"Very well," Ray answered. "Peaches, if you will pllease retrieve Aurelia."

Peaches flew off into his orchard. None of us followed. I didn't want to know where he'd stashed Aurelia's object of attachment. Controlling a djinn only had one final outcome —death.

Chapter Twenty

PHLOX

Goddess, I wanted Leon. My skin itched like it was too tight. We weren't bonded, not in the pixie or vampire way. Being away from him wouldn't be physically dangerous. I wasn't so certain about the emotional aspect of things. The sun was almost down. If I called, Leon would be awake enough to answer. He'd still be down in Lucroy's sanctuary underneath Dusk. He could safely leave soon.

My phone was a heavy weight within a loose pocket. I left it where it was. I wasn't certain how long it would take Peaches to recover Aurelia and I didn't want to rush a conversation. Besides, talking with Leon right now would probably make me crave his presence more. I needed to keep a cool, level head. Especially if a djinn was involved.

Little dots of far-off lights lit up the sky, surrounding Peaches in a twinkling cloud. Dusk had settled in enough for the sprites to begin showing off their true glory.

Peaches's hands were clasped in front of him, holding something close to his chest. I couldn't see what he cradled but could only assume it was Aurelia's object of attachment.

"I've got her," Peaches said as he dropped down beside Lucroy. "Are you certain we have to do this?" Peaches asked Ray.

"Beloved, I do not believe this is a request Hellfire makes lightly."

I didn't think it was truly a *request* but didn't argue with Lucroy.

"Indeed, it is not," Ray answered.

"Okay." Peaches stared down at the dirt covered amphora within his cupped palms. Wendall stepped closer, placing a comforting hand on Peaches's arm. Trinket scurried over and perched on Peaches's shoulder, leaning in and cooing her support.

"Thanks, Trinket." Peaches dug his fingers into her fur, scratching lightly before he sucked in a deep breath and said, "Aurelia, I wish for your presence."

At first, nothing happened. Then a hazy mist eased from the amphora. The Caribbean blue mist coalesced and a figure formed.

"Sweet Gaia. Look at all that ink," Erasmus barely whispered. He moved closer to me, perhaps seeking comfort in the only other one who hadn't met a djinn before.

Erasmus wasn't wrong. The being standing there in combat boots, ripped jeans, tank top, and flannel was bald. Inked markings ran along nearly all her visible skin. Golden hoops and rings pierced through Aurelia's large, pointed ears. Her thick, plush lips pouted, and her eyes dangerously narrowed when she stared at the congregation surrounding her.

"Master," Aurelia gritted out when she stared at Peaches.

"No. Goddess, no." Peaches frantically waved his hands in front of his chest, Aurelia's object of attachment clasped in one hand. "Please don't call me that. I'm no one's master. Or, at least, I don't want to be. Please, Aurelia, call me Peaches."

Some of the hostility leaked from Aurelia's tense posture.

Beside me, so quiet I doubted anyone else could hear, Erasmus stuttered, "That's...strange."

Personally, I thought the whole thing was strange and ignored him.

"You promised me rest, Peaches. And yet, you've called me back...already." Aurelia glanced around the area probably noting no one had changed since the last time she'd seen them.

"I'm so sorry about that," Peaches apologized.

"It was not his desire." Ray stepped forward. "I felt it necessary and for that, you also have my apologies, Aurelia."

"And my thanks," Wendall jumped in, rushing to Aurelia and pulling her into his arms, hugging her tight. Aurelia stood there, arms at her sides, eyes wide, and expression deeply confused. "You saved me. And you made it so Ray and I can be together for a long time by increasing my fairy DNA. I can't thank you enough." Wendall offered a final squeeze before pulling away. Aurelia continued staring at him as if he were a puzzle she wasn't certain she wanted to figure out.

Wendall appeared unfazed. Hopping from Peaches to Wendall, Trinket nestled in close, cooing her thanks as well.

Wendall stepped back and sheepishly said, "I'm sorry if that made you uncomfortable. I wasn't sure if I'd ever get a chance to thank you properly."

"And that is the reason I was awoken? So you might...thank me?"

"I wish," Vander huffed sounding exhausted. Aurelia's attention immediately snapped to the warlock.

Instead of Vander answering, Ray stepped closer, once more wrapping his arm around Wendall's side. "It appears as if another might be looking for a djinn of their own."

Aurelia's large eyes blinked while her expression remained blank, as if she were awaiting the real reason she'd been disturbed.

When nothing appeared forthcoming, Ray continued, "Djinn history has either been lost or purposefully forgotten. We seek information only, Aurelia."

"And you believe this is a concern I share?" Aurelia sounded one part puzzled and two parts irritated. Call me crazy, but I didn't think an annoyed djinn was a positive sign.

Gaze shifting from Ray to Peaches, Aurelia's posture stiffened again when she asked, "Is this something you wish?" She didn't call him Peaches, but Aurelia didn't call him master either. Small steps were important.

Peaches wildly shook his head. "No. I won't make you tell us anything." Peaches shot Ray a pointed look. "Not even if that's what others want." Peaches gripped the amphora tight, and I noticed Lucroy took step forward.

"If that is my beloved's choice, then he has my full support."

"And mine," Wendall quickly followed before lifting his watery blue eyes to Ray. "Listen, I know this is important, but if Aurelia doesn't want to discuss her species' past, then we need to respect that. We made her a promise and that's important. I'm sorry, Ray, but I can't ask Peaches to force her."

Ray's fingers carded through Wendall's wavy blond hair, lightly skimming his scalp. "If those are your feelings, I will respect them."

Witnessing a fairy defer to anyone less than 100 percent fairy, was...odd. Maybe Aurelia thought so too or perhaps it was the collective agreement that for once in her djinn life, she wouldn't be forced into action. Whatever the reason, her demeanor instantly changed. Relaxing significantly, Aurelia's stone-cold features also eased. I wouldn't go so far to say she smiled, but she had a lot more in common with the Mona Lisa than she'd had about two minutes ago.

"Very well," Aurelia said. "What is it you wish to know? I cannot guarantee I will have the answer and even if I do, I will decide if I wish to impart the information." She glanced Peaches's way and at his nod, Aurelia inhaled deeply and added, "However, I can promise not to lie. If I answer, it will be the truth as I understand it."

"More than acceptable." Peaches beamed. "Thank you, Aurelia."

With a barely perceptible nod in Peaches's direction, Aurelia turned her attention back on Ray. "What is it you wish to know?"

Ray didn't hesitate. "Do you know how many djinn were created?"

"Twenty-seven," Aurelia answered without hesitation. A collective groan went through our group.

"Twenty-seven. Shit," Parsnip vocalized. "That's a lot of djinn. Are they all active?" Parsnip glanced around our circle before settling his gaze on Aurelia.

"Do you mean, are they all awake and within a master's possession?" When Parsnip nodded, Aurelia shrugged. "That is beyond my knowledge. We are not aware of each other on a subconscious level. I do not *sense* other djinn. Generally, we make our presence known to one another."

"Do djinn fight each other?" Vander asked.

Inhaling deeply, Aurelia's gaze turned distant. "When we were first created, but it was quickly deemed futile." Waving a dismissive hand, Aurelia calmly answered, "Djinn are equal. There were never any winners or losers. It was a waste of energy and time."

I swallowed hard and spoke for the first time. "You mean, djinn can't destroy other djinn?"

Aurelia's gaze locked on me and this time she did grin. I couldn't decide if it was malicious, curious, or fond. I figured I was safest to assume it was the first. "Another pixie? Your group becomes increasingly curious, Hellfire Rayburn."

I'd argue that we weren't exactly *Ray's group* but that seemed like foolish semantics at this point.

"In answer, no, we cannot *destroy* each other. Nothing can *destroy* a djinn," Aurelia confidently stated.

"Um...I'm not sure that's true."

Every set of eyes bore down on Erasmus. Shoulders rounded, hands stuffed in his pockets and head hanging, Erasmus back tracked. "Like I said, I'm not sure it's true. It might be but..."

"But what?" I asked. "What do you know?"

"And what are you?" Aurelia stepped closer. Her movements weren't necessarily aggressive, but I didn't like her increasing proximity. I wasn't sure if Erasmus's shifting feet were a sign he felt the same or if he was nervous because of his earlier statement.

Eyes slipping closed, Aurelia's chin jutted out slightly. Multiple tattoos came to life, glowing in the early evening. It almost looked like she was scenting the air or maybe just concentrating really hard. Either way, whatever she did didn't give her any further answers. Her eyes snapped open, and she glared. "Are you part of a species or are you a single anomaly?"

"Uh, I suppose I'm part of a species." Erasmus glanced from Aurelia to Vander.

Clearing his throat, Vander said, "Erasmus is a necromancer. He is warlock born. They did not exist when you were created. It is very possible you have never crossed paths with them as necromancers are uncommon."

"Necromancer?" Aurelia sounded more curious than judgmental. "Similar to the priestess, Muriel?"

Erasmus shook his head. "Yeah, no. I mean, maybe a little, but not really. We both deal with the dead, but my talent lies in a slightly different area."

Vander stepped in to clarify. "Necromancers bring back

the dead's consciousness. That's not something priests or priestesses can do."

"Except with me," Wendall chimed in. "I was a little different because of my fairy blood."

Aurelia's eyes narrowed. "I am uncertain I understand the finer points, but I do not believe it is of any significance."

Erasmus's foot shifting increased, and he rubbed the back of his neck. "Well, in this case, I think it might be really significant. Then again, I'm not entirely certain."

Ray moved closer and Wendall followed. Honestly, I think everyone tightened their circle around Erasmus.

"Explain," Ray demanded.

Erasmus glanced at all of us before settling his gaze on Peaches or more precisely, what Peaches held within his hands. When he asked, "Can I see that?" and pointed at the amphora, everyone stiffened and the anxiety spilling into the night increased.

"Absolutely not," Lucroy answered first.

"I'm sorry, Erasmus," Peaches offered, "but I can't just hand Aurelia's object of attachment over to anyone."

"Oh!" Erasmus waved his hands in a placating manner. "Sorry, I didn't mean it like that. I just need to get closer. I don't actually need to touch it. I mean, touching it might help, but I think I can figure things out without physical contact."

Figure what out? I glanced around, wondering if I was the only one completely lost.

"Just give me a minute." The first hint of irritation colored Erasmus's words. "I've had this weird feeling since Peaches brought that amphora out of the woods. If I can get a closer look, I'll be able to clear this up. I think." Erasmus cocked his head to the side, thinking. "Sorry, I'm not trying to be obtuse on purpose. I've never met a djinn before or been around their object of attachment. This is all new for me too."

Peaches looked to Lucroy first, followed by Ray. Neither seemed to have any direct objections. Then he asked, Aurelia. "Do you mind if he takes a closer look?"

Aurelia's lips twitched into the hint of a smile. "I do not. Thank you for asking."

"Of course," Peaches answered before flying closer, Lucroy hot on his heels.

Holding out his cupped hands, Peaches moved the amphora a little closer. I wasn't a witch, warlock, fairy, or brownie. As far as I was concerned, the lump of ancient clay Peaches held was little more than an antique.

It was way more than that to Erasmus.

"Holy shit. I didn't know that was possible." Erasmus held his hand closer, palm outstretched but just shy of physical touch. Licking his lips, Erasmus's wide eyes darted from the amphora to Aurelia before he asked, "How were you created?"

Aurelia's lips curled into a snarl. "Witch magic."

Erasmus nodded. "Yeah, I know that much, but I mean, how did the witch create you?"

Aurelia's animosity fled and she was left blankly staring. "I am not a witch. I do not know."

Vander said, "We'd need Mattie here to give a full account or tell us as much as she knows. I'm no witch either, but I can tell you there are layered spells. The closest analogy would be an onion. Thankfully, Aurelia's restrictions are on the outermost layer and the easiest to break. Deeper down, at her very core, is her connection to her object of attachment. That one would take days to reach and break. Why do you ask?"

Erasmus's attention was glued to the amphora. "And all djinn have an object of attachment," he stated more than asked.

Aurelia still answered, "Yes."

"And whoever has possession of it controls you?" Erasmus asked.

"Yes," Aurelia hissed.

"And when you touch the object?"

"I am pulled back inside. I am incapable of moving my object on my own." Aurelia sounded infinitely disappointed by this fact.

"Interesting." Erasmus continued staring at the amphora. "Like I said before, I've never seen anything like this. I didn't know it was possible." He swallowed hard. "That's probably a good thing. I don't think this kind of information would be beneficial if let loose into the world."

"And what information would that be?" Ray calmly asked.

Erasmus opened his mouth before slamming it shut. His gaze took on a shifty air.

"Erasmus." This time, Ray's tone was stronger. "While I may not force Aurelia's voice, I have no qualms forcing yours."

Erasmus stood tall, shoulders back and expression hard. "Are you threatening me?"

"You may take it as you wish. The existence of djinn are a threat to this world and possibly Fairy. While djinn themselves are not the exact threat, those who would seek their power to use for nefarious means are. Djinn were created as weapons, and unfortunately, those who seek them do not have noble intentions. Make no mistake, this issue is of the utmost importance to my queen."

"Aunt Silvidia wants the pixie trafficking ring shut down yesterday." Wendall backed Ray up. "And if the reason for the ring has anything to do with finding a djinn, then I think we already know that the one searching has the morals of a... Well, I can't think of anything to tag right now. The point is, this individual doesn't care about life and is willing to squander it to their end goal. Someone like that should never have access to a djinn, and if they do find one, then it will be bad. Really bad." Wendall swallowed hard. "We got really lucky with Aurelia. I wouldn't want to push that luck."

"And if there is a way to defeat a djinn, then that knowledge would be immensely helpful," Parsnip said.

Erasmus appeared torn. I wasn't sure if it was Ray's threat or Wendall's plea. Whatever it was loosened Erasmus's tongue. "That," he said, pointing at Aurelia's amphora, "is way more than it appears." With a grumbled head toss, Erasmus said, "I'm not sure exactly how a djinn is created, but I can tell you they didn't start out that way. Most likely witches had to have something to work with, a base living organism. Don't ask me how, but they tore the life from that living creature and if Aurelia's amphora is anything to go by, they ingrained it into their object of attachment.

"You mean... What exactly are you saying?" Wendall asked, words breathy.

"Plain and simple, Aurelia's object of attachment contains her consciousness and life force. Some might say it contains her very soul."

Our circled group grew deathly silent. Only the far-off sounds of Peaches's sprites mixed with crickets, bullfrogs, and the wind whispering through the trees could be heard. Erasmus's verbal bomb destroyed everyone's ability to speak.

Chapter Twenty-One

Leon

"You look a damn sight better." Johnny clucked his tongue as I walked up to the bar.

"Thank you. I feel much better as well." The gnawing hunger hadn't completely dissipated, but it was far more tolerable. I didn't feel like I might snap Johnny's neck for simply existing. That was a definite improvement.

"'Bout time," Johnny groused. "I've got enough to worry about without adding your health to that list." Walking off, I heard Johnny's whispered mumblings regarding *stupid, arrogant vampires*. The words weren't said out of malice but worry.

"Ditto to what Johnny said." Lizbeth made her way down the bar while wiping a glass clean. "I'd ask if you want a glass of blood, but it looks like you've already dined tonight."

I hadn't dined yet tonight, but my pre-dawn meal had been heaven-sent and still maintained me. Phlox and I hadn't had nearly the time we needed to discuss the situation. He'd fallen asleep not long after I finished feeding and he'd been gone before I woke. There was a note on the side table clearly explaining his destination and the reason for his absence. I was exceedingly grateful I'd shown Phlox how to leave Lucroy's safe haven. Getting out was much easier than getting in.

"Thank you, Lizbeth. I appreciate your consideration." Lizbeth's lips twitched until finally giving way to a smile.

"Damn, Johnny really is right. It's good to have you back to your old self, Leon. I'm not sure what changed, but please don't let that happen again. I like working here. It's the best job I've ever had and part of that is due to who runs the joint." For a human, Lizbeth had perfected an excellent glare. Even her bubblegum-pink hair didn't deter from the seriousness of her statement.

"Apologies if I caused you distress."

"It's okay. Just don't do it again." Lizbeth threw me a wink before walking away.

Dusk wasn't officially open yet. The sun had only recently gone down and the bar wouldn't open its doors for another two hours. Johnny and Lizbeth were here, along with a smattering of other employees, getting the bar prepared. Phlox obviously wasn't back from his meeting yet. I was disappointed but not overly upset. He'd been considerate enough to leave a note.

Pulling out my phone, I shot Phlox a quick text, asking if he knew when he would return. When I didn't get an immediate response, I placed my phone back in my pocket. With time to kill and my mind more settled, I decided to look through Dusk's accounts. I'd been unable to focus the last few days and hadn't kept up properly with my duties. The minimal time I'd allocated to the task most likely had questionable errors.

After a quick trip to Dusk's small office, I settled in the corner booth and got to work. Accounts were tedious and not terribly interesting. Laptop nearby, I entered numbers into accounting and inventory programs. Nothing was terribly askew. Johnny really could run the bar without me.

When one of my nestmates silently walked up to the booth, I took up the position Johnny could not readily fill. With Lucroy gone more often, I'd assumed the position of liaison with our nestmates. I would solve problems where I could and if not, I would bring the situation to Lucroy's attention.

"Antonia, what may I assist you with?"

Antonia sat down across from me and that's how I spent the next hour, listening to nestmate's concerns.

———

On my way back.

Those words were simple and sparse, yet they settled the frayed nerves slowly eating away at my calm. Phlox was gone far longer than I thought he'd be. His text gave nothing away beyond the fact he was tired, if the exhausted emoji was anything to go by.

On the heels of Phlox's text was one from Lucroy. He too, it seemed, was on his way to Dusk. I wasn't sure if Peaches would accompany him or not. I also wasn't certain if Phlox had eaten much before he left. Even if he had, my beloved needed nourishment.

With that thought in mind, I caught Lizbeth's attention. The bar was open now, but it was still early and a weekday so not as busy. While we didn't regularly serve meals, we did have snacks. When Phlox arrived, I would inquire what else he wanted and order it to be delivered.

"Phlox will arrive shortly. A glass of orange juice and whatever snacks are available would be appreciated."

"You got it." Lizbeth headed back to the bar and disappeared into the back. I'd seen Phlox drink orange juice before and thought it a better choice than water.

I busied myself with some final computer entries and was just finishing when a cloud of bluish-gray pixie dust entered my eyesight. Phlox's twittering wings not far behind.

My grin was automatic, just shy of showing fang, as was the lightening of my chest. "Phlox." That singular word was sweet as honey dripping from my lips.

"Leon."

I took back my earlier thoughts. The sound of my name spoken in Phlox's soft voice and was far superior. What wasn't better were the dark circles under his eyes and the pallor shading his skin.

Holding out my arm, I motioned for Phlox to settle in beside me. He snuggled in close. "I missed you today," Phlox said, making my heart skip a beat. "I know you couldn't be there. The sun was way too high in the sky when the meeting started. We also conducted a fair bit of business outside. I mean, you could have come for the end." Phlox scrubbed his hand over his face, and I brought the glass of orange juice into his visual range.

"Oh, thank you." Phlox grabbed the glass and downed its contents before reaching for the nearby chip basket. "I should have eaten more before I left but I didn't get a lot of notice. The phone rang and Peaches told me to haul ass to his orchard."

"Peaches said that?" I inquired. It did not sound like his normal MO.

Phlox grunted. "I got the feeling he was quoting someone else. Probably Ray, although I doubt he used those exact words either. Most likely Peaches paraphrased the intention."

"It was that dire?"

Another glass of OJ appeared on the table and I barely had time to whisper a word of thanks before Lizbeth was off, attention already on another table. She'd set a glass of water beside the juice.

"I'm not sure. I think it was to accommodate Erasmus's schedule. Although I believe that might be shot to hell now." Phlox groaned. "You are not going to believe what happened."

"Indeed, Frost is correct." Lucroy walked up to the end of the table. Peaches was absent. However, Ray and Wendall were there.

"I already lived this once. I don't need to rehash it. I think Trinket and I will head to the washroom. I could use the busy work to take my mind off things." Wendall placed a kiss on Ray's cheek before asking Phlox, "Do you want to come with me or would you like to stay here?"

"I'll head back and help in a minute. I'd like some time with Leon if that's okay."

Wendall grinned and nodded.

"Lucroy, I believe you and Frost are more than capable of filling Leon in on tonight's happenings. I will leave you to do so while I do the same with my queen."

"You're going to visit Aunt Silvidia?"

"Would you like to come along?" Ray asked.

Wendall appeared to consider the offer before finally shaking his head. "Not this time. Like I said, I don't really want to rehash what just happened. I think Aunt Silvidia will understand. Let her know I'll come visit soon."

"As you wish. I will walk back with you to your station."

With his hand on Wendall's lower back, Ray guided them both through the growing crowd until they disappeared behind the bar and into the room beyond.

"It seems we are all on similar missions," Lucroy coolly stated. "I dropped Peaches off at Philodendron's home on my way here. He will relay the matter to Alpha Voss."

Phlox quickly informed me why Sedrick and Phil were not

at the meeting, finishing by saying, "I think Peaches wanted to check in on Ruthie too."

"I am certain the child is on the mend," Lucroy stated, not unkindly. "She is a dire wolf and the toughest of her werewolf species."

I figured Lucroy was correct. Still, Ruthie was a child and Peaches loved her like a niece. It was only natural he'd be concerned.

Starting on his second glass of orange juice, Phlox waved his free hand in Lucroy's direction. "Feel free to get Leon up to speed."

Lucroy cocked an eyebrow but did as instructed. I sat there, listening and wishing I'd been present. This necromancer sounded intriguing. I would have also enjoyed witnessing Sylvie's unmitigated pain.

Lucroy's tale was entertaining until the topic of djinn entered the conversation. The thought that another was actively seeking one out was a horrific concept.

"You are certain it is a djinn they are after?" I asked.

"No," Phlox answered instead. "I mean, I don't think we're certain. It's just what makes the most sense. What fits." Phlox's lips twisted in thought. "Honestly, I don't know what else it would be."

"Nor I," Lucroy answered unhelpfully. "And if it is something else, then I doubt our situation will be improved. The thought of anything being more powerful than a djinn is truly frightening."

As a six-hundred-year-plus vampire who'd found their beloved in a nature pixie and now no longer even feared the sun, hearing Lucroy Moony admit he was scared of anything was eye-opening.

"And yet, we still do not know who this individual is?" I asked, gaze shifting from Lucroy to Phlox.

"No," Phlox huffed. "Ray says Hamish is still working on

Sylvie's computer. Although he did get a message from Hamish earlier this evening. I think Hamish might have found something. Chances are it's not just the fairy queen Ray will visit tonight."

"Let us hope Sylvie's computer bears fruit." Lucroy's dark eyes locked on mine when my attention was pulled to the edge of the bar room. "Leon?"

"Arie's minions have returned," I answered. They were coming in every night now.

"The same ones that left the note?" Phlox asked.

"No. There are only two this time and neither one was here that evening." I'd yet to hear if Alpha Voss knew anymore regarding the note left. None of us were certain if it were a true cry for help or trap. From what I understood, Arie Belview was prohibited from harming Sedrick Voss or anyone Sedrick considered part of his pack. However, Arie might be able to get around that restriction if it was proven that Sedrick instigated the incident. Arie could claim self-defense which might clear the way for him to evade his fairy law oath.

"Lizbeth is currently taking their orders. I doubt it will be more than one beer each, if that." Sometimes they simply ordered water.

Lucroy's vampiric stillness intensified. Given his current position, Lucroy couldn't see the wolves. Having spent the last two centuries with my king, I knew he was deep in thought and allowed him the time. Lucroy would speak when ready.

Phlox didn't know that and slumped further into my shoulder. I cherished the small weight.

"Wait until you hear the rest," Phlox mumbled, words slightly slurred. "If you think what Lucroy's already said is—"

"When did Arie's wolves begin coming in more frequently?" Lucroy asked, cutting Phlox off. My beloved appeared little more than slightly miffed.

"I would need to speak with Johnny, but I believe it was midwinter. Why?"

Lucroy went silent again before asking, "Was it after the incident with Arthur Stover?"

I contemplated the question. When you were essentially immortal, time became an interestingly fluid concept. Beyond the daily rise and set of the sun, time was of little consequence. The seasons blurred, the days and weeks even less distinct.

"I believe so," I answered. "Although, again, Johnny would know more precisely."

"The night Alpha Belview came into Dusk, when he was interested in Wendall's unique zombie status, I believe you were part of that conversation, were you not, Leon?"

While time might move in shifting tides, a vampire's memory for particular incidents within that timeframe was crystal clear. "I was. Although I did not arrive until after Aurelia appeared."

"Do you remember what Arie said?" Lucroy's tone could freeze the tropics.

"Of course. Are you looking for a specific comment?"

"Aurelia," Lucroy answered.

"He was surprised. As most of us would be. He commented that djinn were little more than myth. I believe he was shocked to be in the presence of one. I believe it is also fair to say he was annoyed to be so out of the loop. The fact I knew of Aurelia's existence and thought little of the fact grated."

Lucroy's attention suddenly shifted to Phlox. "When you were captured, you said Sylvie was speaking with someone regarding Leon's worth."

I easily recognized Phlox's rumbled growl. His inner cat was very upset. "It wasn't a phone conversation, but over the computer. Whoever she was talking to wanted Leon dead and offered to pay for the recorded images of his demise." By the time he was done speaking, Phlox's eyes glowed yellow and his words were little more than garbled hisses.

"Pardon me, Leon. I believe I need to have a word with Sedrick." Lucroy easily slid out of the booth and headed for the hall leading to the parking garage.

I quietly watched him go. Phlox stood on the booth seat, body completely turned and wings fluttering. "What the hell was that about?" Phlox waved a hand in the general direction of the parking garage. "That was hardly a proper goodbye and he didn't even finish telling you what happened tonight."

While I wasn't certain what was on Lucroy's mind, I knew he had a good reason for his actions.

Phlox spun around and flopped back down on the seat beside me. Arms crossed, he huffed. "I suppose it's up to me now." Uncrossing his arms, Phlox's tension dissipated into lethargy. Slumping, he ran his fingers through his hair. "You have no idea how badly I want to shift right now."

Sliding closer, I grabbed Phlox's hand and entwined our fingers. "You do not need to speak further about tonight if you do not wish. I can hear it from another or you can tell me later when you're feeling up to it. If you desire to shift, I have a perfectly good lap you can lie on."

Phlox's lips parted, eyes wide as he stared up at me. I hope it wasn't premature, but I swear I saw adoration sparkling in their deep blue depths.

"You really wouldn't mind if I laid in your lap?"

"Not even a little," I reassured.

Phlox's lazy, appreciative grin lit me up from the inside. I almost believed I could survive on that look alone.

"I'll definitely take you up on that later." With a regretful sigh, he said, "But right now, I need to be a responsible agent and fill you in on the other tidbit of amazing information we learned tonight. I don't think Erasmus was keen to tell us, but after a bit of *persuasion*, he dropped a big-ass bombshell."

I was all ears and leaned down when Phlox lowered his voice. I could barely make out his words above the pounding music setting Dusk's atmosphere.

"First off, necromancers are scary as fuck. Turns out, they might be more useful than we originally thought. Do you remember what Vander said the other night about necromancers, witches, and warlocks? He said that back in the day, witches and warlocks procreated and it was only after their falling out over djinn that they stopped doing that, turning to humans to keep their species going."

"I remember that, yes."

"So, as it turns out, necromancers weren't even a species when djinn were created. They came along later as a product between warlocks and humans."

"That follows, but I fail to see the importance."

Phlox licked his dry lips. "I didn't either. I didn't even think much of it when Aurelia didn't know what Erasmus was. None of us thought much about it until Erasmus said he didn't think djinn are as indestructible as previously believed."

My eyebrows shot high. "How so?"

Phlox cringed. "You know that all djinn have an object of attachment?"

I nodded. "Yes, Aurelia's is an ancient amphora."

"Exactly. Well, it turns out that object is a little more special than anyone thought."

I could not imagine how that could be true. My barely raised eyebrows must have expressed my disbelief.

"Yeah, I know how you feel," Phlox said, running his fingers through his hair, tucking it behind an ear. "Goddess, I could murder a burger right now." Phlox's stomach growled in agreement.

My eyebrows did more than barely tilt upwards. "Meat? I have never seen a pixie eat meat before, not even you."

Phlox shrugged as if it were unimportant, or perhaps, he

didn't want to make a big deal of it. "I'm part Pallas's cat shifter. I'm mostly a vegetarian, but sometimes I crave something a little bloodier. I think my blood donation early this morning might have something to do with it. Although Peaches doesn't crave meat, so my guess is it has more to do with my shifter side." Gaze drifting to the side, Phlox cautiously asked, "Does it bother you?"

"That you eat meat sometimes?" I asked incredulously.

"Yeah. I know that's not very pixie-ish behavior. I've been careful over the years not to eat it in front of other pixies. Bless Auntie Tandra. I think it hurt something deep in her soul to buy it for me, but she did it anyway."

The more I heard about Phlox's auntie Peltandra, the more I desired a direct meeting. "I care not what you eat, Phlox. I only care that you are properly nourished and happy. I would slaughter whatever livestock you crave."

Phlox's nose wrinkled. "That should sound gross and yet it makes me all warm and fuzzy inside. I'm not really sure what that says about me."

"It says nothing negative. Now, do you have a preference from where food is ordered?" I pulled out my phone and found a food delivery app. Phlox listed what he wanted and from where and I happily placed his order.

With my beloved's needs on the way to being met, I turned the topic back to Aurelia. "You mentioned Aurelia's object of attachment is even more significant than earlier believed. You have piqued my curiosity."

Phlox took another drink of juice before nodding. "It's not something any of us knew. The way Vander and Erasmus talked, it's something only a necromancer would be able to determine." Phlox cringed. "I swear, the witches of old were some twisted women. I don't mean to be species-ist and condemn a whole generation, but those ladies needed a serious reboot of their moral compasses."

Curiosity is a precious gift vampires do not take for granted. "Do tell."

"Did you ever wonder how djinn were created?" Phlox asked. "I mean, we know they were created by witches and a shit ton of twisted magic, but where did they get the raw materials?"

I blinked, my mind blank.

"The bodies, Leon. Where did they get the bodies? I mean, they had to come from somewhere. It's not like they threw a bunch of ingredients together, popped it in the oven, and out came a djinn." Phlox shook his head. "Honestly, I'm kind of embarrassed I never thought about it before. I think Vander and Ray were more pissed at themselves than the rest of us." With a huff of irritation, Phlox said, "They killed them. The witches... They murdered perfectly healthy humans. But worse than that, they used that soul, that human's very life essence, to create their object of attachment."

My body stilled as I made zero attempt to feign life. The implications were... I could not fathom the words.

Phlox took my silence for the unholy disbelief it was. "Erasmus figured it out. I'm not entirely certain how necromancer's abilities work, but Erasmus dumbed it down for us. Necromancers can find the detached spirit. They zero in on the lifeforce and drag it back to the body. It's a very specific specialty and Erasmus could tell there was something hinky about Aurelia's object of attachment. Goddess, Leon, Erasmus could literally feel Aurelia's soul in it. Can you believe that shit?"

I wasn't certain which part Phlox found unbelievable. The fact witches might be capable of such atrocities or the fact that Aurelia's soul was well and truly bound to an earthly object. Which made me wonder, "What was Aurelia's reaction? Was she aware?"

Phlox violently shook his head, scattering his hair. "She

had no idea. I mean, she knew the object is special and specific to her, but she didn't know it contained her soul. Aurelia doesn't remember a life before becoming a djinn. Vander and Erasmus aren't certain, but the best guess is that djinn creators found a body—a living human, and essentially hollowed it out, leaving little more than a shell behind. Vander described it like stripping a house down to the studs and redecorating it to suit your needs and tastes. Vander didn't seem one hundred percent certain, but he thought the analogy was close enough. Erasmus agreed."

If I'd required breath, I would have inhaled deeply. As it was, I maintained my stillness. "Earlier, you mentioned that Erasmus believes djinn aren't as indestructible as we imagined. I assume it has something to do with this latest revelation."

"Oh yeah." Phlox's eyes widened, his earlier tiredness temporarily gone. "Erasmus isn't certain, but he thinks a djinn's object of attachment is their Achilles' heel. It's something witches back in the day never would have considered because necromancers didn't exist when they created djinn. That soul, that lifeforce that's trapped within the weave of Aurelia's amphora has the power to break every single spell held within Aurelia's body"—Phlox snapped his fingers —"just like that."

Few situations truly stunned me. I'd thought finding my beloved would be the culmination of unexpected revelations. By far, it still held the spot of most joyous. However, this newest piece of information attempted to rise to a similar occasion.

"Before, when Professor Arthur Stover controlled Aurelia, Vander and Matilda attempted to unravel her magical bindings. I believe they described it as a layered onion. The deepest connection was to Aurelia's object of attachment. Vander and Matilda both said it would take days, perhaps weeks, to sift through all the layers."

"Maybe for them, but Erasmus seems convinced that it can be done a hell of a lot quicker. While he can't be certain, Erasmus believes all it would take is releasing a djinn's soul and returning it to their body. According to Erasmus, there's no stronger magic than the soul. Souls trump any twisted witch spell. Pulling that soul out and placing it back in the djinn body will unravel everything, essentially making them powerless."

I sat there, staring into my beloved's generous blue eyes. "Could it truly be that simple?"

Phlox cocked his head. "I'm not sure, but if it is, that's a game changer. Ray and Vander convinced Erasmus to hang around a little longer. He's staying with Peaches and Lucroy for the time being. Besides Phil's home, it's the safest place, and at least this way, Erasmus has a whole orchard he can get out and explore."

"They are concerned for his safety?"

"Wouldn't you be? If this gets out, whoever's got a hard-on for a djinn of their own is going to be royally pissed off. They've put themselves at a lot of risk in search of a djinn and spent loads of money in the pursuit. If they find out a necromancer can upend their plans..." Phlox's words faded.

I didn't need him to finish. I could easily see the bloody road that information led to. Necromancers had human lifespans. They suffered from human ailments and shared their mother's fragility. I had not considered that disadvantageous. Given my current knowledge, I saw it for the flaw it truly was.

Chapter Twenty-Two

PHLOX

Leon was quiet the rest of the evening. He watched me eat my burger and fries, making certain I finished the entire meal before allowing me out of our corner booth. When finished, I managed to beg off so I could help Wendall in the washroom and cleaning up the tables. While I was tired, the busywork helped keep my mind off today's batshit-crazy revelations.

My mind was full to overflowing. I was still unpacking Leon's declaration. I was a vampire's beloved. I didn't doubt his belief. That wasn't a word vamps threw around willy-nilly. If Leon thought I was his beloved, then I was. Simple as that.

What wasn't so simple was how I felt about it. The idea was growing on me, but I needed to make certain that growth was fruitful and not akin to mold on stale bread. So far, Leon was being exceedingly generous. He wasn't pushing the point, and I appreciated his consideration.

"Are you nearly finished?" Ray suddenly seemed to pop out of nowhere, asking Wendall if he was ready to leave. When I jumped and dropped a glass, Wendall and Ray looked at me. Trinket's eyes widened and the way she chittered made me think she was laughing at me. Wendall didn't so much as flinch when Ray spoke.

"Don't worry," Wendall soothed. "I reacted the same way the first few times Ray *appeared*. I don't think he means to do it." Wendall casually shrugged, as if he wasn't certain and cared even less.

"Apologies, Frost. It is as Wendall says." Ray barely flicked his gaze in my direction before honing in on Wendall. Softness filled those crimson ringed irises. "Do you require more time or perhaps more help?"

"No. I think we're about done. Did you get Aunt Silvidia filled in?"

"I did. I also had an interesting meeting with Hamish." Ray didn't elaborate and I didn't ask. Fairies weren't known for their altruistically sharing ways. When he deemed the information important enough to share, Ray would do so then and no sooner.

"Go on." I made a shooing motion with my hand. "There's just half a bin left. I can take care of it."

Wendall chewed his bottom lip, looking uncertain. "Are you sure? I don't mind staying if—"

"Go," I ordered. "Seriously, this is nothing."

Wendall's smile made the miniscule work worth it. "Okay. Thanks, Frost. I'll see you later."

By way of goodbye, Trinket unwrapped her tail, dipped it in the dirty water, and splashed me.

"Trinket!" Wendall scolded. "That's not very polite."

The little scuttlebutt didn't take the scolding to heart. Tapping her hidden feet, Trinket shifted from side to side, cooing and twittering madly.

"I swear, sometimes you act like you have no manners at all." Wendall's words might have been harsh, but his tone was filled with unwavering love.

"It's fine," I said, wiping the dirty water from my face.

Wendall shot me a skeptical glance but in the end accepted my capitulation. "If you say so. Thanks again for finishing up."

"No worries. Go on and get some rest." I'd heard fairies didn't need nearly the amount of sleep or rest that other species did. Given Wendall's mixed human/fairy genes, I had no idea where he fell on that scale.

With a small wave goodbye, Wendall followed Ray through an atmospheric tear. I had no idea where they called home. I imagined it was somewhere in Fairy but wasn't certain. If someone else knew, they hadn't told me. Maybe I'd ask Johnny sometime. Right now, I had enough minutiae clogging up my brain.

I spent the next few minutes attempting to quiet my mind. I somehow managed a modicum of success and was finishing the last glass when Leon poked his head through the door and asked, "Are you nearly done?"

"Almost. Just this last one," I assured.

He came the rest of the way into the washroom and leaned against a nearby counter, doing that stillness thing all vampires had in spades.

My pulse quickened. I couldn't figure out if it was disturbing or endlessly flattering being the center of someone's attention. I was straddling the fence, leaning ever so slightly in the flattering direction.

Emptying out the sink and wiping down the area, I finally turned my attention to my would-be paramour. I gave Leon the same attention he lavished on me. I figured mine might be a little more clinical as I was still concerned about his health. He'd fed from me late this morning, before the sunrise, but I doubted it was enough.

"Are you hungry?" I asked. There was no sense beating around the proverbial bush.

"I am always hungry for you," Leon answered, leaving me confused.

"Are you talking about my blood or something a bit more carnal?" After Leon fed, I'd passed out and had to leave before he woke up. Sexy times had been placed on hold.

Leon smirked and offered up a completely unhelpful "yes."

I threw my dirty towel at him. It hit Leon's chest and fell limply to the floor. My face was flushed and burning hot. I doubted my body had time to replenish all the blood Leon relieved me of but there still seemed to be enough to turn my face into a tomato.

Leon's low chuckle made my toes curl and did funny things to my heart. I didn't think the heart was supposed to jump rope like mine felt like it was doing. Closing the distance between us, Leon leaned in and nuzzled my neck. I briefly tensed before relaxing into his gentle touches.

"I will never take what you do not freely offer, Phlox. Be that your blood or your body. You hold my leash. I am yours to command as you will."

"Shit," I whispered through my disbelieving lips. "That's a lot of power. I'm not sure I want it."

"Whether you do or not is unimportant. It is yours regardless of your desires."

I inhaled, pulling Leon's scent into my core. My inner shifter rolled in it, purring and making an embarrassing fuss. I spent far more time as a pixie than a Pallas's cat. My cat was fully on board with Leon's claim. My pixie side was holding up the show.

I wanted to let Leon bite me. It seemed natural and yet the fear remained. It wasn't that I was afraid of the pain, it was that I was afraid that if it hurt again, that would mean it would always hurt. I wanted what Peaches described. I wanted Leon's bite to affect me the same way. Fearing that wouldn't be the case, or more precisely, confirming that fear, kept me from offering. Right now, I still had hope. If Leon bit down and the pain was the same, that hope would fizzle. I wasn't ready to take that chance yet.

Pulling away, I said, "I need a shower. I needed one before Trinket's idea of a goodbye, but now I smell like dirty dishwater on top of my other stink."

"You smell nothing short of delicious to me, but I understand your desire for cleanliness. Would you like to shower in your apartment or downstairs?"

Leon's shower was far more impressive than the little cubbyhole in my apartment, but all my toiletries were there, and it seemed silly dragging them downstairs. The way things were going, maybe I just needed to move all my belongings into Leon's cubbyhole.

"As long as you don't mind damp hair, I won't be long," I promised.

"Take your time. The sun doesn't rise for another eighty-seven minutes."

I wondered if I'd ever get used to Leon's very specific time-stamp regarding the sun's movements.

"I'll be back in plenty of time."

"And I'll be waiting," Leon promised.

I raced upstairs and took the fastest shower of my life.

Leon's teeth tugged the edges of my bleeding wrist. He wasn't as ravenous this time. He also didn't take as much. Leon cradled my body, holding me as if I were the most important creature in existence. It was a heady sensation. I'd always felt loved. Auntie Tandra made certain of that. But the love of a parental figure was wholly different than this. I'd had lovers before, mostly brief dalliances here and there. Nothing that lasted more than a few weeks to a month or longer. I knew down to my very core this was different. I realized that before Leon confessed twenty-four hours ago.

Licking my wrist, Leon closed the wound, speeding the healing. I felt slightly lightheaded, but nothing like yesterday.

"Thank you," Leon reverently said. "Those words are a pale reflection of my true feelings. However, they are currently all I have."

"They're enough." With my head resting on Leon's chest, I thought back to our earlier conversation as well as my thoughts while washing glasses. I could feel the press of Leon's firm cock against my rear. My own sex was in a similar state. I could easily turn within Leon's arms and sate that desire. I'm not sure why I didn't. I only knew that, although it would undoubtedly feel good, it wasn't what I needed.

Suddenly, it was crystal clear what I wanted. I only hoped Leon had been truthful earlier. Clearing my throat, I ignored Leon's obvious desire and said, "Did you mean what you said?"

"You will need to be more specific."

"Sorry." I wasn't sure why I was nervous. Maybe it was because I didn't share my shifter side with a lot of others. Leon had seen it a couple of times. But this situation was different. "About being okay with me shifting and laying on your lap." My cheeks warmed. I hadn't even done that with Auntie Tandra. Sometimes I'd shift and sit at the opposite end of the couch, but I never crawled into her lap. I'd never wanted to do something like that with anyone else, not like I did now.

Leon was eerily quiet before he finally answered, "I would be honored if you would do so."

I thought *honored* was a stretch but appreciated the sentiment. With a deep inhale, I focused on my inner cat, pulling it forward. I'd been told there was a shimmer of light when I shifted but it wasn't something I could see. Auntie Tandra offered to record my shift so I could see it, but that wasn't something I was interested in.

Stretching, I eased into my new form, relishing the feel. My purr was instantaneous. Leon's slender fingers had to dig deep. My fur was thick and plush, the cooler temperature of Lucroy's underground home a welcome reprieve from the sweltering heat of summer.

"Beautiful." Leon's whispered praise filled up all my hollow spaces. Kneading my paws, my thick claws dug into Leon's pants. I was careful not to dig too deep. I didn't want to hurt Leon, but his pants felt good between my toes. I wanted him to smell like me and rubbed my cheek over his chest, reaching up and rubbing his neck and whatever skin I could reach.

Leon's thick chuckle matched my purr.

"I do not know why I was blessed with you as my beloved, but I will not question or doubt it." Leon sounded confident. "I will never allow another to take you from me. Should you wish to leave on your own, I will not stop you. But should it not be your wish, there will be no hope of survival for the culprit."

I hadn't thought it possible for my purrs to gain in volume, and yet, that's exactly what they did. Nestling in, I curled up in Leon's lap and soaked in the peace.

We stayed that way until near sunrise. Leon rose, picking me up with him. He didn't ask me to shift back to my pixie form. Leon carried me to the bed and laid me on his chest. His fingers only stopped stroking me when the sun grew higher in the sky, suppressing my mate with its power.

Chapter Twenty-Three

I knew the moment my consciousness stirred that I'd woken earlier than typical. The sun was still well into the sky. Early afternoon wasn't a time I'd experienced in centuries. Phlox was still on my chest, curled up and peacefully sleeping. I'd never imagined waking up with a cat on my chest would be so fulfilling. Then again, Phlox wasn't a typical housecat.

While I was conscious, my limbs still felt heavy and it was difficult to open my eyes. I'd been roused, but functioning was a different matter. If I didn't have Lucroy's experience as a blueprint, I would have found the situation odd. As it was, I assumed Phlox's blood was beginning to have the same effect on me as Peaches did on Lucroy. Although they had different affinities, Phlox was a nature pixie, same as Peaches. Was it just nature pixies' blood that allowed vampires more time in the light? Was it all pixies? Only time would tell. I also wasn't certain if I would have the same sun tolerance as Lucroy. He was three hundred years older. That might factor into the situation.

I was not so foolish as to go running into the sun.

Quickly lulled back to sleep, I remained where I was, soaking in the feel of my beloved's trust and desire to be near me.

It was later in the day when I woke next. The sun wasn't so high in the sky and would set soon. My body was still sluggish, but not as heavy as before. Phlox was no longer in his Pallas's cat form and lay on his side, arm thrown over my chest, his fingers lightly teasing my side. My hand found its way to his forearm, my fingers dancing across his flesh.

"Good evening, Leon." Despite being in his pixie form, Phlox's voice rumbled with a low purr.

"Good evening, beloved." The word tasted sweet on my tongue. Almost as sweet as Phlox's blood. I had no idea how Lucroy had taken but a few sips of Peaches when he began experimenting.

Phlox stretched before pulling his knee up and draping it over my thigh. I could feel the heavy weight of his cock resting against my hip. My own responded in kind.

"Would you like some help with that?" Phlox asked as his hand inched downward, cupping me.

"Only if it is something you desire." The thought of pushing Phlox to do anything he didn't truly want made me physically ill.

"I think I can tolerate it." Phlox pushed up on one elbow and winked. The grin lighting his face appeared truly wicked. "Are you awake enough to appreciate it?" he asked with a raised brow.

"Most definitely." I was fully conscious and becoming increasingly aware by the second. My body felt like it was on fire. Phlox's touch was like a shot of oxygen to that flame, making it burn ever brighter.

"Good." He leaned in, peppering my face with kisses. They started out whisper soft and grew in intensity. "I might not want to drink your blood, but I do enjoy nibbling."

Phlox's hand slid under my sleep pants. I'd stopped wearing underwear over a hundred years ago, which gave him easy access.

"Hmm, is this for me?" Phlox's tongue rasped up my cheek, rougher than I expected yet oh so delicious.

"Everything is for you," I managed and meant every word.

Phlox's movements briefly halted before starting again. "I can't figure out if that makes me hot as hell or scared out of my mind." His warm breath tickled my ear.

"I do not wish to frighten you."

"I know. But it's a lot of responsibility. You're giving me a lot of power, Leon. I don't take that lightly."

"And that is why it is freely given." Had Phlox felt differently, he would not be my beloved.

"Fucking hell," Phlox muttered, his hand picking up speed as he ran it up and down my shaft. Phlox's hips undulated as he rubbed himself on my thigh. His pants and groans grew, rivaling any sound I uttered. His pleasured moans drove my pleasure, filling me with heated desire.

"Are you close?" Phlox panted.

In answer, my back bowed as I arched off the bed, shooting cum into Phlox's talented hand.

"Oh shit, I'm—" Phlox's filthy groan filled the room and soon I felt the warm wetness of his release pressing against my thigh. It would cool soon and become uncomfortable. Regardless, I couldn't make myself move.

Phlox's long, content sigh made me even less inclined to clean up. "That's definitely something we should repeat in the future." Crawling up my body, Phlox's wings stretched out behind him, fluttering and covering us in a magical haze of dust. If pixie dust didn't dissipate, the world would be covered in it.

Long tendrils of silken hair draped across my body, falling to the side and spreading out along the bedsheet. Phlox's lazy, contented grin stared down at me. "I thought about doing that earlier this morning, before the sun rose." His cheeks pinked. "Peaches said that he and Lucroy typically have...intimate times during or after a feeding." Reaching down, Phlox cupped my now flaccid cock. "I knew you were interested. Thanks for not pushing it then. I'm not sure why, but I really needed to spend time with you in my other form first. I wish I could explain it, but I don't know that I can." Phlox sounded far too apologetic.

"I have no regrets regarding what we did or did not do. I have rarely experienced the level of peace and contentment having you near me gives. I cherish your cat form. You may feel free to shift and lay on me or beside me whenever you desire." Phlox could shift and just run around the room like a mad kitty for all I cared.

I hadn't realized Phlox was tense until my response eased him. "Thanks, Leon." Phlox's tongue darted out and licked a strip along my lips. The roughness was gone, making me think he'd partially shifted his tongue earlier to make it raspier.

Rearranging his body, Phlox grimaced. "I can't believe I just came in my pants like a teenager."

"I do not believe I am in any better condition. I also believe I am far older than you and thus my situation is more embarrassing."

Phlox threw his head back and laughed before slapping the bed and moving off me. I wasn't sure if he pushed his body up or if his wings lifted him.

"Come on, Leon. Let's get cleaned up before I have to do the walk of shame up to my apartment for fresh clothes. Maybe I'll get lucky and Johnny won't be in yet."

I gave Phlox a questioning glance.

"Yeah, I know, but a pixie can hope."

Hand grasping my wrist, Phlox pulled me to the bathroom

and started the shower. It was possibly the best shower of my long life.

***

Phlox's hope wound up being misplaced. Johnny was indeed already at the bar when we made our way upstairs. Thankfully, it was only Johnny. Lizbeth would be in soon. Johnny took one look at Phlox's soiled pants, raised his head, sniffed, and then broke into a smile that took up his entire face.

"Not a word," Phlox threatened before darting upstairs.

Johnny tossed a towel over his shoulder and soon peals of laughter filled Dusk. It was a joyous sound, one that I was not inclined to make in front of anyone except, perhaps, my beloved.

"I'm happy for you, boss-man." Johnny's hooves happily stomped behind the bar. He was on his riser and near eye level.

"Thank you, Johnny."

"Maybe we'll get another permanent pixie out of the deal." He tossed me a wink. "One that actually works in the bar and doesn't just drink all the honeysuckle mead."

My happy façade instantly faded. Most wouldn't be able to read vampiric expressions well. Johnny wasn't *most*.

"What put that frown on your face?" Johnny asked, leaning an elbow on the bar and coming closer.

My gaze instantly traveled to the stairway leading to the upstairs apartment. "I am uncertain if Phlox will want to stay."

"*Phlox?*" Johnny's nose scrunched in thought. "Is that Frost's real name?"

"It is." In inwardly cursed my slip. "He requested I call him Frost in front of others. I should not have spoken his true name aloud." I wasn't certain if it was meant to be a secret for a reason. What I did know was it was one of Phlox's requests and I had just broken it.

Johnny waved me off. "I ain't tellin' no one. It's a nice name, though. I like it."

I liked it too.

"But what do you mean he might not want to stay? I've seen that look before—on Mr. Moony. Never thought I'd see it on another vamp, especially one so soon, but I'd bet a decade's wages that Frost is your beloved."

"Your monetary future is secure," I promised, admitting Johnny was correct.

"Then what's the issue? He's not bonded to any land is he?" Johnny's concerned brows drew close as he shot a glance upstairs. "If so, he's been gone from it a long time."

"He is not bonded as Peaches is," I reassured. "Frost is, however, a happily employed pixie. He is an agent with the Magical Usage Council and enjoys his work. It is not a profession that allows him to remain in a singular location."

Johnny's eyes widened with awareness. Licking his lips, worry filled Johnny's once happy eyes. "What does that mean exactly?"

"I am uncertain. All I am aware of is that if Frost will allow, I will not be parted from him for long."

Johnny blew out a deep breath. "I get it. I just hope some kind of compromise can be found. I don't like the thought of losing you and I know the boss won't either. Have you spoken to Lucroy?"

"Not fully," I admitted.

"He'll understand," Johnny confidently answered.

"I know." And I did. Even if Lucroy hadn't experienced what I was going through firsthand, he still would have been understanding. That was the kind of vampire he was. It was why I did not wish to leave his side. It was why the Southeast vampire nest was one of the fastest growing in not only the

United States, but the world. Our admission requests grew daily.

"Speaking of the boss, I got a call earlier. Lucroy will be here early tonight." Johnny became deadly serious. "I didn't like the tone in his voice. Oh, I know, you vampires try and hide your feelings and you do a damn fine job of it. I've just known you both too damn long to miss the obvious. Or, well, I suppose what seems obvious to me."

"You believe something more has happened?" I asked.

Johnny grunted. "When doesn't shit happen? And yeah, I'm pretty sure he found something out. Wendall's not scheduled to work today, so I'm not sure if he and Ray will show up or not."

"I suppose we will find out soon enough." Worry was rarely productive. The emotion was making an unwelcome comeback where Phlox was concerned. I'd thought I'd managed to nearly eliminate worry from my emotional catalogue. Finding my beloved proved worry was a far more difficult foe to slay than I'd previously thought.

My phone buzzed with a text. The words were simple. Phlox was grabbing a bite to eat and would be down when he was sated.

When I glanced back up, Johnny's grin was back. "Yeah, I've definitely seen that look before."

"As have I." Lucroy's smooth tenor eased through the otherwise empty room. "It pleases me to see you so settled, my friend." Lucroy's palm clasped my shoulder and offered a gentle squeeze. "Marian would have been overjoyed."

Familiar sadness flared, but it was tempered knowing Lucroy was correct. My maker would be happy for me. I only wished Marian had found what Lucroy and I had. If so, she would still be with us.

"Where is Frost?" Lucroy asked, scanning the Dusk's interior.

"Upstairs. He needed a change of clothes, and I just received a text that he is going to eat prior to coming back down."

Johnny snorted but didn't share his knowledge regarding why Phlox was in need of fresh clothes.

"Have you learned something new?" I asked, making Lucroy still.

"I have. And what I do not know for certain I suspect. I spoke with Sedrick and Ray last night and they, unfortunately, agree with me."

"That doesn't sound the least bit ominous," Johnny dead-panned. "You wanna talk privately or should I stay?"

"Your presence would be appreciated," Lucroy answered. "I value your opinion."

"As do I," I agreed.

Johnny's cheeks pinked but otherwise he remained silent.

"You left rather abruptly last evening. Does this have anything to do with why?" I asked.

"It does." Lucroy sat next to me, elbows on the bar, hands folded, and chin resting within. "As you are aware, Leon, where vampires are concerned, time becomes a fluid entity. Nights run together and are often lost to us. That is the only excuse I can offer for not making connections earlier." Lucroy's eyelids slid closed and when he opened them again, crimson colored their margins. "Arie Belview is a weed I should have pulled long ago."

Johnny's lips pulled back in a sneer. "Alpha Belview. What has that jackass done now?"

"As usual, nothing we can currently prove, only speculate. I am concerned that by the time we can prove anything, it may well be too late."

"Too late for what?" Phlox flew down the stairs, settling his bare feet on the floor when he reached the bottom. His dust wouldn't bother Lucroy and me, but he abstained for Johnny's sake.

I scooted my bar stool to the side, giving Phlox room. Instead of grabbing another chair, he hopped onto the bar and sat, feet dangling as they swayed back and forth. His bare ankles were too tempting, and I wrapped my hand around the closest one, rubbing my thumb along his flesh. Phlox sucked in a quick breath.

Ignoring my obvious affection, Lucroy answered, "There is a fair possibility Alpha Arie Belview is the mastermind behind the pixie trafficking ring."

This time, Phlox's inhale was more hiss than pleasure. "You have proof?"

Lucroy gave a miniscule head shake. "Circumstantial more than anything direct."

Johnny's grunt mimicked my own feelings. "Of course. Fucking asshole alpha." Tossing his towel on the bar, Johnny pointed a finger Lucroy's way. "He doesn't even deserve the title. He uses his pack as cannon fodder and doesn't give two shits when they lose their lives in his service. Sedrick would never act that way. Hell, you're a vampire king and you don't even act that way." We all knew vampire kings and queens weren't known for their altruistic ways. They protected nest holdings, but it was more in service to themselves than those they considered nestmates. Lucroy Moony really was different.

"Agreed," Lucroy answered. "Regardless of our mutual opinions, Arie Belview will hold his alpha position until successfully challenged. That is shifter law and fairy law does not dispute it. As much as we all wish it weren't so, Arie Belview is an imposing and powerful alpha. Precious few alphas could best him and that would be assuming Arie fought fair, a situation I am not willing to bet on."

Johnny reluctantly agreed. "Sedrick could probably take

him, but I don't want to think about what would happen if he lost. And if he won…"

"He would be in charge of a pack he doesn't want," I finished.

"Exactly." Johnny blew out a frustrated breath. "That pack's gotta have a shit ton of issues by this point. I wouldn't envy anyone that position."

Phlox followed our conversation, silently taking everything in until he finally said, "I'm not nearly as familiar with Alpha Belview."

"Consider it a blessing," Johnny said.

Phlox gave Johnny an appreciative grin before becoming serious again. "What's the circumstantial evidence?"

"Sylvie's computer, for one," Lucroy answered. "Hamish was unable to exactly pinpoint who she was communicating with, but he can track it back to within a one-hundred-mile radius of Rutherford Haven."

"Seriously?" Phlox asked, leaning in enough that his silken hair brushed my arm.

"There is also the matter of what was discussed and Sylvie's contact's answer." Lucroy glanced at me before saying, "We all know Leon wasn't supposed to be taken. He was an unexpected passenger during Frost's capture. When Sylvie tried to turn error into opportunity for profit, her contact's answer was death." Crimson flooded Lucroy's eyes and Phlox's inner cat growled. Johnny patted Phlox's leg in sympathy. It was humbling knowing I would have been mourned by so many.

"Yeah, that pisses me off too. But like you said, Leon wasn't expected. At that point, he was an unknown." Johnny cocked his head to the side, truly contemplating the matter. "As much as I hate to say it, considering the illegal activity they were involved in, killing Leon doesn't sound that out of character."

"While that may be true," Lucroy agreed, "the offered price for proof of Leon's death was not. Her contact *wanted* Leon dead. They wanted proof and were willing to pay handsomely for it. Leon has survived long enough to have created enemies on his own. He is also my second, so Arie Belview is not the only possible culprit. However, the vast majority of those enemies are not located so near my territory."

"If they were vampire—"

"I would have eliminated them," Lucroy stoically answered.

Johnny agreed. "Damn right you would have."

"So," Phlox said, "what you're saying is that Alpha Belview is the only one within your territory, or at least within the one-hundred-mile radius, that would react that way."

"Precisely," Lucroy answered. "And then there is the matter of Arie's wolves frequenting the bar, along with the timing."

My hiss rivaled Phlox's cat. "Aurelia."

"Precisely," Lucroy confirmed against Johnny's muttered "shit".

Phlox raised his eyebrows in question, and I explained. "Last night, Lucroy asked me when Arie's wolves began frequenting the bar."

"It was after Aurelia's appearance," Johnny quickly filled in. "Maybe not straight away, but soon enough."

"Unfortunately, Aurelia made an appearance in front of Arie Belview," I explained. "From his reaction, it is safe to assume he was under the same assumption as the rest of us, that if djinn ever truly existed, they were no more. Djinn have mostly been relegated to modern-day fairy tales and little more."

"More like nightmares," Johnny said.

"Most fairy tales do read more like nightmares." Phlox

stared down at his bare toes, their nails so dark blue they nearly appeared black.

"True enough," Johnny easily agreed, then the full horror of the situation hit him. "You mean to tell me Arie Belview is after his own djinn?" Color fled Johnny's face, leaving him blanched and pasty.

"Worse. What I am telling you is that we believe Arie Belview has found a djinn." Lucroy's voice was devoid of all emotion. I envied the ability. Maybe that's what three hundred more years into your second life gave you—the ability to eliminate the abject horror and fear your imminent death brought.

Chapter Twenty-Four

PHLOX

Found one? I processed those two words again and again and yet they still made no sense. Or, perhaps, my brain just couldn't cope with the terrible meaning and didn't want them to compute.

"Tell me you're lying," Johnny begged.

"Then I would be lying to you, Johnny."

"I'll take that lie." Johnny swallowed hard and I reached out a hand to steady him. I understood how he felt. "Sweet goddess above. That's... I can't even find the words."

I could. "If he's found one, then why are we all still alive?" I wasn't sure if Alpha Belview would come after me straightaway, but if he was out to get Leon, then I knew where I'd be, and it wasn't cowering in a corner.

"An excellent question," Lucroy answered. "Of course, it is not certain he truly has the djinn in his possession."

"Then why do you believe he's succeeded?" Leon asked what I was thinking.

"Again, Sylvie's computer. During her communications with her contact, they made it clear they would be stepping away from the smuggling ring. She was very upset about this until she was reassured others would fill the void. Her contact simply stated he'd gotten what he needed out of the endeavor and had other, more pressing, concerns to attend to." Lucroy maintained his emotionless tone.

I slumped, shoulders rounded and wings lax. "All this loss of life..." I could hardly fathom it. "All this suffering...for money." I spat the last word like the curse it was.

"Money was only the means to his main, end goal," Lucroy corrected me. "If we are to presume the mastermind is truly Arie Belview, then he used his ill-gotten gains to fund his djinn search. Possibly, he's used those same funds in other nefarious ways."

"His pack," Johnny said, voice fading. "That note Sedrick got. Do you think it was the real deal?"

Lucroy silently contemplated the question. "I believe it is possible. Arie has become a single-minded alpha. Revenge is a dangerous obsession that often harms the wielder as well as the recipient."

I'd seen enough ravages of revenge to know Lucroy was all too correct. "You think he's abusing his pack to get what he wants?" I asked.

"He's done it before," Leon answered. "It was a much smaller scale, but if revenge is truly Arie Belview's one and only mission, then he would care little for who his quest destroyed, even his own pack."

"That's"—I wasn't sure what to call it besides—"very un-werewolf like." I could see it in vampire nests, but weres took care of their own. They were very pack driven with a hierarchy designed to protect the pack at all costs. The way Alpha Belview was suspected of acting was as wrong as an alpha werewolf could get.

"I think that note was a true cry for help." Johnny sounded like he was talking more to himself than the rest of us. "I might be wrong, but if what you're saying is true, Arie's pack might finally have had enough."

"I believe that was true long ago," Leon said, and the barest tinge of sadness colored his words. "When a group is under stress, they find ways to cope. The abnormal becomes normal and acceptable given the confines of their situation. And then things change. The situation becomes untenable. Those coping mechanisms no longer function, and the group implodes. There is always a tipping point. I believe Arie Belview's pack may have reached that precipice."

"Most likely, you are correct." Lucroy's eyes had long ago changed back to their typical obsidian darkness.

We quieted. I know I needed a minute to digest what I'd learned and assumed Leon and Johnny felt similarly. Finally, Leon asked, "I assume Ray has informed Queen Silvidia."

"He said he would after we spoke. I have not heard back from him yet."

"Do you think she'll interfere?" I asked. "From what you just said, there isn't absolute proof. Will she act without it?" Fairies were all about the law, even their queen. Most of the time, that was a good thing. I'd hate to think what our world would be like if fairies viewed themselves above the laws they set into place or if there were no law to abide by. Some thought fairies created laws and adhered to them out of a sense of boredom or perhaps to try and get one up on each other in a way that didn't leave another dead. Others thought it was to avoid conflict with brownies. Brownies were nonviolent as a general rule, but I don't think anyone wanted to test that theory if they felt truly threatened. Fairies were smart enough to realize that.

Personally, I thought it was a combination of both.

"When do you expect to hear from Ray?" I asked.

Lucroy's dark eyes blinked before he answered. "I am not certain. Time moves differently in Fairy."

"Shit," Johnny repeated, echoing my sentiment.

"Indeed," Leon agreed before asking Lucroy, "What preparations are we making?"

"I've spoken with Peaches, Philodendron, and Parsnip. According to Aurelia, pixie bonds are difficult to break. She cannot speak for all djinn, but she said if she were ordered to harm a pixie while they were in their bonded safe zone, she would need to find a creative way to do so. Should Alpha Belview truly already have a djinn in his possession, it is fair to believe he will go after Sedrick and Philodendron first."

"They're staying within their home," Leon correctly assumed.

"They are. I understand Ruthie and Dillon are not pleased, but they understand the danger."

Given their ages, I didn't envy Phil trying to keep the two youngsters entertained indoors for goddess knew how long.

"Peaches will stay within his orchard. I will stay there as well." Lucroy didn't sound as pleased about that.

Johnny chuckled. "Bet you had to promise him that so he'd stay put."

Lucroy nodded. "Perceptive as always, Johnny. Aurelia has agreed to remain awake. I do not know if she will offer more aid or not. At this point, it does not appear that she will detrimentally interfere. Erasmus has agreed to stay as well."

I perked up at that and wanted to ask more questions, but Lucroy quickly added, "Peaches asked Vander, Parsnip, and Byx to stay at the orchard also. They've agreed for the time being, but I am uncertain how long they will remain if the situation drags on. Vander does have a business to run, and Parsnip has a television show he is contractually dedicated to." Lucroy tilted his head and he appeared to contemplate something before he said, "We are uncertain how effective Parsnip's bond will be protecting them. We believe it would be strong enough to keep Vander safe, but—"

"But his bond doesn't necessarily protect him," I surmised. Social pixies rarely formed bonds and it was always with another individual instead of land or a home.

"Correct. Vander and Byx can help protect Parsnip through magic, but Aurelia says magical manipulation is far easier to break through."

I wondered about Vander and Parsnip and asked, "Would Alpha Belview come after them?" The history in this little corner of the world was varied and difficult to grasp.

Johnny chuckled before clearing his throat. "Yeah, well, you see, Vander kind of insulted Arie by not taking a job."

"What kind of job?" I innocently asked.

Leon answered. "Alpha Belview *requested* Vander severe a pixie bond. In particular, a home-and-hearth pixie bond."

I sucked in a heated breath and claws sprouted, digging into the bar surface and adding my own bit of graffiti. "That's...at the very least, that would be punishable by death." Why in the hell was Arie Belview still alive?

"As with everything, it's only suspicioned Arie was behind the commission." Johnny sounded as angry as I felt.

Eyes wide, I'm sure they glowed yellow. I was furious. To think someone would stoop so low, to condemn a pixie to that kind of unspeakable death. Arie Belview had no soul. I was convinced. Before coming to Rutherford Haven, I'd heard the Belview name. The Magical Usage Council was well aware of a portion of the crimes he was accused of. It was also aware of the challenge that had taken place between Alpha Belview and Alpha Voss. At this point, it was believed Alpha Belview would run afoul of his oath and fairy law would eliminate him. Evidently, the alpha was a little too cunning or perhaps devious. Or maybe he was just lucky. I didn't know. All I knew was that Alpha Belview needed to be taken out.

Lucroy's dark gaze danced from Johnny to me. His typically emotionless voice held a tinge of sympathy when he said,

"There is some chatter. Hearsay mostly. Some say Arie Belview managed to find a warlock willing to attempt such an endeavor."

My claws dug into the bar surface and my lips pulled back. I could feel my teeth lengthen. I was ready to rend Alpha Belview into little more than chunks of flesh too small to make a good stew.

"As I said, it is merely hearsay." Lucroy said nothing regarding my loss of control.

"Beloved." I wasn't certain when Leon stood, but he was suddenly by my side, eyes level with mine.

"He can't do that," I hissed. "I will shred him before he has the chance."

Leon's cool hands gripped my face, holding me steady. If it were anyone else, I would have lost my shit at being held down. "And I shall assist you in that endeavor."

"We all will," Johnny reassured. I had no idea what the faun thought he could do, but the conviction those words were spoken with eased my inner cat. "Phil's my friend," Johnny continued, fury echoing through every word. "It's past time Arie Belview was put down."

"Here! Here!" Lucroy echoed.

"Don't leave us out." Wendall slid through the swinging door leading to the washroom. Trinket on his shoulder, her feet pattering back and forth, mouth open and letting loose high-pitched yips. "Trinket wants in on the action too. She might be small, but don't underestimate her." Wendall sank his fingers into Trinket's fur, vigorously rubbing.

"Only the foolish would do so." Ray exited the washroom behind Wendall. His words brought a grin that nearly split Wendall's face.

Lucroy stood and asked, "What is Queen Silvidia's ruling?"

Ray and Wendall came closer, standing beside Johnny. "My queen has deemed Arie Belview an imminent threat."

Imminent threat sounded promising. "So, she's taking action?" I asked. When fairies intervened, it typically wasn't pretty. A slap on the wrist wasn't their way of handling situations. Death and utter elimination were more the fairy idea of justice. I suppose it made sense considering they rarely got involved in minor squabbles. When fairies stepped in, especially their queen, the shit had truly hit the fan.

Wendall huffed, fisting his arms on his hips. "She would if she could find him."

"What?" Johnny and I said in unison.

Ray's fingers clenched and the fire constantly ringing his pupils expanded. Heat pressed against my skin. It wasn't enough to burn, simply raise the temperature.

"It seems Arie Belview has disappeared." Ray's voice was deathly quiet, its icy tendrils in stark contrast to the heat emanating from his body.

"Disappeared?" Johnny's mouth fell open. "How in the hell does one disappear from the Fairy queen?" Johnny's gaze snapped between Lucroy and Ray. "I mean, she's fucking powerful as..." He waved a hand in the air. "Honestly, I've got nothing to compare her to. She's powerful, and let's leave it at that."

Ray's eyes slid closed, and he inhaled deeply. Wendall gripped Ray's bicep before entwining their fingers. Giving Ray a chance to pull himself together, Wendall answered, "That's a good question. My aunt's really angry." Wendall swallowed hard. "I, uh... That's the first time I've seen her so mad. It's scary."

"She would never injure you," Ray said defensively.

"Oh, I know that. I didn't mean to imply otherwise. I'm just saying that Johnny's not wrong. Aunt Silvidia is scary powerful and if she can't locate Arie, then—"

"Then he's found what he was looking for," Lucroy coldly answered.

"I fear you are correct," Ray agreed. "I believe we must all accept the idea that Alpha Arie Belview is indeed in possession of a djinn."

"Goddess save us," Johnny prayed.

My stomach cramped, filled with knots and squirmy discomfort. "I need to alert the Magical Usage Council," I stated, tone flat. I didn't want to make that call. Being the bearer of Armageddon-level news wasn't all it was cracked up to be.

Despite my words, I sat there and made no reach for my phone. Disbelieving silence filled the air, surrounding us in a fog of uncertainty. That silence was broken by Johnny's tapping hoof. His fingers danced along the bar surface, adding another beat. With a head shake, Johnny asked what was probably on all our minds. "If Arie's got a djinn at his beck and call, then what the hell is he waiting for?"

The collective, oppressive silence was answer enough. None of us knew the answer.

Chapter Twenty-Five

Leon

There was an edge riding all of us tonight. I doubt Dusk's patrons noticed the change. Lizbeth kept sending Johnny inquiring glances, but she held her silence. Phlox spent the better part of the early night on the phone with the Magical Usage Council. He'd told me they'd called an emergency meeting to discuss the matter. He felt they were appropriately alarmed. Phlox also got the distinct impression they had no idea what to do. I could easily sympathize. We'd barely escaped our last meeting with a djinn. I did not want to contemplate our chances when faced with another, especially one leashed to Arie Belview.

The sad truth was that we hadn't *defeated* Aurelia. We had Wendall's kind nature to thank for our continued existence. I did not believe that strategy would work to our favor this time around.

Phlox slipped by, bin on his hip as he cleaned another table. He shot me a warm grin as he walked past. I wanted to return it but couldn't muster the energy. I'd stopped just short of begging him to go to Peaches's orchard and stay there. I'd thought it safer than Phil and Sedrick's. At least Peaches had a djinn by his side. And Erasmus was there too. No one knew if what he proposed would truly work or not. Understandably, Aurelia had declined acting as guinea pig.

"Stop frowning," Phlox scolded as he walked past again. "You're starting to freak out your nestmates."

I was uncertain if Phlox was correct or not. I did not believe I'd allowed my emotions free enough reign for my fellow vampires to pick up on anything. Lucroy and I'd discussed the situation and felt it best to keep them in the dark. For now. They were as helpless as the rest of us when it came to djinn. Neither Lucroy nor I had any idea if we should attempt normalcy or not. To our knowledge, Arie was unaware of our suspicions. Would changing our routine draw out his attention quicker? And if so, was that a good or bad thing? There were far too many unknowns for comfort.

I followed Phlox to the wash station. Wendall wasn't scheduled tonight. I wasn't certain the avenues he and Ray were currently pursuing beyond attempting to locate Arie. And if they did locate him, what would they do? Could Queen Silvidia best a djinn? It was another wholly unacceptable unknown.

"Is there nothing I can say to convince you to move to Peaches's orchard?" Discussing the situation would be a waste of breath had I required air.

"Are you going?" Phlox asked.

"No. I must stay here and do what I can for the nest. Lucroy would be here as well if it were not for Peaches."

"Then I'm staying too. End of discussion." Phlox aggressively cleaned the glass in his hand, slamming it onto the drying counter with more force than necessary. "I'm not leaving you, Leon. Period." He picked up another glass, repeating the process.

Leaning against the counter, I stared at Phlox's soapy

hands and forearms. They were so slender and appeared far too delicate for comfort. While my pixie was strong, he was more vulnerable than I would like.

"Don't look at me like that," Phlox hissed.

"Like what?" I asked.

"Like you're trying to commit everything about me to memory. Like you're afraid this might be the last time you see me. Like you think something's going to happen."

My shoulders rounded as I slumped into the counter. "Forgive me, but you have never experienced a djinn firsthand."

"I met Aurelia," Phlox countered, chin up and jutting out.

"So have I. It is fortunate she was not attempting to kill you when you met her."

Phlox's throat moved with his harsh swallow. "I read the report."

A light grunt escaped my lips. "I doubt the writing did the experience justice." I also imagined facts were purposefully omitted.

Phlox set more glasses in the soapy water before pulling his hands out and drying them. "I doubt it did too. I'm sorry you went through that. I don't have a death wish, Leon. I just can't leave you." His large, dark blue eyes stared up at me. "Would you leave me if the situation were reversed?"

"Of course not." I rubbed my hands up and down his arms. Phlox's wings fluttered, filling the space with dust. "You are my beloved. You are everything to me."

"And you don't believe I feel the same?" Phlox cocked his head to the side, his hair falling over one shoulder.

I stilled, the full weight of his words hitting home. "I would not presume to know the extent of your feelings." I knew Phlox thought of me fondly. He did not wish my death and agreed to feed me. He even found me sexually stimulating, but those things did not automatically mean what I wanted them to, what I felt for him.

Placing his palm over my slowly beating heart, Phlox's smile was soft. "I'll admit, I wasn't certain how I felt when you first told me. I knew you were special, that it broke something inside me to think of you in pain or starving to death." With a wink he added, "And you're dead sexy. I knew that from the first time I laid eyes on you." Inhaling, Phlox shifted close enough to lay his ear where his palm had been. "And then I got to know you better, the kind of vampire you are. You never pushed. You took what I was ready to give and never made me feel like it wasn't enough." I felt his grin through my shirt. "I've never laid in anyone's lap before. My inner cat was never comfortable with the idea. Pallas's cats aren't very sociable. They're wary and don't trust easily. My cat trusts you. Completely. My pixie side just took a little more time to come around."

I couldn't speak. I didn't even want to blink for fear when I opened my eyes again this would all be a dream.

On tiptoes, Phlox leaned up while I bent down, meeting him halfway. The gentlest press of flesh met my lips. Phlox's tongue flicked against my skin, parting my lips. Heeding his request, I opened my mouth and Phlox's tongue delved deep. I lifted him into my arms, cradling his body close. Phlox's wings sped and dust consumed us.

Pulling away, Phlox gasped. I would need to use caution. While I didn't require air, my beloved did. Now eye level, Phlox's gaze fixed on mine. "Don't ask me to leave you again, Leon. I won't do it. I'll never leave you. Even when all this shit is done and over with, I'll still be by your side. I'm not sure what we'll do about my work, but we'll get it figured out. Love is too important not to try."

"Love." That singular word left my lips on barely a whispered garble.

"It's all I've got. Is it enough?"

"More than enough. More than I could ever hope for." I squeezed my beloved, holding on for dear life.

"Hey, Johnny told me to let you know we're running out of glasses, so stop sucking face and get busy." Lizbeth's laughter followed her out the door.

Allowing Phlox to slide through my arms, my pixie's feet landed on the floor while I stared at the swinging door. "Perhaps I should speak with Lizbeth. She is getting a little cheeky for a human."

Phlox smacked me with a wet towel. "You'll do no such thing. I like her. So do you."

My beloved wasn't wrong. I was pleased Lizbeth felt comfortable enough to jest.

Going back to his glasses, Phlox said, "Why don't you make yourself useful and take the clean, dry ones out?"

"As you wish, beloved."

Phlox huffed but his cheeks pinked, and I thought he was more flustered than irritated by my comment.

Doing as told, I refilled the empty areas behind the bar. Dusk had its usual crowd, minus Arie's wolves. So far, we'd yet to be graced by their malodorous appearance. I mentally berated myself. Werewolves didn't necessarily smell bad. It was a different odor that didn't always agree with my palate. I'd gotten used to Sedrick's musky scent. I simply didn't care to put as much effort into Arie Belview's pack.

Heading back to the washroom, I began drying glasses.

"They'll air-dry soon enough," Phlox offered.

"It is something to keep my hands busy and occupy my mind," I confessed.

"I understand. I hate waiting. Especially now that we've got an idea what's going on." Phlox glanced up and asked, "Do you know if Hamish has made any more headway with Sylvie's computer? We're pretty sure Alpha Belview's the mastermind, but there are other guilty parties that need brought to justice."

Justice, in this case, would be death. "I am unaware. If the culprits' names have been discovered, I've no doubt justice will be swift. Perhaps that is what Hellfire and Wendall are currently doing."

Phlox's washing momentarily halted. "You think Ray would take Wendall with him for that?"

I considered the question. Wendall's nature was gentle, however, he was aware of the consequences of the pixie ring. "I believe Wendall would agree with the punishment. However, I believe he would also make certain the sentence is fulfilled quickly and without the level of pain others would undoubtedly inflict."

"Wendall's version of mercy. I understand."

While Lucroy and I had an agreeable relationship, I do not believe I'd ever found another's company this easily companionable. Not even my maker, Marian. It was oddly humbling and immensely calming. Being around Phlox was so incredibly easy. It was as if we'd known each other for centuries instead of mere weeks.

"Have any of Arie's wolves shown up yet?" Phlox asked, pulling me from my peaceful mental space.

"No."

"Is that good or bad?"

"I do not know." I was not even certain why they'd been coming before. Lucroy thought it was a way of keeping an eye on us. Dusk was a hub of activity for the different species. With Wendall still working part time, Ray was often here. Sedrick and Phil made the occasional appearance, as did Vander and Parsnip when they were in town. While Lucroy wasn't in Dusk as often as he once was, he stopped by enough that any given week he was here at least two to three times.

I wasn't sure what knowledge Arie Belview hoped to learn.

Perhaps he was simply making certain our routines did not deviate from the status quo. That made the most sense to me. Arie wanted a heads-up if we figured out what he was doing. If that were the case, then perhaps it was good we were keeping up the peaceful façade. Not that Arie had sent any of his minions into the bar tonight to make certain.

Reevaluating my earlier statement, I amended, "I believe it might be a poor sign."

Enough time had passed that Phlox gave me a quizzical glance. His eyes widened when he caught my meaning. "Bad that Arie didn't send any wolves in tonight?" Phlox rightly guessed.

"Yes. Although I am frustratingly uncertain."

Phlox's sigh sounded soul deep. "You and me both. Scratch that—you, me, and everyone else in the know. The Magical Usage Council feels just as impotent as the rest of us. I got a text earlier. They can't find Alpha Belview either. So far, they're trying to be discrete in their inquiries. If Arie's really got a djinn at his control, they don't want to give him an excuse to use it." Phlox frowned. "I think maybe I just insulted djinn by calling them *it*. Do you think that's the right way refer to them?" Phlox shook his head. "I'm still not really sure what djinn are. I mean, Aurelia's alive—"

"More alive than vampires or zombies," I offered.

Phlox gave me a withering stare. "That's very debatable. What I'm getting at is that according to Erasmus, Aurelia's original essence is tied up in her object of attachment. I know we've only got her to go on, but most likely that's the case with all djinn. Goddess, those witches murdered others to form djinn. It's hard to believe."

Given the witches of today, Phlox's disbelief was understandable. There were always rotten apples in every species' barrels. Letty Fox was proof enough of that. However, as a general rule, I believe witches learned their ancestral lessons where craving more power was concerned. Djinn caused far more death and grief than expected. It was a price their community continued paying for.

"I wish Matilda knew more," Phlox lamented. "Or any of the witches on the Magical Usage Council for that matter."

Vander spoke with Mattie earlier. She'd been just as horrified as the rest of us to learn where a djinn's body came from. While Mattie knew more than the average current witch regarding djinn, that damning fact had been carefully hidden or, perhaps, completely erased.

"As do I. Perhaps it is for the best that knowledge has been lost."

Phlox nodded slowly. "Yeah. I can see that." He blew out a breath, shifting his hair from his face. Without thought, I ran my fingers through his hair, tucking the troublesome strands behind a pointed ear.

"Thanks." Phlox shot me a shy but grateful grin before leaning into my cupped palm. A rumbling purr rose from deep within his chest.

"It is my pleasure," I easily answered.

Phlox's purrs increased, the sound filling the small washroom and bathing us in a brief, peaceful, reprise. It wouldn't last. Both of us knew that. Regardless. We drowned ourselves in the moment of contented bliss, willing it to hold as long as possible.

Will and fate are often two opposing foes, constantly battling against each other. Unfortunately, will is rarely the victor.

Chapter Twenty-Six

Leon and I enjoyed two days of strained peace. It was a little after four p.m. when my phone rang. The ringtone told me it wasn't Auntie Tandra. It wasn't the Magical Usage Council either. Leon stirred, his fingers immediately tangling within my fur. I'd shifted into my cat form and was perched on his chest. If we hadn't been on Armageddon's edge, I would have ignored the call and allowed it to go to voicemail. Given current circumstances, I couldn't do that.

Stretching, I shifted back to my pixie form and answered the phone with a sleepy, "'Ello?"

"He's made his first move."

I sat up, sliding off Leon's chest. Sheets wrapped around my lower body, I placed the call on speaker and allowed Vander's voice to filter into the room. "I've got you on speaker," I said. Leon's awake enough to listen."

"Hey, Leon. Sorry it's so early for you, but I didn't want to wait," Vander said. His tone was deep, cool, and calm with just a hint of anxiety. With voices like that, had warlocks been so inclined, they would have made great school principals.

"It's fine," Leon said huskily. "It is not the problem it once was." Leon's fingers raked through my hair, fanning it out across his chest as he continued laying on his back. "What has happened?"

"Nothing bad. Yet." Vander inhaled deeply. His voice was more distant, and I thought he was talking to Parsnip or maybe Byx when he said, "I'm getting to that." Vander huffed before he said, "As predicted, the first shot came at Phil and Sedrick."

"Are they okay?" I asked, not attempting to hide my worry.

"They're good. It wasn't a direct attack. Probably more of a fact-finding mission. Phil said he felt a something pushing at his bond."

"*Pushing at it?* What does that mean?" I asked.

There was a rustling sound on Vander's end and the next time someone spoke, it was Parsnip. "Phil said it was kind of an itchy feeling. He said it didn't really hurt but was uncomfortable. The best he could describe it was like someone poking at the edges of his bonded area."

"Around the house?" Leon asked.

"Yeah. The Voss household is locked down tight. Phil's bonded with the house and a bit of the land extending away from it. When Phil told Sedrick what was happening, Sedrick ran out of the house. He stayed within the bonded area but wanted to see if he could sniff them out."

"Did he?" I asked.

"Kind of. Sedrick said he didn't recognize all the scents, but there was a hint of Arie Belview. Not enough to think he was that close by, but enough to let Sedrick know that whoever it was, they'd been around Arie recently." Parsnip huffed. "It's recon if you ask me. He's looking for weak spots."

If that was the case, Alpha Belview was going to be sorely

disappointed. There was no stronger magic in the world than a pixie's bond. I swallowed hard. I wasn't as certain of that statement as I'd once been. Aurelia said she couldn't get through a pixie bond, but also said there were creative ways to get around it. There was also the concern that Vander's contacts came through with a possible warlock who'd agreed to try and figure out a way to break a pixie bond. If they'd succeeded... Goddess, I didn't even want to think what that could mean.

Vander and Parsnip must have placed their phone on speaker also because Vander's voice came through next. "I agree with Parsnip. Most likely it was a test of some kind."

"That means that Arie must still be close by," Leon said, finally propping himself up on his elbows. Leon's pale chest was displayed, his washboard abs tight in his crunched position. My mouth watered and my inner cat preened. I was this gorgeous creature's beloved, and he was my mate. Leon McMillan was a fine catch.

"Unfortunately, no." Parsnip sounded exhausted. "According to Aurelia, the individual holding their object of attachment can be halfway around the globe and it wouldn't matter. Djinn can transport to wherever they want, just like brownies and fairies."

"Damn," I muttered. "Do we really think Arie is on the other side of the earth?"

"No." Vander sounded adamant. "That fucker enjoys doling out pain. He's vindictive and when the final strike comes, he'll want to be there to witness it. Arie Belview won't be able to help himself. He's all about the gloating, about the power, and about others knowing it was him that got the best of them. There's no way he'll be able to stay away."

"Agreed," Leon quickly answered. Since I didn't know Alpha Belview like the others did, I would easily take their word for it.

"What about Peaches's orchard?" I asked. "Anything from him?"

"Not yet," Parsnip said. "But I imagine it's just a matter of time before—" Parsnip's voice cut off. "Hold on, we're getting another call now from Peaches. It's on my phone so we can keep communication open with you. Peaches, what—" Parsnip's words cut off again. I couldn't hear what Peaches said but Parsnip's occasional grunts and groans told me it probably wasn't great.

While we patiently waited, Leon's fingers continued sliding through the ends of my hair, lovingly combing the darkened tips. The gentle tug on my scalp was near coma inducing.

"Looks like we were right. Peaches just told me the same thing happened to him not five minutes ago." Parsnip's voice was full of anger. "Where does this jackass get off playing with others like this?"

"Don't try and understand it, babe," Vander soothed. "You'll just give yourself a headache."

Apparently agreeing, Parsnip blew out a frustrated breath but let his tirade drop. "Just like Phil, Peaches is okay. He said no damage done. Evidently, the sprites were in an uproar and are flying about, checking the boundary."

"What about Aurelia?" I asked. "Did she make herself known?" She'd said djinn couldn't necessarily sense each other which led me to believe she'd have to purposefully reveal herself.

Parsnip answered, "Peaches said she remained quiet. Arie Belview knows about Aurelia, but I don't know if he's aware she's at Peaches's orchard."

"That's an interesting thought," Vander said.

"Very interesting," Leon agreed. "None of us made it known that we gave Aurelia's object of attachment to Peaches for safe keeping. Perhaps that is what the other djinn is truly looking for."

I considered that. "It might be."

"As much as I'd like it otherwise, Arie Belview isn't unintelligent," Vander said disappointedly. "You could be right. It would make sense that once Aurelia was in our possession, we'd keep her object of attachment somewhere safe. The best option would be with a bonded fairy. Phil or Peaches would make good choices. Sending it to Fairy might have been an option too."

"Wendall didn't want it," Parsnip quickly added. "I don't think he could stomach the idea of being another sentient being's *master*. We all would have been okay with Wendall taking over Aurelia's keeping. Peaches was the next logical choice. Phil and Sedrick have werewolf children in the house," Parsnip explained. I couldn't say I disagreed with their decision-making process. I didn't think the Magical Usage Council had been aware of Aurelia's resting area, but I understood the reason for the secrecy.

"And what of Erasmus?" Leon asked. "Can he tell if this djinn is similar to Aurelia?"

All of us were operating on the hopeful theory that all djinn, along with their objects of attachments, were made equally and thus equally vulnerable.

Parsnip remained silent for a beat before he answered, "He believes so." There was a lot of hesitance in that statement.

"What's wrong, Parsnip? Has Erasmus changed his mind? Does he now think returning the djinn's essence to their body wouldn't work or wouldn't incapacitate them?" I asked, picking up on the tone change.

"Nothing. Not really. It's just... Erasmus isn't sure the djinn would survive the process. Returning their essence might be an immediate death sentence. There's a chance they'd immediately age. Given that djinn are centuries old...they'd be dead nearly the instant their essence is returned. And even if that doesn't happen, if they return and age doesn't catch up with them, it will negate all their magical power. Erasmus believes all their magical bonds will be shredded, leaving them what they were."

"Human?" Leon asked.

"Maybe. Probably." Parsnip didn't sound all that certain. "It's Erasmus's best guess. Aurelia looks basically human, or at least, humanoid. Her ears are a lot larger and there are some other changes, but Erasmus thinks that's due to the magic filling her up. At the end of the day, none of us really know for certain."

"Fuck," I whispered. "Is there anything we do know for certain?"

There was a pause before Vander said, "Arie Belview's a jackass. I know that for certain."

Parsnip choked before bursting into laughter. I grinned, fighting the giggle filling my belly. Finally giving up, I joined in the vocal laughter. It was either that or cry. I, for one, would rather laugh in the face of catastrophe.

"A very true sentiment," Leon agreed. While he didn't openly laugh, his lips tugged in a distinct grin just short of showing fang.

Our giggling fit fizzled and while I felt a little lighter, I was still worried. I'd be an idiot not to be. "You two take care," I pleaded. "From what I understand, Vander, you're on Arie Belview's shit list too."

"And proud of it," Vander answered with confidence. "I find the company on that list most agreeable."

Leon shook his head while I palmed my forehead. Warlock Vander Kines was one of a kind.

"You stay alert also," Parsnip warned. "Arie's not a fan of Dusk or Leon. Hell, he's not a fan of the Southeast vampire nest. I don't think you'll be first on his list, but you won't be far down the line. Then again, if he manages to take care of his first few targets, I doubt they'll be much you can do beyond running and I don't imagine that will do you a lot of good either. I think if Arie gets that far, the world in general is pretty much screwed."

"I would never run," Leon answered, offense clear in his voice.

"Me either." The very thought pissed off my cat. Pallas's cats and pixies might be small, but we were the epitome of mighty.

"Didn't think you would," Vander reassured. "Stay safe. We'll call you when something else happens." I noted Vander said *when* not *if.*

Wings spread, I lowered myself, draping my back across Leon's chest. "This is a clusterfuck."

"Hmm, I have encountered many such instances."

"Me too. I still think this one's a little different."

Leon's fingers danced across my scalp, lulling me to slumber. As my mind drifted, I said, "It sounds like Erasmus's plan might work, but he's reluctant to implement it."

"Understandably so. Although I have yet to meet the necromancer, he sounds like someone afflicted by virtue. He would not take the possibility of killing another lightly."

"The djinn might not die," I said.

"True, but even still, returning to an unmagical state, with all its mortal shortcomings, may not be something a djinn desires. I highly doubt there will be time to ask for their opinion on the matter."

I cringed realizing how correct Leon was. "I don't suppose I'd want to be in that position either. But if I had to choose between them and you, that decision would be very simple."

"As it would be with me, beloved."

I fell asleep like that, tossed over Leon's chest like a ragdoll, his fingertips raking along my scalp, petting me in my pixie form.

Lucroy called shortly after sundown. I woke hearing Leon's voice on the phone. When he ended the call and placed the phone back on the side table, Leon sat there, elbows on bent knees and staring into the dark.

As I rubbed his back, Leon leaned into my touch. "What did he say?" I asked.

"My king has ordered Dusk closed for the foreseeable future. Lucroy is concerned."

I sat up, scooting until my front was pressed against Leon's back. "Did something else happen?"

"No. And that is the way Lucroy wants it to stay. He is concerned that Dusk will be seen as a soft target. It would be a much easier mark than Peaches's orchard or Phil's home. Attacking Dusk would be an understandable strategy. Injuring his nestmates would be an excellent way to draw Lucroy out. Possibly Sedrick as well."

"It makes sense in a sick, twisted way." Leon remained quiet and I wondered what else Lucroy had said. "Is there something else?" I wrapped my arms around Leon's middle, hugging his granite-like body closer.

"I've been ordered to Peaches's orchard. While my king cannot order you also, I would ask that you accompany me."

"Hey, I already told you—where you go, I go. I didn't want to hide out in Peaches's orchard before because you weren't planning on going. I've got no problem if you're there too."

While it was barely noticeable, Leon's body relaxed. "It will be a crowded place. Evidently, Ray has asked Phil, Sedrick, and the children to go there as well."

I pulled back, moving so I could see Leon's turned face. "Why? Phil needs to stay at home. He's bonded and can't be away for long periods of time. Besides, his home should be as safe as Peaches's orchard." I was truly confused and concerned.

Leon's fingers ghosted across my cheek. "That is true. However, it appears that Ray has discovered corroborating evidence that Alpha Belview did indeed find a warlock willing to attempt breaking a home-and-hearth pixie bond. According to Vander, the charm would need to be specific to a home-and-hearth pixie and, therefore, would not translate into usage on a nature pixie such as Peaches. Ray is concerned this warlock has made enough progress to be a danger."

I sucked in a deep breath. "Can Queen Silvidia find this warlock and eliminate him?"

"She has tried, but just as with Arie, he cannot be found."

The litany of curses that flew from my mouth would have either horrified or made Auntie Tandra proud. I wasn't entirely certain which. What I did know was that I needed to call her. She was still in the dark regarding current circumstances, but I wasn't certain when I'd get another chance and needed to let her know I might be going off the grid for a bit.

"But what about Phil's bond with his home?" I still wasn't sure how Ray planned on getting around that sticking point.

"Phil is also bonded to Sedrick and the children. He will be fine for a longer period of time as long as they are with him. Should he need to make a trip home, Ray plans on transporting him there and back. Lucroy mentioned that is how Ray plans on getting them to the orchard to begin with. Traveling otherwise is considered too dangerous currently."

"Yeah, they'd be much easier pickings as soon as they left Phil's bonded area. I stand by what I said earlier: This is a clusterfuck."

"I offer no disagreement."

Sliding off the bed, I stretched my arms high, arching my

back and sighing into the movement. Leon's hungry eyes followed my every motion. Lowering my arms, I walked into his space. Leon's knees parted, allowing me easy entry.

"Are you hungry?" I asked, cocking my head.

Leon's desperate gaze tracked the length of my neck. It was as bold move on my part, or, at least that's the way it felt. It was past time to make this offer. I trusted Leon. I needed to have faith in that trust. I needed to have faith in him.

"Beloved, you do not need to—"

"I know I don't *need* to. I want to." My personal wants and desires were the key. Leon would do nothing without that reassurance.

Leon's fingers twitched before his body stilled. "I do not wish to harm you."

I slipped onto Leon's lap, my legs draped on either side of his thighs. "And that's why you won't." Carding my fingers through his hair, my dull nails skimmed across his scalp. "It'll be different than the last time." I grinned, pushing all my trust into my eyes. "Peaches says it's amazing." He'd actually used a lot more colorful words than that. "I want the full vampire beloved experience."

For the first time, I didn't have to swallow down my fear as it no longer existed. "I'm not scared, Leon." He could read my emotions and knew it to be true. "We don't know what's coming. You need to be strong and I . . . I want to know what it feels like to truly give myself to you."

For a lot of species, that would mean sex. Not so in the vampire world.

Leon's eyelids fluttered as his eyeteeth elongated. "Beloved," the word whispered through his parted lips like a prayer.

Instinct tilted my head, exposing my neck further. Leon's warm breath drew goosebumps. His tongue sweeping across my heightened skin sent shivers of pleasure racing down my spine before Leon's teeth pierced my skin. The pain was instant, but it was immediately swamped by unmitigated pleasure. Had it not been for Leon's firm hold on the back of my head, I would have lolled backward.

Indistinct gasps of desire breezed past my parted lips. My cock thickened and I couldn't stop grinding against Leon if my life depended on it. My whispered pants grew in sound as well as frequency. Lost in a sea of pleasure, I groaned as my body found release, cuming in my pants.

Body lax, I realized Leon was licking the wound, sealing my skin and healing my languid body.

"Holy shit," I managed. "That was . . ." I didn't have the words and settled on, "wow."

Leon's soft chuckle reverberated against my skin. "Am I to presume this bite was preferable to the first time?"

"Yeah. That's safe to say." Easing away from Leon's body, I stared into his crimson ringed eyes. "You know, I think it might be a good thing that it hurt the first time."

Leon's lips twisted into a frown. "How so?"

I gave my soiled pants a pointed look. "If it had felt this good, I would have had to walk around Sylvie's compound with *this* in my pants. That would have been embarrassing and uncomfortable. And can you imagine what Ray would have thought?" I shook my head. "Nope, best this didn't happen then."

Leon's grin barely hinted fang. "I concede your point, even though it still pains me that I brought you harm."

Speaking of pain . . . "Would you like me to take care of that for you?" I asked while palming Leon's firm cock. "I'll even unzip your pants and everything."

Leon's jaw tightened and his eyes briefly flashed full crimson. "As much as I would enjoy that, Lucroy was most adamant that haste was of importance, and I need to notify the staff as soon as possible."

"Shame," I said.

"I promise we shall address this need in the near future."

Pulling away, I stripped off my dirty pants, allowing them to fall to the floor. Adding a sway to my hips, I felt my long hair sashay across my bare ass as I walked away. While I understood where Leon was coming from, that didn't mean I couldn't make him regret his actions. Leon's low, rumbled growl let me know he well and truly understood his loss.

Chapter Twenty-Seven

Johnny advised me he was capable of contacting the rest of
the staff. He'd asked what excuse we were going with, and I'd
left the decision in his capable hands. Johnny would spin a
believable tale. Most likely he would point to some mainte-
nance issues or the like. Most would buy the excuse and those
that did not would wonder in silence. He would also place the
notice on the doors and create a social media post. Stragglers
would appear, but their numbers would be few.

Lucroy and I'd long ago set up a communication chain
within the nest. It was relatively easy alerting our nestmates
that Dusk would be closed for the foreseeable future. We also
let them know that it was more dangerous now and to use
caution and keep a low profile. Our nestmates would be easy
pickings for a djinn under Arie's control.

Lucroy asked if Phlox and I could pick up more food for
everyone. Vander and Parsnip were on their way. Byx had gone
to stay with some of her brownie relatives, much to her
dismay. I was certain Vander would relay Byx's arguments

later. Perhaps in support of the brownie, Phlox wore the meerkat hair clips she'd gifted him.

We'd already stopped at the store and were winding our way through the country when Phlox's phone rang. I recognized the tone as the Magical Usage Council. He answered after the second ring.

"Yes, we're on our way now. I think we should—" Phlox's heart rate spiked, and his hand gripped the phone tighter.

"Say that again." Phlox's anxiety changed, anger taking its place. "You can't ask me to do that," he flatly stated.

I continued driving, keeping one ear on Phlox's wellness while we continued toward Peaches's orchard.

"Let me rephrase it," Phlox hissed, his voice slightly slurred through his dropped feline teeth. "I won't do that." His grip was so tight I thought the phone might shatter. "Why? Because he's my mate, you moron. You cannot ask me to leave my mate behind. I won't do it and Leon will not abandon his king."

My grip on the steering wheel tightened. Phlox told me he loved me, but he'd never referred to me in the shifter way as his mate. "It's not important when it happened," he flatly stated. "Yes, I'm sure!" Oh, he was furious at that question. "You're a mated werewolf shifter. How dare you ask me that!"

Phlox settled back against his seat. His wings desperately tried fluttering but kept hitting the back of the seat. Crossing his arms, he huffed. "I know I'm only half shifter, but I'm telling you, my cat recognizes Leon as my mate. And what's more, I'm Leon's beloved." Those words rang with pride.

"You think?" Phlox asked in disbelief. "Yeah, that was a dumbass *request*. No, I'm aware this is news to you. Even if it weren't I'd need to stay. My mission is to stop this damn pixie trafficking ring and that's exactly what I'm going to do. Arie Belview is the apex of that pyramid and needs brought to justice. He's going to pay for the pixies he's helped capture and kill. Not to mention all his other crimes. When that moment happens, someone from the council needs to be present and it might as well be me."

Phlox silently sat there, nodding and grunting now and again. Few words were spoken and soon enough, he ended the call. "Stupid idiots," Phlox lamented. "The sheer nerve. Ordering me back to headquarters. As if I'd just pick up and leave my mate." He hissed before huffing. I doubted Phlox had any idea what he'd just admitted. I considered leaving the comment alone but couldn't.

"Mate?" I quietly questioned.

Phlox's head whipped my direction, his long hair flying around his shoulders. Mouth parting, his cheeks flushed deep crimson. Finally clearing his throat, Phlox answered, "I didn't realize it until recently. I don't...I don't always understand what my cat's trying to tell me. We don't always communicate the best. It's a work in progress."

Reaching across the console, I offered my hand. Phlox readily accepted the gesture, and I entwined our fingers. "I am honored your cat views me as such."

Phlox's grin lit his face. "I figured you would be. Well, maybe not honored, but I thought you'd be pleased. I have to say, my inner Pallas's cat is nearly impossible to tolerate right now. The damn thing's preening. Gloating too. It wants to rub all over you."

I raised Phlox's hand, peppering kisses across his knuckles. "You may do as you desire. I relish your touch no matter your form."

"You..." Phlox was at a lovely loss for words. His cheeks puffed before he blew out a heavy breath. A soft chuckle passed with that breath of air. "I have no idea what to make of you, Leon. Who knew you were such a romantic?" Phlox winked. I doubt anyone before would have accused me of such affection.

The road narrowed when I turned down the dirt lane leading deeper into Peaches's orchard and territory. I knew the moment we passed through his bonded barrier. The magic washed over me in welcome greeting. Phlox's eased posture let me know he felt the same.

Phlox was a nature pixie and I briefly wondered if he desired something similar—a territory to call his own. He'd never mentioned it and had a more wandering spirit than other nature pixies. Pallas's cats claimed territory as well, but I doubted it was the same. In time, I would learn the answer.

Another vehicle I didn't recognize came into view and I assumed it was Vander and Parsnip's transportation. Phil and Sedrick's truck would be absent considering Ray planned on collecting them himself. I had a moment to wonder if they were here yet when two wolves tumbled through the distance. No, make that three. One was gleaming white, the second tawny gray-brown. The third wolf was much smaller and darker gray. They nipped at each other's heels before heading off into the surrounding orchard.

"Looks like the Vosses are here," Phlox said, leaning forward and staring out the window. "Goddess, I don't think seeing them like that would ever get tiring." Nose scrunched, Phlox said, "I thought there were just two children."

"There are," I answered before opening my door. The humid night air sat like a wet blanket against my skin.

"Damn, it's still hot," Phlox complained while pointlessly fanning himself. "Who do you think the other wolf was?"

"I am unaware." Moving to the back of the vehicle, I pulled out bags of food. Phlox did the same on his side. "I would imagine we are about to find out."

"You two need some help?" Phil asked. Sprites danced around him, diving here and there as they consumed his pink dust.

"There are a couple more bags back here," Phlox answered.

When Phil reached in and grabbed them, Phlox offered his thanks.

"Here, give me some of those." Sedrick's resonant voice echoed through the still night.

"I've got them." Phil leaned in and kissed Sedrick's cheek, just above his scruff. "Thank you though."

Sedrick's cheeks pinked, their heightened color barely visible above his dense scruff.

"We saw a third wolf," Phlox said, the question hanging in the air.

"Here, give me the perishables and I'll take them inside while Sed fills the two of you in."

Before I could offer a protest, Phil deftly grabbed the food and headed inside.

"He's very quick." Phlox echoed my thoughts.

Sedrick grunted. "Tell me about it. I've never met anyone like Phil." Sedrick's words overflowed with fondness. "I can't figure out how I managed without him." Now he sounded truly perplexed. "It's like my life started the day he walked into our home." I didn't think Sedrick spoke to Phlox and me. I doubted he even realized he said the words out loud.

Phlox and I silently waited while Sedrick's wandering mind returned. Inhaling deeply, Sedrick's musing turned deadly serious. "That other wolf is a child from Arie's pack." A low, rumbled growl rose from deep within Sedrick's belly. "He came to the house today. Poor kid looked half-starved and was filthy from head to toe."

"He just showed up?" Phlox asked, glancing questioningly. "I mean, where's his home? Did he travel far?"

Rubbing at his beard, Sedrick gave a shallow nod. "Not sure exactly how far, but there's at least thirty miles between my place and anyone associated with Arie Belview's pack. Shawn, that's the kid's name, traveled in his wolf form. The kid can't be more than seven or eight." Sedrick's bent head shook back and forth. "No one sends a child out like that unless they are beyond desperate. That note was the real deal."

"The one left at Dusk?" Phlox asked.

"Yeah," Sedrick said with a sigh. "Things in Arie's pack have well and truly gone to shit. Or maybe they've always been shit and now it's just gotten to the tipping point." Sedrick's growl reverberated and his eyes shown amber. "According to Shawn, Arie's keeping prisoners."

"Prisoners?" I asked.

"Pixies?" Phlox asked in alarm.

Sedrick flinched. "No. Worse than that, according to pack law. He's keeping members of his own pack prisoner...or basically the equivalent. I always wondered how in the hell Arie kept his pack so loyal." Sedrick huffed. "Shawn's too young to understand everything, but he knows enough and was told to repeat certain information to me."

Phlox's eyes rounded, reminding me of his Pallas's cat form. "He's keeping his owner pack locked up?"

Sedrick gave a slow nod. "In a way. Of course, Arie's dressed it up and put a shitty smelling bow on the whole damn thing. According to Shawn, nearly every family in the pack has someone who's given the *honor* of living in the pack house."

"Honor?" I lifted a single eyebrow. "I get the impression it is not viewed in such an esteemed light."

"It's a way to control the pack. Family is everything to werewolves. We don't abandon family. Arie found a way to keep his pack members under his thumb and bent to his will. He's got someone they love close by, living under his roof, punishment near at hand should someone step out of line. That's why no one in Arie's pack leaves. It's why they're so damn *loyal*."

"Only it's not loyalty," Phlox said. "It's blackmail and fear. Sweet goddess above, that is deviously cruel."

"Arie Belview summed up in only two words. Congratulations, Frost." Sedrick tipped his head in mock appreciation.

I stared off into the distance, my vampiric eyes easily seeing into all the shadowed nooks and crannies. "And that young wolf, he came to you of his own free will?"

Sedrick followed the direction of my gaze. "His mother sent him. She knows it's a risk. Shawn told me that Arie has his grandfather, but before his grandad was taken, he told his daughter, Shawn's mother, to forget about him and get Shawn out." Sedrick swallowed hard, his eyes pinched, and lips drawn in pain. "I can't even imagine the guts that took or the sacrifice."

"She sent him to you." Phlox's voice was soft. "She sent him to you to protect."

Sedrick's nod was painfully slow. "Looks that way." He grimaced. "I just hope... Things are a little uncertain. I'll do my best to keep him safe, but—"

"But the future's a little sketchy right now," Phlox finished.

"To say the least."

The bags in Phlox's hands rustled as he shifted them. "The Magical Usage Council will want to know about this. If what Shawn says is true—"

"It is," Sedrick snapped.

"Then it goes against shifter law and won't be tolerated." Phlox sounded resolute.

Lucroy's voice washed through me like cool water. "If it can be proven. Alpha Belview does seem to exceed in the area of deception." Lucroy walked past Sedrick, coming to stand before me. "I assume the situation with Dusk and our nest is settled."

"As much as possible," I answered truthfully. "I believe we have done what we can."

"And that is the best any of us can hope for. Thank you,

Leon. As always, you've proven my faith in your abilities is well placed. I could not have chosen a better second."

Pride consumed me, warming my eternally cool blood. "It was my honor and privilege, my king." Lucroy and I were rarely this formal. Something in the atmosphere called for the it.

Lucroy's lips lifted, offering a rare grin. "I am comforted you are here. I did not like the idea of you being so far away and unprotected."

"Thank you."

"You have nothing to thank me for, Leon. It is I who am grateful."

"What are you grateful for?" Parsnip asked, flying out of the house at lightning speed, Vander following at a far more sedate pace. "I find it difficult to believe there is much regarding the current situation to be grateful for, so if you've found something, I'm all ears." Flying high, Parsnip's arms crossed over his middle, his chin raised in defiance.

"You'll have to forgive him," Vander said, tossing a thumb in Parsnip's general direction. "To put it bluntly, Byx is pissed I *asked* her to go to a relative's house. She zapped me no less than three times and I swear Byx cracked more than a few finished charms when she screamed at me before transporting out of the shop. I better survive the next few days or Byx will never forgive herself."

"Why?" Phlox innocently asked.

Parsnip flew lower and grinned. "Because, her last words—calling Vander a 'moronic warlock with a death wish'—will haunt her memories. She's not totally wrong, but neither one of us wants her taking that to the grave."

"If things get dicey, I'll shoot her a text or something," Vander said, drawing disbelieving stares from all of us. "What? Why are you all staring at me like that."

Parsnip rolled his eyes. "If things go to hell in a handbasket, I'll dial her number myself and you can *talk* to her."

"How is that different than what I said?" Vander sounded genuinely confused.

"I'll explain it to you later." Parsnip flew down, eye level with Vander before he ruffled the warlock's dark hair, a placating smile tilting his lips.

Peaches and Phil left the small cottage, coming out to meet us.

"What did we miss?" Peaches eagerly asked.

"Only that Vander's an idiot," Parsnip said before adding, "but I love him despite his shortcomings."

Vander snatched Parsnip out of the air, tickling his sides. Parsnip's uncontrolled giggles filled the air and briefly lifted the ominous haze coating each of us like oppressive oil.

Turning from their genuine affection, I asked, "Is Erasmus still here?"

The smile left Peaches's face. "He is." Waving a hand toward the orchard, he said, "He's somewhere out there. I think he's tired of us."

Lucroy moved closer to his beloved. "I believe the necromancer has much weighing on his mind. With that said, I do not think Erasmus is used to this much company."

"Most necromancers are loners," Vander agreed.

"And Aurelia?" Phlox asked. "Is she still...awake. I'm not really sure if that's the right way to say it." Phlox looked at Peaches for confirmation.

Peaches simply shrugged. "I think that's as accurate as anything. Aurelia refers to it as sleeping when she's inside her object of attachment. Saying she's awake when outside of it sounds right. To answer your question, yes, she's awake. I'm not really sure where she is currently."

Panic attempted to claw at my insides. "You are unaware

where the djinn is?" This sounded beyond reckless. Peaches's casual disregard indicated he felt otherwise.

"I don't control her every movement. I don't *want* to control her."

Lucroy stepped in and explained. "Peaches still has Aurelia's object of attachment. As long as that is the case, Aurelia's powers are restricted to his wishes. I believe she is enjoying her reprieve."

"It's the least we can do," Peaches adamantly defended. "I told her she could rest and here it is, just a few months later, and I woke her up already."

My thoughts regarding djinn were restless. While I understood they were sentient beings, and, perhaps even more tragic than initially thought, I also saw them for the powerful weapons they were meant to be.

Wolf yips sounded far in the distance, drawing Sedrick and Phil's attention. "Sounds like they're having a good time," Phil said warmly.

"I'm glad," Sedrick answered. "Dillon and Ruthie have been troopers, but they're getting cabin fever. It's good to stretch their legs. They're also distracting Shawn. After some food and rest, he became anxious. Burning off some of that youthful energy is good."

We remained quiet, listening to the distant sounds of Dillon, Ruthie, and Shawn. Absently I wondered if the wolf children were anywhere near Erasmus or Aurelia.

Sedrick chuckled. "I think Phil and I will be hearing about traveling by fairy transport for the rest of our lives. Dillon especially seemed taken by the idea. Honestly though, I think he was a little disappointed. All we did was step through an atmospheric tear at our home and step out into Peaches's orchard. It was like walking through a door."

Speaking of fairies..."Where is Hellfire Rayburn?" I asked.

Lucroy answered, "Ray and Wendall went to Fairy. Ray believed Queen Silvidia would be interested in Shawn's tale."

Phlox's nose scrunched. I'd learned that expression meant he was thinking. "I'm not sure what Alpha Belview has done to his pack falls under fairy law. That's more in the Magical Usage Council's wheelhouse. Mind you, it wouldn't break my heart if Queen Silvidia decided to make an exception in this case."

"Fuck that," Sedrick rumbled. "I want first crack at Arie. If he weren't such a fucking coward, this shit wouldn't even be happening. We could have met in the challenge ring and been done with it months ago."

Phil stiffened but remained silent. From what I understood, the outcome of such a match was not a forgone conclusion. As it was, Sedrick barely defeated Arie Belview's designated second.

Vander ran his black-tipped fingers through his hair and said, "I think at this point, we'd all like a—"

"Ah, here you are."

Everyone froze, each pair of eyes drawn to a pleasantly malicious voice none of us recognized. Those who required air for existence sucked in plentiful quantities. Phlox immediately slid by my side, feet landing on the ground. Phil's feet were also planted on the dirt. Peaches and Parsnip remained aloft.

Lucroy took a measured step forward, placing himself in front of the group. Peaches followed, staying by his right side. "And you would be?" Lucroy drawled, voice devoid of all emotion.

Our *guest* smirked. "I thought it would be obvious what I am."

"Of course it is, but that was not my questions. I asked who you are. Or would you prefer we simply refer to you as *djinn*?"

Chapter Twenty-Eight

Djinn.

Having met Aurelia, it was obvious what stood just beyond Peaches's boundary. Devoid of any visible hair, the male's body was covered in ink. His ears were larger and lay flat against his head. Metal hoops pierced his lobes and ran through his nose. He was large, in every conceivable way. The djinn struck an impressive figure—tall, broad, and well-muscled. Those impressive muscles were on full display as his only scrap of clothing was a navy patterned, Scottish kilt.

"He is called Janus." Aurelia appeared from seemingly nowhere. "As time is meaningless, I am unaware the last occasion we saw each other."

Janus grinned. Unlike Aurelia, his teeth were shark-like, filed into sinister points. "Aurelia. I heard you were slumming it with a bunch of pixies." Janus tilted his head, expression cast in mock sympathy. "Unfortunate for you."

Aurelia lifted a single brow. "That depends on how you define the word *unfortunate.* I would not consider the likes of your current master an improvement upon my situation."

Janus's grin grew. "Now see, that was always the difference between you and me. I happen to like the wolf's black soul." Rolling his shoulders, Janus flexed his impressive physique. "He's got some truly horrific plans. It is a relief, finding a master who knows how to wield one of us."

While my heart stuttered, Aurelia seemed unruffled. "He is a master, just like all the others. The decisions are not yours. You are a mere puppet with another pulling the strings."

Janus's grin thinned and his eyes briefly flared, along with half a dozen tattoos. "I cannot argue that point. However, he will prove more entertaining than most."

"And when he no longer proves *entertaining*?" Aurelia prompted.

"Then he will die, just like all the others. To be honest, I am looking forward to the challenge. In the meantime, I expect he will use me to great and terrible effect. Now, if you'll excuse me, I have a *master* to get back to. See you again soon."

As quickly as he appeared, Janus was simply gone before I could blink.

"Aurelia." Lucroy's tone was cold.

"It is unfortunate Janus is the one that was found. Even in the beginning, he was...unstable."

"Unstable how?" I asked.

"Out of all of us, Janus was the first to eliminate his creator witch. While all djinn hated our creators, I am uncertain we would have turned on them as quickly if it weren't for Janus being the first. He showed us it was a viable option." For the first time, Aurelia flinched, the barest hint of emotion leaking through. "Out of all of us, Janus carries the fewest restrictions. His creator's death sparked *concern* within the remainder. Our creators became increasingly paranoid and abusive."

"I'm so sorry," Peaches said sincerely. "I promise I will never do something like that, Aurelia."

Eyes narrowing, Aurelia ran her gaze up and down the hovering pixie. "Time will bear the truth," she finally answered. I suspect everyone but Peaches understood the underlying threat.

"I'll do right by you. I swear." Peaches flew higher, clutching Aurelia's object of attachment close to his chest.

Aurelia didn't comment. She simply stared at the space Janus had recently inhabited. "Janus will not act as I did. He has always enjoyed bloodshed and the violence that causes it. He will not attempt to find work-arounds to Arie Belview's orders. He will enact them with gleeful expediency."

I swallowed hard, feeling that lump of saliva ache down my throat. Leon was statue still at my side. Only his lips moved when he said, "We must find a way to remove Janus's object of attachment from Arie's possession."

Peaches's wings fluttered faster. A few sprites dove in and munched on his dust, but most had disappeared back into the surrounding woods. If they were smart, they'd remain there for the foreseeable future. "But how do we know what that even is? It could be anything. It took a minor miracle for us to figure out what Aurelia's object was."

Lucroy asked, "Aurelia, do you know what Janus's object is?"

Silence descended again. Aurelia's arms crossed under her ample chest. Staring Peaches in the eye, she asked, "Is that an official wish?"

Lips parting, Peaches appeared momentarily torn before finally shaking his head. "No. I won't make you do anything. I would appreciate your help, but I won't force you."

Head tipping to the side, Aurelia inhaled deeply before releasing it in slow measure. "It is a dagger. By today's standards, I assume it would appear ancient and I do not know its current condition beyond the assurance that it is still intact. If it were not, then Janus would be no more."

Now that we understood a djinn's soul, their very life essence, was woven into the fabric of their object of attachment, that fact made more sense.

"Arie Belview will not need to have the object on him to control Janus," Aurelia reminded all of us while pointedly staring at the amphora clasped within Peaches's fist. "It is merely important he be the last to touch the object. Arthur Stover was far too paranoid for it to be out of his possession. That is not always the case. As long as it is stored somewhere safe, where no other knows its location, those who do not carry our object are wiser than those that do."

"Point taken." Peaches glanced at Lucroy and said, "I'll be right back," before flying into his orchard. When he returned, no doubt the amphora would be gone.

I turned to Sedrick and asked, "What do you think? Will Alpha Belview have it on him or not?"

Sedrick's facial muscles tightened as his hands fisted. "I give it a fifty-fifty chance. Sorry, but I'm not sure. Arie is paranoid, but he's also deviously smart. He'll figure out holding onto the object isn't smart."

"Indeed, Alpha Voss is correct." We all turned when Ray and Wendall joined our group. I wasn't certain where or when they entered Peaches's protective boundary.

Immaculate as ever, Ray strode forward, a slightly more rumpled Wendall by his side. "Hey everyone," Wendall offered a small wave. "Sounds like we missed something." Trinket hopped on Wendall's shoulder, flicking her wet tail. Water droplets flew from its tip, landing on Sedrick.

"Sorry about that." Wendall blushed before turning his attention to Trinket. "I can hear the children in the orchard. Go on. I'm sure they'd like to play with you. Just be mindful of your teeth. Okay?" Trinket skittered down Wendall's body, leaping to the ground when she reached his hip. Tail flying in the wind, she scurried into the woods, heading toward the sound of the children's playful yips and howls.

Wendall's turned back gave us all a view of his soaking shirt.

"What happened to you?" Parsnip asked, flying closer and inspecting the sopping shirt. "You look like you did a trust fall into a lake and Ray let you down."

Ray's eyes narrowed and Wendall's cheeks flared. Glancing down at his feet, Wendall shuffled back and forth a little before raising his oceanic eyes and answering, "I've been trying to get in touch with my fairy side. Aunt Silvidia thinks I've got more potential than originally thought. I was working on manifesting my wings while Ray filled Aunt Silvidia in on what's going on with Alpha Belview's pack."

"And that made your back wet?" I asked, sharing a confused glance with Parsnip.

"Yeah. My wings are water."

My head jerked. "*Water?*" rang out in questioning unison.

Ray answered, "Fairy wings reflect our innate nature. Mine are fire. Hamish's are plant life. Wendall's sire, Prince Hanon, had an affinity for water. The ocean rolls through his eyes as it fills his wings."

Wendall's flushed cheeks deepened. "Ray used a lot prettier words than I would have, but essentially that's it. I'm just not very good at it."

"Yet," Ray corrected. "You are very young and new to your fairy side. Queen Silvidia is most impressed with your progress. As am I."

Wendall's blush turned atomic. "That's very nice. Currently, all I seem to be able to do is manifest a wet shirt."

"You will improve," Ray said with utmost confidence.

"Thank you." Wendall's words were whisper soft, his rolling eyes filled with affection. That affection dwindled as he returned to the topic at hand. "Aunt Silvidia's even more pissed than before."

"She is quite angry," Ray agreed. "Out of courtesy, my queen will contact the Magical Usage Council, but she has directed Hamish and me to rectify the situation with all due haste. Currently, the only issue tying our hands is an unknown djinn."

"Not unknown," Sedrick growled before waving a hand in Lucroy's direction. "Mind filling him in?"

In answer, Lucroy gave Wendall and Ray the rundown on what had just happened. As he spoke, it occurred to me that Aurelia was no longer present. Her appearances and disappearances were beginning to grate.

"She's gone," I leaned in and whispered into Leon's ear as Lucroy continued speaking.

"So she is," Leon answered. Although barely audible, a thread of tension strung those brief words together. I found his irritation oddly comforting.

"I don't like it," I said.

"Nor I. However, I do not see how we can change the matter."

I huffed. "I still don't like it."

Leon's arm wrapped around my waist, pulling me in close. I found his unyielding body even more comforting than his words. It was a solid show of support. This vampire, my mate, wouldn't leave me. Come hell or highwater, Leon would be by my side. We'd either make it out of this mess together or meet the afterlife as a united duo. I didn't relish the thought of dying and thinking of Leon passing from his second life nearly doubled me over in pain. However, there was comfort in the knowledge that we were bonded. Where one went, the other followed. Life and death intertwined in a coupled dance.

I tuned back in when I heard Lucroy say, "I do not find Aurelia's opinion of Janus comforting."

"Understated as usual," Vander quipped. "And yet, I find I can hardly disagree. I'll just add she about scared the piss out of me."

"I second Van's thoughts," Parsnip agreed, holding up his hand in a physical show of support.

"I'll bet Phil and I third and fourth that," Sedrick agreed. "What do you think, Ray? Will Arie have that fucking object of attachment on him or not?"

My heart dropped when Ray answered, "Unlikely."

"Fucking shit," Sedrick growled. "I was afraid you'd say that." Phil ran his hand up and down Sedrick's bicep, offering him comfort.

"Is there a way we can track it down?" Phil asked. "Could Aurelia?"

Peaches flew out from the edge of the woods in time to hear Phil's question. "She said no." Peaches pulled to a stop beside Lucroy.

"No, she won't tell us or no she can't do it?" Phil asked, echoing my own confusion.

"No, she can't find it," Peaches clarified. "We talked while I was out hiding her amphora. She's really very helpful when in the correct frame of mind. I don't think Aurelia likes Janus, but at the same time, she won't be that helpful." Peaches's anticipated the next question. "From what I understand, djinn aren't very effective against each other."

"That's...that seems counterintuitive," I said. "Why create them then?" I'd assumed witches were trying to outdo each other—get a leg up on their enemies.

Peaches shrugged. "I'm not sure Aurelia knows. From what she told me, witches tried using them to battle each other but found it nearly pointless. Djinn are indestructible. They can't be defeated, at least not back then. They can't even destroy each other."

"Erasmus," Ray said. "Is he still nearby?"

Eyes briefly slipping closed, Peaches nodded. "He's still within the confines of my territory. He's...the trees tell me he's very troubled. Along with the sprites, they've been keeping an eye on him."

"That must come in handy," Parsnip said. "I'm impressed." Truth radiated through that statement. As a nature pixie, it was possible I could one day have the same thing, although not all nature pixies found a place that synched with their magic. Currently, bonding with a piece of earth wasn't my ideal. I traveled too much to make it work. Maybe one day that would change, but for now, I was happy being an unbonded nature pixie. My mate was more than enough. More than I ever expected.

"It is comforting," Peaches answered before he flinched.

"Beloved?" Worry pierced Lucroy's voice.

Sedrick's rumbled growl echoed Lucroy's concern. "I hear them, Peaches."

"Hear what?" I asked. Flying, I twirled, attempting to see what made Peaches's flinch and Sedrick's wolf spark.

Leon and Lucroy's heads snapped up, crimson flooding their onyx eyes. "We've got company," Leon said.

"Lots of company," Peaches amended. "They can't get inside my barrier, but all land is connected and the area surrounding my bonded territory is screaming a warning." Peaches placed the palm of his hand to his temple. "This isn't good."

"As if I expected *good*." Vander's tone dripped with sarcasm. "You let us know what we can do, Peaches. This isn't all on you."

"Vander is correct." Ray's attention turned toward the dirt road leading to Peaches's orchard and the cottage contained within. Only the enemy didn't simply come up the road, they walked through the surrounding prairie and woods. Arie's pack slipped through the darkened night, surrounding Peaches's boundary, barely a toe length away. At that distance, they had to feel the unwelcome prickle of his magic.

A string of large, dark SUVs lumbered up the road, dipping and swaying along the uneven ground. The first rolled to a stop and the were of the hour stepped out.

Sedrick's body cracked, his transformation close at hand.

"Easy," Phil whispered, and Sedrick calmed. At least for now.

Alpha Arie Belview looked good, if not a little wild around the edges. He was a broad individual and his bulk pulled at the bespoke suit that bunched and stretched across his chest. Alpha Belview's thick, chestnut hair and beard were peppered with gray. His cheeks were filled out and his posture was one of smug ease.

The same could not be said for most of his pack. While some appeared well fed and hearty, the majority were too lean. Not emaciated, but whipcord raw with haunted, shifting eyes. Others simply appeared resigned, as if they'd rather be anywhere else than standing on the edge of a bonded pixie's territory.

"Janus," Arie said and suddenly the djinn appeared, as starkly underdressed as before. Janus said nothing, simply stood beside Arie, anticipation lighting his wicked grin.

But it wasn't Janus's appearance that made Vander swear, it was the appearance of a warlock, one with a mere smattering of gray at his temples. This warlock was young.

"That's a bad sign," Vander grumbled before striding forward. Despite his halting hand gesture, Parsnip followed, a barely audible "as if," echoing from Parsnip's lips as he darted past me.

"What the fuck are you doing with the likes of him?" Vander shouted, waving a hand in Arie's general direction. "Sweet Gaia, I don't even want to think of what he asked you to do, let alone the possibility that you agreed."

"Ambrose is a very talented warlock," Arie answered, glee filling every word. "Much more talented than you."

Far from offended, Vander scoffed, waving off the dig. "I doubt that. He's younger and stupider. Most likely he's got ability, but whatever he's got, he threw his life away when he agreed to try and do what we all know you want."

Ambrose was already sickly pale. I hadn't thought it possible for him to get any whiter and yet that's exactly what Vander's words achieved.

Alpha Belview's laughter slithered across my skin and wormed its way into my soul. With glinting, amber eyes, he turned his gaze on Sedrick and Phil. There was far too much pleasure in that stare, too much unmitigated joy.

"Where are my grandchildren, Sedrick?" Arie hummed. "Close by, I've no doubt. We stopped by that little hovel you call home first. I wanted to give you and your...pixie"—Arie sneered the last word, as if calling Phil a pixie was laughable —"a gift."

"We don't need jackshit from you." I don't think any amount of cajoling on Phil's part could calm Sedrick's wolf.

"Oh, I am perfectly aware of that," Arie answered.

"Alpha Arie Belview, you are precariously close to breaking your oath, sworn on fairy law. I would advise choosing your following actions carefully, however, I believe we both know that you have already committed far worse crimes." Ray stepped forward. Heat radiated from him as he slid past. Wendall didn't go with him. He stood his ground. Trinket came running from the forest, shimmying up Wendall's leg and settling on his shoulder, her tail firmly wrapped around his bicep. The ground shook as Ruthie and Dillon followed, still in their wolf forms. The smaller wolf, the one I figured was Shawn, stayed by the tree line, unsure what to do. I was glad the boy stayed where he was—out of sight and out of mind.

Alpha Belview threw his head back and laughed. At least two-thirds of his surrounding pack flinched at the sound.

"You amuse me, Hellfire Rayburn." Arie's grin was positively dripping with arrogance. My eyes flew wide. I'd never heard anyone so boldly insult a fairy.

Ray's eyes swam with fire. "A curious response. A foolish one as well."

All traces of humor fled as Arie's facial features hardened. "It is you who are foolish. The end of fairy law—no, the end of Fairy itself is close at hand." Thrusting out his arm, Arie made a sweeping motion in Janus's direction. "I finally found something more powerful, and I hold its leash."

Janus's eyes narrowed and a handful of tattoos flared. Alpha Belview appeared far too self-absorbed, caught up in his own self-aggrandizing to notice. It was a dangerous oversight. Even if Arie won the day, the creature he hung his victory upon would one day be his destruction. Arie Belview either couldn't or wouldn't see it. More likely still, Arie's arrogance wouldn't allow him to believe he'd meet the same fate as all Janus's previous masters.

Sedrick's rumbled growl vibrated up my spine. "Your stupidity will be everyone's downfall."

"*Stupidity?*" Arie mocked. "I'm hardly an idiot. I'm an entrepreneur." Arie's chest puffed with pride. "When I'm told something is impossible, I see it as a challenge." Arie's grin was back, more wickedly pleased than before. "Take pixie bonds, for example."

Everyone stiffened. Parsnip and Peaches dropped, temporarily grounded by fear.

But Arie wasn't looking at them, his eyes had a single target. "I understand my grandchildren have become rather fond of your pixie, Sedrick. You might want to send them away. I doubt you'll want them to see this."

Sedrick strode forward, Dillon and Ruthie flanking him,

all three standing before Phil. Dillon lunged and snapped, growling low. Ruthie took on a wide-based stance, ready to spring at a moment's notice, all of them determined to protect Phil.

With a casual shrug, Alpha Belview said, "Suit yourselves. Ambrose."

It was all the warlock needed. Raising his hands, sigils danced in the air, floating around a large uncut diamond. Words I didn't understand spilled from Ambrose's lips, drifting into the night, leaving a swath of pain in their wake.

"Fucking shit," Vander cursed. "Don't do it. Don't—" Vander's words were drowned out by Phil's scream.

Chapter Twenty-Nine

My ears rang with Phil's wail, but that pain was nothing compared to Sedrick's howl. That howl quickly magnified when Dillon and Ruthie joined their uncle's horror-stricken one.

"Phil!" Peaches darted to his friend's side. Phil was on the ground his body contorted into the fetal position, his arms wrapped around his middle and fingers balled into the fabric covering his heart.

"Phil. Baby, tell me what's happening." Sedrick grabbed his mate, hauling him onto his lap and holding him close. On his knees, Sedrick rocked Phil, pushing pink strands of hair away from Phil's pale, sweaty face. Ruthie licked the sweat away while Dillon frantically paced, unsure what to do.

"Moon goddess, he's... I can feel our bond breaking. It's shredding, thread by thread." Sedrick choked on a sob. His body shook as tears fell on Phil's face. Wings limp, Phil lay there, unable to speak. Frantic trembling shook his body.

"Ambrose!" Vander screamed. "Stop this. No amount of

money is worth this." Vander pointed at Phil and his surrounding family. "You're killing him."

Ambrose stood there, eyes wide as he took in the fruits of his labor. The warlock almost looked shocked, as if he hadn't expected his efforts to work this well. Or maybe he simply hadn't contemplated what breaking a pixie bond truly meant.

A torrent of fire flew from Ray, aimed directly at Ambrose. The fire slid through Peaches's barrier, Ray's aim true. Janus stepped in front of Ambrose, blocking the deadly fire.

Arie Belview was the only one enjoying the scene, glee in his manic eyes. Burning wolf-bright, those eyes glowed amber. "Wishes are beautiful, especially with a djinn backing them up. Janus was instructed to protect Ambrose."

Janus appeared curious but otherwise bored. Most of Arie Belview's pack stood there, horrified expressions haunting their gaunt faces.

"You're welcome to step outside the barrier." Arie threw his hands wide. "Maybe I'll make a different wish this time. Without Janus's protection, Ambrose is easing pickings."

Ambrose jumped back, eyes flying impossibly wide upon realizing he'd been demoted to bait.

"How in the hell did Ambrose's casting get past Peaches's barrier?" Parsnip asked Vander.

"The casting itself wasn't aimed at an individual, but a magical bond. Peaches's barrier probably didn't see it as a threat." Vander's jaw ground and his fists tightened. I had an idea what was coming. So did Parsnip.

"Don't you dare," Parsnip ordered. "As soon as you step outside that barrier, you're dead. You know that."

"And if I do nothing, then Phil's dead. Sedrick will follow. This is warlock business. It's my responsibility."

Parsnip flew high, staring Vander in the eyes. "Then I'm going with you."

"No, you—"

"Shut up! I'm going with you." Tears rolled down Parsnip's cheeks. With fisted hands, Parsnip wiped them away. I stepped closer to Leon's side. He wasn't necessarily warm, but Leon's touch was soothing.

"This can't be happening," I muttered. Leon said nothing but I caught the mutual glance he shared with Lucroy. I knew what was coming and wanted to find an argument against it but couldn't. It was the right decision.

"I'm not letting you go out there alone either, so don't even think about telling me to stay put," I said before Leon could verbalize his and Lucroy's silently brewing plan.

Leon's lips tilted into a barely there smile. "I would not dream of doing so, beloved."

Despite the situation, or maybe because of it, my chest warmed. "Damn right." Blowing out a deep breath, I said, "If we're doing this, we better get to it."

Turning in unison, we walked to Vander's side. Lucroy was by Leon's side. Peaches was still by Phil's tortured and fading body. Time was running out.

"Are we ready?" Ray asked.

"No," Parsnip answered. "But when has that ever stopped us from doing something immensely stupid?"

"Never," Vander answered. "Gaia, I love you," he said, voice low.

Parsnip clasped Vander's hand, entwining their fingers. Leon's hand found its way into mine. Wendall was by Ray's side, Trinket on his shoulder, gaping maw open, rows of teeth on full display.

"Feel free to rip out as many throats as you want," Wendall instructed Trinket.

"I do not think that will be necessary. Yet." Aurelia's voice echoed none of the surrounding chaos and pain. "I believe this is who you want." Aurelia stood there in her ripped jeans, combat boots, tank top and flannel shirt, one shoulder bare to the humid summer night air. Pushing Ambrose forward, the warlock stumbled, nearly falling on his knees.

"Holy shit," I stammered, mouth open. Leon slid a single finger beneath my chin, closing my gaping jaw.

"Aurelia?" Wendall asked, gaze flicking from the djinn to the warlock she'd neatly snatched.

Aurelia's narrowed eyes scanned each and every one of us. "I am fulfilling Peaches's earlier wish," she simply answered, and yet, that explained nothing.

"My beloved made a wish?" Lucroy sounded just as confused as the rest of us.

"He wished for me to do what I wanted," Aurelia stated.

It was a dangerous wish. I wondered if Peaches understood just how dangerous.

Phil's fresh scream sliced through our inaction. When Ray took a step forward, flaming sword held high, Vander placed a hand on his arm and said, "I've got this." Striding forward, Vander's darkened fingers flew through the air at lightning speed. "Better warlock my ass. Young, stupid, and dangerous is more like it." Done with his casting, Vander slammed a hand into its center. The diamond holding Ambrose's spell shattered, glimmering pieces falling to the ground like sparkling rain.

Phil's cries subsided into heart-wrenching whimpers until an even more disturbing silence took hold. Dillon's and Ruthie's echoing whines added unwelcome background music.

Safe for now, we crowded around the Voss werewolf pack. Arie's screams of fury sounded from outside Peaches's boundary. Ignoring his growing ire, all our concern was for Phil. He still appeared horribly ashen, and his skin was slicked with cooling sweat. I could hear the frantic beat of his heart, the rhythm far too rapid.

Dillon shifted, naked as the day he was born. Kneeling beside Phil, Dillon ran his fingers through pink strands of hair. It was the only part of Phil that didn't look faded.

"Uncle Sed..." Dillon's lower lip wobbled. He was still a child. Ruthie too. They'd already suffered the loss of their mother and father. The fear wafting off the young shifters was palpable. "Is Phil...?" Dillon couldn't finish that scary sentence.

Sedrick gripped Phil tight, but the pixie remained unconscious and limp. "He's going to be fine, Dillon." Ruthie nuzzled in, licking Phil's face again. Sedrick's fingers fisted her fur. "He's going to be just fine."

I noticed the tremble in Sedrick's arm. Phil wasn't the only one physically suffering. They were essentially double mated. Sedrick's wolf had claimed Phil and Phil's home-and-hearth pixie nature had bonded to Sedrick. While Phil had suffered the brunt of the blow, Sedrick wasn't well either.

"Philodendron needs to go home," Ray said.

Peaches's wings fluttered, spreading golden-yellow dust. "Ray's right. We need to get Phil back to his home. Sedrick, Dillon, and Ruthie need to go too. Phil's bonded to all of them. He'll stand the best chance if he's surrounded by that bond. It will help heal him, just like my land heals me."

"I'll take him," Wendall said, pulling our attention to him. "I've been working with my fairy side. I can create a portal. Ray should stay here. He's better in a fight than me." Swallowing hard, Wendall's gaze latched onto Ray's. "I don't want to leave you, but I think I should stay with them. If something happens, they'll need a quick exit and—"

"And your plan is sound," Ray answered, skimming his fingers through Wendall's wavy blond strands of hair.

"Trinket should stay with you. She'll give 'em hell."

"I would be honored to fight alongside the scuttlebutt." Without further prodding, Trinket hopped from Wendall's shoulder to Ray's. Her prehensile tail immediately wrapped around Ray's arm, holding tight. Twittering, Trinket sounded distressed.

"It'll be okay." Wendall scratched her side. "I'll see you soon. Right now, I need to get Phil home."

Legs shaking, Sedrick picked up Phil, cradling him in his arms and close to his chest. "I'm sorry. I want to stay, but—"

"Take care of Philodendron," Lucroy said. "And yourself. Allow us the pleasure of dispatching Arie Belview. You have already paid enough for his trespasses. Let your pack carry some of your burden."

Sedrick sucked in a harsh breath. "An alpha never had a better pack. Pixies, vampires, warlocks, fairies, humans, dwarves... No alpha has ever been prouder, or more grateful. Thank you, Lucroy."

Stepping beside his king, Leon answered, "It is our pleasure, Alpha Voss."

"Ditto on that," Vander answered. "And don't worry about Ambrose. He's out for the count. Activating that shitty charm took a lot out of him. When I shattered the damn thing, Ambrose went down like a sack of potatoes. He'll be out for a long time and when he does come around, he'll wish he were still out cold." With a head shake, Vander lamented, "Damn waste of talent."

"Bye, Ray." Going up on tiptoes, Wendall planted a heated kiss on Ray's lips. "Don't do anything stupid. If you do, Aunt Silvidia will kick your ass. And if she doesn't, then I will." With a final squeeze, Wendall's fingers trailed down Ray's arm before those same fingers lifted, creating an atmospheric tear. With the support of Dillon and Ruthie, Sedrick carried Phil across the threshold.

Before they could vanish completely, Dillon yelled into the forest, "Come on, Shawn." The smaller gray wolf darted from the orchard edge, disappearing behind Dillon right before the tear closed.

With the loss of the wolves and Wendall, our numbers significantly dwindled. Peaches shivered, rubbing his hands up and down his arms. The balmy summer night wasn't the cause of his chills. When I saw him physically flinch, I knew he was in pain too.

"Beloved?" Lucroy's hands took hold of Peaches, stilling his actions. "What is wrong?"

Peaches grabbed his forehead. "He's trying to break through." When Peaches raised his head, his eyes were pinched, and deep grooves marred his forehead. "Arie won't succeed, but what he's doing doesn't feel good."

Lucroy's neck popped, unnaturally twisting from side to side. Talons erupted from his fingers, their touch whisper soft against Peaches's exposed skin.

"You realize he won't stop," Vander bluntly said. "This time it was Phil. Next time it will be Byx or one of your nest-mates. Maybe Johnny or Lizbeth. Arie will keep dangling carrots just outside Peaches's barrier, attempting to lure us out and pick us off one at a time. And while he's doing that, he'll make Peaches's life as hellaciously painful as possible."

"The warlock is correct," Aurelia said plainly. "Rarely have I seen a soul as dark as that alpha's. His core is rotten, and he spreads that rot like a disease. Janus will be all too happy to aid in that endeavor." Aurelia's gaze was distant, staring into the night. "There is only one thing Janus values more than death and destruction."

I started to ask what that was, but Aurelia had already walked away, headed toward the edge of Peaches's barrier.

"Aurelia," Peaches yelled after her. "I wish for you to protect yourself." Peaches bit his bottom lip and scratched at his arms. I knew what the order cost him and yet he'd done it for Aurelia. Djinn had little power if not under the direct command of a wish.

Twisting her head just enough to see her grin, Aurelia said, "Your wish is appreciated and shall be enacted without hesitation."

"What's she doing?" Parsnip asked, hovering closer to me.

"I've no idea," I answered. "Any thoughts, Peaches?"

"No, but Arie pulled his pack back. They aren't trying to breach my barrier any longer so I'm grateful." When I glanced at Peaches, he was slumped against Lucroy's side.

"You really wished for Aurelia to 'do as she liked'?" Vander asked.

"I did. It seemed the right thing to do. It's the closest I can come to giving her a modicum of freedom," Peaches answered.

"Beloved, Aurelia herself said it is unwise to free her."

"Yeah, I know. I just... I can't stomach thinking of anyone enslaved like that. It's wrong."

"No argument here," Vander agreed. "It's just a dangerous gambit, that's all."

Leon's lean body stiffened, and his fingers tightened against my side. "Yeah, I know," I said, confirming his silent agreement with Vander.

Ray remained eerily quiet. Trinket shifted on his shoulder —a coiled snake ready to strike. I wanted to ask what he was thinking, but I swallowed my words when Aurelia reached the edge of Peaches's boundary and spoke.

"Is this the path you truly desire, Janus?" Aurelia asked.

Janus walked forward, stopping just on the other side of the barrier. Arie's face flushed and his cheeks puffed. Lips pulled into a snarl, I figured it was killing him that Janus made a move without his specific authorization.

Janus's gaze slipped past Aurelia, staring each and every one of us down. "I'd say you've gone soft, but you always were the weakest of us." Janus's beefy arms crossed over his chest. "You lack the necessary instincts to do what's required."

Aurelia tilted her head to the side. With her back to us, I couldn't see her expression, but her voice was bland when she answered, "I rarely saw the necessity in what was *required* of me. Only the waste of it all." Hands stuffed into the deep pockets of her camo pants, Aurelia rolled her shoulders. "As a courtesy to one of my own, I will offer this warning: Djinn are not as indestructible as once imagined. I was asked to speak with you, to see if there was any hope of salvaging your current state. If so, then every effort will be made to preserve you. If not..." Aurelia shrugged. "The choice is yours."

Janus gave an expectedly suspicious smirk. "A new low, even for you. We are too powerful to have use of lies."

"I am well aware."

Janus's smirk temporarily fell but it returned with frightening speed when Arie said, "Janus, I wish for you to do everything in your power to destroy Peaches's barrier. Use whatever means. Kill anyone not associated with me or my pack."

Janus's grin widened into a teeth-revealing smile. "With pleasure, master."

Hands spread wide, Janus stared Aurelia in the eyes as the ground beneath our feet shook. Anyone with wings took to the air. Leon's legs widened, bracing himself.

"Goddess, he's ripping apart the ground," Peaches gasped.

"I'll dig deeper than your precious boundary. And when I find the end, I'll lift the earth, tipping it upside down and destroying the land you love." The glee lighting Janus's words shivered down my spine, shaking me more than the ground.

"Do not say I did not warn you, Janus," Aurelia said before she winked out, disappearing into the night. In her place stood a wholly different creature. Aurelia brought the necromancer onto the playing field.

Head bent and shoulders rounded, Erasmus deeply sighed and said, "I'd hoped it wouldn't come to this."

Erasmus. Necromancer. Untested and untried savior. Our only hope had finally shown. I slid my fingers under Leon's shoulders, ready to pull him off the ground. I wasn't certain my small body could hold him aloft. What I was certain of was I would expend every ounce of will to make sure I kept Leon safe.

My fingers tightened when Erasmus showed, gripping just shy of pain. "Goddess, is he really going to—"

"I believe he is," Leon answered. "The question is, will it truly work?"

Regardless, the ground steadied as Janus got his first look at a necromancer. Head cocked to the side, Janus asked, "What are you?"

"Something you haven't seen before. Something that didn't exist when you were made." Raising his head, Erasmus's dark, sweat-laden hair matted against his neck. "To be fair, I'd never met a djinn before Aurelia. It was a rather eye-opening experience."

Arie's temper flared. "I did not wish you to talk the enemy to death. I told you to destroy Peaches's barrier."

Janus's eyes narrowed and his jaw ticked. "I will fulfill your wish in due time."

"You will do it now!" Arie shot forward, grabbing Janus's arm and attempting to twirl the djinn his direction. "I've waited long enough. I've been mocked and disregarded, and I'll have no more. I am Alpha Arie Belview, and I will have my revenge." Arie's bellow rattled the surrounding trees. Most of his pack cringed, rolling in on themselves in an attempt to appear smaller and less noticeable.

"I'm afraid you're going to have to wait a little longer, Alpha Belview," Erasmus calmly said. "To answer Janus's earlier question, I'm a necromancer and—"

"I don't give a shit what you are," Arie slung back.

"You should." Erasmus's tone was deadly quiet. "You should care a great deal."

Arie's mouth snapped, his eyeteeth slipping past the edge of his lips.

"Despite being a necromancer, or maybe because of it, I value life a great deal. I don't take lives; I bring them back, temporary as those lives might be." Erasmus's inhale lifted his shoulders. "Janus, a great and terrible wrong was done to you. To all djinn. I wasn't certain, just from meeting Aurelia, but now that I've had a chance to feel you out, I'm surer than ever. Your life was stolen from you, woven into an object that has kept you trapped. The good news is that I'm about to free you from that trap. The bad news is that I'm not at all certain what that will do to you. I'll apologize ahead of time if you find the experience painful."

Only now realizing the potential danger, Janus retreated a step. "You're lying."

"I don't think so. If I am, then it's not intentional. Either way, let's find out together."

Without further conversation, Erasmus raised one hand and said, "Ah, there you are. Time to come home." The faintest glow lit the area in front of Erasmus's outstretched hand. Seconds ticked by and I thought perhaps we'd all overestimated what Erasmus was capable of. That fear dissipated when Janus's mouth opened in a silent scream. Head thrown back, body contorting, Janus's body lunged forward, as if being shot in the back.

Chapter Thirty

LEON

Shocked silence filled the air. Janus's body hovered and then collapsed as if the strings holding him were suddenly severed. The inked tattoos covering his skin evaporated like they'd never existed. Still broad and large, Janus's ears became small, like a human's. Curled into a ball, he lay there on the ground, shivering but alive.

Arie stared, mouth opened and eyes wide with disbelief. Alpha Belview recovered first and ordered, "Janus, I wish you to rise."

Nothing happened.

"Janus! You will do as your master commands."

Aurelia appeared again, this time outside the barrier, kneeling by Janus's side. "He no longer has a master to command him." Looking up at Arie's seething face, Aurelia remained calm. "I believe he was warned. As were you." Standing, her attention turned to Erasmus. "It is as you said it would be. The magical bindings were destroyed when you returned Janus's soul. He is alive and...human." Aurelia said that last with a bit of confusion. No one still living knew if all djinn were created from humans or if witches used other species. Given the similarities between Aurelia and Janus, most likely Aurelia's original form had been human also.

"You...y-you can't," Arie muttered. "It's not possible."

"I believe you have just been proven wrong," I answered, most likely echoing other thoughts.

"No." The word started out low and grew in strength. "No!" Arie growled.

"I do not believe Alpha Belview takes defeat well," Lucroy said, tone icy.

Peaches huffed and taunted, "You'd think by now he'd be better at it."

Arie roared and when he turned, his arms were covered in fur and claws sprouted from his fingertips. "You think this is the end? You think you've defeated me?"

Vander sighed, long and deep. "He's right, you know. This shit will keep going until he's dead."

"Alpha Belview's sentence under fairy law is clear," Ray answered. "Peaches, while your aide has been appreciated, I believe it is time to leave its safety."

"Be my guest, but also be careful," Peaches answered eagerly. "There are still a lot of wolves out there and not many of you."

"There's plenty of us," Parsnip said, flying high and chest puffed out. "Besides, it's clear most of his pack doesn't want to fight."

"Shawn's mother might be out there," Peaches reminded us.

"Damn," Vander cursed. "Your beloved has a point, Lucroy. I hate killing the innocent."

"Then try and just knock them out," Parsnip answered. "We'll sort out who's who later."

"Easier said than done," I said while allowing my transformation to overtake me. While not as tall as Lucroy, my vampiric form was impressive. When I glanced in Phlox's direction, I had to look down. My beloved had already shifted. Puffed up, he appeared twice his actual size. Claws digging into the ground, it was clear Phlox was ready to rend flesh from bones.

"Shit, that's what he is?" Peaches said, flying lower. "Dylan and Ruthie will be sorry they missed this. He's so freaking cute." Directing a hand Phlox's direction, Peaches yanked his fingers back as Phlox bared his teeth and swatted.

"I do not believe that wise, beloved," Lucroy said while coming to Peaches side.

"Do not underestimate him due to his size," I defended my beloved before leaning over and raking my talons through his thick fur. Pleasured pride rolled through me when Phlox easialy allowed the action. "Stay close," I whispered.

Phlox's low, grumbling answer was somewhere between a hiss and meow.

The sound of tearing fabric met my ears. Arie's pack shifted while the alpha himself did a partial shift, appearing like something out of a horror film. Remaining bipedal, it was a form only strong alphas could hold. Sedrick should be here. He should have the pleasure of bringing Arie Belview to heel. But Sedrick Voss had learned a lesson Arie Belview never would. Love was far more precious than hate and revenge. Sedrick was where he was needed, where his life resided, where his soul came alive.

Arie's words were garbled when he spoke. "Pathetic, hiding behind a pixie's power."

Peaches's opened his mouth, but Lucroy's taloned touch silenced him. My king understood as well as me nothing Peaches said would make Arie Belview understand. His words would be wasted.

"Kick his pompous ass," Peaches said.

Lucroy answered, "With pleasure."

Stepping through Peaches's barrier was as easy as walking down a street. His magic swept over me, its welcoming strength inviting me back when I wished. As soon as we were on the other side, Arie raised his head and howled. His pack answered that call and came running. It was impossible to tell a reluctant wolf from an eager one.

"Look at their weight," Vander said as he formed a sigil and slammed his hand into it. "Remember, the reluctant ones didn't appear as well fed." The wolf running at him fell to the ground, knocked out but still alive.

I wasn't sure judging by weight alone was wise, but it was better than nothing. A large, fully fleshed out wolf leapt at me. Twisting, I drove my talons into its underbelly, tearing through entrails and ripping them out as I pulled away. The wolf went down, rolling on his side and quickly bleeding out.

Phlox sped past me. Jumping high, he latched onto the back of a smaller wolf, this one appreciably leaner. Teeth sinking in, Phlox shook his head and sank his claws deep. As the wolf attempted to buck him off, I grabbed it and slammed its head to the ground. The blow was hard enough to knock the wolf unconscious, but not deadly.

We tried weeding through the onslaught, but they kept coming. I'd just pulled my talons out of a large chest when something slammed into my side, nearly driving me to the ground. A sharp, stinging pain ripped through my side. Twisting, I managed to throw my attacker off. I barely held in my surprise when I turned and saw it was a very human Janus, wielding a wicked dagger. Fresh blood leaked from a split lip, my own borrowed blood dripping from the blade in his hand.

Janus's grin no longer held a mouthful of razor-sharp teeth, but it was just as wildly sadistic. Maybe more so with its touch of desperation.

"I'd forgotten," Janus huffed, breathing labored. "I'd forgotten what I was before that witch found me." Janus's smile widened. "I was a killer before." He laughed gleefully. "That's why she chose me. I was mercilessly deadly even before she made me what I was." Holding up his dagger, Janus gazed at it lovingly. "She used my favorite weapon as my object of attachment. I didn't remember that, but I do now." Janus tilted his head and stared at the night sky. "I might be human, but I'm still going to kill you." Twisting the blade, he pointed at my head. "A vamp can't live without their head or heart. You're too fucking easy to kill."

My side ached but was already healing. Crouched low, I readied myself for the attack. Janus took a single step before he screamed. Scrambling around his back, Janus turned, and I could see Phlox. His claws were deep in Janus's skin, as were his teeth. Climbing Janus's back, Phlox made his way toward the tender flesh residing along Janus's neck. I knew what he meant to do and moved to help him.

Phlox's claw and my talon met, each sliding through Janus's thick neck, slicing through each carotid artery. Blood spilled like lava down Janus's chest, soaking his skin. Janus blinked, fingers clawing at the open wounds. But it was too late. Far too late. Janus was already dead, his mind simply hadn't caught up with the physical blow.

Leaping off his back, Phlox landed on all fours before running in my direction. I picked him up, placing his smaller form on my shoulder, holding him much as Wendall did Trinket as we watched the light die from Janus's ancient eyes.

It was a rather uneventful end to a magical life. When I glanced up, Aurelia stood in the background. She'd chosen not to engage in the fight. A mere spectator. Her expression was unreadable as she looked down on Janus's unmoving body.

A shot of fire flickered to my right, pulling my attention to Ray as he trapped a group of wolves within a flaming inferno. It was a cage they had no hope of escape from. Trinket was nearby, tail wrapped around the slender neck of a smaller wolf.

The wolf bucked and ran but eventually its legs went out from under them, and they fell to the ground, unconscious.

I searched for our main target, finally finding Arie Belview in the back of the fray, using his pack as a living shield. They had no choice but to fight. Some of them obviously relished the bloodshed while the majority only obeyed Arie's command for fear of what would happen to their loved ones. It was clear that Arie Belview would offer his entire pack to slaughter for the chance of survival. While we strived to save those who did not truly wish to fight, it was becoming increasingly difficult to adhere to those high ideals. Keeping them alive took far more effort than dispatching them.

Jumping from my shoulder, Phlox shot into the melee, and I followed. We worked our way toward Vander and Parsnip. I'd wondered what use Parsnip would be. The pixie flew just out of wolf reach, scattering dust in his wake. Enough dust made it close enough to the wolves to induce sneezing fits. The distraction gave Vander enough time to formulate a sigil and put them to sleep. It was a surprisingly effective system.

Lucroy's body flashed through the heart of the pack, breaking them up as if they were little more than pool balls.

Ray's arm raised, blazing sword lashing out and slicing through a heavy body. The scent of burnt fur hit my nose and made me cringe. Raising his arm again, Ray suddenly stopped, his body turning and stilling.

A heavy weight fell across the land. The sounds of battle dwindled as the oppressive feel hit each and every creature. The night went deathly silent. Not even the wind dared breathe.

"My queen," Ray reverently said, flaming sword disappearing into the ether.

Queen Silvidia's arrival stilled every snarl, rooted every paw, and grabbed every creature's attention. A crimson, nearly see-through gown barely covered her small body. White hair flowed around her shoulders and flowers bloomed throughout. Queen Silvidia's peach eyes swirled as they glanced around the carnage.

"It appears as though you have been very busy, Hellfire." Queen Silvidia's voice was like liquid honey, dripping and sticking to every pore. Phlox leapt into my arms, and I cradled him to my chest. His deep, resonating purr rumbled through my skin.

Queen Silvidia's bare feet gently walked along the ground. Flowers bloomed within thickets of bloodshed. When she reached Ray, Queen Silvidia slid her fingers against his cheek and warmly smiled. "You have done well, Hellfire. As expected."

"And you, my queen?"

Queen Silvidia's smile scrunched her eyes. "Oh, I had my own bit of fun. Hamish was quite cross with me for being so hands on." Twisting to the side, Queen Silvidia waved her hand. "You may come out now. Let your loved ones see you are safe and well."

A head cautiously peeked out from the atmospheric tear floating near the ground. That head led to a body, others just as cautiously stepping through, their stunned eyes wide and fearful.

Yips and joyful howls erupted as wolves shifted back to their humanoid forms. Shouts of unexpected happiness filled the silence as loved ones collapsed into each other's arms, sobbing with released anxiety.

"It was just as the young wolf, Shawn, relayed," Queen Silvidia said. "They were locked inside rooms. Gilded cages meant to keep his pack under tight reign. Pathetic," Queen Silvidia spat, her eyes narrowed and gaze traveling to where Arie stood. "I have never seen an alpha sink so low."

Arie backed away, shoulders bent, and teeth bared. He

snapped in Queen Silvidia's general direction, but the action was little more than base theatrics. The wolves standing between Arie and the Queen of Fairy slinked away, tails tucked between their legs. Low, pleading whimpers replaced angry growls. Lunging, Arie snapped at his fleeing pack. Clearly, their loyalty only ran so deep. Self-preservation was a far more powerful motivator.

Ignoring Arie for now, Queen Silvidia's gaze tracked the blood-soaked field. "Wendall?" she questioned.

"He is safe, my queen." Ray quickly explained what happened earlier. Oppressive power radiated from Queen Silvidia like oceanic waves. Holding my ground became increasingly difficult.

"Is this warlock still alive?" Queen Silvidia asked.

Vander cleared his throat. "He is. Unconscious, but still breathing. Activating that charm took a lot out of him and when I destroyed it." Vander shrugged. "I think the magical backlash was a bit much."

"You will give this warlock to me." It wasn't a request.

Vander's jaw worked and his eyebrows scrunched. "He... he's very young."

"Youth is not a defense," Queen Silvidia answered. "But I will take your thoughts into consideration. I will also consult the victims of his crime."

Vander lowered his head. "Thank you, Queen Silvidia."

Queen Silvidia's answer was quiet dismissal. "Now, to finally deal with this unworthy alpha."

Arie made a move, lunging not toward Queen Silvidia, but in the direction of the surrounding woods. Queen Silvidia's tinkling laughter danced down my spine.

"How amusing." She sounded genuinely joyful.

Arie didn't get far. He ran into an unyielding, invisible wall. Enraged, he howled and immediately ran the other direction, only to have the same thing happen again. Alpha Arie Belview was trapped in a prison of his own making.

Continuing forward, Queen Silvidia didn't bother stepping around the dead and dying. Her gentle feet did not shy away from the carnage, but stepped upon their flesh, using it as her own, gruesome red carpet.

"You were given a chance, Alpha Belview," she calmly said.

Arie's snarls and howls increased in volume before going eerily silent. He still wailed his frustrated anger, but it could no longer be heard.

"My, my. You are a loud one." Queen Silvidia shook her head. Everywhere her hair touched, fresh blossoms appeared. Spreading her arms wide, Queen Silvidia motioned at the blood-stained ground. "Such wastefulness. And for what? Your worthless pride? Power? Revenge? Tell me, Alpha Belview, what has such endeavors gained you?"

Arie threw his head back. I imagined the wail of his howl but was thankful I could not hear it.

Queen Silvidia continued walking toward him. "Nothing. It has gained you nothing. Your daughter is dead. Your grandchildren want nothing to do with you. Most of your pack loathe your very existence. The Belview name will forever be associated with greed, death, and arrogance. And you are about to die. So much potential and yet you threw it all away for nothing. Worse than that, you orchestrated the death of dozens of pixies in your quest for the source of ultimate power." Queen Silvidia's gaze landed on Janus's dead body. Aurelia still stood in the background, silently still and cautiously observing.

Deeply sighing, Queen Silvidia waved a disinterested hand in Arie's direction. "Perhaps fairy law needs a refresh. One such as you should have been eliminated long ago."

Phlox stiffened within my arms. Fairy law could already be

brutal. I doubted any of us relished the thought of it becoming even stricter.

Arie threw his body against the barrier imprisoning him, headless of the self-harm he caused. It should have been satisfying. Instead, it was pathetically disturbing.

"Enough," Queen Silvidia ordered and Arie's body stilled but his eyes remained wide. "Let us be done with it."

I'd expected some type of motion, a hand gesture, something that would indicate Queen Silvidia's intentions. Instead, all she did was turn, disregarding Arie Belview's gasp before his neck twisted, snapping his spinal cord and dropping the powerful alpha to the ground. This time, the silence emanating from Arie's direction wasn't caused by magical manipulation.

Alpha Arie Belview's reign was over. His chest didn't rise, and his black heart no longer beat. Just like Janus's death, Arie Belview's was disturbingly quick and simple. Death remained the great equalizer. There would be no second life offered to Janus or Alpha Belview. They'd squandered the ones gifted to them and had not earned a second opportunity.

Dismissing Arie's corpse, Queen Silvidia made her way back to Ray. "My father would be terribly disappointed in me."

"My queen?"

"I am afraid I have little interest in the torture he loved so dearly." Queen Silvidia stared at her empty palm. "It has never held such appeal to me. I find the whole thing...tedious."

Ray gave a discrete bow while the rest of us held our collective tongues.

"I trust you can sort out the rest?" Queen Silvidia asked Ray.

"Of course."

"Thank you, Hellfire."

I thought that would be it, that the Queen of Fairy would

leave us. Instead, she walked toward Peaches's barrier, stopping just outside it. "Peaches, may I enter?"

"Oh!" Peaches fluttered about, spreading golden dust everywhere. "Yes. Please do." He waved her inside.

"Thank you. You have a lovely orchard. I would enjoy returning when the situation is calmer."

"As long as you mean my land no harm, you are welcome anytime," Peaches answered easily.

Queen Silvidia smiled, and her peach eyes glowed. "A most generous offer. Now, if you will allow, I will remove this warlock from your presence." She stepped toward Ambrose, his body still unconscious and prone on the ground.

Peaches's appeared alarmed and his eyes immediately sought out Vander. Queen Silvidia interrupted Peaches's concerns. "He will be taken to Fairy but as promised, I will withhold judgement until I've spoken further with Warlock Kines and Philodendron. Is this acceptable?"

I thought Queen Silvidia asked more out of politeness than true need. Had she wanted, Ambrose's body would already be in a holding cell deep within Fairy.

"More than acceptable," Peaches said.

"Excellent. I will take my leave then." Creating a new atmospheric tear, Queen Silvidia walked toward it, Ambrose's body hovering close behind. "Hellfire, please tell my nephew that I am sorry I missed him today but look forward to seeing him soon. Do not be a stranger." With that, the Queen of Fairy walked through the atmospheric slit and disappeared. The window sealed behind her.

The oppressive curtain Queen Silvidia brought with her dissipated with her absence. Familiar night sounds filtered back in, erasing the surreal atmosphere.

"Damn, djinn and the fairy queen." Erasmus leaned against an apple tree, Aurelia oddly close by. "Pops is never going to believe this."

"Sweet Gaia save us all," Vander lamented. "Nikodemus will hold this over my head for the rest of my life."

The universe quickly answered Vander's painful lament. Phone ringing, Vander pulled it from his pocket and groaned. "Speak of the devil."

Erasmus just laughed.

Chapter Thirty-One

PHLOX

"I promise, we're fine," I reassured Auntie Tandra. I typically kept Auntie Tandra in the dark about my missions, even when they were over. But this one was different. She'd been worried sick about the pixie trafficking ring and needed to know it was shut down. Auntie Tandra was expectedly upset when she learned the part I'd played.

"I hate thinking of you in that much danger," Auntie Tandra said. "You know I hate your job. At the same time, I'm also so damn proud of you I want to go shout from the rooftops what you did."

"Auntie Tandra, you can't—"

"Oh, I know I can't do that, but it doesn't stop me wishing I could. Besides, you know me, I'd post it on social media first." Auntie Tandra giggled. "I'm joking. Well, not about wanting to post it, but you know I wouldn't do that."

Thankfully, I did know.

"So, when do I get to meet your mate?" she asked, all coyness gone and tone deadly serious. "I need to make certain he's treating you right. A vampire," Auntie Tandra clucked.

"Who would have thought? Certainly not me. Not that I'm judging. As long as you're happy and he's treating you like the gem you are, then we'll get along fine."

Warmth flooded my chest, and I grabbed the fabric over my heart. "Thanks, Auntie." I knew she'd understand. Not all pixies would, but Auntie Tandra wasn't like that. My happiness truly was all that mattered to her.

I checked the time and reluctantly said, "I need to get going. The party should be starting soon, and I don't want to miss it."

"No, no. I don't want to keep you. Thank you for calling and telling me what you can. I can't tell you what a relief it is to know this particular pixie ring has been dismantled. Others will most likely pop up."

"And I'll be there to shut them down," I promised.

Auntie Tandra inhaled deeply. "That is and isn't a comforting thought. Regardless, I'm so proud of you, Phlox. Perovskia would be too. Your mother would be brimming with pride. Have a good night. I love you, Phlox."

"Love you too, Auntie."

Auntie Tandra blew a kiss across the phone line before the call ended. I sat on the edge of Leon's bed, kicking my feet back and forth as I stared at the darkened screen. My fingers swept the mark on my neck, making me shiver. Despite our exhaustion after the showdown with Arie Belview, Leon and I'd come back to Dusk and claimed each other. Leon sported my mating mark, and I was equally marked as his beloved.

That had been a little over a week ago. Queen Silvidia acted quickly, and fairies tracked down each and every member of the pixie trafficking ring Arie Belview was responsible for. Those individuals were promptly dispatched. Over a dozen pixies were rescued in time. Seven weren't so lucky but their bodies were found and returned to their loved ones. Countless others were unaccounted for. Queen Silvidia, along with the Magical Usage Council agreed to continue working until all their fates were discovered. Of course, we knew they wouldn't be found alive, but it was important to bring their bodies home.

I'm not certain whose idea the party was. Lucroy offered to host. Dusk would be closed tonight to all but his nestmates and Sedrick's pack. We'd waited for Phil to recover. From what I understood, Phil was unconscious for two days. He'd gotten steadily stronger and was now well enough to leave his bonded home for a few hours.

Peaches also suffered. While he wasn't away from his bonded land, that stunt Janus tried to pull by ripping the ground apart had done a lot of damage. Peaches spent the earlier part of the week repairing the land's foundation. Lucroy stayed at Mulligan's Orchard, watching over and taking care of his beloved.

Vander was also tired. Parsnip called a few days ago, agitated worry making him grumpy. Evidently, Vander extended himself a little too far and had taken four days to fully recuperate. Byx wasn't pleased either, but like Parsnip, she was more concerned than angry.

As far as I knew, Erasmus was long gone. He'd taken off shortly after Queen Silvidia. I'm not certain what his frame of mind was. His actions hadn't killed Janus. In fact, I believe returning Janus's soul would have allowed him to live out a full, human life, if he'd chosen to do so. But that wasn't Janus. Whether djinn or human, his soul was a black pit of violent desire.

Erasmus offered to do the same for Aurelia. So far, she'd declined. However, Peaches said Aurelia had an odd fascination with Erasmus and continually stalked the necromancer. Peaches didn't seem nearly as concerned as the rest of us regarding this development. Well, Wendall didn't act too concerned either. I would have felt more at ease if Aurelia wanted to go back to sleep.

She didn't. Aurelia was on a loose leash. Time would tell if that was wise or not.

The double door leading to Lucroy's underground sanctuary opened. I easily recognized Leon's light footfalls.

"Beloved?" Leon called out even though I knew he could hear my heartbeat and knew exactly where I was.

Hopping off the bed, I flew into Leon's open arms. My inner cat and I were in heavenly agreement when it came to Leon's touch.

"Did your phone call with your aunt go well?"

"Very well." I didn't tell Leon that Auntie Tandra was proud of me. I didn't think I'd be able to contain my tears if I did. Instead, I said, "She wants to meet you."

Leon pulled back, eyes slightly widened, and eyebrows raised. "Should I be concerned?"

"No. She'll love you just like I do." Wrapping my arms around Leon's neck, I flew up and slammed our lips together. Leon's fangs nipped my lower lip and he groaned when my blood hit his tongue.

"So infinitely delicious." Leon's purr rivaled my cat's.

I nuzzled Leon's neck, rubbing my cheek along his mating mark. I easily felt the fruits of my labor as Leon's cock thickened against my thigh.

"If you keep doing that, we shall miss the party," Leon gasped.

"Is that such a bad idea?" Right now, I didn't think so.

"My king would be disappointed, but he would understand."

I'd learned that disappointing Lucroy wasn't something that sat easily with my mate. He did not love Lucroy Moony as he did me, but Leon respected Lucroy and was loyal. It was one of my mate's best qualities.

Reluctantly, I let Leon go and said, "We'd better head up there before I change my mind."

Flying, I kept ahold of Leon's hand as I made my way up the stairs. When the doors opened, music filled the stairwell, laughter hot on its heels.

Ooh, Peaches was right. Johnny's cousin made the best honeysuckle mead. I sipped the sweet nectar and leaned back. My wings spread flat and wide against the back of the booth we'd all crammed ourselves into. Currently, I was content where I was. Peaches and Parsnip were out on the dance floor, flying high and spreading dust everywhere. A large group of dwarves were dancing underneath, just out of range of their falling dust. Johnny and Lizbeth ran the bar. They'd sent the other employees home given the smaller crowd.

Phil leaned against Sedrick. He looked nearly normal. I thought the area under his eyes still appeared a bit bruised, but his pink hair glimmered in Dusk's low lights. They'd brought Dillon and Ruthie with them tonight and the children were out on the dance floor with the dwarves.

"They're having a good time," Phil lazily said while one of his fingers toyed with the diamond and platinum choker wrapped around his neck.

"Moon goddess only knows what kind of language we'll be subjected to." Sedrick's voice was fondly gruff. "Burt and Ollie aren't the best influences."

"It could be a lot worse," Vander offered before taking a large drink of burnt rum. "I'm always amazed Byx turned out so well. Georgiana gave her a strong base foundation that even I couldn't ruin."

"Idiot," Byx said before sending a zap Vander's way. He jumped and rubbed his arm, but Vander's grin said he wasn't upset. "I'm gonna go join the dwarves." Byx downed her soda before she looked at me and said, "Phlox—is it okay if I call you that instead of Frost?" Byx looked around the table before her eyes settled on me. "I mean, if you're staying and all . . ."

I'd shared my true name with everyone shortly after the battle with Arie. Most were used to calling me Frost. I wasn't particular to either name and answered to both. Truthfully, I only cared what Leon called me.

"Phlox is fine," I easily answered.

Byx gave a firm nod before scrunching her fingers in a gimme motion. "I think those meerkat hair clips still need a little work. Give them to me before we leave, and I'll see what I can do."

I touched the sleeping meerkats. That was mostly what they did. I didn't mind so much. They were still super cute.

"You guys need any refills?" Wendall asked, a light bin of dirty glasses balanced on his hip.

"Sit down and take a load off," Vander said, slapping a nearby chair.

Trinket cooed but Wendall shook his head. "Maybe later. I need to get back to the washroom." Wendall's grin widened. "Ray's washing the glasses. I need to make certain he's not screwing it up."

Laughing, Wendall wove his way around the dwarves, wiggling his hips as he made his way past the bar and into the back.

"Fucking hell, I'd like to see that," Vander said. "*The* Hell-fire Rayburn—dishwasher. What we do for love." Vander fingered the ring on his finger. It was lit up crimson and burned bright.

"Never a truer statement spoken," Lucroy said as he came around from the back of the booth. His gaze settled on Peaches, a soft, fond smile tilting his lips. Settling into the booth, Lucroy's gaze momentarily strayed to Leon and while his fond smile changed, the light in his eyes did not.

"Speaking of true statements," Sedrick started, leaning forward and sounding serious, "I can't thank you enough for what each and every one of you did. Without you, Phil would—"

"No thanks are necessary, my friend," Vander quickly cut in when Sedrick's voice wobbled. "Ambrose was desperate and naïve. Not every warlock has a Georgiana to keep them on the straight and narrow."

"Queen Silvidia came to the house," Phil said. "She asked if I wanted Ambrose killed." Phil swallowed hard and shook his head. "I...I didn't know what to say. I mean, I know what he did and that he was trying to kill me, but I couldn't..."

Sedrick palmed Phil's cheek. "Of course you couldn't. You wouldn't be Phil if you did."

"You're not mad?" Phil asked.

"Never," Sedrick quickly answered before leaning in and kissing Phil.

Vander's elbows landed on the table as he leaned forward. "Ambrose was an idiot, but like I said, he's young. Honestly, I don't think he fully understood what he was doing or its ramifications. Manipulating magic is like that. There are a lot of things you can do, but that doesn't mean you should. Some of us learn that sooner than others." Vander took another drink before slamming his empty glass back on the table. "Ambrose is going to stay in Fairy for a bit. I've agreed to take him in when Queen Silvidia deems it appropriate for him to leave. Fuck knows when that will be. From what I understand, time moves differently in Fairy. I could be dead before that day comes." Vander huffed but didn't seem overly concerned about it.

"How does Parsnip feel about that?" I asked.

"Relatively okay." Vander grinned and leaned back while

pointing a black tipped finger in Sedrick's direction. "Besides, I'd say I got off easy. I've just got one wayward warlock to wrangle, unlike some of us at this table."

Sedrick's growl rumbled through his chest. "By pack law, Queen Silvidia should be the new alpha. She's the one that finally killed that asshole." We all knew it grated on Sedrick, that he'd been denied the honor of dispatching Arie Belview. "Regardless, somehow I've still been saddled with digging through the Belview pack trauma."

"It's not the Belview pack any longer," Phil corrected. "It's the Voss pack, and it's Dillon and Ruthie's legacy. You will make it a pack worthy of respect and of your niece and nephew." Phil's tender smile matched his gentle touch as his fingers raked along Sedrick's beard. "Arie's pack is so desperate for honorable leadership. You're the perfect alpha for the job."

I couldn't have said it better. "The Magical Usage Council agrees and has offered whatever support they can give." I wasn't really certain what that was, but the offer had been made and I wanted to make sure it was relayed.

"Will you have time, with the mine as well?" Lucroy asked.

"I've spoken with Burt and Ollie. That land belongs to the dwarves as much as it does me. We're still working out the details, but I'm planning on turning it over to them. They'll have majority stock in the mine. I hired Ray to take care of the legal details."

Lucroy smirked, barely short of showing fang. "And how is Hellfire faring now that he is back to doing menial legal work?"

"Damned if I know," Sedrick answered while pulling at his beard. "Fairies are hard to read."

"Not that hard," Phil said. "Ray is happy, although I'm sure that has a lot more to do with Wendall than legal work."

Johnny walked up, placing fresh glasses of honeysuckle mead, burnt rum, and a beer for Sedrick on the table. Leaning in, Johnny whispered, voice just high enough for all of us to hear. "Wendall told me that he and Ray agreed to officially share their bonds." Johnny glanced over his shoulder. "Wendall was all kinds of embarrassed when he told me, but you know how that kid is. Don't worry, I plan on pestering him. I'll know when the deed's done and when it is, I expect congratulations all around." Johnny pointed a finger at each of us before trotting off.

"Well, I'll be damned." Vander grinned, wide and bright. "It's about time."

Leon's fingers found mine, entwining together and squeezing tight. Bonds were important. Bonds of love. Bonds of friendship. Bonds of comradery. When I was assigned this mission, I never dreamed I'd find all three.

Glancing at Leon, there was no doubt where I belonged. My mate would never try and cage or change me. When the Magical Usage Council sent me on the next mission, he would be right there by my side. Johnny could run the bar without him, and Lucroy and Peaches agreed to open the orchard to Lucroy's nestmates when they needed their king.

Leon was mine and I was his. We'd make Rutherford Haven home base, but it didn't hem us in. Everyone needed a touchstone, a place where they felt welcome and safe. Rutherford Haven would be that for us. It would be the physical representation of the love we held for each other in our hearts.

Without giving it much thought, my clothes fell away as I transformed into my Pallas's cat form. Crawling onto Leon's lap, I dug my claws in and kneaded his pants. Purrs rumbled through the air and Leon's slender fingers slipped into my thick fur. There was no place I'd rather be. No place that had ever felt safer. No place I'd ever felt so warm.

Leon was my mate, and I was his perfectly peculiar pixie beloved.

Epilogue

ERASMUS

Some graveyards were more peaceful than others. On a scale of one to ten, with one being blissfully silent and ten being rave level ear piercing, I'd place Trinity's Holy Cross Cemetery at a two. Soft murmurs of souls long gone filtered in and out of my brain like soft elevator music. Overall, their hums were content and distant with the passage of time. The dead were like that. The more time passed, the quieter they became. Only the truly pissed or wronged souls retained their loud tenor.

My witching hour walk would have been far more peaceful if I'd been alone. Unfortunately, I'd gained a rather unique shadow since visiting Rutherford Haven. I doubted anyone else could claim the willing company of a djinn.

"Your work is very morbid," Aurelia stated flatly. There was no judgement. She was merely stating the facts as she saw them. Her words were a variation of similar statements she'd made over the past few weeks.

"To some," I answered, mimicking my own familiar answer. I didn't bother telling Aurelia that I wasn't technically on a job. I'd finished that work earlier in another cemetery. That plot of land had been a level nine. It was loud and made my head pound. Many of the graves were less than a decade old and their inhabitants were not a content group.

While my paying job only entailed speaking with one particular soul, the others chattered away, vying for my attention. It had been difficult keeping them away long enough to concentrate on Antony Livingston.

I smirked at the memory. Mr. Livingston was a firecracker in life and death. He was none too pleased his grandchildren exhumed his body and even less happy they'd hired me to interrogate him.

Antony's grandchildren were typical clients—greedy. Stocks, bonds, jewels, and cold hard cash were *missing*, and they wanted to know what their grandfather did with it. I knew the answer as soon as I walked over his grave. Antony Livingston had literally taken his fortune with him to the grave. The end of his casket was packed with his wealth. I'd only needed to open the upper part of the casket to speak with him. His wealth was safely concealed at Antony's feet.

I could have forced him to tell his grandchildren the truth. I didn't. Instead, I'd first asked Antony why he'd hidden the valuables, not where. His soul could do nothing more than tell me the absolute truth, and that truth was coldly brutal. Some used wealth for good. Some squandered it. Some used that money to do nothing but sow evil. Antony Livingston's grandchildren fell into that latter category.

After learning the truth, I'd laid Antony's soul to rest, closed the casket, and walked away. I'd also returned the entirety of my retainer. I didn't want a cent from Antony Livingston's relatives. Threats, curses, and violent outbursts followed me out of that cemetery and drove me into the comforting arms of Trinity's Holy Cross.

The cool comfort of an old graveyard was akin to taking a

warm bubble bath. Tension eased and my muscles loosened. My brain quieted and my skin felt less prickly. With every step, I left a little more of my anxiety behind.

"Do you believe those men will follow through on their threats?" Aurelia asked, amping my anxiety back up a couple of notches.

I shrugged. "Not if they know what's good for them. I already sent Pops a text. He's making the appropriate *notifications*." It was handy having a powerful warlock in your back pocket. My warlock also happened to be my father, Nikodemus Holland.

"I see." Again, there was no inflection, just quiet acceptance. I'd yet to figure out why Aurelia kept popping up in my world. I should feel threatened and yet I didn't. If she'd wanted, Aurelia would have taken me out by now. She had reason to do just that. I was one of the few who knew the secret to her demise, and I was the only one who knew that had the power to act on that knowledge. It would take less than five minutes to return Aurelia's soul to her body, eliminating all the magical manipulation that made her the powerful djinn she was.

I'd offered to return Aurelia's humanity. She'd no longer be bound to a master, her will would be her own. She'd be able to live a life of her own choosing and making. She'd also be mortal and without a drop of magic. If I'd been in her shoes, combat boots once again, I'm not certain what I would have done.

As for Aurelia, she'd declined, but I got the feeling the idea wasn't completely off the table. Maybe that's why she'd been following me around.

Walking across another grave, I was hit with a wave of sadness. The woman buried below was young when she passed. She'd been buried with her stillborn baby cradled within her arms.

Shaking away the morose feeling, I asked, "How is Peaches?" Peaches was Aurelia's current *master*, not that he acted much like one. In fact, he'd given Aurelia a very loose leash. Possibly too loose. So far, Aurelia hadn't given him cause to reign her back in. I wasn't sure what would happen should that situation change.

"He is fine. Rutherford Haven has calmed considerably since Alpha Belview's demise."

I grunted. "Couldn't have happened to a more deserving guy."

"His soul was very black," Aurelia said by way of agreement. She'd never acted as if Janus's death was my fault. I'd returned his human soul, destroying his djinn abilities and making him mortal again. Janus had taken that second shot at life and quickly thrown it away by attacking Leon. Turns out, humans, no matter how strong and deranged, don't stand much chance against three-hundred-year-old vampires and their shifter beloveds.

While Arie Belview had been alive, I hadn't been able to see his soul. I'd gotten a glimpse of its ugly filth after Queen Silvidia killed him. That brief glance was more than enough.

"I'm glad he's—" My words caught as something else slammed into my brain. Trinity Holy Cross Cemetery was old and wasn't accepting any new customers. So why was a freshly deceased soul screaming so loud I was on the verge of a migraine?

"Shit," I cursed, bending over and placing my hands on my knees. I breathed through my nose and attempted to throw up some mental shields. Given my location, I'd complacently allowed them more slack than typical.

"Erasmus?" Aurelia shifted closer but did nothing more than that.

My gaze raked the ground until I saw the disturbance. "There." I pointed, walking toward the worn headstone. It was tilted to the side, the ground having shifted over the past century. Just past the new moon, it was too dark for me to see the ground well. Taking out my phone, I turned on the flashlight app and scanned the freshly turned earth.

Inhaling, I let loose another, "Shit."

"What is it?" Aurelia asked.

I pointed to the ground. "A grave should only have one body. This one has two and its latest occupant has been in residence, one, maybe two weeks." Rubbing my temple, I frowned. "And from how pissed off they are, I'd bet whoever's down there met an untimely, grisly end."

"Are you implying they were murdered?"

"I'm more than implying, Aurelia. Whoever's down there was definitely murdered."

L ook for Erasmus's story coming out Summer/Fall 2024

Like What You've Read?
If you've enjoyed reading *Purrfectly Peculiar Pixie*, please take
the time to leave a review. Reviews help readers find works
they might enjoy and help support authors.
Reviews are priceless gifts.

Available and Coming Works by MJ May

The Reaping Covetous Series:
Sow What You Reap: Reaping Covetous I
Dead Women Tell Tales: Reaping Covetous II
Dying to Reap You: Reaping Covetous III
Brother's Keeper, Brother's Reaper: Reaping Covetous IV
Ashes to Ashes: Reaping Covetous V
Pushing Up Roses: Reaping Covetous VI
Reaping Consequences: Reaping Covetous VII—End

M/M Fantasy Romance: Perfect Pixie Series
Perfectly Imperfect Pixie
Perfectly Perfect Pixie: Peaches's Story
Perfectly Charmed Pixie: Parsnip's Story
Perfectly Perplexing Zombie: Wendall's Story
Purrfectly Peculiar Pixie: Phlox's Story—End

M/M Mystery Romance: Maverick Insurance Mysteries
No Good Deed
Goes Unpunished
The Road to Hell
Paved With Good Intentions: Coming Soon

M/M Fantasy Romance: Necromancer Series: Spin Off from
the Perfect Pixie Series
Erasmus (title forthcoming): Summer/Fall 2024

Acknowledgments

I'm not sure if it takes a village to make a writer, but I believe it takes a village to make a writer's books more enjoyable. My village consists of friends, coworkers, editors and proofreaders, and two- and four-legged family.

Many thanks to Hannah VanVels Ausbury for being my editor and turning my writing into something infinitely more enjoyable to read.

The book cover for *Purrfectly Peculiar Pixie* was done by cheriefox. As always, Cherie did a great job and made the cover beautiful.

Longtime friends can be hard to come by and, in my case, are exceedingly rare. I will be forever grateful that Kathy and I sat down across from each other almost thirty years ago. Biology lab wouldn't have been half as fun without her, and my life would have been infinitely duller had either of us picked a different seat or table. Thank you for reading my raw writing, even when the genre isn't one you would usually pick.

My furry, four-legged family is my sanity, heart, and home. I have no idea how people live without pets; I only know that I would simply be existing, not living, without mine. Newton and Fennik are my compasses. They humble me, remind me the world isn't always as fucked up as it seems, and give me a smattering of hope the human race can do better. Or at the very least, that the human race needs to do better.

Author Bio

MJ May lives in the Midwest with her cat, Newton, and dog, Fennik. She is passionate about her furry children, the wild birds eating her out of house and home, and her garden. MJ May is a firm believer that changing the sheets on your bed with a housecat involved should be an Olympic event. Scores should be based on speed, accuracy, creative cursing, and how many times you have to toss a cat off the bed.

Connect with MJ May at her website: https://blogaway withmjmay.com.

www.ingramcontent.com/pod-product-compliance
Lightning Source LLC
Chambersburg PA
CBHW031116160726

47991CB00004B/1412